Elizabeth Moon joined the US Marine Corps in 1968, reaching the rank of 1st Lieutenant during active duty. She has also earned degrees in history and biology, run for public office and been a columnist on her local newspaper. She lives near Austin, Texas, with her husband and their son.

Find out more about Elizabeth Moon and other Orbit authors by registering for the free monthly newsletter at www.orbitbooks.co.uk

ELIZABETH MOON

THE DEED OF PAKSENARRION

BOOK 1

SHEEPFARMER'S DAUGHTER

www.orbitbooks.co.uk

An *Orbit* Book

First published in Great Britain by Legend Books 1997
Reprinted by Orbit 1997, 1998, 1999, 2001, 2003

A CIP catalogue record for this book
is available from the British Library.

ISBN 1 85723 640 8

Printed and bound in Great Britain by
Mackays of Chatham plc, Chatham, Kent

Orbit
An imprint of
Time Warner Books UK
Brettenham House
Lancaster Place
London WC2E 7EN

THE DEED OF PAKSENARRION

BOOK I

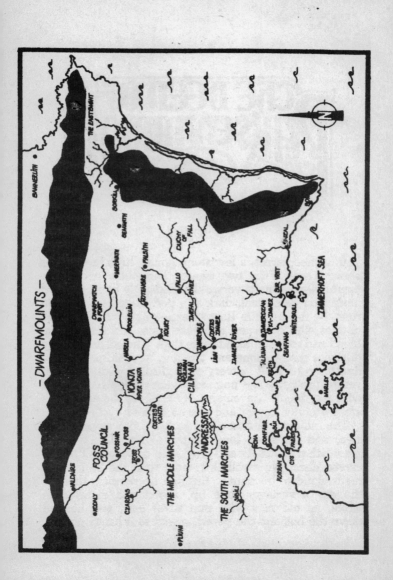

Prologue

In a sheepfarmer's low stone house, high in the hills
above Three Firs, two swords hang now above the
mantelpiece. One is very old and slightly bent, a sword
more iron than steel, dark as a pot: forged, so the tale
runs, by the smith in Rocky Ford—yet it is a sword, for
all that, and belonged to Kanas once, and tasted orcs'
blood and robbers' blood in its time. The other is a very
different matter: long and straight, keen-edged, of the
finest sword-steel, silvery and glinting blue even in
yellow firelight. The pommel's knot design is centered
with the deeply graven seal of St. Gird; the cross-hilts
are gracefully shaped and chased in gold.

The children of that place look at both swords with
awe, and on some long winter nights old Dorthan,
grandfather of fathers and graybeard now, takes from its
carved chest the scroll that came with the sword and
reads aloud to his family. But first he reminds them of
the day a stranger rode up, robed and mantled in
white, an old man with thin silver hair, and handed
down the box and the sword, naked as it hangs now.

1

"Keep these," the stranger said, "in memory of your daughter Paksenarrion. She wishes you to have them and has no need of them." And though he accepted water from their well, he would say no more of Paksenarrion, whether she lived or lay buried far away, whether she would return or no.

The scroll Dorthan reads is headed *The Deed of Paksenarrion Dorthansdotter of Three Firs*, and many are the tales of courage and adventure written therein. Time and again the family has thrilled to the description of Paksenarrion in battle—the littlest ones pressing close around Dorthan's knees, and watching the sword on the wall. They are sure it glows slightly when those tales are read.

And always they ask, the little ones who never knew her, what she was like. Just like that in the scroll? Always so tall, so brave? And Dorthan remembers her face the night she left, and is silent. One brother thinks of a long-legged girl running down errant sheep; the youngest remembers being carried on her shoulders, and the smell of her hair. Besides this, legend is all they have.

"She's dead," say some. "She must be, or they wouldn't have sent her sword."

"No," say others. "She is not dead. She is gone where she doesn't need *this* sword."

And Dorthan turns to the end of the scroll, which solves nothing . . . for the *Deed* is unfinished, ending abruptly in the middle of a stanza.

And one of those children, the little ones, has climbed from stool to table, and from table to mantelpiece, and touched with a daring hand the hilt of each sword . . . and then climbed down, to dream of songs and battles.

Chapter One

"And I say you will!" bellowed the burly sheepfarmer, Dorthan Kanasson. He lunged across the table, but his daughter Paksenarrion sidestepped his powerful arm and darted down the passage to the sleeping rooms. "Pakse!" he yelled, slipping his broad leather belt from its loops. "Pakse, you come here now!" His wife Rahel and three smaller children cowered against the wall. Silence from the sleeping rooms. "Pakse, you come or it will be the worse for you. Will you go to your wedding with welts on your back?"

"I'll not go at all!" came the angry response.

"The dower's been given. You wed Fersin Amboisson next restday. Now come out before I come in."

Suddenly she stood in the mouth of the passage, as tall as he but slender, long blonde hair braided tightly. She had changed to her older brother's clothes, a leather tunic over her own shirt, and his homespun trousers. "I told you not to give dower. I told you I wouldn't wed Fersin or anyone else. And I won't. I'm leaving."

Dorthan glared at her as he wrapped the belt around

3

his right hand. "The only place you're going, you arrogant hussy, is Fersin's bed."

"Dorthan, please—" began Rahel.

"Quiet! She's your fault as much as anyone's. She should have been spinning at home, not running out on the moors hunting with the boys."

Paksenarrion's gray eyes glinted. "It's all right, Mother; don't worry. He'll remember someday that he's the one who sent me out with the flocks so often. Father, I'm leaving. Let me pass."

"Over my dead body," he grunted.

"If need be—" Paksenarrion leaped for the old sword, Kanas's sword, over the fireplace. As she lifted it from the rack, the belt caught her shoulders with its first stroke. Then she was facing Dorthan, sword in hand, with the firelight behind her. The sword felt easy in her grip. Startled, Dorthan jumped back, swinging the belt wildly in her direction. Paksenarrion took her chance and ran for the door, jerked it open, and was gone. Behind her came his furious bellow, and questioning calls from her brothers still working in the barns, but Paksenarrion did not slow or turn until she came to the boundary stone of her father's land. There she thrust her grandfather's sword into the soil.

"I won't have him saying I stole it," she muttered to herself. She turned for a last look at her home. Against the dark bulk of the hill, she could see light at the open front door, and dark figures crossing and recrossing the light. She could hear voices calling her name, then a deep bellow from Dorthan, and all the shapes went in at the door and shut the light in. She was alone, outside the house, and she knew, as well as if she'd seen him do it, that Dorthan had barred the door against her. She shook herself. "It's what I wanted," she said aloud. "So now I'd better go on with it."

The rest of that night she jogged and walked down the well-worn track from her father's farm to Three Firs, warmed by the thought of the coming adventure. She went over her cousin's instructions time after time, trying to remember everything he'd said about recruiting sergeants and mercenary companies and training and drill. In the first light of dawn she walked into Three Firs. Only in the baker's house did she see a gleam of light behind closed shutters, and a plume of smoke out the chimney. She smelled no baking bread. She could not wait until the first baking came out unless the recruiters were still in Three Firs. She walked on to the marketplace. Empty. Of course, they might not be up yet. She looked in the public barn that served as an inn. Empty. They had left. She drew water from the village well, drank deeply, and started off again, this time on the wider track that led to Rocky Ford—or so her cousin had said; she'd never been beyond Three Firs.

As daylight came, she was able to make better time, but it was nearly noon when she came to the outskirts of Rocky Ford. The rich smells of cooking food from the inns and houses nearly made her sick. She pressed on, through what seemed to her like crowds, to the market square in the town's center. There she saw the booth that Jornoth had told her to look for, draped in maroon and white silk, with spears for cornerposts. She paused to catch her breath and look at it. On either side, a man-at-arms with breastplate, helmet, and sword stood guard. Inside was a narrow table, with one stool before it, and a man seated behind. Paksenarrion took a deep breath and walked forward.

As she reached the booth, she realized that she was taller then either of the men-at-arms. She waited for them to say something, but they ignored her. She looked inside. Now she could see that the man behind the table had gray hair, cropped short, and a neatly trimmed mustache. When he looked up at her, his eyes were a warm golden brown.

"This is a recruiting station for Duke Phelan's Company," he said as he met her gaze. "Were you looking for someone?"

"No. I mean, yes. I mean, I was looking for you—for

a recruiting station, I mean." Paksenarrion reddened with embarrassment.

"You?" The man stared a moment, then looked down briefly. "You mean you wanted to join the Company?"

"Yes. My—my cousin said such companies accepted women."

"We do, though not so many want to join. Look— mmm—let's get a few things straight before we start. To join us you must be eighteen winters old, healthy, with no deformities, strong, tall enough—you have no problem there—and not too stupid. If you're a drunkard, liar, thief, or devil-worshipper, we'll throw you out the worse for wear. You agree to serve for two years beyond your basic training, which takes four to six months. You get no pay as a recruit, but you do get room, board, and gear as well as training. Your pay as a private in the Company is low, but you'll share any plunder. Is that clear?"

"Aye," said Paksenarrion. "Clear enough. I'm over eighteen, and I'm never sick. I've been working on the moors, with sheep—I can lift as much as my brother Sedlin, and he's a year older."

"Mmm. What do your parents think of your joining an army?"

"Oh." Paksenarrion blushed again. "Well, to be honest, my father doesn't know that's where I am. I—I ran away."

"He wanted you to wed." The man's eyes had a humorous twinkle.

"Yes. A pig farmer—"

"And you wanted someone else."

"Oh no! I didn't—I don't want to marry at all. I want to be a warrior like my cousin Jornoth. I've always like hunting and wrestling and being outdoors."

"I see. Here, have a seat on the stool." While she sat down, he fished under the table and came up with a leather-bound book which he laid on top. "Let me see your hands—I have to be sure you don't have any prison brands. Fine. Now—you like wrestling, you say. You've arm wrestled?"

"Surely. With my family, and once at market."

"Good. Give me a try; I want to test your strength." They clasped right hands, and on the count began to push against each other's resistance. After several minutes, with neither moving much, the man said "Fine, that's enough. Now let's go left-handed." This time he had the greater strength, and slowly pushed her arm to the table. "That's good enough," he said. "Now—was this decision to join a sudden one?"

"No. Ever since Jornoth left home—and especially after he came back that time—I've wanted to. But he said I had to be eighteen, and then I waited until the recruiting season was almost over, so my father couldn't trace me and cause trouble."

"You said you'd been on the moors—how far from town do you live?"

"From here? Well, we're a half day's sheep drive from Three Firs—"

"Three Firs! You came here from Three Firs today?"

"We live up the other side of Three Firs," said Paksenarrion. "I came through there before dawn, just at first light."

"But that's—that's twenty miles from Three Firs to here, at least. When did you start from home?"

"Late last night, after supper." At the word, her stomach rumbled loudly.

"You must have gone . . . thirty miles, I don't doubt. Did you eat in Three Firs?"

"No, it was too early. Besides I was afraid I'd miss you here."

"And if you had?"

"I've a few coppers. I'd have gotten some food here and followed you."

"I'll bet you would have, too," the man said. He grinned at her. "Give us your name, then, and let's get you on the books so we can feed you. Any girl who'll go thirty miles or more on foot without stopping to eat ought to make a soldier."

She grinned back. "I'm Paksenarrion Dorthansdotter."

"Pakse-which?"

"Paksenarrion," she said slowly, and paused until he had that down. "Dorthansdotter. Of Three Firs."

"Got it." He raised his voice slightly. "Corporal Bosk."

"Sir." One of the men-at-arms turned to look into the tent.

"I'll need the judicar and a couple of witnesses."

"Sir." The corporal stalked off across the square.

"We have to have it all official," the man explained. "This isn't our Duke's domain; we must prove that we didn't take advantage of you, or force you, or forge your signature . . . you *can* sign your name, can't you?"

"Yes."

"Good. The Duke encourages all his troops to learn to read and write. Now—" he broke off as a man in a long maroon gown and two women arrived at the booth.

"Got another one before the deadline, eh, Stammel?" said the man. The women, one in cheesemaker's apron and cap, and the other with flour dusting her hands and arms, looked at Paksenarrion curiously.

"This young lady wishes to join," said Stammel shortly. The man winked at him and took out a stone cylinder with carving on one end. "Now," Stammel continued, "if you'll repeat after me in the presence of the judicar and these witnesses: I, Paksenarrion Dorthansdotter, do desire to join Duke Phelan's Company as a recruit and agree to serve two years in this company after recruit training without leave, and do further agree to obey all rules, regulations, and commands which I may be given in that time, fighting whomever and however my commander directs."

Paksenarrion repeated all this in a firm voice, and signed where she was directed, in the leather-bound book. The two women signed beside her name, and the judicar dripped wax underneath and pressed the stone seal in firmly. The cheesemaker patted Paksenarrion on the shoulder as she turned away, and the judicar gave Stammel a final wink and leer.

"Now then," said Stammel. "I'm Sergeant Stammel, as you may have gathered. We usually leave a town at noon; all the rest of the recruits are at the Golden Pig and have eaten. But you need something in your stomach, and a rest before we march. So we'll wait a bit. From here on, you're a recruit, remember. That means you say 'yes, sir' and 'no, sir' to any of us but other recruits, and you do what you're told with no arguing. Clear?"

"Yes, sir," said Paksenarrion.

An hour later, seated by a window, Paksenarrion looked curiously at the other recruits lounging in the courtyard of the Golden Pig. Only two were taller than she: a husky youth with tousled yellow hair, and a skinny black-bearded man whose left arm had a tattooed design on it. The shortest was a wiry redheaded boy with an impudent nose and a stained green velvet shirt. She spotted two other women, sitting together on the steps. None had weapons except a dagger for eating, but the black-bearded man wore a sword-belt. Mostly the recruits looked like farm boys and prentices, with a few puffy-faced men beyond her experience. Only the men-at-arms and the recruiting sergeant were in uniform. The others wore the clothes in which they'd joined. She finished the sandwich in her hand and started another; Stammel had told her to eat hearty and take her time. She had downed four sandwiches when Stammel came in again.

"You look better," he remarked. "Is there a short form of that name of yours?"

Paksenarrion had been thinking about that. She never wanted to hear her father's "Pakse" again. Her great-aunt, for whom she was named, had been called Enarra, but she didn't like that, either. She had finally decided on a form she thought she could live with.

"Yes, sir," she said. "Just call me Paks, if you wish."

"All right, Paks—ready to march?"

"Yes, sir."

"Come on, then." Stammel led the way to the inn courtyard. The other recruits stared as she came down the steps. "This is Paks," he said. "She'll march in Coben's file today, Corporal Bosk."

"Very good, sir. All right, recruits: form up." The other recruits shuffled into four lines of five persons each, except that the first file was one short. "Paks, you march here." Bosk pointed to the last place in the short file. "Now remember, at the command you all start off on the left foot, march in step, keep even with the rank on your right, and don't crowd the man ahead." Bosk walked around and through the group, shifting one or another an inch this way or that. Paksenarrion watched him curiously until he bawled suddenly, "Eyes front, recruits!" At last he was through fussing (as she thought to herself) and stepped back.

"Good enough, Bosk," said Stammel. "March 'em out."

For the first time in her life, Paksenarrion heard that most evocative of military commands as Bosk drew in a lungful of air and shouted: "Recruits. Forward . . . MARCH!"

The afternoon's march was only four hours, with two short rest-breaks, but when they halted, Paksenarrion was tireder than she had ever been. Besides the recruits, there were six regulars (Stammel, Bosk, and four privates) and four mules that carried the booth and supplies. In the course of the afternoon, they reviewed (and Paks learned) the correct way to form up, begin marching, and turn in column. She now knew her file number and who the file leader was, and had learned to keep an even distance behind the man in front. Tired as she was, she was in better shape than one of the puffy-faced men. He groaned and complained all afternoon, and finally fell in a faint at the last rest-break. When cold water failed to rouse him, two privates hoisted him over one mule's pack and lashed him there, face down. When he came to, he begged to walk, but

Stammel left him there, groaning piteously, until they made camp.

Paksenarrion and the next newest recruit were set to dig the jacks trench at the camp. This was the tall yellow-haired boy; he told her his name was Saben. He had dug the night before, too, and knew how long to make the trench. As they walked back into camp, the tatooed man sneered, "Here come the ditchdiggers— look like a real pair, don't they?"

The man who'd fainted snickered appreciatively. "It took 'em long enough. I'd say they weren't just digging ditches."

Paksenarrion felt her ears steam, but before she got her mouth open, she saw Stammel, behind the others, shake his head at her. Then her file leader, a chunky dark youth named Coben, spoke up.

"At least neither of them sneaked ale and collapsed like a town bravo, Jens. And as for being ditchdiggers, Korryn, it's better than graverobbing—"

The blackbearded man jumped up and his hand reached for the sword he no longer wore. "Just what d'you mean by that, Coben?"

Coben shrugged. "Take it as it fits. Digging jacks is something any of us might be assigned—I was, and you will be. It's nothing to sneer about."

"Young puppy," muttered Korryn.

"Enough chatter," said Bosk. "Fall in for rations."

Paksenarrion was glad to find that after supper they were each issued a blanket and expected to sleep. She had no problem. She woke early and stiff, and had made her way to the jacks and to the river to bathe before a bellow from Corporal Bosk brought the others out of their blankets. The regulars, she noticed, were already in uniform: did they sleep that way? She folded her blanket as the others did, and turned it in to the privates to load on a mule. This morning she stirred porridge in one of the cookpits; three others were supervised by Saben, Jens, and the red-haired boy in velvet.

A bowl of porridge, hunk of brown bread, and slab of dried beef made an ample breakfast, and Paksenarrion felt no ill effects from the previous day's journey. She was, in fact, happier than she'd been for years: she was a soldier at last, and safe from her father's plans. When she found that Jens and Korryn had been told to fill in the trench, her mood soared even higher.

"I don't mind digging them, if they'll fill them," she whispered to Saben.

"Nor I. That Korryn's nasty, isn't he? Jens is just a drunk, but Korryn could be trouble."

"Recruits. Fall in!" yelled Bosk, and the day's work really began.

In the next few weeks, as they traveled toward the Duke's stronghold where their training would take place, Paksenarrion and the others became more and more proficient at marching and camp chores. They picked up new recruits in most of the towns they passed, until their group numbered thirty-eight. Already friendships had begun among some of them, and Paksenarrion had heard her shortened name enough to feel comfortable with it. Despite having little time to talk, she knew that Saben, Arñe, Vik, Jorti, and Coben were going to be her friends—and that Korryn and Jens would never be anything but enemies.

Stammel changed the marching order every few days, so that they all had a chance to lead a file as well as follow. Marching in front, where she could not see the motley clothing of the rest, Paksenarrion imagined herself already through training and headed for a battle. She could almost feel a sword swinging at her side. Around that corner, she thought, or over the rise—the enemy is waiting. She pictured grim-faced troops in black armor—or maybe orcs, like those her grandfather had fought. Bits of the old songs and tales ran through her mind: magic swords, heroes who fought and won against the powers of darkness, enchanted horses . . . When she marched in back, however, the visions failed, and she wondered how many more days they would be on the road.

At last Stammel told them that the stronghold was less than a day's march away. They halted early, beside the river, and spent the rest of the daylight getting as clean as possible. Paksenarrion did not mind the cold water, but others who tried to make do with a casual swipe at face and hands were ordered back in to do the job properly.

Next day Stammel put Paksenarrion, Saben, Korryn, and Seliast at the head of the first squad files: the tallest recruits. They marched without effort now, and almost without thought, rhythm even and arms swinging. As they came over the last rise, to see the blunt stone walls of the stronghold rise from a narrow plain, squads on the parade fields were shifted out of their way.

Paksenarrion, marching across that space in front of a whole army (as it seemed to her) suddenly felt she couldn't get any air. Only the habit of days on the road kept her from bolting from so many eyes. She blushed a fiery red and kept marching.

Chapter Two

"All your personal belongings you turn in to the quartermaster; he'll put 'em in a bag with your name on it and store them in the treasury. We'll issue your training uniforms today, and if you want to keep your old clothes, they'll be stored too. You'll be issued everything you need." Stammel turned to greet a gnarled older man whose arms were full of burlap sacks. "Ah, Quartermaster . . . good to see you."

The man glared at the recruits. "Hmmph. Another bunch of beginners. And how much sentimental trash have they brought to take up space in storage?"

"Not so much; we've been on the road eight days since the last pickup."

"Good. I'll need a clerk."

"Bosk'll do it." Stammel gestured to Bosk, who came forward and took a handful of tags from the quartermaster. "File one, step up one at a time, give your name, and hand over your gear."

Paksenarrion stepped forward, unbuckling the belt on which her sheathed dagger hung. Bosk had already

15

written out her tag, and handed it to the quartermaster, who fastened it to a sack and waited for her contribution. She held out belt, dagger, and the kerchief with her savings—eighteen coppers—in it.

"Are you going to keep those clothes?" he asked, eyeing her brother's trousers, which had slipped down her hips without the belt.

"Y-yes, sir."

"Amazing. Well, go get your uniform, and bring your clothes back here. Quickly, now."

Paksenarrion looked around to see where she should go; Stammel waved her toward a doorway on the left. There a man and woman presided behind tables heaped with brown clothing. Paks strode quickly across the courtyard, hoping her trousers would stay up. Behind her she heard Korryn's nasty chuckle and whispered comment.

When she reached the tables, she saw stacks of plain brown tunics, socks, and low boots. The woman beckoned her, and grinned. "You're a tall one, right enough. Let's see—" and she began measuring Paks with a length of knotted string: neck to waist, waist to knee, shoulder to elbow to wrist. "Here—" she held out a tunic, after rummaging in the pile. "This should do well enough for now. Change."

Paksenarrion took the tunic, stripped off her shirt and trousers, and pulled the tunic over her head. The cloth was not as scratchy as the wool she was used to. The sleeves were just short of her elbow, and the hem almost reached her knees. It felt more like a dress cut short than anything else.

"Try these boots," said the woman. Paks put on a pair of the heavy brown socks and eased her feet into the boots. They were short. The woman offered a larger pair. These fit well enough. "Here's a belt for you, and a sheath. You'll be issued the dagger later." The belt, like everything else, was plain brown; the buckle was iron. Paksenarrion took her old clothes back to the quartermaster, feeling silly with the tunic rippling around her bare thighs.

"Ooh, look at the pretty white legs she has." She was sure that mocking whisper was Korryn or Jens, and hated herself for blushing as she handed the clothes to be sacked away. But Stammel heard the whisper too.

"Korryn," he said. "Who told you to talk in ranks?"

Paks, returning to her place, dared not look at Korryn's face as he replied: "No one, Sergeant."

"Perhaps you need reminding that you are to do what you're told and nothing else?"

"No, sir." Korryn did not sound as confident as usual. "But, sir, such a pretty sight—"

"If a pair of legs can make you forget your duty, Korryn, you'll have to be better taught. I don't care if the Marshal-General of Gird's Hall in Fin Panir walks through the lines stark naked and tweaks your beard— you pay attention to me, and not to her. Is that clear?"

"Yes, sir." Korryn sounded sullen. "But—"

"No buts!" growled Stammel.

In less than an hour, Stammel's group of recruits was outfitted in the recruit uniform. They moved into one of the big barracks rooms, with Bosk and Devlin, another corporal, assigning bunks.

"File leaders will rotate from week to week for the first month or so," said Devlin. He was taller and thinner than Bosk, and looked as if he would smile more easily. Right now he was not smiling at all. "File leaders bunk here, by the door," he went on. "File seconds here, then thirds, fourths, and so on. You'll change your bunk as you change your place in the files. Now: each bunk has the same bedding, and this is how you'll make it up." The corporals demonstrated, then pulled the bedding apart. "Your turn; get busy." As the recruits struggled with the bedding, they walked from place to place, explaining and criticizing. The long, straw-stuffed pallet had to be patted into an even rectangle, muslin sheet stretched tightly over it, and the brown wool blanket folded in one certain way at the foot. Paksenarrion finally achieved an acceptable bunk, and stood beside it waiting for the others to finish. Her legs still felt chilly and exposed, and she was hungry. Most of the others looked as uncomfortable as she felt.

At last they were all done. Corporal Devlin went to fetch Stammel, and Bosk moved around the room, positioning recruits beside each bunk, ready for inspection.

Stammel came to the door.

"Ready?"

"Ready for inspection, sir," answered Bosk.

Stammel began with the file leaders, checking the bunks first. Then he looked at his recruits, twitching a sleeve into place, here, asking about the fit of the boots, there. When he had made his way all around the room, he returned to the doorway.

"You'll present like this for inspection every morning before breakfast," he said. "And at any other time it's ordered. You'll receive your file positions here, when that's changed, so that you'll go directly to your file position in formation in the yard. Immediately after an inspection, you'll parade in the yard, and you'll march everywhere in formation—to eat, to drill, to work. You'll have a quarterglass after morning call to visit the jacks, dress and make your bunks; I'll expect every one of you to be in place when I come in." He beckoned to Bosk and Devlin, and left the room. Most of the group stood still, but a few left their places and started for the door. Bosk returned, and the rash ones halted.

"And who told you that you were dismissed?"

They stared at their feet.

"Those of you out of position, stay there. The rest of you are dismissed."

Paksenarrion gave silent thanks that she had not moved, and went quickly out to the yard. There she found the other recruit units drawn up in formation, and Stammel waiting. She aligned herself on the others, wondering what was happening to the unfortunates who had been held back. Beside and behind her the ranks filled. At last they were all in position. The corporals reported to Stammel, and after a moment he glanced at the other sergeants.

"Go ahead, Stammel," called someone from far down the row. "Take yours in first."

They were marched across the courtyard to a building with windows opening on the yard. Paks could smell cooked meat and bread. There Stammel sent them in, one file at a time. Once inside, she was urged along by a private who directed her to the serving line. There she found a stack of bowls, another of trays, and a bin of blunted knives. She took a tray, bowl, spoon, and knife, and moved toward the impatient cooks. A dipper of some kind of stew went into the bowl, and a half-loaf of bread, hunk of cheese, slab of salt beef, and an apple went on the tray. As she came off the serving line, another private directed her to a table in one corner. Soon her file was seated along the bench, and the tables were filling in strict order. A cook brought over a large jug of water and a cup to their table. Paks took a tentative bit of stew. To her surprise, it was tasty, savory with onions and vegetables. It had looked like a lot on her tray, but she found herself polishing the bowl with the last of her bread before she knew it.

"Well," said Stammel from behind her. "How do you like army food?"

"Seems good enough to me, sir," said Saben, from the next table.

"You'll eat a lot of it." Stammel moved away.

The first night in barracks, after so many nights on the road, was horrible. It was stuffy. It smelled. Paksenarrion jerked awake several times in alarm, only to find that she was safe in her bunk: someone had walked past the doorway. It was neither as light nor as dark as the roadside, for the dark was thicker, an indoor darkness, and the light was clearly of human origin. Several people snored, and their snores echoed off the stone walls. She missed the comfort of the old shirt she usually slept in. The new nightshift she'd been issued was scratchy. ("We're civilized," Stammel had said to those who protested against wearing a nightshift. "Besides, it'll be cold soon.") Paks had scarcely fallen asleep after her last alarm when a terrible clangor broke out: Corporal Devlin with the triangle that announced morning call.

Paks rolled out of her bunk and made for the jacks down the corridor. Then back to the room, to struggle with her bunk. She peeled off the nightshift, hoping that Korryn's eyes were occupied elsewhere. No one said anything. Everyone around her was as busy as she was. She unbraided her hair, combed it with the bone comb she wore looped into it, and rebraided it smoothly, wrapping the tip with a thread from her tunic. She didn't know what to do with the nightshift. Bosk came to the door; Paks caught his eye and he came forward.

"What do we do with these?"

"See that ledge? Fold it neatly and put it there." Bosk went around the room to tell the others. Paks tied her bootlaces, straightened her belt and empty sheath, and smoothed the sheet on her bunk one last time.

Devlin came to the door. "Ready?" he asked Bosk.

"As they will be."

"Recruits, prepare for inspection!" yelled Devlin. Paksenarrion stood where she thought she should be and stared straight ahead. Stammel entered the room, and began on the other side. He found something wrong with each person: blanket folded wrong, sheet crooked, pallet misshapen, boots laced unevenly, hair uncombed, tunic crooked, nightshift folded wrong, dirty fingernails (Paks felt a stab of panic and almost looked at her hands), untrimmed beard, messy bunk (he was only two bunks away, and Paks was sure she could not stand the suspense), nightshift *under* the bed weren't you *listening*, recruit? And then it was her turn. She felt herself begin to blush before he said a word. She heard—she did not look—him thump the bunk. He looked at her from all sides, grunted, and finally said, "Tunic's wrinkled in back," and walked out.

"Dismissed," said Bosk, and Paksenarrion headed for the yard, beginning to wonder why she'd gotten into this.

She wondered even more in the next weeks. She enjoyed the marching drill, which kept them moving about the wide fields in intricate patterns for several hours every morning and evening. It wasn't fighting, but it was soldierly, and expected. What she didn't enjoy was the other work. Bedmaking, cleaning, and dishwashing were among the things she'd left home to avoid. If she'd wanted to be a carpenter or a mason, she grumbled to herself one day while working on repairs to the stable wall, she'd have apprenticed herself to one.

Others felt the same way.

"We haven't even seen a sword yet," complained Effa. "I signed on to be a fighter, not drag rocks around all day."

"Well—surely we'll get into that," said Saben, as he hoisted one of the despised rocks into place. "I mean, the place isn't full of workers, so they must have become fighters and gone to war."

Korryn gave a sneering laugh. "Fine reasoner you are! No, they'll keep us as laborers as long as they can, and then try to skimp on our training. As long as they can count on fools like you to join every year, they don't care how many die."

Paksenarrion snorted. "If we're fools for joining, what about you?" The others laughed, and Korryn scowled, slamming a rock into wet mortar so it splattered them all.

"I," he said, "already know how to use a sword. I don't have to worry."

"You will if you don't get busy," said Bosk. They all wondered how long he had been listening.

The closest they came to anything that Paksenarrion recognized as weapons training was hauk drill. Every day they spent two hours with the hauks, weighted wooden cylinders that looked somewhat like maces.

"I know what you want," said Armsmaster Siger, as he supervised the drill "You want swords, you think, and spears. Huh. You couldn't wield a sword for a quarterglass yet, none of you. Get that up, recruit—higher, that's right. Thought you were strong, didn't you? And you're all as weak as new-born lambs—look at you sweat." Siger was a gnarly, dried-up old man who looked old enough to be anyone's grandfather.

Paks had began to doubt they would ever get to real weapons—week after week, they swung the hauks: over, under, sideways. And then one day they arrived to find practice swords laid out: wooden, and blunted, but swords. Siger stood behind the row of swords like a potter behind his wares.

"Today," he said, "we find out who's making a warrior. File one, come forward." Paks led her file out of formation. "All right, file leader, are you ready to face a sword today?"

Paks took a deep breath of excitement. "Yes, Armsmaster."

Siger glared at her. "Ha! Eager, are you? You innocents are all too willing to shed your blood. Very well—pick up the first one in line—yes—that one."

Paks could not help grinning: a sword in her hand at last. She waggled it from side to side.

"No!" roared Siger. "Don't play with it, fool! It's not a toy to show off with. A sword is to kill people with, nothing less."

Paksenarrion blushed scarlet.

"Now—hold it just like the hauk in position one. Yes." Siger scooped up one of the other practice blades. "This is an infantry sword, short enough not to get in the way in formation. It's used to stab and slash. Now, file leader—the motions are the same as for hauk drill. Proceed."

Paks was puzzled but willing, and began to move the sword through the remembered sequences. As she did so, Siger's blade met hers, tapping it first lightly, then harder. Paks began to watch his blade, thinking back to Jornoth's sketchy lessons, and forgot all about the sequence of hauk-drill. Excitement rose in her, and she began to swing the blade harder, trying to force Siger's blade aside. Suddenly his sword was not there to be tapped; instead it rapped her sharply on the ribs.

"Ouch!" She was startled, and having lost her rhythm was whacked twice more before she regained it. Uncertain, and a bit angry, she glared at Siger, who gave her a mocking smile.

"That was the flat of the blade," he said cheerfully. "Next time it'll be the edge; keep to the drill, recruit."

Paks bit her lip, but returned to the drill pattern, meeting Siger's blade with a crisp smack. He increased the pace, and she struggled to keep up, irritated by his smile and by the snide remarks of Korryn behind her. Again Siger rapped her ribs, sore now from the earlier blows, and Paks erupted furiously into wild strokes that hit nothing—until a sharp blow in the midsection knocked the wind out of her, and she dropped the sword and sprawled painfully on the ground. Korryn laughed.

"Always a mistake to get angry," said Siger, over her head. "You've a lot to learn before trading killing blows. Catch your breath, now." His voice chilled. "As for you, recruit, that thinks it's funny, we'll have you next, if you please."

Paks gasped a moment or two, and clambered up.

"Still want to learn swordplay?" Siger asked.

"Yes, sir. It's—it's harder than it looks, though."

Siger grinned. "It always is, recruit; it always is. Now you've been blooded, I want you to put on a banda next time." He jerked his head toward a pile of white objects like cushions. "Not you—" he added as Korryn moved toward the pile. "I want to see if you think it's funny when I whack *your* ribs."

Korryn glared at him and snatched up a sword with practiced ease.

"Ah-h. An expert, is it? You've handled a blade before?" Korryn nodded. "We'll see, then. You need not confine yourself to the hauk drill if you think you can do more." But Korryn began with the standard movements, holding his sword easily. "I'd say you were used to a longer blade, recruit," commented Siger.

Abruptly Korryn changed from the drill pattern, and a complicated rattle of blade-on-blade resulted; Paks could not see just what had happened. Korryn tried a quick thrust, but the short sword did not reach Siger, and Siger's blade rapped Korryn's shoulder. Korryn scowled and pressed his attack again, using his height and longer reach, but he could not touch the Armsmaster, who kept up a running commentary.

"Taught by a fencing master, weren't you? You like a thrust better than a slash. You handle that blade like you did most of your fighting in alleys. It won't do for us—you might as well forget it, recruit, and start learning it right." And with that Siger began a furious attack that forced Korryn back, and back, and back around the practice ring, taking blow after blow, until Korryn lost his grip and the sword flew out of his hand. Effa caught it in midair.

"Now," said Siger, the point of his sword at Korryn's waist. "Is it quite as funny when it happens to you? Let's hear you laugh."

Korryn was white with rage, breathless and sweaty.

"Sir," he said finally. Siger gave him a slight smile and nodded.

"Novices, that have never handled a sword, them I expect to get drunk on the excitement and do something stupid—and I thump them well for it. But those who claim to know something . . . Go wait for your turn again, recruit."

Each of them went a round with Siger without protection, and each received a complement of bruises. Then he showed them how to fasten the bandas, the quilted canvas surcoat worn for weapons practice.

"Your turn again," Siger said to Paks. "Ready? Are you sore enough?"

Paks grinned. "I'm sore, sir, but I'm ready. I hope."
"You'd better be. Now start with the drill."

This time Paks handled the sword with more assurance, and kept the cadence as even as she could. "Better," admitted Siger. "Painfully slow, but better. Speed it up, now, just a little. Keep the rhythm." The blades clacked together. Again, again, again. "Now a bit harder—not too much at once." The shock of contact was making Paks's hand tingle; her arm began to tire. Siger shifted around her, and she had to turn and strike at the same time. The ache spread up her arm. Whack. Whack. Sweat trickled down her face, stinging in her eyes. Siger moved the other way, and Paks turned with him, but she lost the rhythm. Quick as a snake's tongue his blade tapped her ribs. "Enough," he said. "You're slowing down again. Give the blade to someone else, and go work with the hauks awhile."

Once they began drilling with wooden blades, they also began to learn other weapons. By the time they marched south, Siger said, they would have a certain minimum proficiency with short-sword, dagger, bow, and spear.

It was the spear that offered the most difficulty. As usual, it had seemed simple, just thinking about it. A long pole with a sharp end, to be poked at the enemy. No fancy strokes—simple. Effective. Surely it was easier than a sword; if nothing else you could hang onto the thing with both hands.

"We don't use polearms often," said Stammel. "We're a fast-moving, flexible infantry, and swords are better for that. But we do train with 'em and we use them sometimes. So. First you'll learn to carry something that long without getting all tangled up in it. Remember those reeds we gathered last week you were so curious about? Well, they've been drying in the storelofts, and you'll each take one."

Soon they were back in formation, each with a twelve-foot reed in hand. Stammel had shown them how to hold the mock spears upright; now he gave the command to move forward. Five of the reeds tipped backwards. The butt on one tripped the recruit in front of the careless carrier. When he stumbled, his reed swung out of control and hit the file leader on the head.

"Pick 'em up—don't stop, come on! You've got to hold them firmly—don't let 'em waver. Keep in formation, there. Stay in step or you'll trip each other."

The reeds dipped and wavered as if a wind blew them as Stammel led the unit to the far side of the parade grounds. By the time he called a halt, most faces were red.

"Now you see what I meant. The only easy thing about spear work is how easy it is to mess up the whole formation. If you ever see one of the heavy polearm companies, like Count Vladi's, you'll see how it should be done. Now—you've got to learn how to shift those things about. Together, or you'll all be tangled together. So just holding them upright, we'll practice turning in place." He called for a right face. Two recruits let their reeds lag behind the turn, and the tips bumped neighboring reeds. "No! Hold them absolutely steady when you turn. Keep 'em straight. Try it again."

After a dizzying few minutes of facing left, right, and about, the unit could turn in place without any wavering of the reeds. Stammel wiped his face and glanced at the corporals. They were trying not to grin. Far across the parade grounds, he could see another unit practicing. It looked worse than his, he thought.

"Next step is the slope," he said. "Don't move anything until I've explained. First, you'll put the butt a handspan behind the right foot of the man in front of you; file leaders, that's an armspan in front of you. Then slowly tilt the reed back over your shoulder—you have to be careful not to let the butt slip forward. Then your left hand grips two spans below the right, and you lift it onto your shoulder. That gives enough clearance in front for marching. Don't let it swing free; use your grip to hold the butt end down. Bosk, show them how to do it."

Bosk came forward and took Paksenarrion's reed from her hands. He held it upright, and demonstrated the facing movements they had practiced: the end of the reed, far over his head, scarcely quivered when he turned. Then he loosened his grip and let the butt end slide toward the ground, tilting the reed as it slid so that it grounded an armspan in front of him. While his right hand steadied the shaft, his left hand reached below and lifted; the reed rose, keeping the same steep slant. When his left hand reached his right, he shifted the right quickly to the lower grip.

"That's the position you want," said Stammel. "Now, show 'em how to move with it."

Bosk strode forward, the reed steady on his shoulder, not waving or dipping with his stride. When he turned, they could hear the whirr as the end of the reed sliced the air. He made a square, then returned the reed to an upright position and handed it back to Paks.

"Ready——" said Stammel. "Ground the butts——" Paksenarrion felt the length of reed quivering as she tried to let it slide slowly through her hands, aiming the butt somewhat ahead of her right foot. It bumped the ground.

"It's too close to you," said Bosk. "Slide it out further." Paks slid the butt along the ground until Bosk nodded.

"Now tilt 'em back along your shoulders," said Stammel. Paks let the top of the reed fall back slowly. The butt came off the ground, but she pushed it back before anyone said anything. Some were not so lucky. Stammel and the corporals were yelling at those who let the reeds get out of control. At last all were in the correct position.

"Left hands down," said Stammel. "And lift, but keep it under control. NO!" he roared. Paks heard a smack and a yelp of pain as someone's reed landed on someone's head. Her own wavered as she tried to shift the grip of her left hand. "Steady!" Paks let her eyes slide sideways to see how others in the front rank were doing. Everyone seemed to be in the right position. "Now—bring them back vertical again. That's right. Now slope 'em back—no— No! Control it, don't let it get away from you."

This exercise was repeated again and again until the whole unit could shift the reeds from vertical to sloped position without getting out of position. Paksenarrion's arms ached, and her palms tingled unpleasantly where the reed slid back and forth.

"We're going to march back with them at slope," said Stammel. "And you'd best not look as foolish as the other units, either. Anyone who drops a reed—" he scowled at them.

They managed to make it back to the courtyard before the others, without dropping anything but sweat. By the time the other units were in and halted, their own reeds were safely on the ground.

Gradually their weapons skills improved. They took fewer—but never no—thumps from Siger, and the spears seemed more manageable. After Paks took the skin off the inside of her left arm during archery practice, she learned to keep her elbow braced correctly. They all suffered a variety of lumps, cuts and scrapes, but the only serious injury in Paks's unit was Mikel Falsson, who fell from the wall while working on repairs and broke both legs. He recovered, but with a bad limp, and eventually went to work in the armory.

"He was lucky not to lose either leg," said Devlin. "That was as nasty a break as I've seen." Paks shuddered, remembering the white ends of bone sticking out.

"If there'd been a Marshal here—" began Effa. Devlin interrupted.

"No. Don't say that. Not here. Not in this Company."

Effa looked puzzled. "But I thought Phelan's Company recruited mostly Girdsmen—doesn't it?"

"Once it did, but not now."

"But when I joined, and said I was a yeoman, Stammel said it was good."

"Sergeant Stammel, to you. Oh yes, we're glad to get Girdsmen—the more the better. But there'll be no Marshals here, and no grange or barton."

"But why—?"

"Effa, leave be." Arñe tapped her arm. "It's not our concern."

It was not in Effa's nature to leave be. She worried the question any time the corporals and Stammel were not around, wondering why and why not, and trying to convert those (such as Paksenarrion, Saben and Arñe) who seemed to her virtuous but unenlightened. Paks found these attempts at conversion annoying.

"I've got my own gods," she said finally. "And that's enough for me. My family has followed the same gods for generations, and I won't change. Besides, however good a fighter Gird was, he can't have turned into a god. That's not where gods come from." And she turned her back on Effa and walked off.

Meanwhile, she and Saben and Vik discussed religions in a very different way, fascinated by each other's background.

"Now my family," said Saben. "We were horse nomads once—my father's father's grandfather. Now we raise cattle, but we still carry a bit of hoof with us, and dance under the forelock and tail at weddings and funerals."

"Do you worship—uh—horses?" asked Vik.

"No, of course not. We worship Thunder-of-horses, the north wind, and the dark-eyed Mare of Plenty, though my father says that's really the same as Alyanya, the Lady of Peace. Then my uncle's family—I've seen them dance to Guthlac—"

"The Hunter?"

"Yes. My father always goes home then. He doesn't approve."

"I should think not." Vik shivered.

"City boy," teased Paks. "We gather the sheep in from the wild hunt, but we know Guthlac has great power."

"I know that. It's *what* power—brrr. Now in my family, we worship the High Lord, Alyanya, and Sertig and Adyan—"

"Who are they?" asked Paks.

"Sertig's the Maker, surely you know that. Craftsmen follow him. Adyan is the namer—*true*-namer—of all things. My father's a harper, and harpers deal much with names."

"You're a harper's son?" asked Saben. Vik nodded. "But you've no voice at all!"

"True enough," said Vik, shrugging. "And no skill with a harp either, though I had one in my hands as soon as I could pluck a string. My father tried to make a scribe of me, and I wrote as badly as I played. And got into trouble, liking to fight. So—" he looked at his hands. "So it became—wise—for me to move away, and make use of the skill I did have."

"Which is?" asked Saben slyly.

In an instant Vik had turned, gotten his hold, and flipped Saben onto his back. "Throwing down great lummoxes of cattle farmers, for one." Saben laughed and rolled back up to a sitting position.

"I see your point," he said cheerfully. "But will it work against a thousand southern spearmen?"

"It won't have to. You and Paks will be up front, you lucky tall ones, and you can protect me."

After several weeks of switching places in formation, they received their permanent assignments. "Permanent until you do something stupid," Bosk said. Paks, to her delight, was made file leader. She still had problems with Korryn, who teased and pestered her whenever the corporals weren't around, but aside from that she had returned to her earlier pleasure in being in an army. She did wish that brawling were not forbidden. She was sure she could flatten Korryn, and ached for a chance. But after the formal punishment of three recruits from Kefer's unit who had livened a dull rainy afternoon by starting a fight, she determined to keep her temper. She did not want to lose her new position.

One afternoon a troop of soldiers in the Duke's colors rode up from the southeast, and were passed by the gate guards into the courtyard. The fifteen men, under command of a yellow-haired corporal, were immensely impressive to the recruits. And they knew it, and swaggered accordingly.

"Get the quartermaster," the corporal ordered a recruit from another unit, and the recruit scurried away. Paksenarrion, taking her turn at cut-and-thrust practice with Siger, was tempted to turn and look, but the Armsmaster brought her attention back with a thump in the ribs.

"When you're fighting, fight," he said grumpily. "You be gazing around at everything on earth and heaven, and you'll be buzzard-bait soon enough."

Paks concentrated on trying to slash past his defenses, but the old man was more than a match for her, and talked on without a break as she grew more and more breathless. "Eh, now, that's too wide a backswing—what'd I tell you? See, you left your side open again. Somebody'll plant a blade in there when you're careless. Quicker, lass, quicker! You ought to be quicker nor an old man like me. Look now, I gave you an opening wide as a barn door for a thrust, and you used that same wide cut. Stop now—"

Paks lowered her wooden blade, gasping for breath.

"You're strong enough," Siger said. "But strong's not the whole game. You've got to be quick, and you've got to think as fast as you move. Now let's break the thrust stroke down into its parts again." He demonstrated, then had Paks go through the motions several times. "Let's try that again. Don't stand flat-footed: you need to move."

This time practice seemed to go more smoothly, and

at last Paks's blade slipped past his to touch his side. "Ah-h," he said. "That's it." Twice more that afternoon she got a touch on him, and was rewarded with one of his rare smiles. "But you still must be quicker!" was his parting comment.

Chapter Three

It seemed to Paksenarrion that events had moved with blinding speed. Only that afternoon she had been a file leader, and Siger had praised her. Now she was shivering on the stone sleeping bench of an underground cell, out of sight and sound of everyone, cold, hungry, frightened, and in more trouble than she'd dreamed possible. Even with cold stone under her, and the painful drag of chains on her wrists and ankles, she could hardly believe it had really happened. How could she be in such trouble for something someone else had done? Her head throbbed, and her ears still rang from the fight. Every separate muscle and bone had a distinctive and private pain to add.

It was so quiet that she could clearly hear the blood rushing through her head, and the clink of the chains when she shifted on the bench rang loudly. And the dark! She'd never been afraid of the dark, but this was a different dark: a shut-in, thick, breathless dark. How would she know when dawn came? Her breath quickened, rasping in the silence, as she tried to fight down panic. Surely they wouldn't leave her down here to die? She clamped her teeth against a cry that fought its way up from her chest. It came out as a soft groan. She could not—could *not*—stand this place any longer. Another wave of nausea overcame her, and she felt hastily for the bucket between her feet. She had nothing left to heave into it, but felt better knowing it was there. When the spasm passed, she wiped her mouth on her tattered sleeve.

Her breathing had just begun to ease again, when she thought she heard a sound. She froze. What now? The sound grew louder, but still so muffled by stone walls and thick door that she could not define it. Rhythmic—was it steps? Was the long night already over? She saw a gleam of light above the heavy door; it brightened. Something clinked against the door; it grated open, letting in a flood of yellow torchlight. Paks blinked against it, as the torchbearer set his light in a holder just inside the cell door. Then he pulled the door closed, and turned to face her, leaning on the wall under the torch. It was Stammel: but a Stammel so forbidding that Paks dared not say a word, but stared at him in silence. After a long pause, during which he looked her up and down, he sighed and shook his head.

"I thought you had more sense, Paks," he said heavily. "Whatever he said, you shouldn't have hit him. Surely you—"

"It wasn't what he said, sir—it was what he *did*—"

"The story is that he asked you to bed him, and teased you when you wouldn't. And then you jumped him, and—"

"No sir! That's not—"

"Paksenarrion, this is serious. You'll be lucky if you aren't turned out tinisi turin—you know what *that* is, sheepfarmer's daughter—" Paks nodded, remembering the old term for a clean-shorn lamb, also used for running off undesirables shaved and naked. "Lies won't help."

"But sir—"

"Let me finish. If what he says is true, the best you can hope for—the very best—is three months with the quarriers, and one more chance with a new recruit unit, since *I* haven't taught you what you should know. If you say he's lying, you'll have to convince us that a veteran of five campaign seasons, a man with a good reputation in the Company, would be so stupid in the first place, and lie about it in the second. Why should we believe you? I've known you—what? Nine weeks? Ten? I've known him nearly six years. Now if your story is true, and if you can prove it some way, tell me. I'll tell the captain tomorrow, and we'll see. If not, just be quiet, and pray the captain will count your bruises into your punishment."

"Yes, sir." Paks glanced up at Stammel's stern face. It was even worse than she'd thought, if Stammel thought she could be lying.

"Well? Which is it to be?"

Paks looked down at her bruised hands. "Sir, he asked me to come to the back of the room—he didn't say why, but he was a corporal, so I went. And then he took my arm—" she faltered and her right arm quivered. "And tried to get me to bed him. And I said no, and he wouldn't let go, but went on—" She glanced at Stammel again. His expression did not change; her eyes dropped. "He said he was sure I wasn't a virgin, not with my looks, and that I must've bedded—someone—to be a file leader—"

"Say that again! He said what?"

"That I must have—earned that position—on my back, he said."

"Did he say with whom?" asked Stammel, his voice grimmer than before.

"No, sir."

Stammel grunted. "Go on, then."

"I—I was angry—about that—"

"So you hit him."

"No, sir." Paks shook her head for emphasis, but the nausea took her again, and she heaved repeatedly into the bucket. Finally she looked up, trembling with the aftermath. "I didn't hit him, but I did get angry because that's not how I got it, and I started to—to say bad things—" she heaved again. "—that I learned from my cousin," she finished.

"Drink this," said Stammel, handing her a flask. "If you're going to heave so much, you need something down, ban or no."

Paks swallowed the cold water gratefully. "Then, sir, he was angry for what I said—"

"It couldn't have been *that* bad—what did you say?"

"Pargsli spakin i tokko—"

"D'you know what that means, girl?"

"No—my cousin said it was bad."

A flicker of amusement relaxed Stammel's face for a moment. "It is. I suggest you learn what curses mean before you say them. Then what?"

"He clapped a hand over my mouth, and tried to push me down on the bunk." She took another swallow of water.

"Yes?"

"So I bit his hand, to make him let go, and he did and I got free. But he was between me and the door, and he took off his belt—"

"Did he say anything?"

"Yes, sir. He threatened to beat me, to tame me, and then he swung the belt, and I ran at him, trying to get away. I thought I could push past him, maybe, the way I did with my father. But he grabbed my throat—" her hand rose, unconsciously, "—and hit my face, and—and I couldn't breathe. I thought he would kill me, and I *had* to fight. I had to breathe—"

"Hmmph. That sounds more like the recruit I thought I had. Tell the rest of it."

"I—it's hard to remember. I broke the throat hold, but I couldn't get away, he was so fast and strong. We were on the floor, mostly, and he was yelling at me—hitting—I remember feeling weaker, and then someone was holding my arms, and someone was hitting me. I suppose that was after you came, though wasn't it?"

Stammel's face wore a puzzled frown. "No one hit you after I got there. When I came in Korryn was hanging onto you, Stephi was lying on the floor, and Korryn said he'd just then been able to pull you off. Captain Sejek wanted to hit you, all right, but he didn't." Stammel sighed. "If you're telling the truth, girl, I can see why you fought. But Korryn was there, or says he was, and his story is against yours, as well as Stephi."

"He was there, at the beginning, but he just laughed. I—I am telling the truth, sir, really I am." Paks swallowed noisily. "But I can see why you wouldn't believe me, if you've known him—Stephi?—so long. Only, that's what really happened, sir, no matter what Korryn says."

"If it were only your word against Korryn's—" Stammel paused and stretched, then shifted his weight to the other leg. "Paks, have you bedded anyone here?"

"No, sir."

"You've been asked, surely?"

"Yes, sir, but I haven't. I don't want to. And I asked Maia—"

"Maia?"

"The quartermaster's assistant. I asked her if I had to, and she said no, but not to make a fuss about being asked, like I might at home."

"Has Korryn bothered you about it?"

Paks began to tremble, remembering Korryn's constant teasing, taunting attempts to force her into bed with him. "He's asked me," she whispered.

"Paks, look at me." She looked up. "Has he done more than ask?"

"He—he has sometimes."

"Why didn't you say something to me or Bosk?"

Paks shook her head. "I thought I wasn't supposed to—to make a fuss. I thought I was supposed to take care of it—"

"You aren't supposed to act like a new wench in an

alehouse, no. But no fighter should have to put up with that sort of thing from a companion. When you refuse, they're supposed to drop it; there's plenty enough that are willing. I wish I'd known; we'd have put a stop to that." He paused briefly. "Are you a sisli?"

"I—I don't know what that is. He—the corporal—asked me that too."

"Like Barranyi and Natzlin in Kefer's unit. A woman who beds women. Are you?"

"No, sir. Not that I know of. Does it matter?"

"Not really." Stammel shifted his weight again and sighed. "Paks, I want to believe you. You've been a good recruit so far. But I just don't know—and even if I believe you, there's the captain. Sejek is—umph. You're in more trouble than most people find in a whole enlistment."

Paks felt tears sting her eyes. It was hopeless. If Stammel still thought she could be lying, no one else would believe her. She thought briefly of Saben, who had left before the fight broke out—why hadn't he stayed? Her belly turned again, and she heaved the water she'd drunk into the bucket. She hurt all over, and tomorrow could only be worse. A sob shook her body, then another one. She tried to choke them back.

"Wishing you were back on the farm, Paks?" Stammel's voice was almost gentle.

Her head came up in surprise. "No, sir. I just wish—I wish it hadn't happened, or that you'd been there to see it all."

"Still want to be a soldier, even after this?"

"Of course! It's what I've always wanted, but—but if everyone thinks I'm lying—I'll never have the chance." She retched again.

"Paks, is all this heaving from being in trouble, or what?"

"I—I think it's from being hit, here—" she gestured at her midriff. "It hurts there."

"I thought you just had a black eye and a bloody nose—let's see, can you sit up straighter?" Stammel moved away from the light to her side. "No, keep looking toward the light. Hmm—that whole side of your face is swollen. I can't even see your eyelashes. Your nose is broken, certainly." He touched the swelling very gently. Paks winced. "That *could* be from more than one blow. Do your ears ring?"

"Yes, sir—but it comes and goes."

"What's this gash on your shoulder? He didn't have a blade, did he?"

"No. I think that was the belt buckle. My father's used to do that."

"I wish this torchlight was brighter and steadier," grumbled Stammel. "Lift your chin. Looks like your throat is bruised, too. Does it hurt to breathe?"

"Just a little."

"Well, where else are you hurt?"

"In—in front. It all hurts. And my legs."

"Stand up, then. I'll want a look at the damage."

Paksenarrion tried to stand, but her legs had stiffened after hours of sitting on the cold stone. At first she could not move at all, but when Stammel gave her an arm to pull up on, she staggered up, still unable to straighten. She could not repress a short cry of pain.

"Here—lean against the wall if you aren't steady." Stammel swung her around and braced her against the wall opposite the torch. "Tir's bones, I don't see how you could have half-killed him in the shape you're in." Then he paused, glancing down at his arm and then at the stone bench. "It *is* blood. What did they—"

Paks felt herself slipping down the wall; she could not seem to hold herself up.

"Here, now—don't fall," said Stammel. The warning came too late. Paks lay curled on her side, heaving helplessly.

"I'm—I'm sorry—" she gasped finally.

"Lie still then. Let me look—" Stammel raised her tunic. Even in the flickering torchlight he could see the welts and dried blood on her thighs. Her tunic was ripped in several places. Stammel swore suddenly, words

Paks had heard from her cousin. Then his voice softened. "Paks, I'm going to talk to the captain. We'll get
this straightened out somehow. You can't be faking
these injuries, and their story doesn't hold up when
you're too weak to stand." He put a hand on her shoulder. "Now, let's get you back on the bench. I'll try to
get the captain to let me have Maia see you, but don't
count on it." He half-lifted her. "Come on—help me.
You're too big for me to lift alone."

Paks struggled up and finally made it onto the bench
with Stammel's help.

"I'll be back to check again tonight, and of course in
the morning. You'll be all right, though miserable. Try
not to move around—that may help the heaves—and
don't panic. We won't forget you." With that Stammel
took down the torch, opened the door, and left, taking
the light with him. Paks lay in the darkness, not quite
sure whether she felt better or worse about her prospects.

Stammel came up from the cells looking, had he
known it, as angry as he felt. Bosk waited near the head
of the stairs. When he caught sight of Stammel's face,
his own seemed to freeze for an instant. Stammel, his
mind whirling with what he must do, and quickly,
before the captain went to bed, stopped at the head of
the stairs and beckoned. "Corporal Bosk," he said, and
his voice surprised himself.

"Yes, sir." Bosk was looking at something below his
face—at his sleeve, Stammel realized. He was unrea-
sonably irritated.

"I didn't do it, Bosk; you know better!"

"Yes, sir." Bosk's eyes came back to him.

"We have a problem, Bosk, and little time to solve it.
I want you to isolate Korryn, at once. I want to speak to
everyone who was in that room from the time Stephi
came in until we got there—no matter who, or how
long they stayed—everyone. Separately—I'll use the
duty room for that. And before I talk to them, I want to

know what they've been doing, and what you and Devlin think. But quickly."

"Yes, sir. Do you want me to move Korryn first? And where?"

"Yes. Use that storage chamber down the way, and put a guard with him. He's not to talk to anyone. Is Dev in the duty room?"

"Yes, sir."

"Good. I'll be there. You take care of Korryn and come to me when it's done."

"Yes, sir." Bosk left the recruit barracks to find a guard, and Stammel walked to the duty room down the hall. Inside, Devlin was writing up the log of his watch, frowning. Stammel stepped into the room and Devlin looked up.

"Are they quiet?" asked Stammel.

"About what you'd expect. I thought we were going to have more trouble for a bit: Korryn and Saben. But I made 'em shut up."

Stammel realized that Devlin, too, was looking at his blood-stained sleeve. "Dev, I haven't been beating her—someone else did that."

"Sir. I wouldn't have thought she'd brawl like that."

"I don't think she did, Dev." Stammel paused to listen to feet in the passage behind him. Bosk must have found a guard. Devlin looked confused.

"But sir, they both said the same thing. And Stephi was down."

"Yes. That'll bear thinking on." Stammel heard voices in the barracks; he and Devlin both listened. Korryn, sounding aggrieved; Bosk, sounding grim and certain. Then three sets of footsteps in the passage, going away. Stammel resumed. "Devlin, if I'd asked you this morning whose word to take on something, Korryn's or hers, what would you have said?"

"Well—Paks's, of course. But now—"

"No buts. If it's just Paks against Korryn, we know Paks is more trustworthy. She's never done one underhanded thing yet."

"Yes, but what about Stephi? He's not like Korryn, that I've heard."

"No, that's true, and I've known him as long as you have. But I've seen him in fights—to be as dazed as he was, with no more marks on him—that's not like him. I wish I knew how badly he's hurt."

Bosk edged in the door. "Korryn's safe, sir. And Saben wants to talk to you."

"I'll get to him. You need to hear this too, Bosk. Stephi's story is that Paks jumped him when he hadn't done more than proposition her, right? And that she halfway killed him, except that Korryn dragged her off just before we got there."

The corporals nodded. "He said—or was it Korryn? —that he'd only hit her a couple of times since the fight started, she was so wild," added Devlin.

"Then how is it," asked Stammel, "that Paks is lying down there too weak to stand, covered with bruises and welts?"

"Welts?"

"Yes. Stephi's belt, according to her, and Korryn still had his on, as I recall." Stammel moved restlessly about the little room. "I can't explain Stephi's part in this, but it needs explaining. He's not known as a liar, but—"

"Come to think of it," Devlin interrupted, "most of that story came from Korryn, remember? Stephi hardly said a word—nodded when Korryn said 'isn't that right'—muttered a little, but that's all."

"Still—I've got to come up with answers before the captain goes to bed. We can't spring all this in the morning. Now: Devlin, I'll be using this room to talk to those who were in the room at any time while Stephi was there. I want you to find out, as quietly as possible, whether anyone saw Stephi acting strangely at any time this afternoon or evening. Bosk, you find Maia, Siger, and the afternoon watch commander, and have them meet me in—half a glass. If I'm not through here, come along and I'll step out to meet them in the yard. Got that?"

"Yes, sir."

"I'll speak to Saben first. And remember—keep this quiet."

"Yes, sir." Bosk and Devlin left the room, and Stammel seated himself behind the desk. Almost at once Saben appeared in the doorway.

"Come in, Saben." The tall boy was obviously worried.

"Please, sir," Saben began even before he was all the way in. "No matter what they say, Paks couldn't have done anything that bad. You ought to know that. She never even hit Korryn, and he pestered her all the time—"

"Just a minute now," Stammel interrupted. "You're the one who came to find us, right?"

"Yes, sir."

"I want to know when you first saw Corporal Stephi, and how he acted, and everything you yourself saw him do, or Paks do, until you left the room."

"Yes, sir. Well, this afternoon our unit was having weapons practice with Siger, and that's when he—I mean Corporal Stephi—rode in with the others. My file was waiting turns, and I'd been watching Paks and Siger, but then I started watching the newcomers."

"How did they look?"

Saben pursed his lips. "Very—impressive, sir. Coben and I were saying we hoped we'd look like that. Anyway, Corporal Stephi sent some recruit for the quartermaster, and looked around until he came. He looked at Paks then, sir, but I didn't think anything of it. She is good to look at, and she actually got a touch on Siger." He paused, as if waiting for a comment from Stammel.

"Go on."

"When the quartermaster came out, they talked, and he and all his men took off their swords. I had hoped they'd do a demonstration for us. Then one of the men led all the horses off to the stables, and the corporal went off with the quartermaster. We were through with practice and just cleaning up for supper when I saw him speak to the guard and go through the Duke's Gate. I don't know why—"

"To arrange lodging for his captain, most likely."

"Anyway, I didn't see him again until after supper, in the barracks. Only a few of us were in there; most weren't through with their chores. Paks and I had finished ours before supper. She'd promised to show me how to do a round braid in leather; Siger had told us to start planning the wrappings for our sword hilts. And Korryn was there; he nearly always is. And two or three more. I'd just fastened some thongs together, and was showing Paks, when the corporal came in. He looked around, and saw us, and told Paks he wanted to talk to her."

"Did he seem the same as before?"

"I don't know. A little flushed, maybe, and determined. He gestured Paks to the back of the room, and he had hold of her arm. He sort of pushed her against the bunk in the corner, so she sat down, and he sat down with her, and started talking. Telling her she should bed him, she should be flattered, all that stuff. I could tell she was upset; she got very pink and then pale, and she looked around—but what could we do? He was a corporal. He kept talking louder, and then he said—" Saben stopped abruptly and blushed.

"Yes? What?"

"He said she must have bedded someone, to be a file leader. It was terrible, sir, Paks of all people, and she was really angry. I didn't think he should be acting like that, so I left to find you. Only I couldn't find you or our corporals, for the longest time—I didn't want to yell it out to the whole courtyard—and when I finally asked a guard, he said you were in the Duke's court with the captain. The guard at the gate wouldn't let me in, and at first he didn't want to take a message. I shouldn't have left, I guess, but I didn't know they'd beat her up."

"You couldn't tell. Next time there's trouble, though, get to one of the guards at once to find me. Now, do you remember who else was in the room when Stephi came, and who left before you?"

"Korryn and Jens, Lurtli, Pinnwa, and Vik, I think. Vik left just as the corporal came in; I don't know about the others. I was watching Paks."

"Saben, have you ever asked Paks to bed you?"

"No. I've wanted to, though. But she has enough trouble with Korryn bothering her; I didn't want to be that kind of worry. If she wants it, she'll let me know. We're friends, anyway."

"All right, Saben; you can go."

"Sir, you won't let them hurt her any more, will you?"

"I'm doing what I can."

"But sir—"

"Enough, Saben. Go on, now."

A full glass later, after talking to everyone he'd summoned, Stammel faced his corporals and sighed.

"I'm convinced," he said. "And you are. But I wish it were any captain but Sejek."

"He's a hard man," said Devlin, nodding.

"And stubborn. If he's still in the same mood, evidence won't mean a thing to him. Once he's made up his mind—"

"You can insist that Valichi preside," said Bosk suddenly.

"By Tir, I can! How did I forget that? It's not as if Valichi yielded command to Sejek; he was just not here. And since she's a recruit—of course her commander has jurisdiction." He rose. "Sejek's going to be furious, I don't doubt, but with what we've found, he'll have to agree. I hope." With a wave of his hand, he left the recruit barracks for the Duke's Court.

At the gate, he spoke to the guard. "I need to speak to the captain."

"He's gone up," said the guard. "Are you sure you want to disturb him?"

"He's not asleep," said Stammel, cocking his head at

a lighted window across the court. "I need to see him before he goes to bed."

"About—?"

"Just announce me. He'll see me."

"On your head, Stammel."

"It already is." Together they walked across the court and the guard spoke to the door sentry.

"Very well, sir. Down this passage, up the stairs, second door on the right. Not carrying any weapons, are you?" Stammel sighed and handed over his dagger. "Thank you, sergeant."

Stammel took a deep breath, checked the hang of his cloak, and strode down the passage, up the stairs, to pause in the second doorway on the right. Inside the room, a roomy study, the captain sat writing in the light of a double oil lamp. The captain finished his line and glanced at the door.

"Come in, Sergeant Stammel. Did you check on your recruit?" Captain Sejek's broad, rather flat face rarely showed much expression, and didn't now.

"Yes, sir." Stammel stood stiffly halfway between the door and the desk.

"Well?"

"Sir, I'm not—easy about this."

"Tir's bones, man, no one expects you to be happy about one of your recruits going crazy—it just happens sometimes. Has she calmed down at all yet?"

"Sir, according to the guards who took her down, she made no resistance; she is not violent now."

"Well, she was violent enough. Of course she's big, but I never thought a recruit could mix it with Stephi and come off on top. That man's known to be a tough unarmed fighter. Still, I suppose the surprise—" The captain leaned back in his chair and let the pause lengthen. Finally Stammel broke it, his voice as neutral as he could make it.

"Sir, I don't think that's the whole story."

"Well, Stammel, she'd have some sort of story cooked up."

"No, sir. It's not that."

"Well, what is it? You won't make me like it better by being coy."

"Captain, I wish you'd go and look at her—just look—or send someone you trust—"

The captain raised his eyebrows. A danger signal. "What—has she been drugged?"

"No, sir. Beaten."

"Beaten? You're sure? All I saw was a royal black eye and a bloody nose—maybe broken—but that's nothing."

"No, sir. More than that—a lot more."

"Well, maybe the guards gave her a few licks going to the cells."

"They say they didn't; they say she was quiet." Stammel sighed. "Sir, what she looks like now, I don't see how she could have hurt Stephi much. How bad is he, really?"

"He's in the infirmary; they say he'll live. Has two broken fingers, fingerprints on his throat—I don't know what else. He seemed dazed, couldn't really talk to me, and the surgeon said to let him sleep. But really, Stammel, that doesn't get you anywhere. She attacked a corporal. If she got beaten up, she deserved it."

"I wish you'd look, sir," said Stammel doggedly.

"I'll see her in the morning: not before. You realize there's no doubt she's guilty, don't you? An eye-witness out of your own unit, plus Stephi—don't you?"

Stammel stood perfectly still, expressionless. "No, sir. I think there is a doubt."

"Stammel, what kind of ridiculous story had she come up with?"

"It's not her story, sir; it's looking at her, and realizing that Korryn, the other recruit, must have been lying about one thing at least. She could not, absolutely could *not* have been winning over Stephi in her condition. She can't even stand up—"

"She's faking."

"No, sir. Sir, I know that recruit, one of the best we've had, and she is not faking. That Korryn, he's been walking on the edge since he joined, and if he's lying about having to pull her off, he could be lying about the whole thing."

"What about Stephi?" asked the captain coldly.

"I don't know." Stammel sighed. "I know him too, captain, and he's always had a good reputation. But— something's wrong here, sir, and I don't think we know all the facts yet."

"Have you found out anything?"

"Yes—not enough for a full defense yet, but—"

"Stammel, are you trying to hold out for a formal trial, or something like that?"

"Yes, sir; I am."

"Oh, for—! Stammel, how many days till Captain Valichi gets back?"

"Three or four, sir."

"All your precious physical evidence will be gone by then."

"Not Paksenarrion's. Besides, you could take evidence tomorrow."

Sejek was scowling as he considered this. "Both of us are a bit partisan on this case," he said finally.

"Yes, sir. I wouldn't ask you to accept my assessment. But what about calling witnesses from Duke's East, say, who could come, examine, and present their findings to Captain Valichi?"

The captain thought a moment. "I suppose that could be done, though it seems a waste of time." He glanced up at Stammel. "You realize Val may be just as summary as I would be—"

"Yes, sir, but—"

"But Valichi is the recruit captain, and has jurisdiction. All right, I won't argue on that; you have the right to ask a trial if you think it's justified. Now, who were you thinking of as witnesses?"

Stammel frowned. "I was thinking through the Council members, sir, for those with military background and experience in court. I don't like Mayor Fontaine myself, as you probably know, but he's honest and no fool."

The captain nodded. "He's said much the same about you, Stammel. I never did know what your row was about."

"Least said, soonest mended, sir, and I don't expect he'd say different to that, either."

"Very well. Heribert Fontaine for one. D'you want two or three?"

"As few as may be; I still think something very odd is going on. I thought of Kolya Ministiera for the second. She was a corporal in Padug's cohort at the siege of Cortes Cilwan."

"I don't remember her."

"Fairly tall, dark—graying now, of course—she lost an arm that campaign, or she'd have made sergeant the next year. She has an orchard."

"I suppose I'd better write a summons. Blast you, Stammel, you might have thought of all this a little earlier."

"Sir."

"Your recruit had better look the worse for wear in the morning. Come to that, if you go back to check on her—you were planning to, weren't you?" Stammel nodded. "Well then, I want you to take a guard along— just to keep the chain of evidence quite clear." The captain went on writing. Stammel stood quietly, seething over the implication of that remark. "Here—" said the captain when he had finished. "Send these over to Duke's East tonight. We'll see the evidence—and her testimony, if you want—before breakfast. Have troops paraded by sunrise, and we'll get everything cleared up early on, I should think."

"Yes, sir. I have recruit Korryn, sir, in custody; I'd like him to be examined too."

"Very well; anything else?"

"Yes, sir, there is. I'd like to ask the captain's permission for the quartermaster's assistant, Maia, to check on

Paksenarrion for the rest of the night. She has some knowledge of healing."

"Do you really think it's necessary? No—never mind: you wouldn't be putting yourself into this position if you didn't. Do what you think necessary. Just remember that she is a prisoner, not an honored guest. No one is to enter the cell alone, and the only mitigations to the ban must be lifesaving. I may not have the right to try her, but I can ban her."

"Yes, sir. Thank you, sir."

"Now take those summonses, and let me get some sleep. Dismissed."

"Yes, sir." Stammel took a deep breath as soon as he was out of the door, loosening the knot in his shoulders. He had achieved the concessions he'd come for, far more than he'd expected to get. At the foot of the stairs, he almost collided with the Duke's steward, Venneristimon, whose dark robes blended into the shadowy hall.

"In a hurry so late, Sergeant Stammel?" asked Venneristimon.

"The captain's request," answered Stammel shortly. He never knew quite where he stood with Venner.

"Ah, well—then I won't keep you. I was but going to inquire about the wellbeing of your recruit, the one in trouble."

"Pretty well beaten up. But excuse me, Venner; I must go."

"Certainly. Is it far?"

"Not so far. Sentry—my dagger, please."

"Yes, sergeant. Here 'tis."

Stammel could feel Venner's eyes following him as he clattered down the steps into the courtyard and headed for the Duke's Gate. The guard let him out without comment, and he broke into a jog across the main court. Maia, Devlin, and Bosk were waiting for him in the duty room. He gave them a somewhat grim smile.

"We're a little forwarder," he began. "First of all, he's agreed to a trial when Captain Valichi comes back:

he wasn't happy about it, but he did agree. I have summonses for Fontaine and Ministiera, as witnesses tomorrow morning. Dev, I'll want you to ride over to Duke's East in a few minutes with them. Maia, he's given permission for you to check on Paks tonight, and even mitigate the ban if necessary—but don't push it. You'll have a guard with you, including in the cell. I'd like to know what you think of her injuries—can you tell if she was raped as well as beaten, for a start. Bosk, he wants the troops assembled before sunrise; I'm about to inform the other sergeants, but you see to it for our unit. Paks and Korryn won't be in formation. Jens will, but be ready to take him out."

"Do you have any idea yet what happened to Stephi?" asked Devlin.

"No. Neither does Sejek, if it comes to that. He can't see how a recruit—any recruit—could knock Stephi about enough that he couldn't explain himself. I still don't know how badly Stephi is hurt."

"Are you going to talk to Korryn?"

"Tonight? No. I couldn't keep my hands off him."

"Hmmph. I'll be back in about a glass, barring accidents." Devlin picked up the summonses and turned.

"Don't have any tonight. Want an escort?"

"No, sir. I'll just take the fastest horse I can find." Devlin ducked out of the room.

"Shall I go down now?" asked Maia.

"Yes. She didn't look too good when I was there an hour or so ago. Take some water. I gave her some, ban or no: she'd been heaving and was too dry."

"I'll do that. Do you need to speak to the guards for me?"

"Maybe I should." Stammel led the way from the duty room toward the prison stairs. "Should be some-one around here—ah, there you are. Forli, the captain his given permission for Maia to check the prisoner's injuries during the night, but she's to have someone with her in the cell. Can you see to it?"

"Certainly, sir, but I'll have to confirm those orders with the captain in the morning—"

"That's fine. I know it's unusual, but it's one of the things I went to ask him about. Do you want me to call over one of the reliefs?"

"No, sergeant, I'll take care of that." The guard led Maia down the stairs toward the cells. Stammel walked out into the yard toward the other barracks.

Chapter Four

This time the noise of boots in the hall was much louder. Paksenarrion struggled to sit up as they came closer. It must be morning. Her heart began to pound. Maia had said that Stammel believed her, but Stammel's belief was not enough, she realized. She still didn't know if they would even listen to her side of it. The door opened. Two guards carried torches, and two came into the cell.

"Come on, now," said the darker one. "It's time."

Paks made it to her feet, unsteadily, then stumbled over the bucket. The guards caught her arms to steady her. She was even stiffer than she had been the night before, and her head swam. The guards urged her out of the cell, holding her upright. With every step, the bronze chain rattled on the stone flags and dragged at her ankles. She had never imagined how hard it would be to walk with chains on. She peered toward the stairs—a long way. The guards pushed her forward. She clenched her teeth, determined not to faint. As she walked, her tunic began to pull free from her legs; she could feel blood trickling down as one of the scabs tore loose.

At the foot of the stairs, Paks swayed as she tried to look up. Her right foot would not lift enough to clear the first step. She tried the left, and made it. With the guards' help, she hauled herself from one step to the next, but at the landing she could go no further. She broke into a cold sweat and her vision blurred.

"No sense in this," she heard one of the guards say. "Let's get her on up." She was hoisted between them and carried to the top of the stairs, and then to the barracks entrance.

Although the sun had not cleared the wall, there was ample light to see the precise formations drawn up facing the messhall and infirmary. An open space larger than usual had been left in front of them. The guards turned Paks to the left, and began moving her along the left flank of the assembly. Paks tried to hold herself upright and walk properly, but she could hardly hobble along. Not an eye slid sideways to look at her; she stared straight at the messhall windows ahead. If only this weren't in front of everyone—everyone would see her battered face and ripped tunic. She shivered.

"Just a bit more," muttered the fair guard, holding her up as she tripped over the chain yet again. At last they came to the corner, turned right, and approached the center of the open area. Now Paks could see the bearded man in chain mail—the captain—and the corporal with a mouse under one eye and a bandaged hand, and Korryn. She had caught a glimpse of Stammel, but he was now behind her, at the head of his unit. She was placed in a line with Stephi and Korryn, facing the captain. Behind him were two strangers, a grey-bearded man in a plum-colored robe, and a one-armed woman in brown. Paks shivered again at the bite of chill morning air on her cuts and bruises. The captain stepped back to confer with the two strangers; Paks could not hear what they said. Then he came forward to address the assembly.

"We are met, this morning," he said, "to consider evidence pertaining to an assault or apparent assault yesterday evening by a recruit on a corporal of the regular Company. Evidence is taken at open assembly, so that none can doubt what was seen and heard. This evidence will be presented to Captain Valichi, who has presumptive jurisdiction, on his return. Two witnesses, having nothing to do with any of these being examined, will assess the physical condition of those implicated and hear their testimony. The witnesses are Mayor Heribert Fontaine of Duke's East, and Kolya Ministiera, on the Council of Duke's East. You may proceed."

The two witnesses went first to Stephi, walked around him, and then approached Korryn. After looking him over, they came to Paksenarrion. She tried not to look at them. The woman reached out to touch Paks's swollen face; the touch was gentle, but Paks winced. One of them felt her tunic in back, where it was stiff with dried blood. They walked back to the captain, and spoke softly. He nodded.

"Guards, strip them," he ordered. Paks was suddenly terrified; she began trembling violently.

"Take it easy, now," muttered the dark guard. "They just want to look at all the damage. Be still." Meanwhile the other guard had run a dagger along the shoulder seams of her tunic from neck to sleeve-cuff, freeing it from the chains to fall around her feet. She glanced sideways. Stephi was taking off his own uniform; the guards pulled Korryn's tunic off over his head. Again the witnesses approached them in the same order. Paks waited, trying not to show her fear.

At last they were back to her. Again they walked around her—but this time they spoke to her and each other.

"Tilt your head up," said the woman. "Look, Mayor, that's a bruise, isn't it?"

"Surely—one hand only, I think. Stand up a bit straighter, there—" Paks tried to straighten, but her belly was too sore. "Bruises there, too, and she can't straighten. Can't tell what instrument—could have been fist, foot, elbow—"

"Those welts are clearly from a strap of some sort—"

The witnesses walked back to the captain, leaving Paks shaky and sick. This time they spoke loudly enough to be heard by all.

"That man," the mayor nodded toward Stephi, "has a bruise on the left cheekbone, probably from a fist blow. Two fingers of his right hand are broken. The knuckles of his left hand are skinned and bruised; he also has a bruise on his right shin. We find no other injuries.

"The male recruit has skinned knuckles on both hands, and a skinned knee. We find no other injuries."

The mayor paused to clear his throat. "The female recruit," he said, "has more extensive injuries. A cut two fingersbreadth wide above the left eye, another such cut above the right eye, much bruising of the right cheek and jaw, the right eye swollen shut, broken nose, possible broken jaw, bruised throat, bruises on both upper arms and both forearms, bruised and skinned knuckles on both hands—"

Paks, listening to the list of her injuries, felt the descriptions as an echo of the blows that caused them. She was determined not to faint in front of everyone, but her knees loosened and her head drooped. The dark guard shook her arm. "Don't listen to that," he muttered. "Look up; count the messhall windows. You can make it." Paks stared at the windows, trying to shut out the mayor's voice.

"—two welts across her shoulders," the mayor was saying, "and a gash that could be from a blade or some stiff instrument on a whip. Similar welts on buttocks and thighs, including several more gashes. Bruises on ribs and belly—from hard blows, but with what is uncertain. Bruises on thighs, especially intense on upper inner thighs. Some sign of internal bleeding. The external evidence, captain, is consistent with rape. Additional examination would be necessary to confirm that, if it is an issue."

Paks noticed that the captain was looking at her for the first time; she could not tell if he was still angry with her.

"Have you any additional comments, Councilor Ministiera?" asked the captain.

"Captain Sejek, when one finds a woman beaten up like this, and two men only lightly marked, the usual interpretation is that the men assaulted the woman." The dark woman's voice was brusque, with an edge of sarcasm. "But she is in chains, so I suppose she's charged with assaulting them. On the evidence, without testimony, that's absurd. Even if she started the fight, she didn't do much damage—and she's been well punished. Furthermore, chains are clearly unnecessary. She can hardly stand up, let alone escape. She should be in the infirmary if you want her in shape to stand trial."

The captain nodded. "Sergeant Stammel," he called.

"Sir."

"Convey your recruit to the infirmary; the witnesses will take her testimony later. Guards, you may strike the chains."

"Hold up, now, till we get them off," said the fair guard softly. "Seb'll have to go for a chisel and stone— not long."

Stammel slipped an arm under hers on the other side. "You'll be all right, Paks. Take it easy."

The dark guard came back with his implements, and chiseled off the bent spikes that fastened wrist and ankle cuffs. "There you go. Need any help, sergeant?"

"We'll make it. Keep an eye on Bosk; he may need you."

The guard grinned. "Aha!" He picked up the fallen chains and moved to the side of the courtyard.

With Stammel's support, Paks was able to manage the few yards to the door of the infirmary. Once inside, she slumped against him, shaking and sick again. He swung her into the nearest bunk, and pulled a linen sheet over her. Maia was ready with a bowl of poultices and a jug of numbwine.

As Stammel came back out, he looked square at Korryn's face. Korryn ducked his head and turned even paler than before. Stammel walked back to the head of his unit, impassive.

"Are you ready to take testimony?" asked the captain. The witnesses nodded. "Very well. I'll begin. After supper last night, I was chatting with the recruit sergeants and corporals in the Duke's Court, when one of the guards brought word that a recruit sought Sergeant Stammel because of trouble in the barracks. The recruit stated that Corporal Stephi was involved. Stammel and I and Stammel's two corporals went directly to the barracks. As I came to the door, I saw that recruit—" he pointed at Korryn, "holding the woman. Stephi was lying on the floor with blood all over his face and tunic, and fingermarks on his throat. The woman appeared to have a black eye and bloody nose; she didn't look nearly as bad as she did this morning, nor did she complain of any injury. The recruit holding her stated that he had restrained her from killing Stephi, that he had just then gained control of her. Stephi seemed dazed and was unable to give a coherent story, but did say that he had asked the woman to bed him. The recruit said that Stephi had teased her when she refused, but nothing more, and that she had attacked him. On the evidence, Stephi appeared to be injured, perhaps seriously. I had the woman secured under ban, and set a summary trial for this morning. Sergeant Stammel requested permission to question the woman about her actions, which I granted, and several hours later he appeared with a request for a formal trial, and evidence to be taken today by witnesses."

"Did the woman say anything yesterday? Did you question her then?"

"No. The other recruit did all the talking. She didn't argue. It seemed obvious."

The mayor turned to Stammel. "Is this the way you remember it?"

"Yes, Mr. Mayor. May I amplify?"

"Go ahead."

"When I visited Paksenarrion in the cell, I realized that she had taken more damage than was first apparent. It seemed to me that her injuries made the story told by Korryn—the other recruit—inconsistent or even impossible. Her story made more sense. She said that after she refused to bed the corporal, he had pushed her down on the bunk. She bit his hand. He took off his belt, and threatened her. When she tried to push past him, he grabbed her and she couldn't escape. She remembered being held while someone hit her, but could not remember who it was. This story fit her injuries better than Korryn's. Paksenarrion has been, until this, an outstanding recruit; she has not been known to lie. Korryn had a grudge against her; she has refused to bed him."

"What is her background, sergeant?"

"She's a sheepfarmer's daughter, from the northwest. She ran away from home to join us."

"And this—uh—Korryn?"

"He joined us in White Creek; claimed to have been in Count Serlin's guard, but wanted more—action, I believe he said."

"And his record?"

Stammel frowned. "He has not done anything that would require his expulsion." The unsaid "yet" trembled in the air. "However, he has been the subject of complaint by Corporals Bosk and Devlin, and Armsmaster Siger."

"That's not fair!" Korryn's face twisted in anger. "You favor her; you always have! A pretty face—I'll warrant one of you has bedded her—"

Bosk and Devlin each took an involuntary step forward; Stammel was rigid and white with fury. Before he could say anything, Kolya Ministiera stepped toward Korryn and looked him up and down.

"Hmmph!" she snorted. "A fine—man—you are." She spat at his feet, and turned back to the captain with a swirl of her brown robe. "I suppose we must hear his testimony, just to keep things straight."

"He's out, whatever he says now," growled Stammel.

"Nonetheless," said the captain. "He must speak. And keep to the truth—" he said to Korryn "—if you can, recruit."

Korryn's eyes slid from side to side. "It is the truth—what I said. She went crazy, and started hitting this corporal, and I thought he could take care of her, and I guess he did hit her a few times. Then she got a grip on his throat, and I decided to help him out and pull her off. He'll tell you—" Korryn gestered at Stephi. "I—I thought it was just a bit of fun at first, and then—I did what I thought was right," he said, pulling himself erect. "Maybe I made a mistake—but you can't punish a man for doing what he thinks is right."

The captain and witnesses received this in tight-lipped silence. "Is there," the captain asked Stammel after a pause, "any other witness to all this?"

"That recruit we met coming out of the door—the one who said he was going for help—he should have seen something."

"Where is he?"

"Corporal Bosk," said Stammel. "Escort Jens to the front, please."

"No!" came a squeal from behind Stammel. "I—I don't know anything—I didn't see—I—I just came out—"

"He's a friend of Korryn's," said Stammel, as Bosk half-dragged Jens out of formation to the front.

The captain beckoned to two of the guards. They took Jens's arms and forced him upright. "Now then—what's his name, Stammel?"

"Jens, sir."

"Jens. I expect you to tell us the truth, right now. Did you see a fight involving Paksenarrion, Korryn, and Stephi, or any two of them?"

"I—" Jens looked frantically from side to side; when he met Korryn's fierce gaze he flinched. "I—I saw a little tussle, sir—sort of—"

"A little tussle? Be specific now: did you see it start?"

"N-no—I was—was—uh—cleaning my boots. Sir."

"Did you see any blows struck at all?"

"Well—I—saw—I saw Paks and that man rolling on the floor, and then Korryn said—said go look at the door—" Jens was staring at his feet.

"At the *door?*"

"Yes, sir. He—uh—said I should—should look for the sergeant, sir."

"Oh? And did you?"

"Yes. I looked, but I couldn't see him—I mean, until you came."

"And just what did he tell you to do if you saw the sergeant, eh?" asked Kolya. She moved to his side and jerked his head up. "Look at me! What did he tell you?"

Jens began to tremble. "He said—he said to tell him."

"Tell who, the sergeant?"

"No. Tell him—Korryn—"

"If you saw the sergeant. I see." Kolya backed away. "I don't know about your Corporal Stephi, captain, but that recruit—" she jerked a shoulder at Korryn, "is lying in his teeth."

"Agreed," said the captain.

"And the other one isn't much better," she said with distaste, looking at Jens.

"They'd both better go under guard," said Sejek. "Captain Valichi won't be back for several days, so they can't be confined under ban the whole time, but until tomorrow morning—"

"But—but ask him!" interrupted Korryn. "Ask the corporal! He'll tell you I'm not lying."

The witnesses turned toward Corporal Stephi, who had stood silent through everything. But the captain intervened.

"Before you question him, I want to tell you what happened this morning."

"Very well, captain," said the mayor.

"This morning when I woke, I had a message from the surgeon. Stephi woke last night, and wanted to see me, but they did not call me because it was so late. This morning I went to see how he was, and found that he had no memory of the events last evening. None at all. I did not want to suggest things to him, so I told him only that he would be examined by witnesses about some trouble. The surgeon could find no physical cause for his loss of memory, and as you can see, the blood I saw on him yesterday was not his own. I must say that since he's been in my cohort, he has always been a competent, sober soldier and a good corporal, with no faults against him. I cannot imagine what caused his behavior, but I can swear that it is not typical."

"Is it likely that he would pretend a loss of memory, if he had done wrong?" asked the mayor.

"I think not," replied Sejek. "He has always been honest, in my experience."

"Hmm." The mayor turned to Corporal Stephi. "You have seen the evidence of the injuries suffered by you and others, and you have heard what testimony has been given. What is your understanding of what happened?"

"Sir, I have no memory from just after supper last night until I woke in the infirmary. When I woke I felt strange—dizzy—and of course my hand and the bruises hurt. I asked the surgeon what had happened, but when he found I had no memory, he would not say anything, only that I had been found hurt. I—when I heard this morning—and saw that girl— Sir, I've never beaten a woman so. I've never forced one to bed. I don't understand how I could have—but I saw her injuries. Someone hurt her, and if it was—if I did such a thing—I know what you must do—" His voice trailed away.

"Why did you ask to see the captain last night?"

"Because I was frightened. I wanted to know what had happened—I thought the captain would tell me. And—and I couldn't *remember*."

"But Stephi," said the captain. "You must remember something—maybe just the beginning—you must be able to say whether this recruit is lying." The witnesses stirred but said nothing. Stephi looked at Korryn with distaste.

"Sir—captain—I cannot remember anything. But I'll tell you, sir, he must be lying. What we've seen and heard—"

"You say that even if it condemns you?"

"Yes. Sir, it's obvious. That girl didn't beat *me* up—and honestly, sir, there's no way she could have." Stephi conveyed all the confidence of a senior veteran, sure of his own fighting ability.

"But you can remember nothing?" prompted the mayor.

Stephi shook his head. "No, sir, I don't. But I don't expect you to believe that. You'll want to test me, I'm sure."

"You *must* remember," yelled Korryn suddenly. "You must—I told you yesterday—" He paled as they all looked at him, and he realized what he had said.

"You told him, eh?" said Kolya softly. "You told him *what*?"

Korryn drove a vicious elbow into the midriff of the guard on his left, and as the man slumped forward he snatched at his sword. The other guard drew his own weapon and darted forward, but Korryn was free with sword in hand, dancing sideways and looking for a way out.

"Take him!" roared the captain, drawing his own sword. Stammel charged, unarmed as he was, with Bosk and Devlin behind him. Korryn swung at Stammel, cursing; Stammel barely evaded the blow. Korryn backed, edging toward the unarmed witnesses as guards converged from around the courtyard. Suddenly Kolya slipped behind him and wrapped a powerful arm around his neck. Korryn fell backwards, gasping. She held him until the guards had jerked the sword out of his hands and grabbed his arms.

"If it were my decision, he'd be in chains," she said calmly, dusting her hand on her robe.

"At once," said Sejek. The guards grinned as they dragged Korryn away. "Now, Stammel—"

"Sir," said Stammel. "I'd like permission to dismiss the formation now. They've seen as much as they can learn from."

"I think you're right. Go ahead, but I'll want you for the rest of this."

"Yes, sir." Stammel turned away. The captain, frowning, spoke to the witnesses.

"Mayor Fontaine, Councilor Ministiera, I appreciate your efforts. You will want to take more testimony from both Paksenarrion and Stephi, I presume."

"Indeed yes," said the mayor. "You have quite a complicated problem here, captain."

"You'll remand Stephi to the Duke's Court, I assume," said Kolya.

"Yes. I must. Corporal Stephi—" he gestured to the corporal.

"Yes, sir."

"This must be investigated further. You must consider yourself under arrest from this time. I'll have to see whether Stammel will trust your parole; he's within his rights to refuse it until Captain Valichi returns."

"I understand, sir. I wish I did know what happened."

While they were talking, Stammel had spoken to the other recruit sergeants and the formation had dispersed. He had told his own corporals to take the unit outside to drill. "And keep 'em busy," he said, "until I come out and relieve you. We have a lot to work off. I'll be there as soon as I find out how Paks is, and what the captain is going to do."

So it was in a nearly empty courtyard that the captain turned to Stammel and said, "Well, sergeant, you were right. I wouldn't have thought it, but—"

"Sir, I was sure Paksenarrion was not to blame—but I'm not sure your corporal is. If Korryn gave him something, a drug or something like that—"

"I hadn't thought of that. Something strange has happened—"

"I agree," said Kolya. "And I think this should be discussed in somewhat more privacy."

The mayor nodded. "I'd suggest the Duke's Court, Captain Sejek."

"A good idea. Stephi, get dressed and come with us. Guard, you'd best come too." The captain turned away and headed for the Duke's Gate. Stammel and the witnesses followed him; Stephi pulled on his tunic and came after them, trailed by the guard.

Chapter Five

In the Duke's Court, the little group clustered near the fountain. The witnesses sat on its stone rim; the others stood.

"Tell us first, Stephi, everything that happened yesterday after you left me in Duke's East," said the captain.

"Yes, sir. Well, I came directly here with the men; we didn't stop at all in Duke's East. When we arrived, I asked a recruit to call the quartermaster for me—I don't know what his name was, a stocky brown-haired boy— and had the men put up their horses and turn in their swords. Then I talked to the quartermaster, and gave him your letter, sir, and we went into the storerooms and started marking what we were to take back. Suddenly I realized that it was getting late, and I hadn't told anyone you were coming yet, so I left the quartermaster and went through the Duke's Gate to speak to the steward."

"Had you had anything to eat or drink, Stephi?"

"No, sir, nothing but water. We got here after lunch. But when I'd spoken to the Duke's steward, he asked if

I'd like some ale. Tell you the truth, sir, that's one reason I didn't stop in the village. When I came up here six months ago with a message, the steward gave me some ale while I waited for the reply, and—and I was hoping, sir, he might again. Not that I'd have asked, of course, it being the Duke's own ale. But sir, you know how tasty it is."

"Indeed I do. So you drank ale, then? How much?"

"Well, the steward brought out a ewer and a tankard, and the ewer was full. I poured out a tankard of it, and he left to go back inside and give orders to the servants. It was as good as I remembered, or better. I finished that tankard, sir, and thought of pouring out another. But I thought how strong the ale was, and I didn't want to be drunk—but he'd said to drink hearty, and it was already out of the cask—he wouldn't pour it back in—" Stephi's tanned face was flushed with embarrassment. "So I—well—sir, I poured it into the flask I was carrying, after pouring the rest of my water out. There was maybe a swallow left in the ewer, and I drank that. Then the steward came back, and asked how I liked the ale, and I said fine, and he asked if I wanted more, or something to eat, and I said no, I'd eat with the men at mess, and thanked him."

"Where is that flask now, Stephi?" asked Kolya.

"With my things, I suppose; I took it back to the barn and put it in my saddlebags."

"Go on, then."

"After that, after I put the flask up, it was nearly time for supper. I saw you ride in, sir, and go on through the Duke's Gate, and then I collected the men and we went to eat."

"What did you eat?"

"The usual, sir. Bread, cheese, stew. The men ate the same. I remember feeling a little—annoyed—at the noise. It seemed louder, all that banging and clattering. I wondered if I shouldn't have had that last swallow of ale, but nobody else seemed to notice anything about me, and I was steady on my feet. But then, sir—it's as if I was—was thinking about something else. You know how you do something you've always done, but you aren't thinking about it, and a little later you can't remember if you've done it? I know I left the messhall, but it's just hazy after that. I think I walked out into the court, but I'm not sure even of that. Then—nothing, until I woke in the night, in the infirmary." Stephi looked around at the puzzled faces.

"How long would you say it lasted?" asked Kolya of the captain.

"The violent phase—only a quarterglass or a little longer; the loss of memory seems to be about six hours."

"It's consistent with a potion or spell," said the mayor.

"A potion, I'd say. We don't have a mage in range for this," said the captain.

"I think we need to check the Duke's ale. If someone has tampered with it—" the mayor's long face scowled at them.

"I'll get the steward." Sejek disappeared into the arched doorway of the Duke's Hall, pausing to speak to the guard on the steps. It was some little time before he came out; he had a large flask of tawny liquid, and the steward carried a ewer and tankard on a tray. Venneristimon looked concerned, and was talking as he came.

"I'm quite sure, Captain Sejek," he was saying, "that nothing is wrong with the Duke's ale. It's true that this cask has been tapped some time, but I fail to see how anything could have adulterated it. Perhaps I simply should not have given the poor fellow quite so much. I mean, he *seemed* responsible."

"We'll have to check it, Venner, and make sure. The Duke has enemies enough who might wish to poison his stores." The captain put the flask he was carrying down in front of the witnesses. "I drew this off, myself," he said. "It smelled all right. I had Venner bring out the same ewer and tankard he served Stephi with. Do you recognize 'em, Stephi?"

Stephi reached for the utensils and Venner released

them. He turned the tankard around in his hands. "Yes, sir; it's the same. There's a dent here on the rim, see? And the ewer matched the pattern, same as this one does."

"I was telling the captain," Venner put in, "that of course these things were washed up at once. If there was anything, it would be gone."

The witnesses all examined the ewer and tankard. "It looks innocent enough," said the mayor. "But it could have held anything."

"Let's test the ale," said Kolya.

"Go ahead," said the captain, nodding toward the flask. Kolya picked it up and sniffed.

"Smells like good ale. But I wonder if we could smell a potion, or would the ale cover it?"

Stammel shrugged. "I don't know—I've heard that some potions have a strong smell, but who's to say?"

"Try a single drop," suggested the mayor. "See what happens."

"If I go wild," said Kolya, "don't break my arm; I've got apple harvest coming soon." She sipped the ale. "Tastes good. This is what he serves at the high feasts, isn't it, Venner?"

"Yes, it is."

"Tastes just as it did last year, if I'm any judge. No aftertaste."

"I think the corporal just drank too much," Venner said again. "It is strong ale, and I should not have brought a full ewer."

"It can't be that, Venner; he didn't drink it all," said the captain. "He drank only one tankard—and one tankard of anything wouldn't make Stephi drunk. He poured the rest into his water flask."

"Stephi," said Stammel. "Do you have any sort of potion at all—anything you might have added to that ale later, and forgotten?"

Stephi thought a moment. "Well—" he looked embarrassed. "I do have a—sort of a—a love potion. I got it from an old granny down the other side of Verella.

But—there's not much to it, sir, really, and besides, I didn't take it."

Kolya looked at him. "A *love* potion?"

"It's—it's something my girl and I enjoy—we share it—"

The captain shook his head. "The things I never knew about you, Stephi."

"But it's harmless, sir, really. It's just like a bit of wine, only more so. Just makes the night more fun, is all."

"Still, we'd better check it. It might not be as harmless as you think. Did you get it from the same person this time as before?"

"Well, no sir, I didn't. But it's a simple sort of thing—lots of the grannies sell it. I usually get it from one of the forest-folk tribes in Aarenis, but we were on the road here, and this little old lady asked did I want anything. I'm sure it's all right, sir, and even if it's not, I never took it."

"Where is it?"

"With the rest of my things, in the saddlebags."

"We'll take a look." The captain turned. "Now where has Venner gotten off to? Stephi, who knows where your things are?"

"Any of the men that came with me would know, or I could show you."

"Stammel, why don't you find them for us."

"Yes, sir. Would you want one of the witnesses to come along?"

Sejek shook his head. "Not unless they want to."

Stammel left the Duke's Court and angled across the main courtyard to the stable. Stephi's squad was hanging around the stable entrance, looking wary. He nodded to them.

"We need Stephi's saddlebags," he said. They looked sideways at each other.

"Sergeant—what're they going to do? Stephi's a good corporal—"

"I can't say. We don't know enough yet, and anyway it's the Duke's decision. Now—where are his things?"

A lanky private led the way into the smaller tack room. "That's Stephi's," he said. "The first on that row." Stammel lifted the saddlebags from their peg and turned toward the door.

"Come along," he said, "and tell me who's handled these things."

"Nobody, sir; Stephi came in before supper from the Duke's Court, and put his flask in with the rest, and nobody's been at his things since that I know of."

As Stammel came across the Duke's Court toward the others, he saw Venner coming down the steps from the Hall. He wondered briefly where Venner had been, but dropped the thought as he handed the saddlebags to the captain.

"These are yours, Stephi?" asked the captain.

"Yes, sir. The flask will be in the right one, in a holder, and the potion bottle is in the left one, wrapped in my spare socks."

They all watched as the captain opened the flaps of the saddlebags and took out the contents. He found the flask and set it aside, unopened for the moment. "It has liquid in it," he said. "I can't tell how much." He began rummaging in the other saddlebags, removing a neatly rolled cloak and a comb, then a single sock, then another one, and finally a small cloudy-glass bottle with a glass stopper. "It wasn't in the socks, Stephi," he said as he slid out the stopper. "Phew! What a smell!" He looked up. "It's empty." He passed the bottle to the mayor, who sniffed, wrinkled his nose, and passed it to Kolya. She did the same before handing it to Stammel.

"Is this the same bottle?" asked Stammel as he sniffed cautiously at the opening.

"Yes sir. It looks like it. But it didn't have a bad smell before. May I smell it now?"

"Go ahead," said the captain. "But you wouldn't have smelled it—looks like it had a wax seal around the stopper."

Stephi sniffed the bottle. "It's strange—but it reminds me of something. Just a little. Who could have emptied it?"

"One of your men says no one touched your things, but you, when you came out of the Duke's Court yesterday," said Stammel.

"But all I did was put the flask back. I didn't open this bottle."

"Let's examine the flask," said the captain. He opened it and looked in. "It's not even half full, and the smell's here, too."

Again the witnesses checked for themselves. "If what made Corporal Stephi act unlike himself and forget what happened was in what he drank, then the evidence is that it came from this potion bottle," said the mayor.

"But I didn't open it," Stephi repeated.

"You don't remember opening it," said Kolya. "If it was strong enough magic, you wouldn't remember."

"But I remember going in to supper after putting the flask away."

"Stephi, are you sure you didn't have a few more swallows of ale—after supper, maybe?" Captain Sejek sounded more tired than angry.

"Sir, I—I thought I was sure I'd never do anything like I must have done. I don't *think* I drank any more—or opened the potion. But—how can I be sure? How can I be sure of anything?"

"Stephi—I don't know." Sejek sighed. "I believe that whatever you did was under some kind of outside influence. Right now that potion seems the likeliest to me—it wasn't what you thought. The witnesses will have their own opinions—" He glanced at them.

"We still need the woman's testimony—Paksenarrion's," said Kolya.

"From what Stammel said, I doubt it will help; but go ahead, of course."

"I wonder if we can find out what the potion is," said the mayor. "And I still have a concern for the Duke's ale. Are we sure it is not contaminated? The smell in this bottle is suggestive, but—"

"We could seal it and hope it keeps until the Duke's Court; he'll have his mage there."

"I've marked and sealed the cask," Venner said. As they looked at him in surprise, he pursed his thin lips. "That's why I went back inside. The entire cask will be available for examination at the trial."

"All right, then," said Sejek. "If you, Councilor Ministiera, will take Paksenarrion's testimony, and gather such evidence as might be needed, the rest of us can get back to our business. Stammel—about Stephi's parole—"

Stammel sighed. "Sir, I've known Stephi as long as you—and I trust him. But recruits—especially my unit—won't understand if you leave him free. They know that Paks was chained under ban last night. Korryn's under ban now—"

"Sir, he's right," said Stephi. "I can't believe that I went—crazy or something—and did *that* to anyone, but the evidence is against me. The troops won't like it; they won't understand it, if I'm not under guard."

"I don't say put him under ban," said Stammel. "He's cooperated, we think someone may have magicked him—so don't ban him. But—"

"I see your point," said Sejek, frowning. "Very well. Stephi, I'm sorry, but you'll have to spend your time in the cell. I'll be down to check on you, and you're not under ban."

"That's all right, sir. I understand. I would like—if it's possible—to know how the girl is, and if she's well enough later, I'd like to—to apologize—"

"We'll see, Stephi." Sejek nodded to the guard, and they watched as Stephi was led back to the main court. The captain sighed heavily. "I'd like to get my hands on that granny, whoever she is. Tir's gut, but that's a fine soldier to be dumped in such trouble. Stammel, you'll need to see to your unit, but I'd like to talk to you later."

"Yes, sir. Any particular time?"

"Not until after lunch, at least. It'll take me that long to settle my men and make some kind of written report of this. When you've time, check with me. I may have to put you off an hour or so, but I'll try to be ready."

"Yes, sir." Stammel bowed slightly, and headed for the infirmary, tailing Kolya who was disappearing through the door.

Paksenarrion lay quietly as Maia cleaned and poulticed her thighs; a large cool poultice already covered the swollen half of her face. She'd been given a mug of beef broth and a half-mug of numbwine, and felt as if she were floating a handspan above the bed. She heard the door open, and saw Maia glance up.

"Well, Kolya; do you need to see her again?"

"If she's able. What did the surgeon say?"

"She'll mend. Her eye's all right. She's had numbwine; she'll be drowsy and drifting a bit. Eh—Paks. Come on, Paks, wake up."

Paks swallowed and tried to speak. Not much sound came out. She tried to look at Kolya, but found she couldn't turn her head. Kolya suddenly appeared beside the bed. Paks blinked her good eye. She had not really looked at the witness before. Now she noticed black hair streaked with gray, black eyes, dark brows angled across a tan, weathered face. She blinked again, her eyes dropping to Kolya's broad shoulders, her arm— the sleeve of her robe covered the stump of her left arm.

"She's awake," said Kolya. "So—they call you Paks, eh? I'm Kolya Ministiera, one of the witnesses. We need to take your testimony on this. Can you speak?"

Paks tried again and managed a hoarse croak.

"Water might help." Kolya turned away and reappeared with a mug. "Can you hold the mug? Good. Now drink and try again."

Paks took a swallow or two of water, gingerly felt the

inside of her mouth with her tongue, and managed to say, "I can speak now, Lady."

Kolya snorted. "I'm no 'lady', child: just a pensioned-off old soldier."

"But—didn't he say—you are on the Council?" Paks stumbled over the words. Even after numbwine, it hurt to move her mouth.

"That's nothing but the Duke knowing I'm the Duke's man still. No, I farm now, and raise apples. I'm no fine lady."

"I—I didn't know you were a soldier," said Paks slowly, trying not to look for the missing arm.

"Yes—I was a corporal, same as Stephi, when I lost my arm. Don't look so solemn, child. That was just bad luck—or good luck, if you like, that I lived. And the Duke's treated me well: a grant of land, and a seat on the Council."

Paksenarrion thought briefly of being as Kolya was, beyond warfare, pensioned off to a farm. She shivered. "But—what do I call you, if not lady?"

"Well, if you want to be formal, you could say Councilor Ministiera, but with you full of numbwine I doubt you'd get your tongue around that. Kolya's fine. I won't bite."

"Yes—Kolya."

"Now, Sergeant Stammel gave me the outline of your story, but I still have some questions for you. Had Corporal Stephi spoken to you at any time before he entered your barracks?"

"No—in fact, I didn't really see him before. Only out of the corner of my eye as they rode in, and then Armsmaster Siger thumped me for not paying attention."

Kolya chuckled. "With good cause. Take it from me, you never look aside when fighting. But you didn't see him at supper?"

"No—I was talking to Saben."

"I see. I understand that he showed up in your barracks and said he wanted to speak to you. Then he tried to get you to bed him, and tried to force you when you refused. Is that right?"

"Yes. He tried to push me down. Then when I said some things my cousin taught me, he put his hand over my mouth and I bit him. And that's when he got very angry—"

"He hit you first with his belt, Stammel said—"

"And I tried to get past him and away. I really did, Kolya. I wasn't trying to hurt him, or fight, just get away."

"All right, calm down. He'd be too much for you, I imagine."

Paks began to tremble again. "I—I couldn't get free—and he was hitting me, again and again. I couldn't get my breath, and someone was holding me, so I couldn't hit back or get away, and—it hurt so much—" Tears ran down her face. "I—I'm sorry—I don't mean to cry—"

"That's all right. A hard beating takes it out of you." Even in her misery, Paks noticed that Kolya spoke as someone who knew. "You'll be all right in a few days. Paksenarrion, have you ever bedded anyone here?"

"No." Paks fought against the sobs.

"Have you ever bedded anyone?"

"No—I never wanted to."

Kolya sighed. "Paks, we need to know if you were raped as well as beaten—do you know?"

Paks shook her head. "I—I don't know what it would be like. I know it hurts, but I don't know what kind of hurt."

"Well, then, we'll have to take a look. Maia will help me, and I think another swallow of numbwine won't hurt at all. If you sleep all day, so much the better." Kolya fetched the flask of numbwine and poured some into the mug Paks held. "Drink all of that." Paks swallowed, almost choking on the heavy, sweet wine. In a few minutes she felt a soft wave of sleep roll up around her, and drifted away, unknowing.

A few minutes later, Kolya left the infirmary, and

almost fell over Stammel who was waiting at the door. "Well?" he asked harshly.

"No," said Kolya. "She wasn't. They put enough bruises on her, and if they'd had another two minutes—but as it is, she wasn't raped. That may save Stephi's hide—or some of it."

"It won't save Korryn's," said Stammel grimly. "That was a neat catch you made, Kolya."

"Thanks. Some things I can still do. I agree you're well rid of that one. I wonder if we'll ever know which of them actually did what—probably not. I presume Korryn's will be a public event."

"Very. That—" Stammel growled and spat. "I can't think of a word. Filth. I should have run him out weeks ago."

Kolya tapped his arm. "Now, Matthis Stammel, you know you aren't that kind. You had to have a good reason. I'd better go on and report to the others. Cheer up—she'll be all right in a few days."

"I hope so. She's a good one, Kolya—almost as good as who she looks like—Tamarrion—if nothing goes wrong."

Kolya looked thoughtful. "Does she? I couldn't tell, with all those bruises. You know you can't protect the good ones, Stammel; it ruins them in the long run."

"I know. But this kind of thing—"

"If she's that good it won't stop her. Nothing stopped Tamarrion. Wait and see—I'd best go."

Chapter Six

By the time Captain Valichi returned, Paksenarrion was up, though her right eye was still swollen shut. She had not returned to her unit; Stammel wanted to report to Valichi, and give him the chance to talk to her if he wished, before she talked to her friends. As it happened, Valichi made his decisions on the basis of the witnesses' reports, conferences with Sejek, Stammel, and Stephi, and an interview with Korryn, the last for form's sake only. So one morning Maia helped Paks back into her recruit uniform, now cleaned and mended, and sent her to join the others in formation to witness Valichi's decisions.

Again it was early morning. Paks had scarcely time to find her place before they were called to attention. A heavy timbered framework on a low platform was centered before them; on the right stood the witnesses, and on the left was a quartet of guards near a smoking brazier, one holding a straight razor, and one a whip. Paks recognized the dark guard who had held her. She looked at the razor and whip, and shivered.

She heard the noise of boots and chains as Korryn and Jens were brought out of the building into the courtyard. Memory of her own ordeal made her choke. She thought hard about Korryn, about all the things he'd done, to keep from feeling sympathy she wasn't supposed to feel. After all, she'd wanted to beat him herself, in the past.

The prisoners passed in front of the formation. Jens was hanging back, having to be prodded, half-carried. She could hear his soft fearful moans. It was disgusting. Korryn had new bruises on his face. She wondered who had hit him, and why. Probably the guards, she thought. They halted in front of the platform. Captain Valichi, shorter than Captain Sejek and looking almost square in his armor, moved towards them, facing the assembly.

"You are here to witness the punishment of two former recruits of this Company," he began. "For their crimes they have been expelled from the Company; after their punishment, they will be taken beyond the bounds of the Duke's domains. Should they ever return, they will be liable to additional punishment, as the Duke may direct. Should any of you see them within this domain, you are required to report it to your officers. Their crimes are known to most of you, but I proclaim them. Korryn Maherit was charged with assisting in an assault on another recruit—"

"It's not fair!" yelled Korryn. "It wasn't my fault!" Even before Valichi's command, one of the guards holding him had slugged him.

"—with conspiracy with Jens Hanokensson to prevent detection of this assault," the captain went on, "and with lying to the witnesses called to take testimony in the case. All the evidence and testimony so far indicates that Korryn Maherit did assault and injure Paksenarrion Dorthansdotter, and did instruct Jens Hanokensson to warn him of the approach of any authority, and did attempt to instruct Corporal Stephi of Dorrin's cohort, a veteran member of the Company, in a lie explaining the assault, while Corporal Stephi was temporarily unaware of his own actions, probably through the action of some drug or potion. We have no proof that Korryn Maherit supplied this drug or potion. Jens Hanokensson stands charged with conspiracy with Korryn Maherit to prevent detection of Korryn Maherit's crimes. Both of these men have a bad record in the recruit cohort. The following sentences are imposed by me, as Duke Phelan's lawful representative and cohort commander of recruits. For Jens Hanokensson: five strokes—" Jens moaned again; the guards holding him shook him. "—a shaved head, and expulsion. For Korryn Maherit, the Duke's brand on the forehead, forty strokes well-marked, and expulsion *tinisi turin*." Korryn writhed, trying to break free from his guards. "Strip them," said Valichi. Two of the guards by the platform came forward and ripped the recruit tunics from neck to hem, then turned the prisoners to face the formation. The guards forced Jens to his knees, and the one with the razor stepped up behind him. When he felt the first tug at his cinnamon-brown hair, he yelped and flinched.

"Hold still, ye fool," said the guard. "If ye jerk around, I'll cut ye." Tufts of hair fell; Jens had shut his eyes and was rigidly still. The barber worked quickly and roughly; soon nothing was left of the thick hair and mustache. A few shallow grazes oozed blood on his scalp, which was pale above his tanned face. The guards hauled him up the platform to the posts and crossbar, and bound him to it, feet dangling. Then the guard with the whip mounted the platform behind him.

"One," said Captain Valichi. The whip smacked against his back; Paks saw his face twist in pain. "Two." Another smack. He gave a strangled cry. "Three. Four." The captain paused. "Sergeant Stammel—do you want the parting blow?"

"No, sir. Not for this one."

"Five." The last blow fell. Jens's screams softened into sobs as the guards untied his arms and dragged him from the platform. Paks could see the welts standing out on his back; only one was bleeding. The guards moved him away from the platform and held him facing the assembly.

It took four of the guards to hold Korryn as one of them took the brand from the brazier where it had been heating. Paks looked down. She didn't want to see this. She could hear Korryn's muttered curses, the scuffling feet, the hiss and sizzle as the brand etched his forehead. He gave a short cry, followed by gasping sobs. She glanced up for a moment. The guard with the razor was taking off his hair; Korryn's face was white under its tan. The brand showed stark, a stylized foxhead. Without his hair and beard, his face looked different; he hardly had a chin. His eyes met hers; he snarled a curse at her, and the guards cuffed him. Paks stared over his head; she didn't want him to think she could not watch.

The guards dragged him up the platform—still struggling to break free—and bound his wrists to the crossbar after removing his chains. Then they bound his ankles to bolts Paks had not noticed, and the guard with the razor stepped up to him. Korryn paled even more.

"What are you—?"

"Tinisi turin means shaved—all over—" said the guard, grinning. "Like a shorn lamb, remember?" And shortly the hair on chest, belly, and groin made a heap on the platform. When that guard was through, he stepped back, and the one carrying the whip came forward.

By the tenth stroke, Paks no longer cared what Korryn thought; she stared straight at the messhall windows. No one had reminded her that she might have been on that platform, but she remembered well enough what Stammel had said when he first came to her cell. She loathed Korryn—would be glad to see him gone—but she could not watch. The blows went on—and on— each counted out by the captain's calm voice. They sounded different now. Korryn sounded different too. She tried not to hear that, and lost the count. Suddenly it was very quiet. She looked up. Korryn hung from his bonds, head drooping; she could see the blood streaking his legs and staining the platform below.

"Well, Sergeant Stammel?" asked the captain.

"Yes, sir; with pleasure." Stammel left his place and mounted the platform. The guard handed him the whip, now glistening along its length. Paks watched, fascinated and horrified, as he braced himself and gave Korryn five powerful blows. Korryn's body jerked, and he gave a last scream and fainted. Stammel ran his hand down Korryn's back and returned to his unit, holding his bloody hand out. He faced Paks, and touched it to her forehead as her eyes widened in shock.

"By this blood your injury is avenged," he said, and took up his position again. Meanwhile one of the guards had taken a pot of some liquid and was daubing it on Korryn's back. Then he was untied, and lowered to the ground. His back and legs were covered with welts and blood; the dye in the pot made a blue stain that looked ghastly mixed with blood. A guard checked his pulse.

"He'll do," he reported. "Cold water, sir?" The captain nodded. After several minutes, and a bucket of water, Korryn stirred and groaned. When his eyes opened, Captain Valichi nodded, and the guards pulled him to his feet and bound his hands in front of him. Jens, meanwhile, had been dressed in a nightshift, with a rope noose around his neck; his guards looked to the captain.

"Go ahead; take him out."

"West, sir?" The captain nodded in answer, and the guards led Jens away. Korryn now had a rope around his neck too, and at the captain's second nod, his guards tugged, forcing him forward. He could barely keep his feet. Paks looked away, stomach churning. She heard horses' hooves behind the formation, near the gate, muttered voices. Then the hoofbeats moved away, through the gate, and the courtyard was left in silence.

Captain Valichi looked at them for a long moment. "Some of you," he said with a grim smile, "seem impressed by what you saw—I hope you all are. The

Duke will not tolerate anything that jeopardizes the strength of the Company. In a few months you will be depending on each other in battle. Each of you must be worthy of your companions' trust, both on and off the field. If you aren't, we'll get rid of you. If you injure a companion, you'll be punished. It may be that some of you don't have the stomach for army life; if so, speak to your sergeant. We don't want cowards. Sergeant Stammel, assign a detail from your unit to clean up this mess, and I'll want to speak with Paksenarrion. The formation is dismissed."

In the unit's duty room, a few minutes later, Paks tried to act calm. "Sit down, Paksenarrion," said Captain Valichi. She sat across the desk from him. Her stomach was a solid knot of apprehension. "Have you talked to any of your friends since this happened?"

"No, sir."

"Good. Paksenarrion, you have a good record, so far. This is the first trouble you've been in, and from the evidence none of it was your fault. Stammel did say that he thought you should confine your use of strong language to terms you knew the meaning of—though calling someone a jacks-hole full of soured witch's milk—" Paks gasped and felt herself reddening; the captain smiled and went on, "—is not an excuse for an attack, it can cause trouble. Did you even know that was Pargunese? No? Well, stick to Common or whatever your native language is. Anyway, you're blameless of the brawl itself. Now—you've been injured in the Company, though not, we think, permanently. If you wish to leave, you may. We will give you a recommendation, based on your record, and a pass through the Duke's domain, and a small sum to tide you over until you reach home or find other employment. I can suggest several private guard companies that might hire you with our recommendation. You'll be on light duty until you can see out of that eye again: you may have that long to make your decision—unless you are already determined to leave. Are you?"

"No, sir. I don't want to leave at all." Paks had had a lingering fear that she might be thrown out.

"You're sure?" Paks nodded. "Well, if you change your mind before you're back to full duty, let me know. I'm glad you want to stay in; I think you'll do well—if you stay out of fights like this. Tell me—do you think Korryn was sufficiently punished?"

"Yes, sir." Paks could hear the distaste in her own voice.

"Ah. It bothered you, eh? I see it did. Well, it's supposed to, and if you stay in, you'll see that again—though we all hope not to. Now—about Corporal Stephi. I've agreed, with Sejek, to let him go south for his trial by the Duke. We've kept the scribes busy, and have the witnesses' testimony and the rest written down. We think this will be sufficient, and the Duke won't need to see any of you. We hope. Anyway, Stephi has been quite concerned about you—did Stammel mention it?" Paks nodded; Stammel had told her a lot about Stephi. "He's asked how you were, and he wanted to see you and apologize. He's a good man, really. We're sure that some outside influence—probably magical—affected him that night. But—it's up to you—will you see him before he goes south?"

"Sir, I—I don't know. Should I?"

The captain frowned slightly, lacing his hands together. "It would be kind, I think. He can't hurt you now, you know, even if he wanted to. It won't make any difference to his trial, but it would reassure him, to see you up. You don't have to, of course."

Paks did not want to see Stephi ever again, but as she thought about it, she realized that she would have to, next year in the south. They might be in the same cohort; he might be her corporal. Best get it over, she decided, and looked up to meet the captain's gaze. "I'll see him, sir. But—I don't know what to say."

Valichi smiled. "You needn't say much. It'll only be a minute. Wait here." He rose from behind the desk, and went out, shutting the door. Paks felt her stomach churn. She swallowed once, then again. It seemed a long time before the door opened again. Paks rose as the two captains, Valichi and Sejek, and Stephi came in together, crowding the little room. The mouse under Stephi's eye had faded to a sickly green.

"I'm very sorry, Paksenarrion, for the trouble I caused you," said Stephi. Paks could not find her voice, and merely nodded. "I want you to know that—that I don't do things like that—not usually. I never have before." His voice shook a little. "I—I hope you won't leave the Company, because of it—"

"I won't," said Paks. "I'm staying in."

"Good. I'm glad. I hope you're feeling better."

"Yes." Suddenly Paks found herself wanting to reassure this man, even though he had hurt her. She liked his honest face. "I'm doing well—in a week I'll be fine." He relaxed a bit and seemed to have nothing more to say.

Captain Sejek opened the door and Stephi went out; Paks saw the guard waiting for him in the passage.

"Thank you, Paksenarrion, for seeing him," said Sejek a moment later. "I, too, regret your injuries and the trouble you've had. Stephi will be punished, of course—"

"But sir, everyone's told me it wasn't really his fault," said Paks, before she remembered that Sejek was a captain. She bit her lip.

Sejek frowned and sighed. "Maybe it wasn't, but even so, he injured you. That doesn't change. We punish drunks for their misdeeds, and for being drunk. He'll be punished."

Paks thought of Korryn's punishment and shuddered. "But he's not as bad as Korryn," she persisted.

"No. He's not. But he's supposed to be better—much better—than any recruit. He's a corporal of the regular Company, a veteran. This is not an offense to regard lightly. But that's not your concern—don't worry about it. I, too, am glad to hear that you're staying in the Company; I'll see you in the south next spring." Sejek went out, leaving Paks with Valichi.

Valichi's mustache twitched. "Now that's as close to an apology as I've ever heard Sejek come."

"Apology?"

"Well—he's wishing he'd taken a better look at you before he banned you that night. But Sejek doesn't like to admit he could be wrong—I'll warn you of that. Don't even hint that he made a mistake on this, or he'll be down on you for years. Right now—well, he's convinced that you're acceptable. It helped that you defended Stephi—was that why you did it?"

Paks was confused. "Sir, I—"

"No. You're not the type. Go find Stammel—he's out drilling, I think, on the east grounds—and he'll keep you busy."

Paks walked out, still confused, but happy to be returning to her friends. She joined in marching drill, but Siger barred her from weapons practice. "You can't fight with both eyes open, yet," he said. "It'll be a long time before you're ready to fight with just one." Barracks chores were well within her capacity; when she thought about the cell, or the infirmary, she was glad enough to have them to do.

At first no one said anything about the fight or its aftermath. Saben explained that he had tried to find Stammel, that by the time he had returned, she was already hurt. The others simply avoided the subject. Even Effa forbore to give a lecture on the protection of Gird. This suited Paks very well; she had no desire to talk about the little she could remember. But in the other units, curiosity overcame tact, and as soon as she was back in weapons drill, the questions began. Barranyi, the tall black-haired woman in Vossik's unit, often matched against Paks in drill, went farther than most. She was well-known for her strength of arm and sharp tongue.

"You should have poked an eye out," she began one afternoon, as they walked back to the main stronghold with a load of firewood. Paks shook her head.

"I was trying to get away."

"That's stupid. Anyone can get mauled trying to get away. Attack on your own. If you'd gotten an eye—"

"I'd have been in worse trouble, Barra." Paks checked the mule she was leading, and shoved one length of wood back into place. But Barra had not gone on; she halted her own mule and went on with her lecture.

"No, you wouldn't. He started it; he was wrong. They'd have had to admit that. As it is, they owe you—"

"No, they don't. Besides, they only found out it was his fault because I was beat up worse."

"That's not right." Barra scowled and strode along silent for some distance. "If it's not your fault, they should—"

"Barra—" Natzlin, a slender, pleasant girl with warm brown eyes who had been coupled with Barra before they joined, laid a hand on her arm. "Paks came out well—and if she's satisfied—"

"No. She came out beaten half-dead, and—"

Paks laughed. "By the gods, Barra, I'm not that easy to kill."

"You looked it that morning. A real mess, I tell you—I was ashamed—"

Paks felt a flicker of anger. "You—and why *you*? I was the one out there in front of everyone—"

"You'd always been a strong one, Siger's pet, and there you were, looking like something that'd come from a lockup—"

Paks grinned in spite of herself. "Well—I had—"

"Blast it! You know what I mean! You looked—"

"Gods above, Barra! She doesn't want to think about that now!" Vik shoved his way between them, and winked at Paks. "Don't worry—even bruises and chains can't make you ugly, Paks."

She felt herself go red. "Vik—"

"Like a song," he went on, unmoved. "Did you ever hear 'Falk's Oath of Gold,' Paks? When Falk was taken in the city of fear, and locked away all those years?"

"No. I thought Falk was a sort of saint, like Gird."

"Saints!" snorted Barra from Vik's other side.

"He is," said Vik seriously. "And Barra—I wouldn't scoff at them. Maybe they're far above us—but they have power."

"The gods have power," said Barra. "I'm not like Effa—I don't believe that men become gods when they die. And I'd rather be alive anyway."

"But tell me about Falk," said Paks. "Isn't he the one that wears rubies and silver?"

"I don't know what he wears *now*," began Vik. "He was a knight, a ruler's son, who kept his sworn oath and saved his kin by it, even though it meant years of slavery for him."

"Ugh. Why didn't he just kill his enemies?" asked Barra. "I heard that he spent a year cleaning the jacks of some city—"

"That and more," said Vik. "It's in the song, but you know I can't sing it. My father did, and I know most of the story. You'd like it, Paks—it's full of magic and kings and things like that."

"A magic sword?"

"Oh, yes. More than one. Someday when we've made enough money, we can hire a harper to sing it for us." Vik kept the conversation going until they reached the stronghold, where they broke up into their separate units. Barra shook her head, but stayed away from the topic the next time they drilled together. But others wanted to know what the underground cells were like, and what Stammel had said, and what the corporal had said. Paks fended off these questions as best she could: the cells were cold and miserable, and she wouldn't repeat any of the talks she'd had. Eventually they let her alone.

Meanwhile, Stammel had taken the unit in to help Kolya with her apple harvest. This was their first time to see Duke's East, since they had arrived from the west. In size it was between Three Firs and Rocky Ford. Children playing in the streets waved and yelled at them; the adults smiled and spoke to Stammel. They passed an inn, the Red Fox, and a cobbled square surrounded with taller stone houses, and came to a stone bridge over the little river. Upstream Paks could see a weir and a millpond, and a waterwheel slowly turning. Kolya's orchard lay south of the river, beyond a water meadow where cattle grazed.

Kolya's orchard had more trees than Paks could count; she had never seen such a thing. Her aunt had been famed for five apple trees and two plums, but Kolya had rows of apples, plums, and pears. Only the apples remained so late, scenting the air with their rich, exciting fragrance. Soon Paks was high on a ladder, picking the apples at the top of her assigned tree. It was cool and sunny, perfect weather for the job. Below, in the aisles between the trees, Stammel and Kolya strolled together, directing the pickers and talking.

Paks caught a few snatches of that conversation, between orders to the workers. It seemed to be far removed from apple harvest, something about someone named Tamarrion, who had once been in the Company.

"—wouldn't have happened like that at all," she heard Stammel say. "She would have made sure first, before she called for a ban."

Kolya snorted. "In *her* day, you'd never have brought back someone like Korryn at all, would you?"

"No—you're right about that. But things are different." Paks saw his head shake, far below, then he peered up to see that she was working. She wondered if the mysterious Tamarrion had been a sergeant—even a captain—but something in their tone kept her from asking.

As fall turned to winter, the recruits honed their weapons skills, now learning to use a shield with their swords. They began drilling in groups, one line against another, learning to work together with their weapons. They were allowed to stand guard, first with the regulars, then alone. On guard duty on the wall, with her sword hanging heavy at her side, Paks felt very much the professional. One gray, sleety day, she was on duty when a traveler came up the road from Duke's West, and called the challenge herself. She thought he did not notice that her tunic was recruit brown instead of maroon.

Along with all this, they were introduced to tactics. Paks had thought that after mastering the intricacies of drill, nothing remained to learn about engaging the enemy. She was wrong.

"But I thought we just ran at them and started fighting," said Vik, echoing her thought.

"No. That's the way to get killed, and quickly. None of you will make these decisions now, but you all need to know something of tactics. You can do your job better if you know what you're trying to accomplish." They were gathered around Stammel in the messhall between meals; he began to set out apples on the table. "Now suppose this—here—is the Duke's Company. And this over here is the enemy. Look at the length of lines."

"Theirs is longer," said Saben, stating the obvious. "But we—"

"Listen. Now suppose we engage just as we are. What happens on each end of our line, on the flanks?"

"They can hit the side, too," said Vik.

"If they have enough, they can go all around," Paks put in.

"Yes. That looks bad, doesn't it? But it depends on why their line is so long, and what they're fighting with." He added more apples to the array. "Suppose they've only as many men as we have, so their line is long and thin. We form the square, and we engage one-on-one all the way around. With our depth, we actually have them outnumbered *at each position*. If they're fighting with swords, they won't have a chance. We have concentrated our strength on their weakness —or rather, they have stupidly chosen to make themselves weak all over."

Effa frowned at the table. "So it's better to make the square?"

"Not always. We can't move fast or far in the square—
you remember—" They nodded. "Mobility is important,
too. So is terrain—where is the good ground?" Quickly
he showed them how slope, water, and such hazards as
swamp and loose rock could change the choice of tactics. "It's the commander's responsibility to choose the
best ground—for our side, of course. The Duke's famous for it. But you need to know how it's done, so
you'll know what to watch out for, and which way to
move—"

"But we're under orders, aren't we? We just do what
we're told—"

"Yes. But sergeants and corporals get killed—even
captains. In battle, there's no time to send questions to
the Duke. If the regulars don't know what to do and
why, the cohort will fall apart. Be captured at best.
That's what Kolya Ministiera did—took over her cohort, kept 'em moving together, the right way. That's
why she made corporal so young. If she hadn't lost an
arm at Cortes Cilwan, she'd have been the youngest
sergeant in the Company, I don't doubt. But when she
went down, someone else took over—that's what we
train for."

They looked at each other, wondering. Paks hoped
she would do as well—without losing an arm. The only
thing that frightened her was the thought of ending her
career as a young cripple, with nothing left to do.

Soon the lessons in tactics had gone beyond table
demonstrations to live practice fields. Each recruit unit
made a mock cohort, and they practiced engagements,
disengagements, squaring, flanking, and other maneu-
vers: first without weapons, and then with wooden swords
and shields. In smaller groups they learned to fight in
confined areas: stairs, passages, stables. They made ladders and scaled the walls of the stronghold in mock
assaults, then learned to hold the wall against assaults.
And since the Duke sometimes hired mounts when he
wanted to move his troops rapidly, they learned to ride.

"This is a mule," said Corporal Bosk. Paks thought

that was unnecessary. The mule flicked one long ear. On the ground beside it were saddle, saddlecloth, and bridle. "A mule is not a horse," he went on. That also was obvious. Long ears, mealy muzzle, heavy head, small hooves. Paks suppressed a yawn. Maybe some of the city people didn't know the difference. She glanced around for Vik. "How many of you," Bosk was asking, "have ever worked with mules?" Several hands went up. "You—" he said, pointing. "What's the big difference between mules and horses?"

"Mules can kick anyways," said Jorti, "and they're fussier about their ears, and they're smarter than horses." Jorti's father, Paks remembered, had something to do with caravans.

"Right," said Bosk. "All of that. Those of you that've never worked either will have less trouble than you horse-folk. They are *different*. Mules are more ear-shy than any horse, and if you drag a bridle over their ears, they'll plant a hoof on you. A back hoof. When you're standing in front of 'em." Paks looked at the mule, surprised. It didn't look like it could kick forward. "And they're smart," Bosk went on. "Really smart. A good one'll go farther on worse ground with less fuss—but a mule looks out for itself above all." He picked up the bridle and began to demonstrate how to put it on.

The mule assigned to Paks flicked its ears nervously as she eased the crownpiece over the top of its head. She talked to it as if it were her father's plow pony, but kept a respectful eye on the near hind leg. The mule that kicked Sif had made a believer out of her. She laid the saddlecloth on its back, and, after another look at Bosk's demonstration, set the saddle in place.

"That's right," he said, as he walked along the line. "Now fasten the girth." For that she had to bend down, reaching under its belly. The mule stood as if its feet were bolted to the ground. Paks caught the end of the girth and drew it up. The mule swelled visibly. Paks tugged the girth tight, and pulled again. The mule gave her an inscrutable look out of one amber eye, and shifted its weight minutely. Paks glanced back, and saw the tip of the near hind hoof resting lightly on the ground. Its ears flopped out sideways, swung lazily back and forth. She tugged again at the girth. The mule sighed, without losing an inch of its circumference, and the ears were still. Paks glared at it.

"Dumb mule," she said.

"That won't do," said Bosk behind her. "Mule knows you're nervous. Like this—" He grabbed the mule's reins, gave a short jerk, and yelled "Hai!" into one drooping ear. The mule threw up its head with a snort, ears forward. Bosk thumped it hard in the ribs, and jerked the girth four inches tighter with one smooth motion. "Like that," he said. The mule was back on all four legs, tail swinging gently. "Don't hurt 'em," he went on. "They won't forget being beaten, say, but you've got to get their attention and be firm. Can't bluff 'em, like you can horses."

Eventually they all learned to bridle and saddle the mules, and after hours of painful practice they all learned to ride without damaging the mules or themselves. Paks even grew to enjoy it, trying to see herself on a prancing warhorse instead of a mule. She asked Bosk once if it were the same; his face creased in a grin. "Thinking of that, are you? And you not yet a soldier! Well, Paks, it's about as much like riding one of these old pack mules as playing soldier with a stick-sword is like real warfare. You've a long way to go, girl, if that's where you're going." Paks blushed and kept her dreams to herself after that.

As the cold winter wore on, they began to feel that they were ready to go—ready to face any army anywhere. Some from each unit had left—those frightened or shocked by Korryn's punishment, those injured too badly to continue, and a few more who decided, as the training came closer and closer to actual combat, that they didn't want to be soldiers after all. Some of the recruits—Paks and Barra among them—were surprised that these dropouts were let go with so little dispute.

Why had they had to sign an agreement to stay two years, if anyone could leave at any time?

"Think about it," said Stammel when Paks asked. "Your life will depend on the skill and courage of those beside you. Look at Talis: she was warned along with the rest of you, and she got pregnant anyway. Anyone too selfish or stupid to take birthbane when it's right there on the table at meals isn't going to make a good soldier. As for courage, do you want to chance your life on someone whose only thought is getting away?"

"No, but——"

"No. And they did not know, until they tried the training, that they would fail, or be so frightened. Neither do you. That's why no one's promoted from recruit until *after* we've seen them in battle."

Paks thought about that, and looked at her companions with new intent. Vik—always joking, but quick as a ferret with his blade. Arñe, pleasant and hardworking, never flustered. Saben, good-natured and strong, quick on his feet. Effa, bossy and nosy, but totally honest and fearless. Barra, her nearest rival among the women for size and strength, and Natzlin, her gentler shadow. Quiet Sim, Jorti with his caravan tales, quick-tempered Seli, chill Harbin. Those swords would ward her, or not. Her sword would ward them—or not.

But time to think was short, with the rush of training, and soon the year turned toward spring. The first brief thaw made mush out of the snow on the drill fields; the ground below was still frozen. And then the hints began.

Chapter Seven

The Duke is coming. The Duke will be here next week—no, two weeks—no, three days. Rumors swarmed over the stronghold like hornets, stinging all the recruits with excitement and curiosity. Every square foot of the stronghold was scrubbed, and what the working parties thought clean enough was scrubbed again—and again. They cleaned the stables, oiled every scrap of leather, polished every bit of metal on all the tack. The pits that served the jacks were dug out and limed, and the stinking refuse hauled away in carts to be spread on the hayfields of Duke's West. Along the road from Duke's East, fifty recruits filled holes and ruts and cleaned out the side-ditches. They rolled the surface with a heavy stone cylinder drawn by oxen, using strings and a notched stick to make sure the crown had an even camber. Siger had a group busy oiling the wooden practice blades and scouring all metal weapons; he would not tolerate so much as a fingerprint.

None of the recruits were allowed in the Duke's Court, but from all the bustling in and out it was obvious that the same rigorous preparation was going on there as well. Messengers jogged back and forth between the two villages and the stronghold, staying off the newly worked road to avoid the curses of the road crew.

It had been raining several days, a cold thin drizzle that penetrated without cleansing, but after a shift of wind in the night, the sky cleared. Paks, on duty as recruit guard in the night watch, had spent several miserable hours pacing back and forth on the battlements before the rain quit. She and Coben had complained every time they met at the southeast corner of the wall. The windshift brought drier and colder air; they agreed the exchange was for the better. Now, as the Necklace of Torre, the winter watch-stars, sank to the west, the eastern sky began to glow. Paks looked toward the messhall chimneys—yes, a thin column of smoke, thickening as she watched, oozed from one of them. She thought of the asar, the hot sweet drink the night guards were given as soon as it could be brewed, and blew on her cold hands, looking outward again.

The land around was still a dark featureless blur, but she could see the ridge to the northeast, black against a sky now showing deep blue. It seemed much colder; she stamped as she walked back and forth from the gate tower to the corner. Light seeped into the sky, moment by moment. She could see the planks she walked on, and the remaining puddles, now frozen hard. She could see the paler blur of the road to Duke's East trailing away from the gate. She glanced back at the courtyard, at the messhall chimneys, both smoking now, the smoke torn away in tatters from the tops of the stacks. She looked eastward. A white band showed beneath the broadening blue; only Silba, the dawn star, still shone in the lightening sky. She dropped her eyes to the land, emerging slowly to sight as if it rose from under dark water: the ridge to the east, and the mountains beyond it—the broad reach of the drill fields, sodden with rainwater that reflected the brightening sky. Southward, the road stood out more clearly, swerving to avoid a marshy area, lifting over a hummock of ground between the stronghold and Duke's East.

Sometimes, she remembered, you could see the smoke from Duke's East: the low buildings were out of sight in trees, behind the hummock, but she knew which clumps of trees to watch. It was still too dark. Her legs felt brittle with cold; she did a little jig at the corner, waiting for Coben to finish his circuit so they could talk.

"Gah—it's cold!" he gasped, shivering, as he came close enough.

Paks nodded, dancing from foot to foot, both of them numb. "N-not long," she said. "Did—did you see the smoke? Soon."

Coben grinned. "B-better be soon. Better go on; it's colder to stop."

Paks turned away. It was light enough to see colors now, muted though they were. There was the dark blur of trees along the river—the larger blur of the trees near and beyond Duke's East. When she got to the gate tower, the guard sergeant opened the tower door and beckoned her in.

"Here's something to warm you," he said. "Just came up from the kitchens."

Paks nodded gratefully, too cold to speak, and took the mug he offered. Even in the tower it was cold; steam rose from both mug and pitcher on the table. She sipped the scalding liquid; it burned her tongue. Her hands around the mug began to ache with cold, then warmed enough to tingle. She felt a warm glow inside, and drained her mug. "Shall I take some to Coben?"

"Let him come in, out of the wind," said the sergeant. "You walk both segments for a few minutes, then come for a second dose."

"Yes, sir." Paks rubbed her arms hard a moment, then opened the door and went back out on the wall. It was just as cold. A red streak fanned across the east. Coben was waiting at the corner; Paks waved him in.

He jogged past her with a stiff grin. She walked on, looking east at the nearby slopes, and turned north at the corner to take Coben's place. North of the stronghold she could see more ridges through a gap in the nearest. Orcs laired there, someone had said. West were great rounded folds of moorland that the villages used for sheep pasture. She thought back to the moors above her father's farm. It had been cold there, too, but you could stay in with the sheep at night. Her nose wrinkled, remembering the smell. She grinned to herself. She did not want to be back there, even for a warm place at night. She turned and started south along the wall.

A chip of liquid fire lifted above the eastern horizon, south of the ridge: the sun, a fat red-gold disk. Paks noticed the crisp blue shadows that sprang across the walk from the stones of the battlements. The early light gave the fields below a rosy glow. Evergreens along the river were clearly green, and bare branches on other trees glinted as they swayed in the wind. She looked again for Duke's East. Yes—smoke, now gold-white against a pale blue sky. She looked along the road, idly, then stiffened. She had caught a glimpse of sunlight on something—something that glittered.

She strained her eyes, squinting against the cold. Whatever it was lay between the hummock and Duke's East, where the road itself was out of sight. Another glitter, a vague sense of movement. Paks let out a yell. The guard on the other side of the tower, who had been heading for the west corner, turned and looked at her. She yelled again, and pointed toward Duke's East, then jogged to the tower. The door opened.

"What is it?" asked Coben. "Was I too long?" Behind him, Paks could see the sergeant.

"No—something on the road. On the road to Duke's East."

Coben erupted from the doorway just ahead of the sergeant. "Where?" asked both of them at once. Paks pointed.

"Beyond the hummock—I saw something in the light, something moving."

"I can't see anything," said the other guard, a recruit from Kefer's unit, who had come through the tower. "What were you yelling for?"

"It may be the Duke," said the sergeant. "If she saw anything—we'll know soon enough. Get back to your posts; I'll rouse the others. If it is the Duke," he said to Paks, "I'll thank you for the extra warning. He won't catch us unprepared—not that we were."

Coben went back to the east wall, but kept looking over his shoulder to the south. Paks could not take her eyes off the road, where it came back into view over the hummock. Behind her in the courtyard she heard a sudden commotion, but she was not even tempted to turn around. The tower door opened, and half the complement of regular guards poured out, all armed, to space themselves along the wall. Paks saw two trumpeters waiting in the doorway. The other half of the guards, she realized, had gone out the far side of the tower. The sergeant reappeared.

"Paks, you and Coben come down and parade with your unit."

Paks tore her eyes from the road; the sergeant eyed her kindly. "Go on, now. I know you want to stay and see it, but the Duke likes everything done regularly. All the recruits should be together." Paks nodded, and slipped down the tower stairs to the courtyard. The recruit units were already forming. Stammel was watching for Paks and Coben with another jug of asar.

"Here—you two look half-frozen. Drink this quickly, go use the jacks and straighten yourselves up, and get back here as fast as you can."

They took the jug into the barracks. Paks took down her windblown hair and rebraided it quickly, then downed a mug of asar. She ran to the jacks, rubbing her arms and stamping her feet. It seemed much warmer down off the wall. When they came out, Stammel took the jug and sent them into formation. Corporal Bosk moved out of her place and into his own.

Just as Paks stepped into her position, the trumpets rang out from the tower. She wished she was up there to see. After a breathless pause, the trumpets sounded again; this time she could hear a faint answering call from outside. Captain Valichi was striding around the courtyard, checking each recruit unit in turn. Across the court, Paks could see his horse waiting. The trumpets sounded again. Captain Valichi mounted and rode to the gate. A bellow from the guard sergeant, high overhead. A rumble from outside. The sergeant yelled down into the court: "Captain, it's my lord Duke."

"Open the gates!" ordered the captain. Paks could hear the grinding of the portcullis mechanism, and the great brown leaves on the main gates folded inward. For a moment nothing happened. Then the clatter of horses' hooves on stone, and a figure in glittering mail under a long maroon cloak rode through the gates. Valichi bowed in the saddle.

"Welcome, my lord Duke," he said. The cloaked figure pushed back the fur-edged hood, revealing rumpled red hair above a bearded face.

"Early for breakfast, I'd have thought," said the Duke. "What sharpeyes spotted us this time?"

"A recruit, my lord," said Valichi.

The Duke scanned each of the recruit units; Paks felt his gaze like a dagger blade, cold and keen. Then he grinned at Valichi. "Well," he said, "let's keep *that* one. Good work, captain." He dropped his reins and stretched. "Tir's bones, Val, I'm ready for breakfast if no one else is. It's cold out there, man. Let's get the fire." He lifted his reins and rode through the wide aisle of the formations to the Duke's Gate. Behind him came two youths, also in chain mail, a tall man in flowing robes and a peaked hat, two richly dressed men in velvet tunics edged with fur, and a troop of men-at-arms. One of these carried a pennant on a long staff.

Paks wondered if its polished tip had caught the light, and that's what she'd seen.

Grooms ran out to take the horses; the men-at-arms dismounted as the Duke went through into his court, and led their own mounts to the stables. Horses, Paks noticed, and not mules. The guard sergeant came out of the tower with all but the dayshift guards; he caught Stammel's eye and made a lifting gesture with his hand. Paks could not yet read the hand signals the veterans used, but Stammel grinned. He turned to Paks. "Good eyes. The Duke tries to take us by surprise, and he likes to fail—at that, if nothing else. Where did you see him?"

"I saw something—but I wasn't sure what—between that high ground and the village. It must have stuck up fairly high; could it have been that pennant?"

"Could have been, or a squire's helmet. The sun must have caught it just right—and then you were looking in the right place. Well done, Paks."

Duke Phelan might have traveled half the night to arrive at his stronghold at dawn, but that did not mean he planned to sleep the day away. Shortly after breakfast, he appeared in the courtyard to watch Kefer's unit at weaponsdrill, and by noon he had observed every recruit unit in its work. He said little that any of the recruits could hear, but his sharp glance seemed everywhere at once. In the afternoon the recruits lost sight of him; they were doing two-on-one engagements in the mud, with Stammel's unit the one, and trying to maneuver in the square. None of them had a glance to spare for the wall, or the cloaked figure atop it, watching. The sergeants saw, but said nothing.

In the next week, while the sergeants muttered and fussed over the recruits like hens with too many chicks, the Duke managed to see everything. He appeared in one barracks when the recruits were just getting up, and in another while they were sanding the floor. He walked through the messhall during meals, and even ate there twice. The recruits could hardly choke down their food. He ate as if he liked it, and talked easily to his squires. They all knew by then that the young men in mail were his squires, and one of them a nephew of Count Vladiorhynsich of Kostandan. He was there when Vona's unit made a brilliant reverse in square and threw Kefer's unit off balance, and still there when Stammel's unit managed the same thing, not quite so well, against both the others.

"I wonder if he ever sleeps," muttered Arñe to Paks in the jacks, the one place they were almost sure he wouldn't be.

"I don't know. He was on the wall last night when we came on. Gave the watchword, just like Captain Valichi, but I nearly fell off the parapet."

"And this morning he was waiting in the courtyard when we came out. I wish I knew what he was thinking—"

"I don't." Paks had, in fact, been wondering what the duke had done to Stephi, but she was afraid to ask anyone. Surely Stammel knew, from the men who had come, but— "If I knew," she said in answer to Arñe's quizzical look, "I'd be even more frightened of him."

"It's not like he's *done* anything to anyone," mused Arñe. "But I have the feeling he would. I'd like to be first on the road," she added, bringing up the unspoken thought of all of them. One recruit unit would be chosen to lead the march south to join the Company. The best unit, of course. They all knew who the best unit was—but a little coolness came into the friendships that had formed between recruits in different units.

"Barra and Natzlin think they're getting it," said Paks. Arñe snorted.

"After the way Vona's pulled them off two days ago? They'll have to do something big to make that up."

"Ours wasn't so sharp," Paks reminded her.

"Against both of 'em. Kefer's was only one-on-one. I hope—"

"We'll make it," said Paks, suddenly full of confidence. "We're much better with spears, and we've got four of the best swords—"

That week was, in fact, one long round of contests. Those few who were dimwitted enough not to catch on to that by themselves were forcibly enlightened by their companions. Mock combat the last day was hardly mock: collarbones and fingers, one or more in each unit, snapped under the blows of wooden swords. When the entire recruit cohort was gathered in formation in the courtyard, there were no smiles. For the first time, they were being addressed by the Duke himself, formally.

Paks, in her usual position at the front of the formation, ignored the bruise that had three of her fingers swelled up like blue sausages. It had definitely been worth risking them broken to break the front line of Vona's square. Especially since they weren't broken; the surgeon said they'd bend in a few days. She watched for the Duke. One of his squires came through the Duke's Gate and nodded to Captain Valichi. The trumpeters blew a fanfare; Paks's skin rose up in chillbumps. The Duke strode briskly through the gate, cloak swirling. He spoke to Valichi, nodded, then moved to Vona's unit, on the far side of the courtyard. Paks suppressed a groan. Had they lost to Vona's? But the Duke made no announcement. Perhaps he was just inspecting, as he had twice before. She dared not glance over to see. Her hand began to throb more insistently; the pain edged up her arm. She listened to the rasp of the Duke's boots across the court. It seemed a very long time before the sound came closer. Now he was at Kefer's unit. She could hear that he was, indeed, passing along the ranks. She could even hear the rumble of his voice as he spoke to this recruit or that.

Then he was in front of them, greeting Stammel, and giving a quick glance along the front rank. Paks wondered if he would speak to each of them. She reminded herself of Stammel's instructions: "Say 'yes, my lord,' or 'no, my lord,' instead of just 'sir' as you would for the captain." The Duke came closer, with Stammel now a pace behind him. Paks could feel her neck getting hot. She tried to stare through him to the messhall windows, but he was tall; it was hard to avoid meeting those gray eyes.

"Fingers broken?" he asked her.

"No, sir—my lord," said Paks, stumbling over the honorific and blushing even more.

"Good." The Duke moved on, and Paks heard nothing for some time but the blood drumming in her ears. After Stammel had told them, and she had reminded herself, she'd still said it wrong. When she could hear again, the Duke was already on his way to the front of the formation.

"When you were recruited," he said to them all, "you agreed to stay with this Company for two years beyond your training, and to fight at the orders of your commander. Back then you didn't know your commander. Now you do. All of you have qualified to join my Company, and that means you follow me—obey *my* orders, fight when I tell you to, march when I tell you to. Your sergeants will tell you—have told you, I expect— that I'm hard. That's so. I expect a lot of my soldiers. Skill, courage—and loyalty. To me, personally, as well as to the Company. Now if there's anyone who, after seeing me, can't swear fealty—now's the time to leave." There was a long breathless silence. The Duke nodded. "Very well. Then give me your oath."

Captain Valichi stepped forward to lead them in the oath of service. "We swear to you our hands, our blades, our blood, our breath—the service of the hands, and the service of the heart. May the gods witness our oath of loyalty and be swift to punish the oathbreaker."

"And I to you," said the Duke, "pledge hands and blade and blood and breath. My honor is your honor, before all enemies and trials, in all dangers high and low. The gods witness my oath to you, and yours to me." He looked back and forth at the recruits, and nodded.

"Well, now, companions—" Paks stiffened, surprised

by the change in his voice and address. "You'll soon be on your way to battle. As always, one unit must be first on the road. 'Tis no easy chore to choose among you. Tir knows what I'll do if the Company grows to four cohorts. But the choice is made, and that's for Stammel's unit—" Paks suddenly felt that she could soar high in the air on the breath she drew. She locked her jaw on a yell of triumph. Someone behind her was less careful. To her surprise the Duke grinned. "One yell won't hurt," he said. "Cheer your sergeant, if you will."

And "Stammel!" they yelled, and the walls rang with it.

The Duke rode out the next morning, with a late snowstorm behind him. He had hardly disappeared into the swirling veils before the recruits were hard at work again—this time in preparation for the march south. First they were measured for their uniforms, having changed shape since they arrived. With the maroon tunics went taller boots and longer socks, a long maroon cloak with a hood, and—most exciting—armor. Instead of bandas, they would wear boiled-leather corselets ("Until you can buy something better, if you want it," remarked Devlin.) There were greaves for their legs, and wide bands to protect their wrists. And bronze helmets on top of all.

"Make up your minds," said Stammel, "how you're going to wear your hair. If it's long, I'd say keep it inside the helmet, hot as it is, or some enemy will grab it and throw you. It'll make a cushion." Paks found a way of winding her braid that was comfortable and secure. But the helmet was heavier than she'd expected. So was everything else.

"You'll get used to it," said Stammel. "After you've marched all the way to Valdaire in it, you won't even notice."

It seemed hardly any time at all since the Duke's visit when two of the captains arrived from the south to escort them. A last few days for inspection and packing the mule train that would carry their necessary supplies— and then it was the last night in the barracks. Paks found it almost as hard to sleep as she had the first one.

Chapter Eight

As Paks passed under the gate tower and out into the cold gray light of a late-winter dawn, she felt how changed she was from the girl who had left home those months before. She had not told anyone when her nineteenth birthday came, but she felt the extra year like a wall between her and the past. No one would take her for a farmer's daughter, not with the sword at her side and the skill to use it, not in the uniform of Duke Phelan's Company. Beside and behind her, eighty pairs of almost-new boots beat the same crisp rhythm on the hard-frozen road to Duke's East. Going to the war, the rhythm sang in her head. Going to the war.

By the time they reached the rise between the stronghold and Duke's East, the sun was rising, a brief red glare between the clouds. This was the last bit of known road: the curve into the village past the Red Fox, the square, the bridge. Smoke rolled out of chimneys. As their boots rang on the cobbles of the square, faces appeared at windows and doors. Mayor Fontaine opened his door to wave, along with the row of children that

appeared at his back. Several children ran from houses
to march alongside, singing and yelling, until they were
called back. Beyond the bridge was Kolya's farm and
orchard; Kolya was leaning on the gate, grinning.

"Good luck," she called. "Fight well." Paks glanced
at her, and Kolya winked. Then they were past, and
after another fifty paces the road swung left again,
leaving the village behind to curve through a wooded
swamp, now frozen. After that it climbed, and the trees
fell away. A stone wall bordered the road on the west,
and beyond it Paks saw a herd of shaggy cattle, guarded
by several men in leather capes. All the cattle stared at
them, ears wide, as they marched by. Most of them
were heavy in calf, and looked as wide as they were
long in their winter coats.

They were seven days on the road to Vérella, marching at first through forested ridges that gentled into
farmland sprinkled with villages. The people were shorter
here, and looked heavier; the women wore their
headscarves knotted high, with a peak to one side.
Each night they stopped by a large stone-walled barn
with a fox-head design chiseled into the stone. Stammel
explained that the Duke had built these barns for the
farmers to use, provided they let his troops shelter
there while traveling.

The column settled quickly into the habits of a long
march. Recruits took guard duty in rotation with the
regulars, and hardly thought of themselves as recruits.
They knew the captains now: Pont, junior to Cracolnya,
and Ferrault, junior to Arcolin. As they passed through
the villages, they saw themselves as they were seen:
mercenaries. The Duke's Company. They began to pick
up the news of the road as they neared Vérella.

"Eh, captain," shouted one graybeard. "You're late
this year. They Sobanai is already come by here."

"Seen anything of Vladi's?" called Pont.

"Nay, and I hope not. They don't come this way but
once in a while, and I'm glad for it."

"Why, grandfather?"

"Eh, well—he's too hard for us, that one. Better he go east."

The captain laughed and rode on. Paks wondered who the "Sobanai" were. She watched as two children, screeching to get the soldiers' attention, struck at each other with wooden swords. An older voice called them, angry, and they dropped the swords and ran off.

Then they came to Vérella—the first city Paks had ever seen, Vérella of the Bells, the seat of the Kings of Tsaia. From a distance its great stone walls and towers seemed to sail the river meadows, already tinged with spring green. They had passed slower carts and wagons all that morning, and as they neared the city, they met more traffic: trains of mules, ox-drawn wagons, foot travelers, and horsemen.

The guards at the city gates wore rose and gray, and carried pikes. They marched under the gate tower. It seemed immense to Paks, its opening wide enough for two wagons at once to pass. The way was paved with square cobbles of pale gray stone, and was even wider than the gate. Paks tried not to gawk, but she was distracted by the buildings, tall and many-windowed, and crowded wall to wall, and by the incredible noise and bustle. Against the tall stone walls lay a flotsam of bright canvas awnings over shop windows and street peddlers, merchandise of all sorts piled in alluring heaps—it seemed that only the constant current of traffic kept it from taking over the road itself. She had never imagined such a variety of people and things. Men in long gowns with fur-edged sleeves. A stack of intricately patterned carpets next to a pile of polished copper pots of all sizes. Four men carrying a sort of box on poles, with curtains swaying on the box. A woman in green velvet, on a mule, strumming a hand-harp. A fat child, broad as he was tall, with an axe at his belt—as they passed, Paks was startled to see a waist-length red beard on the child. She gasped.

"Don't gawk about," muttered Bosk. "It's just a dwarf." She had not realized that dwarves were real. She tried to keep her eyes ahead, but it was impossible. They passed a man in red and blue motley carrying a strange skinny black animal with a long tail that wrapped his arm. Two children dashed by, balancing loaves of bread an armspan long. She heard a confused roar from the right, and Stammel yelled a halt. From a side street rode six figures in gleaming plate mail on chargers bigger than the duke's; the street shook to the pounding hooves. Paks felt breathless. She watched Stammel peer down the side street before leading them on. She had never seen horses so big. Were there more?

After another few minutes of marching, the street made a sharp turn left and then right. Here were fewer sidewalk stalls, but a fascinating blend of smells: roast meats, fresh bread, ale, wine, spices. Paks heard her belly rumble in response. The buildings had benches in front of them, and a row of watching eyes followed them down the street. She saw another dwarf, and then two more, on one of the benches.

At a cross street, Stammel turned right into a narrower street the column almost filled. Ahead was a high stone wall, and beyond it the turret of some building. When they reached the foot of the wall, Paks saw that a wide paved area lay before it; Stammel turned left again, and they marched beside the wall for a space. Paks saw no gate, and no guards on the wall. At last it swung away to the right, and they went on, again on a wide street between buildings. There were fewer stalls, and no peddlers. Paks saw a string of mules being led through a gate; she glanced sideways into the gate as they passed it. Inside, stables surrounded a courtyard; she saw another of the great horses, this one led by a boy.

They entered a square with a fountain in the center and trees around the fountain. Here once more were the canvas awnings of shops and sidewalk stalls. A barefooted woman in a short dress struggled with a large jar of water from the fountain. A plump child in a furlined hood trotted behind a large fluffy white dog. Two cloaked men in tall boots strolled near the fountain, hands near the hilts of their weapons. A tall slender figure in gray trotted briskly past the column on a horse bridled in green and gold. It was past before Paks realized that its face was not human.

Past that square they marched down a quiet street with trees planted in the center. Ahead was another gate. The captains, who had ridden ahead, sat chatting with the guards as they marched up. "Everyone still with us?" asked Pont.

"Certainly, sir."

"Very good. I've arranged for a meal outside the gates—you remember the Golden Goose? They call it the Winking Tomcat now: old Penston's nephew inherited it this winter. We're called to meet with the vice-regent; wait for us there."

"Yes, sir. Do you think you'll be long enough to unload the mules?"

"No. Give 'em a feed though. We'll march through to Littlebridge today."

"Yes, sir." Stammel led them through the gates, this time onto a wide stone bridge with a waist-high stone parapet. They were far above the water. Paks looked upstream and saw a dark still surface; she could not tell how fast the water was moving. Another bridge spanned the river upstream; a wall rose from the far bank. Ahead of them, their own bridge pierced the wall at a tower, and again they passed through gates.

Here the buildings were lower, many of them wood and not stone. Paks could see over them to yet another wall. These streets were crowded, but they saw few velvets and furs, and more bare feet. Some people wore wooden clogs that clattered loudly on the cobbles. A pack of lean dogs worried something in a gutter. They passed a row of taverns, reeking of stale beer; only one man huddled on the benches outside. A fat woman in gaudy clothes danced sideways beside the column, showing a trayful of glittering jewelry. Paks heard one of the corporals swear at her; she flung back an oath in return.

At the last wall, the guards waved them through the tall gates, and they came out to see loosely spaced buildings and fallow fields beyond. They passed a tanner's stinking yard, a pen of cattle on one side of the road and a pen of hogs on the other, a field fenced with split rails (which Paks had never seen) holding a dozen horses and a few mules, another field with wagons parked in rows. Ahead on the left was a large stone enclosure with a two-story building in front. On the sign hanging before it was a yellow cat with a ferocious leer. Stammel halted them, and entered the inn. Paks looked around. Across from the inn an open slope of bare ground eased up to a stand of trees. Ahead, down the road, was another building that might be an inn, then a row of cottages.

Stammel came out. "The court's too full," he said to Bosk. "We'll eat over here—" he nodded at the open space. "I'll take the file leaders in for food."

Paks followed Stammel into the inn, excited and curious. It was much larger than the inn at Rocky Ford, larger than any she'd seen. They entered a long low room filled with tables and benches and noise. The landlord, a tall heavy young man with a pale mustache, led them to the kitchen behind, where the cook's helpers were heaping platters with roast meat, bread, cheese, and dried fruit. Paks took a platter and carried it back through the dining room and across the road. The food was good, spiced with strange flavors, and Paks devoured her share. The second rank took the platters back, and they settled down to wait until the captains returned.

"How do you like cities?" Saben asked Paks.

"I don't know—it's not what I thought it would be."

"Did you see that dwarf?"

Paks nodded. "I didn't know they were real, any more. Do you know what was on that horse with the fancy bridle?"

"No. I missed that. We can ask Stammel or Bosk."

Bosk chuckled at their question. "You mean you don't

know? It's a good thing you didn't point. That was an elf, from Lyonya or the Ladysforest, a messenger to the Council."

"Elf—" Paks and Saben looked at each other. "Will we see more of elves and dwarves and things like that?" asked Paks.

Bosk spat. "I hope not. Uncanny, they are, and unfriendly, too. We don't have much to do with them, and the less the better, I say."

"Now Bosk," said Devlin, who had walked up on the conversation. "Elves are good fighters, you have to say that."

"If it's fighting alone, give me dwarves—not that I want them, but they're hard as stone, and tireless. Elves—they'll sing as soon as fight, or go off after some fool idea. And they think they know everything, and have to tell you about it—without answering any question you want answered, either."

"I don't know—" Devlin looked thoughtful. "I've met a few elves—five years ago, that year you stayed north, Bosk, I talked to one. She was uncanny, but beautiful. Sometimes she'd sing in Common, about the Beginnings, and where the elves came from, and battles long ago. It was strange, but very powerful. I liked it."

"Your choice," said Bosk shortly. "And you can't say some elves haven't gone bad—"

"The kuaknom? That may be, but they're all dead."

Bosk snorted. Another recruit broke in. "But won't we go past dwarf lands in a few days?"

"South of here, yes. But we go around the mountains rather than through them. We'll see dwarves on the road between here and Valdaire, but we won't see their caves."

"Are gnomes just another name for dwarves?" asked Saben.

"Gird's arm, no! And remember that, if we see any. The Aldonfulk princedom comes near the road for a day's travel. They're not like dwarves at all, save their love of stone and living underground. You saw that dwarf—wide as he was tall, and so they all are. Gnomes are slenderer, but still short. Good fighters; they're lawful folk, knowing the value of discipline and training. They don't say much, but what they do say you can trust with your life."

"You like them, don't you?" asked Paks.

"Of the elder races, yes. Trustworthy, brave, well-organized. Some of them are Girdsmen." Paks had not realized before that Bosk was Girdish; she looked at him curiously.

The sunlight had dimmed behind thicker clouds as they ate, and now a fine drizzle sifted over the landscape. Paks stamped her feet, feeling the chill.

"I hope we start marching soon."

"We'll have to wait for the captains. I hope they don't linger over their meal."

"Where are they?"

"Probably with the vice-regent. They usually eat at the palace on these journeys; the regents always have some message for the Duke."

Paks wondered what the palace looked like. "Did we pass the palace?" she asked.

"Do you remember that wall we marched beside, before we came to the square with the fountain? That was the palace wall. You can't see the palace itself from outside."

"Have you seen it?"

Bosk shook his head. "No. But Stammel did once, I think. It's just a palace, though, like any other. I've seen the King's Hall in Rostvok."

"That's in Pargun, isn't it?" asked Vik. Bosk nodded, and Vik went on. "I heard it had a room lined in gold, polished like mirrors, and all the guards wore jewelled helmets and a ruby in one ear."

"I never saw a golden room," said Bosk. "But they do wear jewels in their ears, and not just the guards, either. I couldn't say if they were rubies. As for helmets, the ones I saw were good polished bronze, nothing more. Tell you what they did have, though: in the

King's Hall itself, where the King sits and receives ambassadors and such, they had a hanging framework that held—oh—a hundred candles, I suppose. Much like what the Duke's got, so far, only bigger. But all over it, and hanging from it, were little chips that looked like clear ice—much too big for diamonds—and they glittered in the candlelight, and made sparkles of all colors that danced over the whole hall. One of their men told me it was a kind of glass, but I never saw glass anything like that. It was something to see, I'll tell you—all lit up and a hundred colors. Like the sun coming out after rain, or an ice storm, only more so."

Paks tried to imagine such a thing and failed; she had never seen even the Duke's dining hall. She shivered as the drizzle thickened. When she glanced back up the road toward the city, she saw nothing but a cloaked man on foot, trudging doggedly toward the gates. Just as Stammel spoke of moving them into the inn courtyard, they heard a shout.

"Good," said Stammel. "Here's the captains, and we can go on. What I heard of the roads, it'll be a long march."

"What about cloaks?" asked Devlin. "If this gets worse—"

"We'll need them dry for tonight," said Stammel. "If a caravan's stuck in Littlebridge, we may not have shelter for everyone."

The captains rode up. "Sorry we were held up," said Pont. "The vice-regent insisted that we witness the seal on a letter for the Duke. Ferrault will go on, and I'll stay with the column. We'd better march."

Quickly Stammel reformed the unit, and they moved out. Ferrault's bay horse trotted ahead, quickly moving out of sight. The last large building was indeed another inn, this one with a picture of a mounted fighter on its signboard. As they passed, a small group of men lounged out its wide door to stare at them.

"The carrion crows are moving, I see," said one in green, with grey boots.

"Whose are those?" asked another. He had a delicately curled mustache.

"Some northern warlord. Duke something-or-other, I forget. They all ape the nobility, that sort." Paks heard him hawk and spit. "Better they go south to Aarenis and die than cause trouble here, I say."

The others laughed. Paks noticed that Stammel's neck was redder than usual. He said nothing. She wondered if the captain had heard. They marched on, up a rise in a gentle S-curve. The road ran between low walls and hedges, with farmland on either side. Under the drizzle the plowed fields looked soft and black. Most of the cattle were dun, with white markings on their faces. Cottages near the road were stone below and whitewashed wood above; the roofs were slate cut thinner than Paks had seen before. Each cottage had a block of fruit trees behind it.

The next two days taught Paks more than she wanted to learn about bad weather marching. First the hard-frozen road went from greasy to soft mud under the drizzle. As the afternoon and rain went on, the mud deepened, until they were all ankle-deep in thin slop. Paks felt the wet creep into her boots: first the toes, then the sides of her feet, and finally the whole foot, squelch, squelch, squelch with every step. Her socks pulled the dampness up her legs. Drizzle soaked her tunic at the shoulders, until little trickles of rain began to run down her back and sides. She worried about her sword in its scabbard. That was better than thinking about her cold feet. When the road lifted over low hills, it firmed, but in the hollows mud was deep enough to slow them. Paks, in the front rank, could see how it had been churned already by heavy caravan wagons.

As the light faded, Paks began to wonder where they would spend the night. Usually by this time they were already camped. She glanced around. Thick leafless woods on either side of the road, as they toiled up yet another rise. Mud dragged at her feet. Several had stumbled in holes hidden by the mud; some had fallen. At the top, the road followed the ridge, swerving east. The drizzle thickened to a steady light rain, blown by a northeast wind. As it got darker, it was harder to see the road surface. Paks lurched as she missed her footing in the ruts and holes. The road swung right; she felt the change in grade as it dipped. Paks heard the captain coming up, the sucking noise of his horse's hooves in the mud. He rode past her, his horse in mud to the knees, and called to Stammel.

"It's going to be black dark before we make Littlebridge in this muck, and that bad hole's still to come. We're starting to break up in the rear. There's a place to camp along on the right; it'll be out of the wind if it stays as it is."

"Yes, sir. Do you mean that old wanderer campground?"

"That's it. There's a spring straight downhill." The captain wheeled his horse and rode back past the column. Paks noticed that he looked as wet as she felt. She was glad they were stopping soon. The next two hundred paces seemed to take forever. She watched Stammel search the edge of the woods.

"See this path?" he asked. Paks could barely see a dim gap between the trees. "We follow this; it'll open out on a firm slope. Stay on the path; we don't want the tribe angry with us." He led the way, and Paks followed. File by file they slipped into the woods. After a few twists and turns, they came to a large clearing, dim now in the dusk, but easily large enough for all. Paks followed Stammel to the right, and they settled down under a row of cedars to rest. Stammel went back to direct the others. It seemed to take a long time. Paks began to stiffen in the cold, and her belly cramped and growled as if she'd never eaten lunch. She looked back through the trees and saw a flickering light—torches— someone had gotten torches from the pack mules.

The light roused her, and she stood, swinging her arms back and forth. If they were camping, Stammel would want a fire. And the captain had said something

about a spring, and they'd need a ditch—she looked
around for her file, and called them over. The other file
leaders of her unit looked up, listening.

"As soon as we can get a torch," she began, "we can
see to set up. Same assignments as night before last,
except I don't know if we'll be cooking. I'll find out.
Wood gatherers, try to find something dry—at least not
soaked. Everybody up and get working, or we won't
sleep dry." She was sure they would have a miserable
night.

It seemed to take a long time to get organized. Torches
sizzled in the rain, giving barely enough light to see,
until the main campfire finally caught. The clearing was
a slightly irregular oblong, edged all around with thick
cedar trees, and sloping just enough to shed water. Off
to one side was a smaller clearing where Stammel told
them to dig their trench. The tribe, he explained, always used it so. Paks and Malek went with Bosk to find
the spring, down slippery wet rocks until they heard a
frog splash into open water. By the time they came
back, the fire was burning well, and Stammel had them
fill several kettles. Steam rolled up from their wet
tunics. Bosk took the packet of ground roots and herbs
for making sib, and poured it into the kettles.

"It'll be stronger this way, and bitter, but we need it
strong."

Paks stirred the brew with a wooden spoon, enjoying
the fire's warmth. More and more of them were cluster-
ing near the fire to eat their ration of trail bread and salt
beef. Bosk assigned someone to stir the other kettles.

"Here, Paks." Her file-second handed her a share of
bread and meat, and squatted beside her. "I don't think
I've ever been so wet, and had to sleep out."

Paks grunted around the hunk of meat in her mouth.

"You should see Kefer's unit," he went on. "Mud to
the waist, it looks like. I wonder how much more of this
there is."

Paks finished chewing the beef into submission, and
washed it down with a swig of water. "I guess it de-

pends on how long it rains. Lucky for us we were in front today. If they change the marching order—"

Keri looked startled. "They wouldn't. The duke himself said we were the first."

"As an honor, yes. But in this—whoever marches last has the worst of it. It slows us all down, and it's not fair."

"Maybe it will dry off tomorrow."

"Maybe." Paks stirred the brew again, and took a bite of bread. Her right side, near the fire, was dry and hot; she shifted to the other side of the kettle and decided to take off boots and socks. She could dry her socks on the firepit rocks. She struggled with her boots, and had one off and the other half-off when she saw Stammel approaching. She tried to stand, but he waved her down.

"Don't get up. How's the sib coming?" It had begun to smell good. He dipped the spoon in and took a sip. "Another half-hour, I expect. Don't scorch your boots. I wanted to talk to you about the order of march tomorrow."

Her head came up. "You're changing it? I wondered if you would."

Stammel looked surprised. "I didn't think you'd expect it, but yes. It's nothing to do with the honor, you know; it's the mud. The last unit has the hardest time, and slows us."

Paks nodded. "I thought so. How will you change it?"

"We'll change places every two hours—the change will keep any one unit from wearing down, I hope. The mules will go first; with those narrow hooves they have a bad time in soft ground anyway. You'll be the last unit when we start, then move to second and first in rotation."

"Why can't we walk in the fields, when the road's so bad?"

Stammel shook his head. "No. We don't trample fields. It's one of the Duke's rules, and one of the reasons we can travel without trouble. The farmers don't fear to see us coming."

"How far do we need to go?"

"Tomorrow?" Paks nodded. "We're almost an hour's dry walk from Littlebridge, and the next good stop beyond that is Fiveway—a nice day's march in good weather, and I don't know if we can make it in the rain. Depends."

Paks turned her socks over; they were almost dry. "Is it usually like this?"

"Sometimes. There's a lot of rain south of Vérella, all the way to the foothills of the Dwarfmounts. Then it's usually drier, going west and over the pass—not bad at all once we're in the south itself. By then it's summer anyway. But this stretch of road—three to six days depending—is always bad if it rains. You'd think the Council in Vérella would do something, with all the trade coming this way, but they haven't since the old king died. They leave it to the local landholders. And they just leave it."

Paks thought back to the city she'd seen that morning: a very different world from the wet dark clearing. "Sergeant Stammel, why did that man call us carrion crows?"

Stammel grunted. "You heard that, did you? You don't want to listen to that sort. Well—crows follow a battle, I suppose you wouldn't know that—they come to feast on the carnage. And some folks call mercenaries that, as if we were bloodseekers."

Paks thought that over a moment. "But who were they? They had rich clothes. And why did they say that about the Duke? He really is a duke, isn't he?"

"Them? Town bravos is what they looked like. They'd like to be thought lords' sons by their dress and jewels. As for our duke—I haven't heard anyone dispute his title—any time lately, at least. He's duke enough for me, and more worth to follow than some pedigreed princeling that can't sit his horse without a tutor, or draw blade without six servants to protect him." Stammel stopped short, and stirred the fire for a moment. Paks asked nothing more, but turned her socks again.

They were dry, and she brushed the dried mud from them. Stammel tasted the sib again and shook his head.

When the sib was finally ready, Stammel dipped a large spoonful of honey into each kettle. After a mugful of that stout drink, Paks felt warm to her toes. Her unit, being least tired, had the first watch. For the first hour or so the drizzling mist lightened, and Paks hoped it might stop entirely. But heavier rain returned, hissing and spitting in the fire. Stammel brought a length of waxed canvas to lay over their store of wood.

When the watch changed, Paks took her dry cloak from the protected pack with a feeling of futility. Everything was wet. She found a space under a cedar where the tree's thick foliage kept the rain from falling directly on her, but she was sure she would not sleep.

Stammel's call took her by surprise. She had slept the night through despite the damp. She unrolled her cloak and crept out. A wet mass of cedar foliage smacked her in the face. Paks shivered. Around her the camp came slowly to life. She stretched the kinks out of her back, then looked distastefully at her sodden boots, and walked barefoot to the firepit.

The last watch had put porridge on the fire as well as sib. Paks checked to see that her file was up and moving, then took her place in line. Her wet cloak dragged at her shoulders. She wondered if they would pack the wet cloaks or wear them. When she could get near the fire, she turned her back to it, hoping to dry the cloak. The hot food warmed her; she wondered if she could march barefoot, and save her boots. But Stammel explained the dangers of this, and she resigned herself to the discomfort.

Soon they were ready to leave; yesterday's last unit grinned slyly as they filed away through the trees. Only the captain on his horse stayed behind. When they came out on the road, Paks started after the rest. The road surface was churned into uneven mush, like half-eaten porridge gone cold. Their boots sank in several inches at once. Downhill the mud deepened. Rainwater on the surface splashed high up their legs. The next unit was already far ahead, but when Paks tried to pick up the pace, several of them slipped in the mud and almost went down.

She had to slow again; she and the other file leaders began a marching song to keep everyone in step, and that seemed to help. When some ran out of breath, or stumbled, others took it up. The downhill grade eased, but the mud was deeper still. It dragged at their boots; Paks felt her thighs begin to ache from jerking against that pull with every step. Around another turn of road, Paks saw that they'd gained half the distance to the unit in front of them. Then she saw why: it was floundering in a section of road that seemed to have no bottom.

"Tir's brass boots!" growled Captain Pont. "I told them that the next time I mired a troop in this place, I'd fix it myself, then and there." She looked up at him; he was scowling. "Very well—Paks—"

"Yes, sir."

"We're going to put some stepping stones in that mess. See those walls?" He pointed to the drystone walls that bordered the road. Paks nodded. "Get your unit off the road; when they get to the bad spot, take those stones and pile 'em in until you can walk across. Those Tir-damned farmers have made enough pulling wagons out of this hole—we all pay toll on this road anyway, and some of it is supposed to go for repairs."

The edge of the bad patch was obvious: the gaping hole where a mule had gone in belly deep was still there. Already the mired unit was beginning to tear up the wall for stones. The first stones sank at once, but eventually they began to fill the hole. Finally Paks had her unit lay the flat topping stones from the wall over all, and they walked across the hole without sinking.

Beyond that hole, they were back in ankle-deep mud, but the change of pace had rested them. Now they slogged on together, all three units chanting one song after another. "Cedars of the Valley" gave way to "The Herdsman's Daughter" after many verses. On the left, trees thinned to pasture, and across the fields Paks could see a river as gray as the sky. The road edged toward it. Soon she could see a cluster of cottages huddled near the road. As they neared them, the road firmed. Paks could feel gravel through her sodden boots. They came to a paved square, streaming in the rain. Around it were larger buildings: an inn, a tall building with wide doors painted blue and red, several large houses. Stammel halted the column. Paks shifted her shoulders under her wet cloak and wondered if they would get anything from the inn. She looked around. The square was empty but for them; their mules were caked in mud to the belly, and the other units looked as muddy as she was. Her legs ached. She tried to see out the other side of the square, where the road humped itself up—a bridge, she thought. This must be Littlebridge.

A short time later, they marched out, having seen the inside of the inn very briefly, while downing fresh rolls and mugs of hot soup. That interval of warmth and dryness was welcome. All too soon Paks was back out in the rain, lining up behind Vona's unit, with Kefer's behind her.

They started briskly across the square and over the narrow humped bridge beyond it. On the other side were more houses, some large, and craftshops. Then the houses dwindled to cottages flanked by gardens, and the gravelled road softened to mud.

The rest of that day was a matter of endurance. At times the rain slackened, but mostly they marched before a chill, wind-driven rain. Mud was always with them: now thicker, and clinging to their boots with every step, now thinner and splashing like water. They passed sodden little villages, too small for an inn, and wet farms that seemed half-melted into the ground. Every two hours they halted for a brief rest and change of position. By midafternoon, they were numb with fatigue, stumbling along the road like drunks. Paks ached from head to heel. She no longer worried about her sword rusting, or where they would sleep. She put one foot ahead of the other with dogged intensity. As the light faded, her unit shifted again from last to middle, this time with no pause for rest.

"We've got to get them to Fiveway," she heard Stammel say, but she did not look up to see who else was nearby. They started again, lurching in the mud. Soon it was too dark to see anything but the nearest ranks and the road beneath. Then that faded. They marched on in the darkness more by feel than sight. The last singers lost heart and the marching songs died away. Paks could not have said how long they'd marched—it seemed like half the night—when the darkness ahead was broken by a line of dim orange lights. She could not tell how far away they were, nor how big—they were merely blurs that brightened step by step. After awhile, she realized that they were square: windows, she thought suddenly, with lights behind them. At once she felt even colder and stiffer than before.

Soon she could see light reflected on the wet road outside the windows. The road firmed under her feet: gravel again. She heard the crisp hoofbeats of the captain's horse passing on the right. Torches flared ahead, wavering in the wind. By their light she could see wet pavement, the fronts of buildings, the gleam of steel. An abrupt challenge rang out before them. Stammel called a halt. She heard voices, but could not distinguish the words. She shivered. The torches came nearer; now she could see the men holding them, and the armed men behind. She slid a hand to her sword hilt. Stammel appeared, carrying a torch now. In its dancing light his face was strange; she could not read its expression.

"We've got shelter near here," he said. "Vona's unit will pick up food at the inn. Paks, yours will unpack the mules. Follow Devlin; he knows where to go."

Paks did not think she could follow anyone anywhere, but when Devlin came with a torch, she found she could still pick up her feet. They turned down a lane beside a high stone wall, and came out in a field, onto short wet grass. Not far away Paks sensed a large structure looming against the sky. Devlin led them to it: a barn, stone below and wood above, easily large enough for all of them. The mules were already tied along one end, and the skinner had lighted other torches; a warm glow spilled out to meet them.

Once inside, the relief of being out of the wind and rain was enormous. The barn was almost empty, but for hay in one corner. Paks wanted to fall headlong in that hay and sleep, but Devlin prodded her to come unload the mules. She and the others stumbled over and pulled off the packs. Kefer's unit, meanwhile, began placing torches high in wall brackets away from the hay. Then they laid out sleeping areas. Their final chore was setting up lines for drying their wet clothes; the barn had hooks built in, and Devlin handed out rolls of thin cord. By this time, Vona's unit had brought the food, plentiful and hot despite the trek from the inn.

Long loaves of bread that steamed when they were broken—crocks of butter—kettles of savory stew—Paks ate at first hardly noticing what she put in her mouth, but as she warmed up she realized how good it was. Mug after mug of a strange hot drink not so bitter as sib. Bowl after bowl of stew. Suddenly she was nearly asleep, nodding as she sat. She glanced around. Devlin and Bosk were gathering empty platters and pots; she wondered if they would make the trip back tonight to the inn. She met Stammel's eye and braced herself for the order to go back—but he smiled and told her to get some sleep. When she tried to get up, she found she had stiffened from that brief rest. She barely made it to a heap of hay and an empty blanket, falling into a deep sleep before she could review any part of the day.

Chapter Nine

The next morning rain still fell in curtains. Captain Pont decided to delay at least a day, and the barn filled with drying clothes. Everyone was stiff and grumpy at first, but by noon they were all awake enough to be restless. Paks even welcomed a walk through the rain to the inn for food. A caravan bound for Vérella had come in; great wagons blocked the streets, and the inn was full of wet and disgruntled merchants.

"Camped!" she heard one exclaim to the landlord, as she led her file toward the kitchen. "By Simyits, we weren't camped. We were stuck—flat stuck! Gods blast your count or whatever you've got down here! I pay toll on this passage every year, and he hasn't set stone on the road since my father died." Paks glanced at the speaker, a tall, powerful man in mud-stained leather with a gold chain around his neck and a ring in each ear. The landlord, shorter and plumper, had a fixed smile on his face. "You can tell him for me," the big man went on, "that the Guild League can find another way north, if it comes to that." Then Paks was in the kitchen, dodging a squad of agitated cooks to the table where their food was laid ready. She noticed on her way back out that the landlord had escaped from the tall man, and was leading a party of velvet-clad ladies up the stairs.

When she mentioned the incident to Stammel, he laughed. "That'd be the wagonmaster," he said. "Let's see—it might be the Manin family caravan, or maybe Foss Council. Did you notice what they carried?"

"No, sir. What's the Guild League he mentioned?"

"Guild League cities, that is. Those on the north caravan route, not the Immer route." Paks felt that this explained nothing. Stammel noticed her blank look. "Don't you know anything about the south, about Aarenis?"

"It's where some spice comes from, and fancy embroidery," said Paks.

"Umm. That's not enough. We have time for better. Have you heard of the Immerhoft Sea, that lies south of the land?" Paks nodded. Jornoth had mentioned it. "Across the Immerhoft was Aare, the old kingdom. Those people settled islands in the Immerhoft, then sailed on to find a great land they called Aarenis, the daughter of Aare. They settled it, and spread, and the land was divided among great lords and their children. In time they spread to the Dwarfmounts, driving the elves ahead of them, and found passes to the north. That's what we call the south—Aarenis is what it's called when you're in the south—from the Immerhoft to the Dwarfmounts. These same folk settled the western kingdoms of the north."

Paks frowned. "I thought the Eight Kingdoms were settled by seafolk and nomads from the north. My grandfather—"

"Was probably a horse nomad. In part, they were. But all these groups met in the Honnorgat valley. The eastern kingdoms, those below the great falls, have more seafolk. Tsaia and Fintha have more nomads. And Lyonya and Prealith have elves. But most of the folk in

Tsaia and Fintha came from Aarenis long ago." Paks nodded, and Stammel went on. "There's a great trade between Aarenis and the Eight Kingdoms and most of it comes through the pass we'll use, up the Vale of Valdaire. Long ago it came by water, up the Immer and its tributaries. Southbound trade sailed from Immer ports to Aare itself. But Aare is a wasteland now, and the sea trade goes to other lands—I don't know where myself, and the tales are strange enough. Anyhow, for one reason and another, a group of cities agreed to build a new trade route, a land route. Some say the river trade was taxed too heavily by the lords and cities along it, and some that river pirates made it too dangerous. I think myself that these cities traded more with the north, and for that a land route was needed anyway. So their merchant guilds joined in the Guild League, and they built the road and maintain it, and they send their caravans north each year, and we send ours south. The wars in Aarenis come partly from rivalry between the Guild League cities and the river cities and old lords."

"Which side are we on?" Effa had come near to listen, with several others.

"Whoever hires us," said Bosk, leaning on the wall nearby.

Stammel nodded. "He's right. The duke makes a contract with someone—a city or a lord, whoever will pay his price—and that's who we fight for."

Effa looked shocked. "But—surely the duke wouldn't make a contract with just anyone."

"Well—no. We're a northern company, after all: an honorable company. He has his standards. But we've fought for one city against another, and for a lord against a city, and the reverse. It doesn't matter."

"What do you mean, we're an honorable company?" asked Barra. "Aren't all companies much alike?"

"Tir, no! I wish they were. The good ones—mostly northern—agree on some things—we won't harbor each other's criminals or traitors, we won't torture prisoners, we treat prisoners fairly, and so forth. We don't steal supplies from peasants, or destroy crops if we can avoid it. We compete, but we know there's wars enough to keep us all employed; we don't try to kill each other off, except in battle. And that's our business. But there are some others—" Stammel paused, and looked around the group; more recruits had come to listen to him, and Captain Pont lounged nearby. "Captain Pont will bear me out—"

Pont nodded, his long face splitting in a grin. "Surely. The south is full of so-called mercenaries. Most of 'em are robbers that blackmail some poor town into hiring them to keep order. Some are fairly honest hired blades in summer, and robbers in winter. A few are fairly well-organized and independent, but downright nasty—"

"The Wolf Prince—" muttered Stammel.

"Yes—the Wolf Prince. He's definitely a bad one. Uses poison, assassins, and anything else he can think of. Tortures prisoners and sells 'em to the sea-rovers. Takes ransom only in coins or hard jewels, and only within three days. We broke into his stockade one year—were you there, Stammel?"

"Yes, sir." Stammel picked up the tale. "He'd captured a patrol of the Sier of Westland's light cavalry, and chained them all in the open, without food or water. Only three were alive when we broke in; one lived to make it back to Westland, with all we could do."

"But didn't you kill him?" Effa broke in.

"No. He'd gotten away a few days before; we never did know how he got through the lines." Stammel paused, his face grim. "Then there's the Honeycat. Calls himself Count of the South Marches, I think it is, and runs four companies or so along the coast and up the Immer valleys. There's a bad one. We'll probably come against him again this campaign. He's not exactly a mercenary, in the usual sense. He stirs up wars; they say he has factions in every city, and has even bought out some of the guilds. He hates the northern companies, because he can't scare us or bribe us."

"Why is he called Honeycat?"

"It's what he's like, they say—sweet words, soft voice, and then claws in your belly."

"I've heard of him," said Barra suddenly. "Isn't he the one that hung the witwards of Pliuni upside down from the city gates?"

"Yes, but it wasn't the witwards. It was the priests of Sertig's Anvil and the Lord's Hall. That's why five priesthoods have banned him—not that he cares; he believes in none of them. Some say he worships the Tangler or the Master of Torments, and others say he follows the Thieves' Creed. Whichever, he's bad clear through. His captains are as bad as he is."

"Is that why we're going to fight him?" asked Effa. Stammel glared.

"Haven't you been listening at all? We're a mercenary company; we fight for pay. If we do fight the Honeycat, it'll be because some enemy of his hires us. We have nothing to do with good and bad—not that way, I mean."

Paks was still thinking about something Stammel had said earlier. "You said the honorable companies treat prisoners well—"

"Yes. Why?"

"Well—how do we—I mean, isn't it dishonorable to surrender? And for the others? I thought we just fought until—"

"No, no," Stammel interrupted. "We're hired fighters, not fanatic hotheads. We fight hard when we're fighting, but if our Duke or captains tell us to quit, we quit. Right then. You remember that, or you won't make it back to wherever—Three Firs. There's no sense in losing the whole Company out of pride."

"But don't we owe it to whoever hired us?" asked Saben.

"No. The Duke hired *you*—remember your oath to him?" He looked around until they all nodded. "You agreed to obey the Duke, and his captains—no one else. That's where your honor lies. Somebody who has a

contract with the Duke, that's between the Duke and
him. Our honor is between the duke and us."

"It—it doesn't happen often, does it? Being surrendered, I mean, and captured?" Paks still could not imagine it.

"No. Not to us; the Duke's careful. He won't take a
contract where we don't have a chance. But it has, and
it may again." Paks sat frowning at her bare feet as the
talk went on around her. It had never occurred to her
that they might surrender; she did not like that idea at
all. Effa was still arguing, talking about St. Gird and the
honor of a warrior, and Arñe, as usual, was trying to
shut Effa up.

"Effa," said Pont finally, "if you wanted to be that
sort of warrior—a paladin or something like that—you
should have talked to your Marshal about joining a
fighting order—"

"He said I should get experience," said Effa, red-faced.

"You'll get that here," said Pont. "And even Marshals
and paladins, Effa, must follow orders—"

"But they don't surrender! They fight to the death—"

"Not always," said Bosk. "I've known them to retreat:
any good warrior must learn when to withdraw."

"You've seen that?"

"Yes. Think of the legends; Gird himself retreated
once, at Blackhedge, remember? If you finish your
service with us, and join a fighting order, you'll see—
fighting's fighting, Effa—war doesn't change. If Girdsmen
never backed out of a fight, they'd all be dead." Effa
looked unconvinced, but subsided.

Late that afternoon the rain stopped. By next morning, the clouds had cleared. They were on the road
early. When they fetched breakfast from the inn, well
before dawn, they learned that another caravan had
come in the night before, from the east.

"You might's well go across the fields," the landlord
told Captain Pont. "We've wagons wall to wall in town,
and stuck on all the roads in. You'll not harm plowed or

planted ground if you swing east a bit and then south: that's fallow this year."

So they made good time on the turf for some distance. They climbed a long gentle slope. The view opened around them: pastureland nearby, and blocks of woodland in the distance. Something along the woods edge was in bloom; puffs of white that looked like plum blossom. As they topped the rise, Paks noticed an irregular cloud bank to the south and east.

"There they are," said Stammel cheerfully.

"What?" Paks could not see anything cheerful about more clouds.

"The mountains—that's the Dwarfmounts."

"They're not very big," she said doubtfully. "I thought they were big mountains."

Stammel laughed. "They are. We're a long way from them. Keep watching."

Day by day the mountains crawled above the horizon, showing themselves taller and taller. Eastward were the highest peaks, snow-covered from tip to foothills below—but even the western end of the range was higher than anything Paks had seen. The tales went round the fires at night: those dun-colored hills were home to gnomes, the princedoms of Gnarrinfulk and Aldonfulk. The mountains themselves sheltered tribe after tribe of dwarves: Goldenaxe, Axemaster, Ironhand. Rich dwarves, immensely rich with the gold and silver and gemstones they delved from the mountains' roots.

Now the road swung west, along the line of the range, and west again, as they climbed higher into the hills. The mountains seemed to dive into the earth just west of their path. "That's the pass," explained Stammel. "And just beyond is the Vale of Valdaire." Here the road was busy. They passed caravans headed north, great wagons pulled by powerful mules, each with its armed guard atop, and a squad or so of men-at-arms marching before and behind the train. They saw more dwarves, traveling in troops, heavily armed, peering up at the humans suspiciously from under their bushy brows. Elves here and there—single travelers, mostly, but once a small band of elven knights, who hailed the captain in silvery ringing voices that thrilled the ear like harpstrings lightly plucked.

As the road rose higher over every hill, Paks could see behind them the great tumbled rug of forest and field that sloped from the mountains to the Honnorgat. Far away north was Vérella of the Bells, and upriver from that Fin Panir that she had never seen. And somewhere very far north and west, beyond the Honnorgat and at the springing of one of its minor branches, were the moors above Three Firs and the low stone house where she'd been born. The miles to the duke's stronghold had seemed no barrier to return, nor the crossing of the great river, nor the miles since. But when she looked up at the mountains' snowy wall, she felt that crossing them would be to leave the land of her home.

As she mused, someone noticed the blue shadow to the west. Still many miles away, it hung a blue curtain on the sky—the arm of a great mass of mountains that bordered Aarenis on the west. The pass south lay between the two ranges.

The pass itself was easier than it looked. For hundreds of years that road had been worked and reworked; it wound between hills and around them, taking the easiest way up, and only at the last did it lift itself from beside a streambed and crawl over one. At once, having crossed, it returned to the easy path, winding along as it must, among hills now green with spring.

For it was full spring in the south, a lush spring. The Vale of Valdaire lay lovely and green before them, a vast bowl with snowy mountains in the background, green pastures on the uplands, and darker green forests below. From the top of the pass, it took two days to reach the city, but every step of the way was pleasant.

Valdaire, as they saw it gleaming beside the laughing waters of its little rivers, was far more welcoming than Vérella. Its walls seemed more apt to hold up the backs of shops than to form a defense. As they neared it, the road was lined with great inns, each with a huge walled court for the caravan wagons and draft animals. Across the river from the road, on rising ground not far from the city, they saw what looked like a small stone village. Bosk pointed it out.

"That's Halveric Company's winter quarters," he said. Someone bolder than Paks asked what "Halveric Company" was. "Mercenaries, like us. They usually contract with the Sier of Westland, these last few years. A good company, all things considered."

"Where's ours?" someone asked.

"East of the city. We'll go through, just to show you. Now keep it sharp."

Valdaire swarmed with people, and not only merchants and craftsmen, as in Vérella: it swarmed with troops of all sorts. They had been told it was the truce city, but they had not expected so many different colors and badges. Green tunics much like their own, red tunics over black or gray trousers, green leather over brown wool, brown tunics over red—it was bewildering. Riders in chain mail on slender, quick-stepping horses, riders in plate on massive chargers, crossbowmen on mules. Now and again one of them spoke to Captain Pont or Stammel, commenting freely on the recruits' appearance. Paks noticed the strange accents, and the gods they swore by—she had no idea who or what Ashto and Senneth were.

At last they were through the city. On the right was a last inn, The White Dragon. A row of men in leather armor lounged outside it, and stared as the column went by.

"Phelan's new recruits," she heard one of them say.

"Wish they were ours," said another. "That load of blockheads we got this year—"

"Think these are better?"

"They march better, that's something. By Tir, I hope we don't close that contract with—"

"Hssh!" Then the column was past, and she heard no more.

They turned from the road into a lane. Ahead were whitewashed stone buildings, most long and low but three of them two-storied. Paks took a deep breath. This had to be the duke's winter quarters—in a few minutes they would see the veterans for the first time, would find their places in the full Company. They marched closer. She could see people walking around between buildings. No one seemed to pay them any attention. Paks tried not to let her eyes wander as they came between the buildings. The veterans looked incredibly tough. They came to an open space, and Stammel halted them. Almost at once, a voice she did not know bellowed a command, and the Company formed so fast it seemed the bodies snapped into place. Instead of men and women casually walking about or standing in doorways, now there was a compact, precise formation of hard-eyed soldiers. Paks blinked; several behind her gasped. She could feel the veterans' eyes scanning the column. It made her uneasy, like an itch. Then the duke rode out and greeted Captain Pont, and within moments the column was dispersing to the three cohorts of the Company.

All in Stammel's unit went into Arcolin's cohort. He was a tall, stern-faced man with dark hair and bright gray eyes. Arcolin's junior captain was Ferrault, who had ridden with them as far as Vérella: sandy-haired, bearded, both shorter and slighter than Arcolin. Barra and Natzlin and the rest of Kefer's unit were assigned to Dorrin's cohort. Paks was startled to find that Dorrin was a woman. Sejek was her junior captain—and Stephi, then, was in another cohort. Paks was relieved.

The next few hours were even more chaotic than her first as a new recruit. Each novice was assigned to a veteran, and the veterans made it clear that they would have to prove themselves all over again—if they could. Donag, a heavy-set file leader with dour dark brows, gave Paks an unfriendly look.

"Are you the one that got Stephi in such trouble?" Paks froze; she had relaxed too soon. Donag interpreted her silence to suit himself. "I thought so. You ought to be ashamed enough to keep quiet. A good friend he's been to me, Stephi—cause more trouble, and you won't see the north again." He glowered at her a moment longer. "They say you can fight; it had best be true." He led her to her assigned bunk without another word. Paks felt a smoldering anger. She had not gotten Stephi in trouble; it had been his fault. She glared at Donag's back.

The next several days were uncomfortable. They drilled every day, marching and weapons, and it was obvious how much they had yet to learn. Paks had been coasting, as one of the best recruits. Despite Siger's nagging about speed, she had thought she was as fast as she needed to be. The slower veterans were faster. The best—and Donag was one of these—seemed inhumanly fast. She acquired a lot of new bruises, and the only time Donag smiled at her was when he dealt them.

"He's down on you, isn't he?" asked Saben one evening on the way back from supper. Paks nodded. She didn't want to talk about it. She had heard, through the grapevine, what happened to Stephi, and had decided Donag would just have to wear out his resentment. Barra, of course, had noticed and urged Paks to complain. "It's not your fault," Saben went on. "He shouldn't be like that." Paks shrugged.

"I can't stop him."

"No, but Stammel could. Or the captain." That was what Barra had said, too.

"No. It wouldn't work. Just—don't say any more, Saben, please."

"All right. But I'm on your side, remember." He looked worried, and Paks managed a smile, her first in several days, to reassure him.

Later that evening, Stephi showed up in their barracks. Donag smiled at him, and gave Paks a warning glare. She went on with her work, polishing her helmet. To her surprise, Stephi greeted her first.

"Paks—how do you like the south?"

She looked up, startled. "It's very different. It's so hot already."

Stephi smiled. "That surprised me, my first year south. Wait until full summer; you'll think you're melting into your armor. Are you settling in all right?"

Her eyes flicked toward Donag and back. "Yes, very well."

"Good. I expect, though, you've found it a change from being a top recruit—it's usually a shock."

Paks found herself relaxing a bit. Stephi did not sound angry with her, not nearly as hostile as Donag. "It is a change—you're all so much faster."

"If we weren't, we wouldn't be here to teach you," said Donag gruffly. He had walked over while they were talking, and now turned to Stephi. "Have you heard about the contract yet?"

Stephi shook his head. "No. We were out all day in the hills. Have you?"

Donag looked at Paks.

"Don't mind her," said Stephi. "They have to learn about contracts sometime."

Donag frowned, but went on. "I saw Foss Council messengers today, and two of them rode out just after lunch with a squad of guards. And in the city they're saying that Foss Council and Czardas are squabbling over boundaries."

"Huh," grunted Stephi. "Czardas. Let's see—that's a count, isn't it? All he's got is local militia, unless he hires someone—or if Andressat joins him."

"I don't really know yet," said Donag, but he was grinning.

Stephi grinned too. "But it was one of your—umm—good sources?"

Donag just grinned, shaking his head. Paks watched him in surprise. When he wasn't scowling, he had a pleasant face: rough and weathered, but humorous. He caught her look, made a wry face, and went back to his grin. "I'm not always a grouch, no—if that's what you were thinking. And perhaps you're not as bad as I thought—if you behave."

"I'm going down to the Dragon," said Stephi. "Why don't you come, Donag? I'd like to see what other rumors you can pick up."

"Well—I'm on late watch. But if we don't stay long—" He looked at Paks then back at Stephi. "I'll come. But you, Paks don't be blabbing all I told Stephi, and be sure you're ready for watch on time."

"Yes, sir." Paks watched the two men leave with mingled relief and astonishment.

From that time on, she had little trouble with Donag, though he still thumped her during drill until she found speed she had never thought to reach. In those weeks, a few of the younger veterans made cautious overtures of friendship. Paks was glad to spend time with Canna Arendts, whose tales of her first year's battles were much more exciting than Donag's dry instruction. Canna's best friend had died, and she enjoyed having someone to tell her stories to, someone who would listen by the hour. Saben liked her too, and Vik said he liked having a woman around who was not taller than he was—which made them all laugh wildly, the last night in Valdaire, as he craned his neck pretending that Paks and Arñe were seven feet tall. Canna laughed too, dark eyes dancing. She was lean and quick, and Paks felt clumsy and huge beside her.

On the road again, marching south, Paks could think only of the fighting to come. She had thought herself close to fighting before, but this time she was. This was real, marching with battle-scarred veterans around her, and soon the fighting would be real. No more drills, no more instruction. In the back of her head the vision rose of herself with a great sword, leading a charge. She knew it was nonsense, yet—this was a long way from Three Firs. Anything could happen. Almost anything. She was marching as file second to Donag—that had been a surprise. Most of the recruits were slotted further back in the column.

After several days of marching, they came to the fields where the first battle would be fought. Across a wide space was a dark mass: the enemy army.

"Militia," muttered Donag contemptuously. "We won't have much trouble with them, unless they've a surprise for us." Paks did not dare ask how he knew. She said nothing at all. "Just remember that even militia can kill you if you're stupid," he told her. "Stay in formation—remember the strokes—and listen for orders."

To her surprise, they set up camp that afternoon as if it were any other day on the road—except for the surgeons' area. Paks eyed the rows of straw pallets and the neatly-arranged tents with distaste. She had heard stories about the surgeons, too. The recruits got another lecture, from the captains, and then a final one from their own sergeants.

"And after that they expect us to sleep?" asked Arñe. "I can't keep my eyes shut an instant, I know."

"The followers of Gird—" began Effa. Arñe interrupted.

"Effa, you Girdsmen may be all you say—brave, wise, and everything else—but I'm not one of you. If you can sleep, fine. Do it. As for me, if the gods guide my strokes tomorrow, and bring me safe through, then I'll sleep—"

"And I." Saben's face was more serious than usual. "I find I'm thinking how peaceful it is in the cow byres, on a summer's evening."

Paks thought of sheep, fanned wide on a slope and coming together at the foot. The quick light clatter of their hooves, the anxious baa-ing, and the wide silence over all.

The next morning they were wakened before dawn, and barely managed to choke down breakfast.

"Eat, fools," said Donag, scowling again. "You can't fight empty. You'll wear out. And be sure your flasks are full, and drink so you slosh. Hurry now."

And before the sun cleared the low hills east of them, they were standing in formation, swords drawn, waiting.

Chapter Ten

As the sun rose higher, Paks felt sweat crawling through her hair under her helmet. The dust cloud ahead came closer as the Czardians advanced. Somewhere off on the right wing, a confused clamor began: crashing, metallic, and a deep roar that seemed to shake the earth. Her heart pounded; her sword grip felt slippery. She opened her mouth for air. Surely Stammel would tell them if they were supposed to do anything. She watched his unhurried stroll back and forth in front of their ranks. Behind him the mass of enemy came closer and closer. Someone in the ranks let out a sobbing groan.

"Take it easy, now," came Stammel's rough growl. "Remember your drill. I'll tell you when to worry, recruits. And you veterans, stop acting up to scare the new ones. I'll dock you a day's pay, if anyone else tries to unsettle 'em." Paks took a deep breath and tried to relax, flexing her hand on the sword. The noise and the dust came closer. One of the captains trotted along the front of their line and paused to speak to Stammel. Paks saw him nod. Stammel swung round to face them; Paks felt him capture and release her gaze before giving the expected order. At his command they began to march forward, and now the corporals began chanting a ritual encouragement and reminder.

"Stay in formation now, file two; keep your swords up; keep your shields up and ready; steady march, slow march, count y'r cadence, slow march; file three, pick it up; steady march; no crowding there, third and four! Remember your shields, up and out—" And then the front rank was engaged with the enemy, and the noise of battle drowned out their voices. Paks suddenly found enemy swords thrust at her as the first rank moved into the enemy formation.

She blocked one with her shield, and hacked awkwardly at another with her sword. Only her longer reach kept her alive as her more dexterous opponent disengaged and thrust again. She remembered the correct move, this time, and slashed his sword away. The attacker on her left was now fully engaged with her shield partner, so she could use her own shield for protection against the man in front. She blocked another thrust, and tried an overhand swing. Her opponent's shield caught her blade; for a terrifying instant she could not wrench it free. She was wide open to his sweeping stroke; though she deflected it with her shield, the blade slid down and sliced into her leg through the greaves.

Paks staggered as the blade bit in, and that jerk freed her own sword. She lunged straight ahead, thrusting at the man's belly. Her longer reach worked; her sword slid into him. Before she could follow up her thrust, someone ran into her from behind, and knocked her off balance. She fell among the stamping feet and swinging blades, confused by dust and noise. The man she'd stabbed was also down—she saw his face, barely a foot from her own, and the dagger in his hand. She dropped her sword and grappled with his knife hand, trying to free her left arm from the shield so she could draw her own.

Suddenly his arm went limp; she saw another blade deep in his body. She could not see who had done it. She could not see anything but shadowy legs in the dust. She groped about for her own sword and found it, and tried to get to her feet. Bodies shoved at her from all directions. Her eyes were clogged with sweat and dirt; she blinked furiously, then realized she was surrounded by fighters in the Duke's colors. She tried to pick out where she was in formation—or anyone she knew—but nothing was familiar. Out of the whirling dust came more fighters in blue and yellow; around her rose screams and bellows of rage. She found as she thrust at one of the enemy that her own throat was raw with yelling—and still she yelled. Her shield arm ached. Her sword weighed as much as a full-grown sheep. Her left leg was on fire. She kept thrusting, countering with shield, thrusting—her head splitting with the noise and dust. She took in great gulps of air, but found herself choking on dust, coughing, sobbing against the coughs. She nearly went down again, slipping on something underfoot, but someone grabbed her arm and kept her upright.

"Go on! Forward!" yelled someone in her ear, and she went on, squinting through the dust for yellow and blue to strike at, her sword and shield work now mechanical, as in drill.

At last there seemed to be less dust in front of her, and no blue and yellow. Someone grabbed her arm; she raised her sword to strike, but Stammel's voice penetrated the din. "Paks. Stop! Paks!" Her sword arm fell as if someone had cut the tendons. She stood, half-blinded by dust, gasping for breath, shaking—at last she could see Stammel, and met his eyes. "All right, Paks," he said, more quietly. "You're wounded; go to the rear." She could not move. The light failed, as if clouds had come over the sun. She heard Stammel's voice, now urgent, but could not follow what he said.

Someone's shoulder was under her arm, supporting her; someone's hands fumbled at the buckles of her shield. She tried to stop them, but could not seem to move well. Voices talked back and forth across her hearing. Nothing made sense. Suddenly someone shoved what felt like a length of wood into the wound on her leg; she tried to push them away from her, all of them, but found herself lying flat on the ground with no memory of how she'd gotten there. One of the veterans held her shoulders down; sweat dripped off his nose onto her face. When he saw her watching him, he said "Sorry," but went on holding her. Someone else was holding her legs. Her injured leg throbbed fiercely. A surgeon in his dark robes bent over her leg. A hand appeared out of nowhere, with a kerchief dripping water.

"Here," said a voice. "Chew on this." She opened her mouth, and he stuffed the wet rag in. At once something—she thought the same length of wood—bored into her leg. She twisted against the hands that held her, to no avail. The pain went on, and when it finally stopped was replaced by a bath of liquid fire. Paks closed her eyes, grinding the rag with her teeth. Something tugged at her leg—would tear it off, she thought— but ceased before it came loose. She opened her eyes. Tears blurred her vision until she blinked them away. Her leg still throbbed, but farther away—a spear-length or so, maybe. The veteran released her shoulders; the surgeon was already walking away. She gagged on the wet lump of cloth in her mouth, and a hand came to pull it out.

"There," said the voice. "That's over." Paks tried to twist her head to find the speaker, but it was too much effort. "You need some wine," the voice went on. "That will ease the pain." She tried to speak up, to refuse, but a strong arm heaved her head and shoulders up, and a wineskin pressed against her lips. When she opened her mouth to protest, a squirt of wine filled her mouth; she had to swallow. The wineskin was tooled in gold, she noticed, as another squirt of wine filled her mouth—

then another. The pain receded farther, and a dark haze spread across her vision.

Paks woke to darkness and the sounds of pain. Far away to her left was a bobbing yellow glow. She felt light and crisp except for her injured leg, a cold weight dragging at her. The glow came closer, paused, came closer. She realized it was a lantern—in someone's hand—someone coming near. She felt very clever—she knew what was happening, someone was visiting the wounded. Then she realized she could not find her dagger. Had she been captured? She tried to think as the lantern came nearer. Her leg began to throb, but it didn't bother her. She had just decided that it wasn't really attached at all when the lantern paused beside her. She squinted up, trying to see past the light to the person who held it. "Hmm," said a voice she thought she should remember. "Looks a bit feverish, this one."

"How do you feel?" another voice asked.

Paks worked her tongue around in her dry mouth until she could speak. "I'm—all right."

"Do you feel hot?" asked the second voice.

At the question Paks realized that she was cold, cold from the bones out. She started to answer, but a violent chill racked her body; her teeth rattled like stones in a sack. A broad hand touched her forehead.

"Fever, all right," said the first voice. "Best dose her now, and be sure she's checked on. We'll use what we have to on this one."

"She needs to drink," said the second voice. "She's dry. Here, now—" he said to Paks. "We'll lift you up, then I want you to drink all of this."

One of them lifted her shoulders and steadied her head; a jug came to her lips. Paks sipped; it was water. Despite the shaking chill and rattling teeth, she managed to empty the jug.

"Now then," said the voice. "Swallow this." Paks had half-drained the cup before the taste reached her; she gagged and tried to spit it out, but hands restrained her. "Finish it!" said the voice, and she choked down the rest of that bitter brew. "Now a swallow of numb-wine." Paks swallowed that, and the arm behind her eased her back to the straw.

"Sleep well, warrior," said the first voice. Paks felt a hand grip her shoulder, and the lantern moved away to her right; three shadowy forms moved with it.

When next she woke, a lantern was on the ground beside her, and someone was peeling off her sweat-sodden clothes. She grumbled a weak protest, but the person went on, drying her with a rough towel and then easing her into a long linen shirt. "It's fever sweat," a woman's voice said. "You need dry things so you won't chill again." A warm dry blanket covered her, then the woman held a flask to her lips. "Go on—drink this." Paks gulped it down and was asleep almost before her head hit the straw.

A hand on her shoulder and a voice calling her name roused her to sunlight dappling through green leaves. She felt solid to herself, aches and all. Stammel squatted beside her. "Come on," he said. "You've slept long enough."

Paks found her mouth too dry for speech. He offered a jug of water, and helped her raise her head to drink. She tried again; her voice was thinner than usual. "I—forgot the right strokes."

Stammel grinned. "I was going to mention that. Tir's bones, girl, a battle is no place to show off. Why do you think we teach you what strokes work?"

"I'm sorry—" she began.

"Never mind; more weapons drill for you, until you can't forget it. We don't want to lose a good private—"

"What!"

"Well, you did it in a backwards, idiotic way, but you hardly fit the 'recruit' category any more. I hope you realize you very nearly got yourself killed—and why didn't you get that wound bound up before you nearly bled out?"

"I—I didn't know it was that bad."

"Hmm. You don't come of berserker blood, do you? No? Probably just first-battle fever. Vanza, by the way, is sorry he told you to advance when you were already wounded. He says he didn't see it."

"That's all right," said Paks.

"Not with me, it isn't. It's his job to keep track of you novices and get you back if you're hurt. Do you remember how many you killed?"

"I killed? No—" Paks thought a long moment. "No. There's—a lot I don't remember. It's all confused."

"Likely enough. You did well, Paks, wrong strokes and all. Now—you'll be going back with the other wounded to Valdaire in a day or so. The duke expects we'll take out the rest of the Czardians tomorrow or the next day; they've gotten in among those hills southwest of here. Vanza will stay to help with our wounded—"

"Do I have to go back to Valdaire? Couldn't I stay here—"

Stammel shook his head. "No. The surgeons say you won't be up to a route march for several weeks. You lost a lot of blood, and the fever might come back. Don't worry, though—you'll be with us again soon." He gave her a reassuring grin as he stood up. "I'll see you again before you go. Do what they tell you, and heal fast."

Paks had hoped to prove the surgeons wrong, but she could barely hobble a few steps to the wagons when they loaded. She settled into the second of five wagons, bedded deep in straw and braced into a corner against the jolting ride. Four others shared the wagon: Callexon, a recruit in Dorrin's cohort, with his broken leg bound in splints, a veteran with a huge lump on his head who never woke up, a woman named Varñe, from Cracolnya's cohort, who had been burned by flaming oil, and Effa, who had been trampled by a warhorse and would never walk. Callexon and Paks helped Vanza care for the rest at halts. Paks learned how to feed and clean a helpless person, and how to help with bandaging.

The little caravan had been winding between tall trees, shade cool on the canvas-topped wagons. Paks looked out to see whether it was a road they'd marched over, but she couldn't tell. The wagon rolled smoothly; she closed her eyes and dozed off.

She was wakened by a scream and a jolt that wrenched her leg. She opened her eyes to see Vanza hurtling out the back of their wagon, sword in hand. Out the front she could see strange horses and masked riders with black wolf's heads on their red jerkins. Something blocked her view to the right; their wagon's driver was slumped against the iron bow that held the canvas. Two arrows poked through her tunic. The mules had their ears laid flat. As Paks grabbed for the reins, heaving herself over the front of the box, the lead pair surged forward.

She heard a whirr and a thunk, and saw an arrow stand quivering in the wagon box beside her—but she had the reins. She tried to haul the driver inside with one arm; she couldn't get any leverage. The wagon lurched as the mules veered from the track. Another arm appeared beside her: the burned woman.

"I'll get her—you drive!"

"I'm trying!" Paks had driven her father's pair of plow ponies, but nothing like a hitch of four frightened mules. She had a tangle of reins, all too long, and the mules were picking up speed. Suddenly one of the red-clothed riders swerved beside the lead pair and made a grab for their reins. Paks pulled some of her handful, and the mules veered.

"Now I know what those are," she muttered, and reached to shorten the others. The rider glanced up and saw her. He wheeled his horse and came at the wagon, sword raised. Paks jerked the other pair of reins as he neared it; the mules swerved back and the wagon slammed into his horse. His sword hit the iron frame and shattered. Paks hardly noticed. The mules had broken into a panicky run. There were trees everywhere she looked. She couldn't brace herself well enough to pull them in. And her best attempts at steering had the wagon swinging wildly from side to side. All around came wild screeches, yells, the whinnying of horses and braying of mules. An arrow struck one of the leaders. It screamed, and lurched ahead faster. Ahead Paks saw a gap in the trees; the mules galloped toward it, flat out. Too late, Paks saw the dip that steepened into a bank of eroded stone over a stream. The wagon bounced from stone to stone, collapsing with a broken axle in the shallow streambed; the mules were jerked to their knees by the shock. Paks, already leaning over the front of the box, flew forward. Her injured leg slammed against the back of the box, all that kept her from going headlong on top of the wheel pair. She banged her chin on the footboard, and hung there dazed.

"Quick!" said a voice. Someone pulled at her. "Help with these reins. Don't let 'em take off again."

"Mmph." Paks shortened the reins and blinked heavily. Varñe held the reins she'd dropped.

"I've got the nearside reins," the woman went on. "We've got to get them up. Where's the whip?"

Paks looked around and found the whip still in its socket. She slithered over and managed to reach it. She glanced back into the wagon. Most of the hay had bounced toward in their final crash. Callexon still clung to the rear board, bow in hand, his splinted leg apparently straight. He waved at Paks.

"I've got two, so far," he said. "If you can smooth the ride a little—"

Effa and the unconscious man were tangled in the hay. Paks turned back to the mules. All but one were standing already, quietly enough; she flicked the whip at the arrow-struck mule, and it finally struggled up, not too tangled in harness. Paks looked at Varñe. "Do you want me to take those reins?"

The woman gave a wry grin that creased the salve on her blistered face. "Depends—nothing like a little excitement to clear out a dose of numbwine. Maybe I should take all the reins and let you check on the others."

Paks handed over the reins, and slid back into the hay. She found the driver first; she was dead. The veteran with the head injury snored heavily, but Effa was also dead, her stubborn face wiped clean of all expression. Paks tried to straighten the injured man on top of the hay. Her leg hurt a lot; when she looked at it, the bandages were soaked with blood. She burrowed into the hay for the medical supplies, and wrapped more bandages around it. She felt nauseated and faint, and broke into a sweat trying to pull herself back to the driver's seat.

"I see someone," called Callexon.

"We aren't going anywhere," muttered Varñe. "Blast! Not even a sword among us."

Paks took out her dagger. "Calle's got the bow, and I have a dagger—"

"With those, it's not enough. I wonder how many—"

"It's ours!" yelled Callexon. "Hey—Arvid!"

Paks looked back. A limping figure in maroon and white stood at the top of the bank. "Any more alive?" he called.

"Yes—but the wagon's broken."

"So I see." The man limped down the bank, chest heaving.

"What about them?" asked Callexon.

"Driven off for now. Tir's gut, I never thought even the outlaw companies would attack a sick train." He clambered up to peer in the wagon. "Hmmph. We'll have to clear you out before we can mend this. Can any of you walk?"

"I can," said Varñe. Callexon shook his head.

"Let's see." Arvid climbed in and worked his way forward, checking the bodies first, then Pak's leg. "We'd best deal with that." He tore off another length of bandage and tied it tighter than Paks had managed. "Now you," he said to Varñe.

"I'm no worse than I was."

"No? Let me have the reins, and see your hands." He tied the reins to the wagon frame, and looked her over. "You'll do—after a dose of numbwine. Now—" he climbed down. "—to get these mules unhitched."

Paks sank back in the hay and her eyes fluttered shut. She roused to find Vanza beside her, calling her name.

"Yes—what—"

"Paks, we have to move you out of this wagon. We're going to carry you in a blanket—don't struggle."

She felt the blanket tighten around her, then a swooping sensation that made her want to fight her way to her feet. Instead she lay still. Above her were voices, Vanza's among them.

"We'd better send word to the Duke—"

"—that's the fastest. And isn't there a Baron Kodaly or something near here?"

"Yes—off east a bit; he claims this forest. Don't forget—"

"—wheelwright, and a smith, and supplies—"

"—never heard of anything like this in all the years—"

"—Marshals or priests or something, if you can—"

"—what they thought they'd get out of it—"

"—and coffinwood—"

"—forward to Valdaire, too, but we can't spare another—"

Paks sank into unconsciousness.

Her next waking was a confused struggle through dark corridors with shadowy opponents who faded away as she came near. Far ahead was a blur of light and a clamor of sound; she came to it in bursts of random motion. Finally her vision cleared. She was lying on the ground under a tree. The surgeon knelt by her injured leg, shaking his head.

"—don't think I can do more, my lord," he was saying. "Too much blood loss, and this additional bruising—"

Paks felt a cold twinge of fear. Was that *her* leg about which he had not hope?

"Very well," said a voice from above and behind her. "We'll try a healing. Master Vetrifuge?"

"At once, my lord." A gray-bearded man in black and green robes stooped beside the surgeon and laid his hands on Paks's leg. A warming tingle ran from his touch through the wound; it did not hurt. The surgeon bent to look.

"That's better." He looked at her face and found her watching. "She's awake, my lord. We might try the potion."

"Go ahead," said the voice behind her. The surgeon took a small flask from his robes and brought it to Paks. He slipped an arm behind her shoulders and lifted her head until she could drink.

The lip of the flask was icy cold, and the two swallows of liquid in it burned her throat, but gave her the same warming tingle as Vetrifuge's hands. Her leg did not hurt any more, nor the bruises where she'd hit the footboard. Her nausea had gone too. The surgeon's face, watching her, was clear in every line; she could see the dust on his eyelashes. He turned to look at her leg.

"Ah—that's more like it. Rest and food will be enough now. Thank you, Master Vetrifuge."

"My pleasure, Master Simmitt," said Vetrifuge, with a mocking smile. "Glad to know there are yet a few things in which wizardry can aid the science of surgery." The surgeon reddened, and seemed to swell in the neck.

"Others need your skills," said the third voice, with enough bite that both men froze an instant.

"Yes, my lord; right away."

As Paks watched them stand and walk off, a mail-clad figure moved to her side and sat. When she looked back, she was face to face with the Duke himself. Paks gulped. This close she could see a few silver hairs in his fox-red beard; his nose was sunburnt and peeling; his eyes were the gray of sword-steel, just barely blue. Her eyes dropped. His cloak was fastened with a silver medallion; it was dusty. His gloves were gray kid, sweat-stained.

"First," said the Duke, "you need to drink this, and eat a little; then I want to know what happened. What *you* saw." Paks dragged her eyes back up and saw once more the gold-tooled wineskin she'd seen the night of the battle. "Try to sit up." Paks found she was weak, but able to rise on one elbow. She took the wineskin. "It's watered," said the Duke. "It shouldn't knock you out. Here—have some bread." He bit the end off a loaf and handed her the rest. Paks tore off a hunk and took a swallow of wine. She wondered how long she'd slept, and when the Duke had arrived, but under his eye she ate as he directed.

"Now," said the Duke, when she had choked down most of the bread. "Take your time, but tell it all, from the beginning. I want to know everything you can remember about the attack."

Paks blushed. "Well—sir—my lord—I was asleep. Then someone screamed, and the wagon bumped. I saw Vanza jumping out the back, and out the front were riders in red, with a black wolf's head on the front—"

"On the back as well?"

Paks thought a moment. "No—I don't think so. Just the front. Then I saw our driver'd been shot, so I tried to get the reins. The mules were scared. Varñe helped me pull the driver into the wagon. One of the attackers tried to grab the lead mules' reins, but they swerved away—"

"Were you driving, or—"

"Yes, sir, I was—but I wasn't sure which reins were which. It seemed like a lot—I jerked the ones that were tightest, and the mules veered—"

"Go on."

"Then the rider turned and came at the wagon, so I pulled the other reins, and the wagon ran into his horse—"

"What did he look like?"

"The rider? He had a mask on."

"A mask? Not a—wait—have you seen anything but

open helmets? Have you seen a knight's helmet, with the visor down?"

"Yes, sir. Sergeant Stammel showed us that in training. This was different. He had an open helmet over chain mail, but a mask over his face—it was some kind of cloth; I saw it ripple."

"Aha!" The Duke slammed his fist onto his thigh. "Very good. Go on—what else?"

"He seemed heavy—broad in the shoulders. Taller than Sergeant Stammel, I think. He had something on the shoulder of his tunic that glittered. The horse had no barding, but it was a war saddle, and the blanket was black with a red stripe."

"What color was the horse?"

"Light brown, dappled, with a pale mane and tail. All the others were dark, but for the spotted one."

"Spotted?"

"Yes, sir. One was black and white spotted. Now that I think of it, that one was smaller—we went by it in the trees."

"What sort of rider on the spotted one?"

Paks shook her head. "I'm sorry—I don't remember—"

"But you're sure of the horses?"

"Yes, sir—though I don't know that I saw all of them. We were moving too fast, and I was trying to steer around things, but I didn't see the stream until we were almost into it. So I broke the wagon—" Paks faltered, remembering Stammel's lectures on damaged equipment.

"Hmm." The Duke's eyes crinkled. "Are you an experienced teamster?"

Paks looked down. "No sir—my lord."

"That's all right then. Not your equipment." Paks looked up, still worried. "Tir's bones, girl, that wagon's the least of my concerns. I've lost fighters here. A wagon's nothing—you did well. But I want to know who—" he bounced his fist on his thigh for emphasis, "—and why and how anyone would attack a caravan of wounded. No treasure—no ranking prisoners to ransom—

and they must know this'll bring my Company down on them. It's costing me now, but it'll cost them—" his voice trailed off, and Paks almost flinched at the look in his eyes. He glanced back at her and half-smiled. "You were just promoted, right? Paks, isn't it?"

"Yes, my lord."

"Well, Paks, you've had the most expensive healing I hope you'll ever need, and you should be ready to fight in a day or so. The next time you see those red tunics, you'll have a weapon in hand. I'll expect you to fight as well as you did in your first battle." The Duke stood. "No—don't try to get up yet. The surgeon will clear you for that." Paks watched as he strode away, cloak swirling around his tall boots.

Paks looked at her leg, no longer wound in bandages. A red scar showed the line of the wound, but it looked nothing like the deep gash it had been. She wondered what they had done—how it had healed so fast—and why they hadn't healed it that way in the first place. She looked around. The makeshift camp was bigger than she'd supposed. Smoke rose from a fire near the stream crossing; loud clangs revealed a smith at work. Across the clearing, the Duke was talking to a short man in plate mail. They headed for a tent, maroon and white striped. A man in green livery was cooling out a big warhorse still lathered in sweat. Another led three lighter mounts. On the track away from the stream, the remains of the caravan clogged the way. Two burnt-out wagons, one unburned, but missing a wheel, dead mules. As she watched, a group of soldiers dragged a mule into the forest. She wondered what had happened to the other wounded; she didn't see any of them. Had they all died? Callexon hadn't looked that bad— She saw the surgeon and Vanza approaching.

"How do you feel?" asked the surgeon.

"Fine," said Paks. "Can I get up?"

"Yes—you'll be weaker than you think; you lost a lot of blood." Vanza reached down an arm, and Paks pulled herself up. She felt dizzy at first, but it passed quickly.

"Try walking," said the surgeon. She took a step, then another. She felt no pain, but she was shaky. "That's expected," the surgeon reassured her. "Don't push yourself for the next day or so—rest when you're tired. Eat and drink as much as you can." He turned away. Paks looked at Vanza.

"Where are the others? Were they all—"

"No. Not all." He sighed. "We lost more than we should, though. I still can't believe it. No one does this—I knew the Wolf Prince was bad, but even he—"

"Is that who it was?"

"It must have been. You saw the wolf's head, didn't you?"

"Yes. But I'm confused—"

"We all are. Now—all you wounded are being healed, as you were, by the Duke's command. For today, stay close. You can help with food, and that sort of thing, but don't try to do too much—no hauling mules around."

"But—what did that Master Vetrifuge do? And why not do it all the time, if it works so well?"

Vanza stopped short and gave her a startled look. "You mean you don't know about magical healing?"

"No. Effa said something about St. Gird, but—"

"That's different. Or somewhat different. Let me see— first of all, Master Vetrifuge is a mage. Wizard, they're called in the north. Surely you've heard of them?"

"Yes, but—"

"Just listen. Some mages specialize in one sort of magic; healing magic is one particular kind of magic. I don't know how it works—I'm no mage. It's great learning, I've been told, and great power—but whether of a god, or the mage himself, I don't know. But healing mages can heal wounds, if they aren't too bad. Too old, say, or full of fever. Sometimes they can heal diseases, though not so well. But it takes a lot of money. Mages don't work for nothing."

"What about potions?"

"You had that too? Mages make potions, to speed healing. Those are even more expensive; don't ask me why. Our surgeons always have a few of these, but of course they don't use them most of the time."

Paks frowned. "Why not? If wounds could be healed so fast—"

"Because of the cost. Paks, the Duke will have spent the whole contract's profit, I don't doubt, just healing the few of you here. No one could afford to have every wound magically healed. It's cheaper to train and hire new fighters. Our duke is one of the few I've heard of who will use such healing at all for his common soldiers."

"Oh." Paks thought about it. She had no way of valuing things, but it seemed strange that a tiny vial of liquid, however rare, could be more costly than a person. "But what did Effa mean, then?"

"About St. Gird?" Paks nodded. "Well, the gods can heal, if they will. Those who serve them—Marshals of Gird, or Captains of Falk, or whatever—have the power to ask healing of the gods and have it granted. Before my time, the Duke was friendly with Girdsmen—I even heard he was one himself—and had a Marshal with the Company for healing. I've seen men who say they were healed that way."

"Does that cost so much?"

"Well—I can't say. They usually heal their own, and no one else: Marshals heal Girdsman, and Captains heal Falkians. I'd think it would cost, though maybe not in gold. Why should a god give healing for nothing?"

"The gods give rain and wind for nothing, and sunlight."

"For nothing? Surely your people gave back, wherever you're from—" Vanza stared at her. Paks remembered the little shrines by the well and the corners of her father's fields; the tufts of barley and oats, and the lamb's blood they left there. For an instant she felt cold as she realized how close she had come to impiety.

"You're right," she said quickly. "But the gods have the power to give as they choose, whatever gifts we give. That's what I meant, that we give gifts, we do not compel." She hoped that was what she'd meant.

He nodded. "True, no one can compel—but they are honorable, or the good ones are, and generous." He nodded to her and went away. Paks stared after him, thoughtfully. Wizards . . . magical healing . . . somehow when she'd heard of magic potions in songs, she'd never thought of the cost in gold. Or lives.

Chapter Eleven

The next day Cracolnya's cohort marched in. Pont, his junior captain, escorted the survivors back to the Company's camp while the Duke, Cracolnya, and most of that cohort went on to Valdaire.

"I thought the Czardians were defeated," said Callexon. "What happened?"

Erial, the junior sergeant in Cracolnya's cohort, chuckled. "They were. But they'd hired a mercenary band to help them, only it was late. Then the Duke pulled us out—so when their hirelings finally arrived, they quit talking to Foss Council again and decided to fight for it." She paused to wipe the sweat from her face. "Won't do them any good. As long as Foss Council still has three cohorts in the field, and we have two—"

"Who'd they hire?" Varñe's face still looked patchy and pink, but she was otherwise healthy.

"Some southern company. We don't have to worry; they won't be any better than the Czardian militia."

"Unless they've got the Free Pikes," said Vanza.

Erial looked startled. "I never thought of that—they hardly ever hire out."

"Who are the Free Pikes?" asked Paks.

"The only decent southern company," said Erial. "They're from the high mountains in the southwest—I think they call it Horngard."

"That's right," said Vanza. "They don't hire out much— they fight in defense, or if their land needs money. But when they fight—!" He shook his head.

But the Czardians did not have the Free Pikes; they had hired, Stammel explained, a renegade baron of the Sier of Westland and his so-called knights. They were best known for their woodswork—sneaking into enemy lines at night to kill sleeping men, or steal supplies, or start fires—but could put up a respectable fight on the field, as well.

Paks had hardly realized, in the excitement of her first battle, that the Duke's Company was not fighting alone. Now she had a look at the Foss Council militia. They wore short gray tunics over trousers of bright red (from Foss) or green (from Ifoss); they carried short straight swords and light throwing javelins. Foss Council held the right wing of their position; their camp, like the Duke's, was in the forest. Trees ended on a gentle slope, opening on a wide expanse of grass and sedge that faced another tree-shaded ridge some distance away. To the left, the trees made an arc connecting the two ridges; to the right the grassy meadow grew wetter, finally producing a stream that trickled away to the north.

When the next battle came, two days later, Paks was more than ready for it. Someone had made it through the lines; Arñe was in the surgeon's care with a knife wound, and Kir of Dorrin's cohort was dead. Even so, her breath came short as the two lines closed. For an instant she was even more frightened than the first time—she could feel the sickening blow that had opened her leg. She thrust the thought away angrily as the remembered noise and confusion swept over her. This time she was able to keep her head, battering at the enemy stroke after stroke. She was aware of the man beside her, able to adjust her strokes to his so that they fought as a unit. It seemed to last forever: dust, noise, confusion, the rising and falling blades. Then the ground softened under her feet. She realized that they had advanced to the center of the field, where mud churned up instead of water.

Some time after midday, both sides withdrew a space. Paks drained her water flask and wiped sweat from her face. She had come through uninjured. Her stomach growled—a long time since breakfast. They stood quiet in formation: across the way the enemy lines shifted, milling.

"Pass your flask back," said Donag, handing her his. "They'll send water forward." Soon the dripping flasks returned, and they drank. Slabs of bread came forward, then more water. Paks ate hungrily. When she looked again, the enemy seemed a little farther away. She nudged Kiri beside her.

"They're giving back," he said. "Don't look at 'em, and maybe they'll go all the way."

"But what does it mean?"

"Means they don't want to fight the rest of the day. Fine with me—it's too blazin' hot anyway."

And in fact the enemy were soon back in their own camp, and to Paks's surprise they were not sent in pursuit. In the next week, before the Duke returned, they fought several such inconclusive engagements.

"Why don't they want to fight and win?" she asked one night.

"Don't complain," said Donag. "If they wanted to win—I suppose you mean Foss Council?—it'd be our blood on the ground, and not their militia's. Think about it. They want to win, but what they want to win is whatever it is they're fighting about: where a border is, or a caravan tariff, or something like that. If they can convince Czardas to yield on that, without us having to cut our way through the entire Czardian army, so much the better."

"But—" began Arñe, now back from the surgeons.

"No buts," interrupted Donag. "Tir's guts, you idiots! You'll get all the fighting you've stomach for by the time you make corporal—if you live that long. Don't look for trouble. It's your profession—it'll come to you."

When the Duke returned, everything changed again. With Cracolnya's archers, he decided to change ground. Under cover of darkness they slipped far to the left of their previous position. This left a gap between the Duke's Company and Foss Council's troops, and confused the novices almost as much as the enemy. Paks worried about the militia, and even more about what they might think.

"Don't be silly," said Canna. She had seen this before. "They're moving too. It's a trap, if it works, and a good move even if it doesn't."

They made it to the Duke's chosen field without interference, and Stammel explained how it was better for their purposes than the other one.

"He wants to use our archers. So far the Czardians haven't shown us any, so we don't have to worry. But look—the mixed cohort will be up there—" he pointed. "They can't get to 'em on foot or horse, but they'll be in range to feel it when Cracolnya opens up. Just watch it come."

As Stammel predicted, the Czardian forces gave way once the Duke's archers opened on them. Paks, watching the enemy ranks melt away, was glad the Czardians could not counterattack in kind. The Duke ordered a pursuit, and they began several weeks of constant movement and fighting. Although they never fought the Czardians to a finish, each time they met it was on ground of the Duke's choosing, and each time the Czardians slipped away, losing ground, back toward their city. When the walls were in sight, the duke sent two cohorts around to the south, to stop traffic on the southern caravan route, while the other cohort and the Foss Council militia harried the Czardians. A few days after that, the campaign was over. Incoming caravans paid their tolls directly to the Foss Council commander, and he had a treaty to take back to their Table of Councilors.

"You had a good campaign for your first one," Stammel told the new privates in his cohort. "Some set battles—good moving engagements—enough fighting, but nothing really hard. And we'll be doing garrison work or caravan work the rest of the season, so you'll have a chance to learn that."

"What?" Arñe sounded as surprised as Paks felt.

"Yes. Any year a campaign doesn't last the season—which is most years—we're hired as caravan guards or garrison troops for the rest of it. Foss Council wants us to garrison the border forts between them and Czardas, for instance—"

"But—when do we get to go to a city—?"

"He means, when do we get paid?" Vik interrupted Malek.

Stammel laughed. "Ah—thinking like real mercenaries! I expect when Foss Council pays the Duke—which shouldn't be long—it'll trickle down to you. And if we're close enough to a city or town, you might have a little time to waste your pay."

The Duke's scribe sat behind a table as the captains and sergeants set out stacks of coins. The Company lined up in order of seniority, which meant that the new privates, in the back, caught only glimpses of the glinting piles before veterans blocked their view. Paks wondered if any of them had dared ask how much they would be paid. She had no idea what to expect. For that matter, she wasn't sure how many coppers made a silver, or what a silver would buy. She had agreed, with the others, to pay into the Company's death fund. Stammel explained that this paid for having the personal effects and any salary owed sent to the heirs of those killed. But she did not know what that would leave.

The line snaked forward, slowly. When Paks could see the table again, the piles were much smaller. Suddenly she thought of her "expensive healing"—did that come out of her pay? The scribe called her name at last, and she stepped forward.

"Hmm." Captain Arcolin picked up the roll and glanced at it, then looked at Paks. "You were promoted on the first day of the campaign. You've got a small bonus for your actions when the sick train was attacked. Less the contribution to the fund—did Stammel explain the currency?" Paks nodded. He had, but she didn't really understand. The Guild League cities coined under their own marks at agreed weights, with the gold nata, or father, being the coin of greatest value, followed by the gold nas, or son, silver niti (mother), silver nis (daughter), and two sizes of coppers, the page and serf. "Well, then," said Arcolin, "it will be thirty-six nitis for you." He pushed a pile forward.

"I'd advise you not to draw it all," said Stammel. "As long as we're in town, you can draw your pay once a day; you're less likely to lose it to thieves and such."

Paks had never seen so much money; it was hard not to take it all. "How much, then, sir?"

"Take ten, why don't you? That should be enough to make you feel rich. Take two of it in mixed coppers." Paks nodded to the scribe, and he marked the sum she drew beside her name. Stammel counted the coins into her hand. They were heavy; when she dropped them in her belt pouch, it dragged at her belt. She thought of all she could buy, and how soon she could save up the amount of her dowry to repay her father.

"I've never had so much money," said Saben, coming up beside her.

"Nor I," said Paks. "And to think we'll get more next month, and the next—"

"What are you going to buy?"

Paks thought through her list. She didn't know what they had, yet. "I was wondering if there was a place to buy spicebread—"

Saben laughed. "You and I are truly countryborn. I was thinking about clotted cream—that's what they had at fairs near home. I never had but a bit of it, and I could eat it by the bucket. And something for my sisters—ribbons, or something like that. Stammel said it could go north with the Duke's next courier, if it was small and light."

Paks had not thought about presents; she felt guilty. "I'm—saving to send my dowry to my father," she said.

"Dowry?" Saben looked surprised. "I thought you didn't want—"

"To repay it," she corrected. "He'd already given it, when I ran away." She had never told anyone but Stammel the circumstances of her leaving home.

"Oh. I see. But you hadn't agreed, had you?"

"No. I told him I wouldn't wed Fersin, but he thought he could make me, so he gave dower."

"But if you didn't agree, it's not your fault." Barra pushed in beside her.

Paks wished she'd never mentioned it. "No—I suppose not. But I'd feel better if I paid it back. There's my brothers and sisters to think of."

Barra snorted, and Saben asked quickly, "Do you know how much it is?"

"Not exactly." In fact she didn't know anything but rumor: her oldest brother had said it was as much as Amboi dowered his eldest to the wool merchant's son in Rocky Ford, and she thought she remembered what the baker's wife in Three Firs had said about that. Saben looked impressed, and asked no more questions.

When they asked Stammel for permission to leave camp and go into the city, he told them to wait. Shortly before midday, he gathered some of his novices.

"All right," he said. "You've got your pay—come along and let me show you how not to spend it."

Vik shook his pouch, listening to the jingle of the coins. "But sir—I already know how not to spend it. And I have plans—"

"Sure you do. And I can't stop you from losing your last copper, if you're taken that way. But I can show you the safer places to drink, and maybe keep you from being robbed and beaten in some alley."

"Is Foss so dangerous?" asked Saben.

"And who'd attack us? We're armed," said Paks.

"It's exactly that attitude," said Stammel severely, "that loses good fighters every year. With the Company, you're good. But alone, in an alley with thieves—no. If you're lucky you wake up in the morning with a lump on your head and no money. Unlucky, you find yourself in a slaver's wagon with a sack over your head and a brand—or maybe just dead. You youngsters don't know the first thing about cities—well, maybe Vik and Jorti do—and that's why you'll come with me this time."

A half hour later, Stammel led a dozen of them into the wide public room of the Dancing Cockerel. A tall, powerful-looking man in a green apron came forward to greet them.

"Hai! Matthis, old friend—I thought we'd see you this summer. Bringing the new ones in, eh?" The man looked at them keenly. "Duke Phelan's soldiers are welcome here—what will you have?"

"Bring us your good ale, Bolner, and plenty of it. We're in time for lunch, I trust."

"Certainly. Be seated here—unless you wish a private room?"

Stammel laughed. "Not for lunch—are you thinking the Duke's raised our pay?"

"I'd trust you for it, after these years. Besides, what I heard about the Duke's contract, you're getting paid in gold for copper."

"So? You can hear anything, if you listen to all. Besides, what have contracts to do with us—poor soldiers that we are, and dying of thirst in the middle of your floor." A roar of laughter from a table near the wall greeted this, and the tall landlord turned away. "Have a seat here," said Stammel more quietly, and Paks and the others sat down to a long table near the center of the room.

"How much is the ale?" asked Saben, fingering his belt pouch.

"Last time I was here, it was three pages a mug, and a niti a jug. Local coinage. Dearer than some, cheaper than others, but Bolner doesn't water his ale, and he won't take a bribe to drug it, as some taverners will. This is a good tavern, as taverns go. Just remember that any landlord loves gossip, and can no more keep a secret than a pig can weave. Anyone who talks about the Company's business will be explaining it to the captain."

"Hey—Sergeant Stammel!" They turned to see a fat redhead at the table by the wall. "Still taking your recruits about in leading strings?" His companions laughed again.

Paks looked quickly at Stammel. He was smiling, but his eyes were grim. "My dear Lochlinn, if they were recruits I might, but these are all seasoned fighters— merely friends. And how is the Baroness these days?"

The fat man jogged one of his companions with an elbow. "Seasoned? Half seasoned, I should think, close as they cling to you like chicks to a hen. Haw! They're big enough, especially that yellow-headed wench, but—"

Paks flushed and took a quick breath. Stammel's hand beneath the table dug into her elbow. "Now, Lochlinn, we realize it's been so long since you fought you can't tell the fighters from the spectators. But come to our next, and let us show you. And mind you keep civil— this 'wench' as you would say—" Stammel released Pak's elbow and thumped her shoulder lightly with his fist, "—could part you from crown to cod with one stroke. I trained her."

Paks gazed across the room at the fat man's pink face, now a shade paler than it had been. He looked from Stammel to her and made a face, lifting his brows.

"Well, pardon me for plain speaking to an old comrade." Stammel snorted. "What a fierce look she has, too. I had no wish, wolf-maiden, to anger you and risk a blow from that strong arm your sergeant boasts of." He rose from his table and made an elaborate bow. "There—will that content you, or must I attempt some other satisfaction?"

Paks looked down at the table, scarred by many diners. She would gladly have leaped on the man, and killed him then and there. Saben, sitting on her other side, nudged her with his knee.

"We would be content," said Stammel mildly, "to take our ale in peace—and silence."

"You can't order me off!" cried the fat man. Paks suddenly realized that he was both drunk and frightened. "You don't have any right to order me around now, sergeant—I've got soldiers of my own!"

"Tsst! Lochlinn!" said one of his companions. "Let it be, man. Don't start—"

Paks jumped as a tall pitcher and several mugs were dumped in front of her. Two serving wenches, as well as Bolner, were at the table, distributing the ale. Stammel turned away from the fat man to grin at Bolner. "What's the menu today, eh?"

"The usual. Common lunch is slices off the joint, bread, redroots, cheese—we've the kind you like from Sterry, no extra charge to this party. Or special—roast fowl, and we've three in the oven. Pastries. Cella's tarts, plum, peach, and strawberry, but not enough of the last for everyone. Fish—but I don't recommend it; it's river trash this time of year. Leg of mutton—it won't be done for several hours. Soup—there's always soup; comes with the common lunch or the special, or a mug of soup with bread is five pages."

"How much for the common lunch?"

"For this group—if you all take it—well, I'll take off a bit. Say a niti each, ale included."

Stammel looked around at them. "It's good food here. What about it?"

They nodded, and Stammel gave a thumb's up sign to the host, who left the table, calling orders to the kitchen. Paks looked for the fat man, but he was gone, and his friends with him.

"Who was that?" she asked Stammel.

"Who? Oh, him—the fat one?" She nodded. "His name's Lochlinn. Used to be one of ours, years back; he left the Company. Now he's in some local baron's guard. And bed, they say, when the baron's traveling."

"I'd like to—" began Paks, but Stammel interrupted. "No, you wouldn't." She looked at him surprised. "Don't get into fights. Remember that. The rule is the same as inside the Company—there's no good reason short of being assaulted. You get us a reputation for brawling, and we'll all lose by it."

"But what he said about Paks!" Saben scowled. "Why should we let him get away with that?"

"Because we want to come here and eat—or shop in the market—and not be prey to every cutpurse and ruffian, and have the citizens cheering them on when you and you and you—" he pointed around the table, "—are bleeding in the street. Or being hauled off to the lockup by militia. We don't want trouble. We aren't paid to fight over nothing. Tir's bones—we know any one of us could split the fat leech—what difference does it make what he says?"

Paks reached for the pitcher and poured several mugs full. She pushed one toward Stammel and took one herself. She sniffed at it; it smelled much like the ale sold at market in Three Firs.

"Paks, have you had ale before?"

She blushed. "No, sir, not really. Just a few swallows." She took a cautious sip.

"Don't drink much, then. It makes some people quick tempered; you don't need that. Vik, I don't have to ask you." Vik had drained his mug at one swallow.

"No, sir—and how I've missed good ale these long months."

Stammel grinned. "You can spend your pay quickly on ale, if that's your choice. Just keep in mind—"

"Oh, aye—no fighting, no talking—but what about wenching and dicing?"

"Well, if you must, you must. I'd recommend Silverthorn Inn for the one, and here for the other. Whatever you do, stay away from River Lane, across the market, and don't go to Aula's. They'll recommend it at Silverthorn, but don't. All the dice are magicked, and the dwarf will slit your gizzard in a second if you show you notice."

"Yes, sir—perhaps I'll wait for another day."

Arñe laughed. "Adding up the cost, Vik? Homebrew's the cheapest, they say."

"It's not so much my silver I care for as my fair white skin—you know how I dread being ill-marked." The rest laughed. Between sunburn, freckles, and healing battle scars, not much fair white skin was displayed.

"That's all right, Vik," called Coben from down the table. "You can teach me that dicing game—what is it?"

"Don't play the innocent, Cob," said the redhead. "I heard about you with that girl from Dorrin's cohort— was it five silvers, or six, you won from her while she taught you dicing?"

"More than that, my lad, more than that," said Coben, and drained his mug. "I'm a slow learner, I am. Especially when I'm winning."

"Here you are," said Bolner from behind them. He and each of the serving girls carried a platter of sliced roast meat to set out on the table. By the time they had finished stuffing themselves with meat, rounds of dark yellow cheese, redroots, bread and soup, the rest of the room was empty.

"Now," said Stammel. "A last reminder. Don't wander about alone—stay in pairs, at least. Keep alert; Foss has as many thieves and cutpurses as any city. The slavers won't bother you if you stay together. Don't brawl. Keep your mouths shut about the Company and its business, but be polite otherwise. If one of you gets drunk the others bring 'em home. You're all to be back before supper, so the others can go. Clear?" They all nodded.

In the main market square, they scattered into clumps of three or four. Arñe and Coben stayed with Paks and

Saben, poking into every stall and shop along one side
of the square. One sold lace, its white tracery displayed
against dark velvet. Another sold strips of silk, patterned with exquisite embroidery. Paks found a spicebread stall, and managed to stuff down a square of it
despite the lunch she'd eaten. They found a shoemak-
er's shop, displaying pointed-toed shoes in scarlet and
green and yellow, and a bootmaker's with riding boots,
laced boots, and one pair made of three different leathers. Paks stared, and the man came to the door.

"You like those, fair warrior? 'Tis mulloch's hide, and
goatskin, and the skin of a great snake from across the
sea, south of Aare—only a nas, for you."

"No, thank you," said Paks, stunned more by the
price than the boots. He smiled and turned away.

Coben stopped to look at a jeweler's display; the
jeweler's guards dropped their hands to the hilts of
their weapons. Paks looked over his shoulder, eyes
wide. A tray of rings, gold, silver, some with bright
stones set to them. Most were finger rings, but some
were clearly earrings. Another tray held bracelets, and
a single necklace of blue stones and pearls set in silver.

"Look at that," breathed Coben, pointing to one of
the rings. "It's like a braided rope." Paks saw another
that looked like tiny leaves linked together. She wondered what else was in the shop—far too expensive,
whatever it was.

One shop displayed clothing; they could see the tai-
lors inside, sitting cross-legged on their platform. Bolts
of cloth were piled up behind them. Another shop was
hung with musical instruments: two lap-harps, a lute,
something twice the size of a lute with more strings,
and many more that none of them recognized. In a
litter of woodshavings the maker was working on a part,
and smiled at them as they peeked in the door. He
reached a hand to pluck one of the harps and show its
tone. Paks was entranced. She had heard a harp only
twice, when musicians came to the fair.

"Can—can you play, as well as make, them?"

His bushy eyebrows rose. "Of course, girl—how else would I know if I'd made then well? Listen—" He unfolded himself from the workbench, lifted the harp, and ran his hands along the strings. Paks had never heard that music before, but shivers ran up her spine.

"Do you know Torre's Ride?" asked Arñe, nudging Paks forward.

"Certainly—three versions. Where are you from?"

"From the north—from Tsaia."

"Hmm." He paused to adjust a tuning peg. Then the thrilling sound rang out, one of the few songs Paks had learned before leaving home. She found herself humming along; Arñe was murmuring the words, as was Coben. The instrument maker finished a verse with a flourish. "There you are. But are any of you players?"

Paks could have listened all afternoon. She shook her head, and Arñe said "No, sir," and he went back to his bench, shaping a little piece of wood with a small chisel. Paks wondered which instrument it was for, and where it would fit, but was too shy to ask. They left that shop and moved on.

She found the surprise for Saben several shops down. Here were trays of religious symbols, carved of the appropriate stone or metal. Most she did not know. The crescent and cudgel of Gird were familiar, and the Holy Circle, and the wheatsheaf of the Lady of Peace. The sword of Tir was there, both plain and cleverly set with a tiny jewel in the pommel. But whose was the leaping fish, or the tree, or the arch of tiny stars? She looked at tiny golden apples, at green leaves, at anvils, hammers, spears, fox or wolf heads, little human figures clothed in flowers (the swirling hair made the loop for hanging). Here was the antlered figure of Guthlac, and the double-faced head of Simyits, a harp for Garin the patron of harpers, and shears for Dort, the patron of sheepshear-ers and all in the wool trade. Then she saw the little red stone horse, and remembered Saben's words that day in the stronghold. She looked up and found the shopkeeper watching her. She glanced around; Saben was in the next shop, pricing combs for his sisters.

"How much?" she asked. And, "Will it break easily?"

He shook his head. "Not these symbols, lady. And they have all been blessed, by the cleric for each one. They'll bring luck and blessings to those who wear them." Paks doubted this, but didn't argue.

"How much?" she asked again.

"The little horse? The symbol of Senneth, the horse-lord, and Arvoni the patron of horsemen?" Paks nodded. "Five nitis." She was startled and her face must have shown it. He said smoothly, "But for you, lady— you will need luck—for you, I will say four nitis, and two serfs." Paks had never bargained herself, though she had heard her mother and father.

"I cannot spare so much," she said, and looked away, shifting her feet. She sighed. She wanted that horse for Saben, but four nitis—that was four meals like lunch. And she wanted other things, too.

"Three nitis, two nis," he said. "I can't do more than that—" Abruptly Paks decided to buy it. She fumbled in her pouch for the silver.

When she came out, with the horse safely stowed in her pouch, Saben was still looking at combs; Arñe and Coben were rummaging through a pile of copper pots on the pavement. She ducked into the shop with Saben.

"I can't decide," he said, turning to her. "Suli likes flowers, so that's easy—this one—" The comb had a wreath of flowers along the spine. "But for Rahel and Maia, do you think the birds, or the fish, or the fern?" Paks thought the fern was the prettiest, and liked the leaping fish better than any angry-looking bird. He paid for the combs and they walked out. They saw fruit stalls beyond the piles of pots. Early berries, early peaches— they squandered coppers on the fruit, and walked on with sticky fingers. Coben cocked an eye at the sky.

"We'd better be going," he reminded them. They turned back across the square. Paks went to the spicebread stall again, and bought a stack it took both hands to carry. They munched spicebread most of the way back to camp.

As they were going to their posts for duty, Paks gave Saben the little horse. "I remembered you lost your bit of hoof," she said. "I couldn't find a hoof, but maybe the whole horse will do."

He flushed. "It's—it will do well, Paks. Thank you. Was it from the shop next to the comb place?"

"Yes."

"I looked at it, but didn't buy it—you shouldn't have spent so much—"

"Well—" this time Paks blushed. "I didn't—mean I—umm—"

Saben laughed. "You, too? I bargained myself, but I couldn't get him to go lower than three nitis."

"Three!" Paks gasped and began to laugh helplessly.

"What? What did you get it for?" She shook her head, laughing even harder. A veteran walking by stared at her. Finally she stopped, sides aching. Saben was still watching her, puzzled.

"You should have—" she began, and started laughing again. "Oh, I can't! It hurts—you should have got it yourself—you're the better bargainer—"

"You mean you paid more than that?"

"Not much," she said, still laughing. "As—as a fighter I may be good, but at market—"

"Well, the man tried to tell me it was bad luck to bargain over a holy symbol, so maybe it will be better luck this way." Saben grinned. "Tell you what, Paks—the next time you want something, I'll bargain for you."

"Thanks," she said.

"And by the way," he went on, taking a comb from his pouch. "This one's really for you—the ferny one."

Chapter Twelve

Two months later, as Paks leaned against the wall of the courtyard in a border fort south of Kodaly, she felt well content with her position.

"I agree," said Saben, who was mending a tear in his cloak while she sharpened her weapons, "that it's easier than farming. I've no desire to go back to mucking out barns. But don't forget your first battle just because it's gone so well since."

"I know. That could have ended it—like Effa. But that's the chance we take, as fighters. I wish we could see other good companies too. See how they do things, how they fight. We never can see anything but what's in front of us. It's hard to keep the idea of what we're doing—I mean as a whole—in all that confusion."

Saben shrugged. "I just go for what's in front of me. It makes sense when Stammel shows us with sticks and things, but I can't see it with real people. You can't tell what they'll do. All we can do is follow commands."

"But those who give the commands have to know what they're doing," said Paks.

"We're a long way from that," said Saben drily. "Or are you planning to leave and start your own company?"

Paks stopped a moment, and squinted up at the sky. "No. Or—I don't know. I can't say. No, I suppose not—it's a silly thought. I just—just keep thinking about it. I can't stop. Why the captains put us there, or why their commander never used his archers on the flank, like the Duke did. That was stupid, Saben, that last time. They had the archers, but they held them back where they couldn't see. If they'd been in that wood on the right—"

"I'm glad their commander didn't think of it." Saben looked at his mending and tugged the cloth to test it. "Ah. One more chore done. Are you nearly finished?"

"Sword's done. I notched the dagger yesterday."

"I told you you'd honed it too fine. We're on in less than a glass."

"I haven't forgotten. I just want to smooth this—one—spot. No, I'll tell you, Saben, what I'd like. I'd like to make sergeant someday. Years away, I know, and only six in the Company, but—I'd like that."

"Well, if you don't lose an arm or leg somewhere, or get killed outright, you ought to do it. You don't get drunk, or lose things, or brawl, or cause any sort of trouble. And you fight well. Now me—"

"Saben, you're as good as I am. Better, even—"

He shook his head. "No, and you know it. *I* wasn't practicing all morning. I do what I'm told, but I don't care enough to learn every weapon in sight and practice every spare minute. You do."

"You don't need much practice; you're already quicker." Paks took a last stroke with her whetstone, wiped the dagger blade carefully with a scrap of soft hareskin, and sheathed it.

"Maybe. I used to be faster than you—but you've gotten better. The thing is, I've got what I want. A life I like, good friends, enough pay for the extras I want. The only other thing would be—" he slid a glance at

Paks. When she met his eyes, she reddened and looked down.

"Saben, you know I—"

"You don't want it. I know. Not from me or anyone. Well, I'm not asking: just if you did ever change. If it was just Korryn, I mean."

Paks ducked her head lower and stared at the ground. "No. Even before. I just don't feel that way."

He sighed. "I'm glad it wasn't Korryn. Don't worry; I won't bother you."

She looked up. "You never have."

"Good. I still want to be friends. Besides that, you are— Paks, if you ever did have a company, you would be a good commander. I would follow you. I don't think you'll stop at sergeant, if you want more."

Paks blushed, then grinned sheepishly. "Even a warhorse?"

Saben nodded. "Lady Paksenarrion, in shining armor on a great warhorse, with a magic sword—don't laugh at me, companion! Here I'm giving you a good-luck prophecy and you laugh at me. Ha! See if I ever warn you about overhoning your blades again."

"No, but really, Saben—a sheepfarmer's daughter? That's ridiculous!" But her eyes danced to think of it.

"So laugh. Would you rather a bad-luck prophecy? Let's see—"

"No! Don't ill-wish! Let's go; I've got to get ready for guard."

The fort's wall, high above the village, was quiet in the late afternoon. Paks and Saben reported to the sergeant, an Ifoss militiaman, and took their station. West of the fort were the hay meadows, striped with light and dark green as the second cutting dried in swathes. They walked back and forth, watching the road and tracks that converged on the fort, and looking along the rooftops and lanes below. The sun dropped, touching the woodland beyond the hay meadows.

"Good weather—it's nice up here when it's dry," said Paks.

"Better this watch than the day, though. It's been hot. I wonder how long we'll be here."

"I hadn't thought. Do you think the Duke will get another contract this year?"

"Mmm. While you were working out this morning—"

"Go on, Saben."

"A courier came in—from the northwest. Could be Valdaire. Anyway, he went straight to the captain's chambers, Cully said."

"Wonder what that's about. Valdaire."

"Or anything in between. Maybe one of the others has found where that wolf whatever is."

"There's a fight I'd like to be in."

"And I."

They turned at the corner tower and headed south again along the wall. A cool breeze had come with the falling sun; it brought the scent of hay. Paks stretched. "Umph. I've got a kink in my shoulder."

"What from, this morning?"

"Yes. Hofrin had us working on unarmed combat, and I thought he'd tear my arm loose at the shoulder. Somehow I can't get the hang of it. Either I don't turn the right way, or not fast enough—but I keep ending up on the ground."

"Best stick to sword fighting, then."

"I'd rather, really. But Hofrin says—"

"I know what Hofrin says. Everyone should learn every conceivable weapon and unarmed combat, in case you lose your axe, sword, dagger, pike, spear, mace, bow, crossbow—"

Paks chuckled. "It's not that bad. And I enjoy it—or will, when I'm not spending all my time in the air or on the ground."

"I think," said Saben tentatively, "—what I saw when I watched you for awhile, is that you are too direct. You go straight in, just charging ahead, and then—"

"Land in the dust again. You're right; that's what he says, too. I keep telling myself, but when I get excited—bam, there I go. Today, at least, I made it through a few minutes of practice without doing that. Maybe I'll learn."

"I expect so. When—" Saben broke off as they heard a shout from the north wall. By the time the other guards had manned the walls, a trumpet call rang out. Duke Phelan had come; but even at watch-change, later that night, no one knew why. It was more than a day later that Bosk explained.

"Ours wasn't the only bunch of wounded hit," he said. "Reim Company—they're small—lost a wagonful, and the guards for it. A trade caravan was hit, in spite of heavy guard. Golden Company lost some, and they even struck at the Halverics' camp—stupid of them, whoever they are. Anyway, several mercenary companies have each pledged a unit to go hunting, and—"

"We're going!" cried Coben.

"No. We're not." Over the general groan, he said, "The Duke wanted archers. He's taking Cracolnya's cohort, and some of Dorrin's. The rest of us will spread thinner to cover these forts. Half of us will move to the next, where Dorrin's half has been."

Paks, to her disgust, was one of those staying. "Nothing's happened here so far," she grumbled to Saben. "And I'll bet nothing happens now. We'll stay and walk back and forth on the walls while nothing happens, and they get to go find the Wolf Prince or whoever he is, and do some fighting."

He nodded. "At least Coben and those get to go to another fort, and see something new. But I doubt they'll see any fighting there, either."

Both were wrong. In the weeks that they held the line of forts, brigands tried to strike at the villages they guarded and rob the harvest. Every garrison had at least one good fight, and most had more. When the cohort was reunited, before the march back to Valdaire and winter quarters, Paks learned that two more of her recruit unit had been killed: Coben, who had been a friend since her first day as a recruit, and Suli, a cheerful brown-haired girl who was Arñe's friend. Eight of them, altogether, had died in their first year of fighting.

"If we lose this many every year," said Paks solemnly, "we'll all be gone in a few years."

"The—the veterans don't lose so many," said Arñe. Her face was still marked with tears.

"We aren't as good," commented Vik. "We've all made mistakes this year. If we live, we'll learn better."

"But it's not the worst ones who get killed. Not all of them. Coben was good—and so was Effa, and Suli." Paks felt a restless anger, and forgot how annoying Effa had been. "It's not fair."

"No," said Stammel behind them. "It's not fair. There's luck in it too. You have to accept that, to stay a soldier. Skill and courage go just so far, and then there's luck."

"Or the gods' will," said Saben.

Stammel shrugged. "You can call it that—it may be that. From what I've seen it could be either."

Paks was still dissatisfied. "But it still seems to me that the better ones should have more chance—"

"Paks, think. The better ones do have more chance—but no guarantee. Look how close you came to being killed. Three of those we lost were among the least skilled. Ilvin stood up on the wall even after Bosk yelled a warning about crossbows: that was stupid. Coben—I know he was your friend, and he was a good, honest, middling fighter—but he never learned to handle himself against a left-handed opponent, and a left-handed man knocked his shield aside and spitted him. Suli, too, was not as skillful as any of you four—just not fast enough."

"But she was as fast as I am."

"She was back north. Paks, you've been training hard; you've improved. You hadn't gone against her lately because Hofrin knew it wouldn't be any work for you. I know it's hard losing friends. It always hurts. If you stay in, you'll have that hurt every year—I have. D'you think I like seeing youngsters I trained get hurt and die? I won't try to tell you how to take it; you'll have to figure out your own way. The Company mourning, when we get back to Valdaire, will help. But wishing it were fair is no help at all." Stammel walked away, and left them to their thoughts. For a long time they were silent.

There was more to come. The other two cohorts met them two days out of Valdaire, and they heard the tale of the campaign against the Wolf Prince.

"It was bad enough," said Barranyi, with a toss of her black hair. "We marched for days through the woods west of here, up into the foothills, before we came to his stronghold."

"Don't forget what happened in the woods that night, Barra," added Natzlin. She had a bandage around her left arm, and a healing gash on her forehead.

"Oh—yes. One night—I think it was the second— during the first watch, we heard a wild screeching and flights of arrows started falling in the camp. Red Jori— you don't know him; he's a seven-year veteran in our cohort—he was hit in the leg. Others were hit too. We couldn't see anyone, and we were rushing around, with the sergeants bellowing and swearing—and then the Duke himself yelled something I didn't understand. A voice answered him from the trees, and they talked back and forth a bit—still in words I didn't know—and then the Duke told us that it was all over. And I still don't know what that was about, and no one will say!" Barranyi shook her head, glowering.

"Never mind, Barra; tell them the rest of it." Natzlin, as usual, could soothe Barra out of her sulks.

"And how many others were with you?" asked Paks. "We heard other companies were sending troops—"

Barra nodded briskly. "Yes, they did. And that was exciting, meeting those others. Let me think. Reim Company sent about twenty—they're small, Dorrin says. Halveric Company sent a whole cohort of foot, and twenty horse. Golden Company sent—what was it, Natz?"

"Near a cohort, I think."

"And we had some boundsmen from Valdaire; the city's angry that its neutrality was breached, or that's what I heard. Anyway, when we got near the Wolf Prince, we were attacked by horsemen, again and again. If we hadn't had horsemen with us, we'd have been in worse trouble. And Paks, I did see a black and white spotted horse off to one side; I'd bet that was one of his captains."

Paks nodded. "Could have been. Was it smaller than the others?"

"Yes. Then we got to the stronghold itself. Much better designed than those forts we'd been holding. If the Wolf Prince had pulled all his men inside, I don't think we could have broken the place."

"Never regret the stupidity of enemies," said Vik, who had been polishing his helmet as he listened. "There's no gift to compare with it."

Barra glared at him. "I wasn't suggesting that—"

"Please tell us the rest, Barra," said Arñe quickly, "before we die of curiosity."

Barra shrugged, gave Vik a last hard look, and went on. "We had a battle outside the walls, that's all. Fought most of the day. It was hard fighting, but finally they broke and ran for the gate. We got most of 'em outside, but enough were left to make the assault a real fight too. Black Sim, of Cracolnya's, was trying to set a ladder when he was crushed by a rock they dropped. Oh—and Paks, Corporal Stephi was killed too. It was on the wall, after we'd gotten up. Two of our men were down, and he was trying to protect them from a rush; he got a spear through the body." Barranyi looked closely at Paks, who felt a strange mixture of relief and regret.

"And then," said Natzlin, picking up the tale, "we fairly took the place apart. It was ugly. Ringbolts set into the courtyard and on the walls—with that spacing we didn't have to guess what for. Dungeons: nasty, stinking, wet holes—like a nightmare. Bones—human bones. And the servants—" Her voice faded away as her eyes clouded.

Barra nodded soberly. "They were pitiful. Not one without old scars and new welts. So we killed 'em all—"

"The servants?" asked Arñe, startled.

"No, of course not. The Wolf Prince and his men. And the Duke searched his rooms for a reason why he'd attack our caravan and the others—I hear he found nothing. And then we came back, and that's all." She stood abruptly and stretched. Natzlin rose more slowly, tucking back a strand of brown hair. "We'd better go back," said Barra. "We're on watch tonight." The two walked toward their own cohort.

"By all the gods, that one's prickly," said Vik. No one had to ask what he meant.

"She's a good fighter," said Paks, temporizing.

Vik snorted. "Paks, sometimes I think you'd forgive the Webmistress herself if she was a good fighter. That's not all that matters."

Paks felt her face growing hot. "I know that, Vik. But being touchy isn't all that matters, either—Barra's good at heart."

Vik gave her a long green stare, one of the few serious looks she'd had from him. "Paks, for once let a city-born runt give you a bit of advice. It's possible to like bad people, but liking them doesn't make them good." Paks opened her mouth, but he held up his hand and went on. "I'm not saying Barra's bad, exactly, but I am saying you think she's good at heart because you like her and want her to be good at heart. It doesn't work that way. If you don't learn to see people as they are, you'll get hurt someday."

Paks felt confused and angry. "I don't understand. It certainly sounds like you're saying Barra's bad, and she's not."

"No. I'm not really talking about Barra, but about you. Paks, my father was a harper. Harpers have to learn about people, or they can't sing with power. Even though I can't harp or sing, I learned a lot from him—

about people. They're more complicated—being good
at one thing doesn't make them good at something else:
a good fighter can be treacherous, or cruel, or a liar. Do
you see that?"

"Yes, but Barra—"

"I'm not talking about Barra. Listen to me. You've
told us you always wanted to be a fighter, a fighter for
good, right?" He waited for her nod before going on.
"Well, you're so intent on that—you don't see other
things. You see people as good or bad, not in between;
as fighters or not, and not in between. And since you're
basically a good person, you see most people as good—
but most people, Paks, are in between—both as fighters, and as good or bad. And they're different. If you
don't learn to see them straight—just as you'd look at a
sword, knowing all swords aren't alike—you'll depend
on them for what they don't have."

Paks nodded slowly. "I think I see. But what about
Barra?"

Vik threw back his head and laughed. "Oh, Paks!
Barra's all right; she's just prickly, as I said." Arñe and
Saben were both chuckling, and Paks finally grinned,
still unsure of the joke.

Their winter quarters in Valdaire felt like home. Familiar buildings, familiar people. No longer novices,
after their first campaign year, the newest members of
the Company found themselves accepted by the veterans. Among these friends, the Company mourning ceremony, when all who had died that year were honored
at once, brought more comfort than Paks expected.
Canna was now an "old veteran," being past her required two years of service, but, like most such, she
elected to stay in.

Their winter routine was much like training: drill,
weapons practice, barracks chores. Paks spent hours in
the smithy and armory, fetching and carrying, and doing
what the unskilled could do. Some work always awaited
them. Paks took the opportunity to begin learning

longsword, and collected a whole new set of cuts and bruises.

With free time in Valdaire, they found that the salary which seemed so large at first disappeared amazingly fast.

"It's not that things are so expensive," said Arñe thoughtfully one evening in the White Dragon, the Company's favorite inn. "It's that there are so many things, and all we have to do is buy—"

"I know." Paks frowned at her linked hands. "I was going to save most of mine to repay my father, but I keep spending it. But except for coming here with you, I've needed what I've bought—or most of it—"

"We've gotten used to spending," said Saben. "That new dagger I bought—I could have used the Company one. But—I bought it."

"We might as well enjoy it," said Vik. "We're going to spend it one way or another. No use fretting about it."

Paks snorted. "There speaks a man who dices his way to twice his salary."

"Not always." Vik was unruffled. "And if I do, I spend it all. I'll teach you, if you like. I'll even let you start with pebbles."

"No, thank you. I just can't see taking a chance on losing it."

"You take chances when you fight—that trick you pulled on Canna today—"

"That's different." She blushed when Vik laughed. "No, it is. I know what chances I'm taking, in fighting. But with money—"

"You're still a country girl, Paks. That's exactly the difference between city and country—"

"I'm the same way," said Saben mildly. "I can't see throwing money away—or anything else, for that matter." Vik laughed, shaking his red head.

The Duke left, to ride north; they realized that he was going to inspect another group of recruits. Paks was distressed to find that Stammel was going with him.

"What did you expect?" he asked. "It's my year to recruit and train; I saw you through your first year. I'll be back a year from now." His brown eyes twinkled. "And you'd better be here to lick my recruits in shape, you and the rest. Take care—I want to hear good things of you."

"Is Bosk going too?" Paks felt like crying.

"No. He's staying down another year. Devlin wanted to stay north; his wife's had another baby."

Paks had never thought of any of them being married; she eyed Stammel but lacked the nerve to ask him.

While waiting for the new recruits to come down, they had more time off. Paks met a corporal in the Valdaire city militia who had grown up near Rocky Ford—the first person she'd met in the south who knew where Three Firs was. A bowman from Golden Company bought them all ale one night—he was celebrating his retirement, he said—he'd saved enough to buy a farm. Spring came earlier and quicker in the Vale of Valdaire than in the north. As the fields greened, grass ran like green flame up the slopes toward retreating snow. Rivers boiled with snowmelt, roaring and tumbling the rocks in their beds. Tiny yellow and white flowers starred the grass. New lambs scampered among the flocks, flipping their ridiculous tails. Paks was almost homesick when she saw the lambs. Buds swelled on the trees; wild plums flowered by every rivulet. The first caravans clogged the city with wagons and pack beasts, waiting for the pass to open.

Paks had not realized, the year before, that someone left the recruit column to warn the Company camp while the column went through the city. This year, when the courier came, the older veterans explained what to do.

"Just hang about as if you didn't know they were coming," said Donag, grinning. "Keep close to the yard. When the captain yells, throw yourself into position, fast. Whoever's closest, go for the front; never mind your usual position. What counts is speed. They don't know where we're supposed to be, and they'll be too scared to notice. Be sure to keep a straight face—they'll be funny, but don't laugh."

Paks saw the column coming up the lane; she strolled back to the yard, her heart hammering. What would the new recruits be like? Were they as frightened as she had been? And what about the sergeant who would replace Stammel. She watched as they came into the yard and halted, and tensed, waiting for the captain's shout. When it came, she was moving before it ended. Donag was still quicker, and made his usual position before anyone else had a chance at it. It was all over in a moment. They stood silent and motionless, and the recruits' eyes were wide.

Stammel's replacement was a black-haired, green-eyed woman named Dzerdya; Paks thought she looked forbidding. The other cohorts each had a new sergeant, and Bond, senior corporal in Cracolnya's cohort, was replaced by Jori. They had twenty-nine new recruits in Arcolin's cohort alone. Paks was glad to find that she was not assigned a recruit; she wouldn't know what to say to the bright-eyed youngsters who filled the empty bunks.

In the next few days, Paks found Dzerdya nothing like Stammel or easy-going Coben, their junior sergeant. She seemed to have a mind as quick as her bladework, and she demanded instant attention and obedience. Paks was surprised to find that her recruits actually liked her.

"She was my sergeant," said Canna. "Isn't she amazing?"

That had not been Pak's first thought. Terrifying, quick-tempered, hasty, impossible—but not amazing. But Canna went on, not noticing her reaction.

"Wait until you see her in battle. She's so fast you can hardly see her blade. You ought to drill with her sometime."

"She seems kind of—kind of—angry a lot," said Paks lamely.

"Oh, that. She's quick to bite, true, but she doesn't brood on things. Don't worry about it. I don't think she knows, sometimes, when she's scared someone half to death."

In another week, Paks had begun to agree. Dzerdya was strict, and had a tongue like a handful of razors, but she was fair. She obviously cared a great deal for her troops.

This year's contract was very different. "It's a siege," explained Donag, who had used his own mysterious contacts to find out. "The Guild League cities are joining to siege and assault another city, halfway across Aarenis. They're hiring several companies as well as their own militia. I think our contract's with Sorellin, but the others are supporting it."

"What city?" asked Canna.

"Rotengre. Have you heard of it?"

"I think so. Wasn't there a caravan raid near there, last year?"

"Yes. The Guild League thinks that Rotengre harbors brigands—in fact, that the city lives by preying on the northern caravan route between Merinath and Sorellin. Three or four years ago—before your time, Canna— five caravans were totally destroyed. That was the worst, so far as I know, but for the past ten or twelve years the loss has been enormous. Almost as bad as what Alured's done to the Immer River shipping."

"But why do they think it's Rotengre?" asked Paks. "Do the caravans go through there?"

"Look." Donag began to scratch a rough map on the table with the burnt end of a stick. "Here's Valdaire, in the northwest. Now here's the river. It's like a tree, sprouting from Immerhoft Sea in the south, with branches northwest, north, and northeast. Downstream from Valdaire you come to Foss, Fossnir, Cortes Vonja, Cortes Cilwan, and Immervale, where the branches meet. On the north branch, up from Immervale, you've got

Koury, Ambela, and Sorellin. The other branch, to the
east, has Rotengre. Then off in the far northeast,
Merinath and Semnath. And the Copper Hills—"

"Have you been to all those places?" asked Paks,
awed.

"Most of 'em. The Copper Hills, now, that's where
caravans come north from the coast—"

"Why don't they come up the Immer?" asked Vik.
"That other's a long way out of their way, isn't it?"

"You haven't heard yet of Alured the Black?" asked
Donag, brows rising. They shook their heads. "Well—
that's a tale in itself. Used to be a sea-rover he did—a
pirate—and somehow decided to come ashore. He controls a belt of forest near the coast, and he's pirated so
much of the river trade that there isn't any. It's cheaper
to go the long way around than pay his tolls." Donag
rubbed his face with one meaty hand, then went on.
"Like I was saying, the caravan route is north along the
Copper Hills, then west: Semnath, Merinath, Sorellin,
Ambela, Pler Vonja, then Fossnir and Foss and upriver
to Valdaire. The road they've built is something to see.

"The stretch between Merinath and Sorellin is long—
comes fairly close to Rotengre—and that's just where
the caravans have been attacked. A lot of that's forest,
so it's easy enough for brigands to throw off pursuit,
and for Rotengre to claim they live in the forest. But
they trade somewhere, and Rotengre is the obvious
place. Besides, what else can the city live on? It was
never part of the river trade—that branch is too shallow. No good farmland, no mines."

They nodded, staring at the blurred smears of black
on the table. Paks wondered what the country looked
like.

"What is a siege like?" asked Vik.

"Boring," said Donag. "Unless the first assault works,
and we take the city at once, we camp outside and keep
anyone from going in or out. It takes months, and it's
nothing but standing watch and camp work and drill. A
long wait until they get hungry, that's all."

"That sounds easy enough," muttered Saben.

Donag shot him a hard glance. "It's not. They'll have archers on the walls, and stone-throwers. You can get killed walking too close, but if you're too far away they have time to climb down the walls and get away. And it's hard to keep the camp like the Duke wants it for that long. If you don't, you have camp fever taking out half your troops. It's better than a fight every day, but it's not easy."

Canna had been looking thoughtful, tracing the smeared lines with one brown finger. "Does Rotengre have any allies?"

"Ah. That's a question." Donag frowned and rubbed his nose. "Probably yes; somebody must be buying the stolen goods. My guess is they ship it downriver. Koury, for example: it isn't a Guild League city, but it's gotten rich in the past few years—how else? Or cities passed by on the old river route: Immervale, Cortes Cilwan. Or if you want to reach far enough, there's always the Honeycat. Siniava. He wants to rule all Aarenis, they say; it takes money to hire the troops for that. If all this flows back to him—"

"Well, what if they attack us while we're sieging?" Vik looked almost eager.

"Then we'll have a fight. That's why the siege force is so large—just in case. But their allies may not want to come out of cover."

It all seemed very complicated to Paks. The only thing clear was the route they would travel. She thought of lands and cities she had never seen.

Chapter Thirteen

It was a long three days' march to Fossnir, down the river from Valdaire, with a baggage train much larger than the year before. Peach and apricot orchards were still pink, though the plum blossom had passed. Paks missed the more delicate pink and white of apples, and the white plumes of pear. When she mentioned this to a veteran, he said that apples were grown only in the foothills of the Dwarfmounts, or far to the west. Pears did not grow in Aarenis at all.

The road they marched on was wide and hard: great stone slabs laid with a careful camber for drainage into ditches on either side. To one side was a soft road, for use in good weather when the road was crowded. North-bound caravans passed them; one was made up of pack animals instead of wagons. They had a nod and smile from the caravaners. The last guard on one of them looked back and yelled, "I hope you get those bastards!"

"How did he know?" asked Donag, startled, then answered himself. "It'll be those militia talking, I suppose. Can't keep any quieter than a landlord."

The next day after Fossnir, they made Foss, oldest city in Foss Council. Here they left the river, following the Guild League caravan road to Pler Vonja. Villages were spaced a few hours apart along the way, and great walled courtyards for caravans to use were never more than a day's easy journey apart. Wheelwrights, harness-makers, and blacksmiths had their places at each caravan halt; the villages offered fresh food and local crafts.

As they crossed the Foss Council border, they found a large unit of militia ready to go with them. Paks was happy to find that the militia would march behind; she liked her forward view.

Pler Vonja, next in line, was stone-walled, but most of its buildings were wood above the first story: a great forest bordered the city on the north. It had fortified bridges across its little river. The city militia wore orange and black, and carried pikes. Paks noticed a nasal twang in the local accent that made some words hard to understand. The march from Pler Vonja to Ambela took six days; rain and a crowded road slowed them down.

Ambela was built, like Pler Vonja, across a small branch of the Immer, but it had a different look. Its gray stone walls were livened by the red and white banners that stirred above every tower and gate. Some low flower made a bright gold carpet along the water meadows. Farm cottages were whitewashed, brilliant in the green fields. The two hundred foot and fifty horse of Ambela militia that joined the column were all in bright red and white.

Four days later, they came to Sorellin. Much larger than Ambela, it had double walls, the inner one defining the old city. They marched through the west gate, under a white banner with great yellow shears centered on it. The guards wore yellow surcoats. Paks thought it looked as clean and prosperous as the best parts of Vérella and Valdaire; she wondered if it had a poor quarter. Below the bridge she saw two flatboats, loaded with plump sacks, being hauled upstream by mules.

Outside the city again, on the southeast, they found a large contingent of Sorellin militia waiting for them.

After two days in a camp outside the city, they marched again on a very different road. It had never been part of the Guild League system; narrow, rough, and partly overgrown, it had to be practically rebuilt to allow the wagons to pass. Six days later they came out on the gentler slopes that lay around Rotengre and its branch of the Immer.

Even from a distance, Rotengre looked more formidable than the other cities. It looked more like an overgrown fort than a city: high, steep walls, massive towers, all out of proportion to the breadth. It was shaped somewhat like a rectangle with the corners bitten off; its long axis ran north and south, with the only two gates on the short ends. Paks decided that the tales must be true—it was a city built for trouble, not for honest trade.

As the head of their column cleared the forest and started across a wide belt of pasture toward the walls, trumpets blared from the city. A troop of men-at-arms in dark uniforms, their helmets winking in the sun, came out the north gate. The Duke's Company marched on, angling left toward the gate. The Rotengrens halted, and began to withdraw, as more and more of the attacking column snaked from the forest. Ahead, to the northeast, another column came into sight. These wore black, and carried spears in a bristling mass. Paks caught her breath and started to reach for her sword.

"That's Vladi's Company—don't worry about them," called Dzerdya. "We're on the same side."

"I hope so," muttered Donag, just loud enough for Paks to hear.

The compact mass of spearmen kept pouring from the forest, cohort by cohort—five in all, with a smaller body of horse. They turned south, to march along the east side of the city. After them came a troop of cavalry whose rose and white colors were bright even at that distance. Most of the horses were gray; a few were

white. Paks thought they looked more like figures from
a song than real fighters, but she had heard of Clart
Company.

The Rotengren troops had withdrawn completely,
and they heard the portcullis crash down long before
they could have reached the gate. A small party of
riders galloped away downstream, pursued by a squad
of Foss Council Cavalry, but they were clearly drawing
away.

Setting up and maintaining a siege camp was every
bit as hard and boring as Donag had said it would be.
The Duke's Company was positioned west of Sorellin's
militia, just west of the north gate, and around the
angle of wall to the west. On their right flank was the
Ambela militia, covering the west wall. Vonja militia
had the south wall and gate, and Vladi's Company and
the Foss Council troops divided the west wall. Clart
Company patrolled between the siege lines and the
forest.

The Duke and his surgeons had definite and inconve-
nient ideas about siting the camp's necessities, from
the bank and palisade between Rotengre's wall and
their camp, to the placement of jacks trenches. All that
work—dull and unnecessary as it seemed to Paks and
the others—was better than the boring routine of the
siege itself, when nothing happened day after day. Spring
warmed into summer, and the summer grew steamy.
Rotengre troops threw filth off the walls; its stench
pervaded the camp. When it rained, a warm unrefreshing
rain, dirty brown water overflowed the ditch under the
walls and spread the stinking filth closer. No one complained about hauling wood or water, or cutting hay in
distant meadows: any break in routine was welcome.
Tempers frayed. Barra and Natzlin got in a fight with
two militiamen from Vonja, and even Paks agreed it
was Barra's fault. Rumor swept the camps that two
cohorts of Vonja militia were down with fever from
swimming in the river. Pak's captain, Arcolin, rode off
to Valdaire on some errand for the Duke, leaving Ferrault

in command. The cohort found that Ferrault was as strict as Arcolin had been, where camp discipline was concerned. The Duke's surgeons frowned constantly, and swept through the camp inspecting everything.

Muggy midsummer faded to the blinding heat and cloudless days that ripened grain for harvest. Paks thought longingly of the cool north. Food began to taste odd; she thought it was the terrible smell from the ditch under the wall. Dzerdya's orders to get ready for a long march were more than welcome.

"Where?" asked Paks.

Dzerdya glared at her, then answered. "North. Sorellin Council wants us to garrison a frontier fort, and let the militia up there come home for harvest. They've had a big crop this year. It's up in the foothills." She smiled, then, at Paks. "Hurry; we march tomorrow."

"Is everyone going?"

"No; it doesn't take the whole company to garrison one little fort. We could probably do it with half of you—it's only a matter of taking tolls if anyone crosses Dwarfwatch—but no one will, this late."

They started before dawn the next day, taking a road that led directly north, rather than northwest to Sorellin. After a day's march through the forest near Rotengre, they entered a rolling land of farms and woodlots, check-ered with hedges. They crossed a small river on a stone bridge, and then the main caravan route, the same broad stone way they had been on before. Ferrault, reverting to his usual cheerful demeanor, pointed out the carved stone sign for Sorellin, shears in a circle on top of a pillar. The road they followed swung a little right. With every day, the ground rose in gentle waves. They saw more forest and less farmland. They crossed another road, not so well-made: the north route to Merinath, Ferrault said. The hills ahead were higher, blocking their view of the mountains they'd hoped to see. From that last crossroad to the fort was just under a day's march, a day pleasantly cool after lowland heat, through thick forest and over low ridges.

Just south of the fort they cleared the forest and saw mountains looming north, much higher than near Valdaire. The peaks were streaked with snow. Dwarf-watch itself was a well-built stone keep with comfortable quarters around the inner court, and roomy stables in the outer. Its only fault was its lack of water; a rapid mountain stream rushed nearby, but inside the walls was neither spring nor well. Beyond the fort, a high and difficult track crossed the mountains, but as they had been told, no one used it. All the traffic they saw was grain wagons rolling up the road from Sorellin to collect harvest from the foothill farms, and rolling south again. Paks found it a delightful interlude: cool air, clean water, fresh food from nearby farmers who were delighted to get hard cash for their produce. South of the river, backed up on the forest, Paks discovered an enormous tangle of brambles, loaded with berries just turning color. She kept a close watch on them.

One hazy afternoon, she and Saben were taking in the washing they'd spread on rocks near the river. She heard a yell from the wall behind them, then the staccato horn of alarm. They snatched their clothes and scrambled up the rocky bank, racing for the gate around the corner. Paks saw others running too. She slowed for a moment to look back to the road. The front rank of a column marched out of the forest.

"Paks! Come on!" As Paks darted under the gate tower, Dzerdya caught her arm and swung her around. "Don't *ever* slow like that! D'you want us to drop the portcullis and leave you outside? Go on—hurry and get armed."

The barracks was noisy chaos as all the off-duty people scrambled into armor. Still fumbling at the buckles of her corselet, Paks ran back out and puffed up the stairs to the wall. Whatever and whoever the approaching force was, it clearly outnumbered them. She counted three units of foot, each the size of their own cohort, and a troop of cavalry. And—

"What's that?" she asked a veteran.

He grimaced. "Siege engines. Now we're in for it."

"But—who'd be sieging us?" He didn't answer, and Paks moved along the wall to her assigned position near the gate tower. The foremost troops were almost at the river; they wore dark green tunics. It reminded her of some she'd seen in Valdaire during the winter.

"Halverics," breathed Donag beside her. "Now what'd they be doing up here? Could the Duke have sent—no, surely not." Paks glanced at him; he seemed more puzzled than worried. She relaxed, then jumped as the portcullis clanged the last few inches into the stone. Donag gave her a wry grin. "We're in a pickle now. I won't hide it," he said. "If Halveric Company wants this fort, they'll get it in the end. Might be easier if the captain decides to yield."

Paks stared at him, open-mouthed. "But we can't. It's—"

Donag nodded at the siege engines rolling down the slope toward the bridge. "We will sooner or later. We can hold it a week, maybe, if we've water enough. But we'd take heavy losses, and they'd break through in the end. Tir's guts, I wasn't looking forward to being a captive again."

Paks choked down what she wanted to say, and peered over the wall. A rider in green was waving a truce flag; she saw Captain Ferrault's helmet slip from the postern beside the main gate, then his foreshortened form moving forward to meet the rider. She could not hear what they said. She could not have heard it if they'd been beside her; blood pounded in her ears. She watched as they walked back. Her stomach churned. She was sure they could hold—but when she tried to think how long, she thought of the water barrels. How long would it take the Duke to come north, and how could they send word? Her mouth was dry already.

Even so, she was not resigned when Bosk brought

his word. Nor was she the only one who cried, "But we can't quit—just quit. We can't."

"Oh yes, you can." His face looked more wrinkled than before. "We follow orders, remember? When the captain tells us to lay down our arms, we do it. And I don't want any nonsense, either, from any of you."

"Arcolin wouldn't have—" began someone.

"Enough! Arcolin's not here; Ferrault is. And for my money, Arcolin would have done the same."

"But—what will happen?" Vik sounded as worried as Paks felt.

"They'll collect our weapons, and assign us an area. Usually it takes a day or so to list all the equipment and men, and then they'll send a ransom request to the Duke. Then a few weeks to settle terms and collect the ransom, and we'll be released. Usually less than a month, altogether."

"But what do we *do*?" Paks imagined a month in the cells under the fort.

"What we're told—that's what prisoners always do. Halveric Company is one of the best; we've fought beside them, now and again. They won't make it hard if we don't. I expect they'll pass their commands down through Captain Ferrault; it'll be much as usual. No drill, of course, and no weapons practice. We may work the harvest, or some such."

"I'm no farmer," said Canna, tossing her head. "I'm a fighter."

Bosk glared at her. "You're about to be a prisoner. Unless you want me on your back as well as those—" he nodded at the wall, "you'll do what you're told. You worked on the road during training."

"Aye, but—"

"No buts. There's rules for this, the same as for everything else. We agree to behave until we're ransomed; if there's any trouble, it's handled by the officers. Don't talk about the Company to them—mostly they won't ask; it's bad manners. And don't ask about theirs. No one's to run off, or anything of that sort. No brawling, of course. No bedding with them; it lacks dignity. I expect this will be the usual terms, which means they won't confiscate your belongings except weapons, but I'd keep any jewels out of sight just in case."

Paks could tell that most of the cohort was as miserable as she was, coming out the gate onto the fields by the river. They had been allowed to march out wearing their swords, but the familiar weight at her side did not make up for the knowledge that she would draw it only to give it up. She stared straight ahead, trying to ignore the green-clad troops lining the road. At last they halted between two cohorts. She let her gaze wander to Captain Ferrault, who was met by a dark bearded man in plate mail. After a few words, the captain turned to them, his usually cheerful face expressionless.

"Sergeant Dzerdya. Disarm the troops."

"Sir." Dzerdya turned. Paks was glad it was not Stammel; she could not believe Stammel would do it. "Draw your swords and drop them." Paks felt tears sting her eyes as she reached for the hilt of her sword. She blinked them back. The sword slid as easily as ever from its scabbard; she could hear the rustle of all the others. It was impossible that they should drop them. Surely—

"No!" bellowed Coben from behind, breaking into her musing. "No nonsense. Drop them!" Even now, Paks could not drop a sword to its hurt; she knelt to lay hers gently on the ground. She did not know who had prompted Coben's rebuke, but she was glad of it. At least the Halverics would know they were not afraid.

Around then now the Halveric cohorts stood with drawn swords, waiting. Ferrault was talking to the Halveric commander again, who shook his head: once, then again, more emphatically. Ferrault turned back to them. "It seems," he said in a hard light voice, "that our reputation has preceded us. We should take it as an honor that we are required to yield daggers as well as swords. Sergeant, see to it."

Before Dzerdya could say anything, the Halveric commander grinned and spoke; his voice was deep, and his accent made a musical complement to his speech. "It is indeed an honor. For so long as we have respected your noble Duke, so long have we known his soldiers to be spirited as well as brave and skilled. We would not have lives and blood lost where no need is: your men or ours, captain. These will be returned, when each has given parole." He bowed to the captain, and more slightly to the cohort itself.

"All right now," said Dzerdya. Her voice was flat. "Daggers the same; drop them."

As Paks slipped her dagger from its sheath, she felt a heavy cold weight dragging at her. She was not even tempted to use the dagger. It seemed that nothing could ever be right again. To stand unarmed in the midst of armed troops, defeated without a fight, was the worst thing she could imagine. But with the others she marched back, under guard, to await events.

Several days later, Paks had admitted that Bosk was right. Though they slept in the stables instead of the barracks, the change brought no hardship: they ate the same food, obeyed the same sergeants, and suffered only from the boredom of confinement. That would change when they had all given their paroles. Bosk explained that, too: each one would come before Aliam Halveric, the commander, and agree to abide by the rules for captives—or risk being put under guard while the others went free within bounds.

Now Paks was waiting her turn. She felt her heart speeding up, and tried to breathe slowly. Only one man between her and the door. Her hands were sweaty. Vanza came out and winked at her; she was face to face with the door. She stared at the grain of the wood, finding pictures in its twists and curves. Should she give her parole? This wasn't anything like the old songs, where heroes always fought to the death if they did not win, and captivity and defiance went together like sword and scabbard. The door opened. Rauf came out, and the guard beckoned. She took a deep breath and walked in.

Behind a wide desk sat the dark bearded man who had accepted their surrender. Without his helmet and mail he seemed smaller: almost bald, with a fringe of graying dark hair, a round weathered face, broad muscular hands. He gave her a long look from dark eyes.

"Ah, yes," he said. "I noticed you—you didn't want to chance damaging the blade, did you?"

Paks blushed. "No—sir."

"Sign of a good warrior," he said briskly. "Name, please?" He held a pen, poised over the desk.

Bosk had said they should give their names. "Paks, sir."

He ran his finger down the parchment roll on the desk. "Ah—there. You're a first-term, I see." He looked back up at her. "It's harder, the first time you're captured. I daresay it's bothered you."

Paks relaxed a bit. "Yes, sir."

"You signed on to be a warrior, not to surrender," he went on. "Still, it does happen, and it's no shame to know when you're overmatched. We don't think worse of your captain for seeing the obvious. To be honest, we're glad not to have to fight it out, knowing what we know of your Company." He paused; a slight smile moved his lips. "I imagine you've been wondering whether it's honorable to give your parole—" Paks nodded. His smile broadened, not mocking, but friendly. "I thought so. Well, I won't argue against your conscience. I've given mine on occasion—if that matters. It's only until you're ransomed. You may match swords against us another season at the command of your Duke, or quarrel with my men in Valdaire next winter. They haven't been teasing you, have they?"

"No, sir. They haven't bothered us at all."

"That's good. They know, you see, that it might be the other way next time. Now—" he went on more briskly. "I'll need your answer. Can you swear to remain a prisoner under command of my company until ransomed, without rebellion or escape so long as you're honorably treated?"

Paks paused a moment, but she trusted him in spite of herself. "Yes, sir; I agree."

"Very well." His voice held more warmth. "And I and my commanders give our word that you and your companions will be honorably treated, well fed and housed, and be subject to the authority of your captain, under my designated representative only. Now what that means," he continued, less formally, "is that we won't suddenly sell you to slavers, or turn you over to another company of mercenaries. We agree to be fully responsible for your welfare, just as your Duke would be."

"Yes, sir," said Paks. She found this confusing. It seemed like an extra trouble to both sides.

"I'm telling you this because you youngsters need to understand how we northern mercenaries deal with one another under the compact. We are often rivals, and sometimes hired enemies, but we have our own code, which we will not change for any employer. Your Duke and I and Aesil M'dierra started it years ago, and now most good companies abide by it. The others—well, they can be paid to do anything. If we are to stay honorable, the newest members of our companies must understand—and that means you, in your first term. Do you understand that?"

"Yes, sir," said Paks. She met his eyes and surprised a puzzled look on his face.

"You need not answer if you prefer," he said slowly, "but would you tell me where you're from?"

"Three Firs," said Paks promptly.

He looked blank. "Where is that?"

"It's—well—all I really know is it's a day's journey

from Rocky Ford, and west of Duke Phelan's stronghold." Now she was puzzled by his interest.

"Oh. The reason I asked is that you reminded me of someone I once knew; I wondered if you were related. But she came, if I remember, from Blackbone Hill or something like that."

Paks shook her head. "I never heard of that place, sir. It wasn't near Three Firs."

"Well, then—you may go."

Paks nodded, and turned away, surprised at how much better she felt. That evening their daggers were returned to them—with plenty of warnings about misuse. With her dagger once more at her side, Paks felt much more secure. She found her hand returning to it again and again.

Two days later, Aliam Halveric rode away with two of his cohorts marching behind; the siege engines went with them. His captain allowed the prisoners to practice marching drill in small units, and troops of both companies went out on work details for wood, water, and food. The Halverics hardly seemed to be guarding them, as they worked just as hard as the Phelani. They all bathed in the river, and washed clothes along its banks. At first Paks was very stiff with them, but as she saw her sergeants and corporals chatting with their Halveric colleagues, she began to listen. She knew nothing about Lyonya, where most of the Halverics came from. They spoke of elves as if they'd all seen them and worked with them.

As the days wore on, the Phelani were allowed even more freedom of movement inside the bounds Ferrault received from the Halveric captain. Paks saw Ferrault and the Halveric, who seemed even younger than Ferrault, playing some board games in a sunny part of the court one morning. They were laughing together; the Halveric captain shaking his head.

To Pak's delight, small groups could go to the river or the bramble patches without an escort. The huge brambles she had found were now ripe, and she enjoyed the hours she spent picking them. Vik didn't like it—too hot, too prickly, too tedious—but she, Saben, and Canna gathered pail after pail of dark-red berries that both Halverics and Phelani were glad to eat.

Chapter Fourteen

They were deep in the brambles one afternoon, grousing at thorns as they stuffed themselves with ripe berries, when they heard a signal from the Halverics' bugler. They stopped to listen.

"Not for us, whatever it is," said Canna. The signal for their return was four long notes, three rising and the fourth the same as the first.

"Could be a messenger from the Duke," suggested Saben, standing to peer through the tops of the brambles. They were south of the fort, even with the southeast corner of the wall; the road leading west from the gate was visible only for a short stretch.

"I think it's too soon," said Canna.

"What can you see?" asked Paks. She was pouring berries from her pail into a sack they'd brought along.

"Not much. But—wait—do you hear that?"

They did not so much hear it as feel it, a growing rumbling along the road to the south. They could see nothing, because of the angle of the woods, but as Paks stood, she could see sentries moving on the fort walls.

Other work details, nearer the fort, were turning to look back down the road. The sound began to separate into rhythmic components that sounded like horses and marching feet. A deep-toned horn called from somewhere on the road. The Halverics' bugle rang out again. A horseman came in sight around the angle of the wall, riding out from the fort; Paks could see something glittering on his shoulders, and his green cloak. She thought it was the captain's horse, and told Canna.

"Maybe we should go back," said Canna. She bounced up and down on tiptoe, trying to see over the brambles. Paks and Saben could just see through the upper thorny branches.

"Let's wait," said Paks. "Whatever it is—it's odd. And they haven't called us. Look, Saben; isn't that—"

"Troops. Yes. Lots." Out of the trees came a column of men-at-arms behind twenty or so horsemen. "Not the Duke," added Saben. "Whose colors are those, I wonder?"

"What colors?" demanded Canna.

"Just a second; the wind's wrong. Yellow field— something on it in black, but I can't tell what it is. The horsemen—some in chain—one in plate—yellow surcoats. Tir's bones, those men are carrying pikes."

"Pikes? No one around here uses pikes," said Canna. "Yellow and black, and uses pikes—I can't think of anyone within range— "

"He's right, though," said Paks. "It is pikes; I can see the heads glinting in the sun."

"What are they doing?" Canna had given up the attempt to see for herself.

"Marching—no, they're halting. Whoever it was that came from the fort is riding up to the head of the column—I'm sure it's the captain. Let's see—" For a few moments, Paks fell silent as she watched. Nothing moved. "I guess he's talking to someone—passing something across or taking— Now he's backing up. I wonder what— No!" She turned to Saben. "He's down. He fell off his horse. Saben, look!"

"I see," said Saben grimly. "I don't like this."

"Tell me," said Canna, "before I—"

"I think they shot him; they're carrying crossbows. They're moving off the road—going after the work details—"

"But they're unarmed!"

"But they are—and look at the rest—they're marching on the fort. It must be an enemy—"

"But whose?" Canna's face wrinkled in a puzzled frown.

"I don't know. Halveric's, I suppose, but— Oh, no! They're—the devils! The murdering devils—" Paks started to thrash forward through the brambles.

"Paks, get down!" Saben wrestled Paks to the ground. "Be quiet, you fool! It won't help for us to go out there."

"What happened? What is it?" Canna tried again to see.

"Some of our men tried to run. They're down—arrows, I'd guess."

"By St. Gird! We have to—"

"Not you too! Think, Canna! Paks, listen. Be still. What can we do with three daggers? We don't have any armor—they'd shoot us down before we could kill one of them."

"You're right," said Paks reluctantly. "Let me up, Saben; I won't do anything. But we can't just—just run away and let them be killed."

"What about the fort?" asked Canna quietly. "Surely the Halverics will come out—"

"Not if they're smart," said Paks. "That's a big force; I don't think we've seen all of it yet. They'll be lucky if they can hold against assault, let alone mount a sally." Even as she spoke, they heard the bugler again, and the crash of the portcullis rang across the river meadows.

"We can't get back in now," said Saben. "Even supposing we wanted to."

Paks started to look toward the fort, to see how it was manned, but drew back sharply. "They're closer," she

said softly. "On this side of the river." They all flattened under the brambles as best they could. They
could hear the squeak and rattle of harness as the
armed men came nearer, but they could see nothing.
Paks hoped this was true for the men outside as well.

"Ho, there!" cried a harsh voice. "We see you. Come
out or be shot!" They did not move. Paks heard a
rustling crackle as an arrow went into the bramble some
yards away. "Come on out, cowards!" cried another
voice. Another arrow and another, closer. Suddenly an
arrow pinned Canna's shoulder. She made no sound.
The rattle of arrows passed on, was farther away with
each shot. "By the Master, I told you nothing was up
here," said the second voice, complaining.

"Take it up with the lord, then: it was his orders,"
growled the other.

"Nay—I'll do what he says—only those prisoners are
more to my liking—did you see that redheaded girl?"
The voices, still bickering, moved away to their right.
Still they lay unmoving, without a sound. Paks met
Saben's eyes, his face was white with anger. She looked
over at Canna. Canna was blinking back tears; her jaw
was clenched. They waited. A blue fly buzzed around
the spilled berries, then settled on Canna's shoulder.
They heard shouts from the fort, from the men below.
A scream. More shouts. Paks glanced at Saben again,
and raised an eyebrow. He nodded.

With great care they both moved to Canna's side.
The arrow did not seem to be in very deep. "Hope it's
no worse than it looks," murmured Saben. Paks offered
Canna a wad of her cloak to bite, then steadied the
shaft as Saben cut her tunic away from it. The long
barbs of the head were still outside her skin; the head
itself seemed to be lodged in the big muscle between
neck and shoulder. When Paks pulled, the head slid
out easily, followed by a rush of blood. It was both
longer and wider than those used by their own Company. Saben clapped his hand over the wound, squeez-

ing it shut. Paks emptied the berries from the sack, and looked doubtfully at the coarse fabric.

Canna spat out the wad of cloth in her mouth. "Go ahead—it'll do."

"Not too rough?"

"No. Go on."

"Wait a bit," murmured Saben. "Let the bleeding slow. We can't move now anyway." Paks folded the sack into a thick pad after cutting a strip for a tie with her dagger. They heard more confusion of noise from the fort, but nothing closer. Paks wondered how long they should wait before moving. The attackers might send scouts through the woods to pick up stragglers. She spent the time packing her belt pouch with fallen berries. Finally Saben let up the pressure he'd kept on Canna's shoulder. The wound gaped, but the bleeding had nearly stopped.

"Stopped it," he said. "Let's have that pad, Paks."

"It'll start when I move," said Canna ruefully. "By St. Gird, it was plain back luck being hit at all, when they couldn't see." She winced as Paks pressed the folded sack onto her shoulder. "Eh—how are you—"

"Like this," said Paks softly. "Keep pressure on it, and help her sit, Saben." With Saben's help, Canna rolled to her side and sat up. Her face was pale. "Now," said Paks. "Under this arm, and up and around—and again here. There. Don't move that arm if you can help it."

"Good job. Thanks."

"Now what will we do?" asked Saben.

"We've got to get away from here before they make a proper search," said Canna. "And then we've got to get to the Duke."

Paks nodded. "I agree. But Rotengre's a long way—do you know how to find it?"

"I think so," said Canna. "As long as I'm with you—but what about you?"

Saben shook his head. "Not me. I know it's south somewhere, that's all. You, Paks?"

Paks ignored the question at first. "Canna—you aren't leaving us, are you?"

"No. But if this wound goes bad, or we have trouble on the way and I'm killed, I wanted to know if you could find the Duke yourself."

"Oh. I—I think so. At least, I'll recognize the roads when we get there, the crossroads and such."

"Good." Canna shifted, looking around the tiny space in which they lay. "Saben, can you tell what they're doing, and if it's safe to start moving? And Paks, let's get the rest of those berries packed up."

"It sounds like they may be too occupied to worry about us," said Saben. He rose cautiously and peered out the upper level of the brambles. "There's a force on the walls—maroon and green both—the Halverics must have armed our men too. Wise of them. And a lot of troops below the walls, and horses. I think we can go, but we'd better stay down. Canna, can you crawl with that arrow wound?"

"As opposed to lying here to be captured by those barbarians, certainly. It's a good thing our tunics are dark. But let's eat what we can of these berries before we go." They stuffed handfuls of juicy berries into their mouths, gaining strength from the sweet juice. In a few minutes, Canna started them moving toward the trees. She sent Saben ahead, and Paks followed her, bringing one pail full of berries. They had buried the other under fallen leaves, in hopes that searchers would not find evidence of their presence.

Paks could see that Canna was having a hard time crawling; several times she stopped, swaying, but she never fell. Luckily their explorations during the berry harvest had left little trails running here and there almost to the forest edge; they did not have to force a new path. Canna managed to keep moving, and at last they fought free of the thorns. It was growing dusky; they could see fires twinkling on the meadow below.

They pushed through the hazels that fringed the woods and moved on into the darker shelter of the trees, now walking upright. When they found a sheltered hollow, they settled in to make further plans. Even in that dimness, Paks could tell that Canna was paler than usual.

"At least we've got full waterflasks," she said quietly. "And we've got some berries. I have a lump of cheese. What about you?" Saben had a hunk of dried meat, but Canna had only the berries she'd put in her belt pouch. "We can cook in the berrying pail," Paks went on.

"If we have anything to cook," said Saben. It was almost too dark to see. "Canna, how are you doing?"

"Could be worse—" Her voice was shaky.

"You'd better have the cheese and meat," said Paks. "That's what they told me when I lost a lot of blood: eat to make it up." Canna protested, but Paks was firm. "No—you need it. Saben and I can eat berries. You're the one who will slow us down if you don't recover." She handed over her cheese, and Saben gave Canna the meat. They ate in silence; Paks and Saben, already full of berries, ate little.

"I wonder what they'll be up to tonight," said Saben at last.

"Not much, I hope. I suppose it depends on how far they've marched today—and how the assault goes." Paks suddenly found herself yawning, though she was not at all sleepy. She pushed thoughts of her other friends aside. "How glad I am, Canna, that you said we should bring our cloaks to lay over the thorns. It's going to be cold out here." It was already hard to believe how they had sweated under the brambles.

"Shouldn't we try to get farther away?" asked Saben.

"No—we'd just blunder around and make noise in the dark, and we might get lost. What do you think, Canna?" Paks remembered that Canna was senior to them.

"I think you're right. It's too dark. Though I wish we could find out what they *are* doing, to tell the Duke.

And who they are." She sighed. "But that's even more dangerous. We don't know these woods well enough, and we can't risk capture." She paused, then went on in a different tone. "I know neither of you are Girdsmen, but—I wish you would join me in prayer. At least for the confusion of our enemies."

"That I'll go along with," said Saben. "But won't Gird be angry if non-Girdsmen pray in his name?"

"No," replied Canna. "He welcomes all honorable warriors." She reached into her tunic, the cloth rustling as she moved, and pulled out her holy symbol. Paks heard the faint chinking of the links of the chain. "Holy Gird, patron of warriors, protector of the weak, strengthen our arms and warm our hearts for the coming battles. Courage to our friends, and confusion to our enemies."

"Courage to our friends, and confusion to our enemies," repeated Paks and Saben. Paks felt strange, calling on one she did not follow, but surely such a simple request could not be misunderstood. She heard the chain jingle as Canna replaced the medallion, and reached to help Canna wrap her cloak around her injured shoulder. She added her own.

"I'll take first watch," she told Saben. "You sleep."

He rolled up in his own cloak and lay next to Canna. Paks sat with her back against a tree, listening to the noises from the fort, and trying to imagine what they meant. She wondered which of her friends had been killed, and which were in the fort—and who had been captured. And who was the enemy—and why here, at the end of the road? Ferrault had said that the worst they could expect was brigands robbing the grain wagons—yet first the Halverics, and then this army, had marched up to take the fort as if it were important. Why?

She slipped her knife from its sheath and tested the edge. It had dulled on the cloth, as she'd feared. She felt for her whetstone, then paused. The sound would be distinctive if anyone heard it. Still, a dull knife—she decided to take the chance. She moved the blade lightly across the stone. Not too loud: good. It would take longer, but she had time.

When her blade was sharp, she put the stone back in her pouch and the dagger back into its sheath. She looked for stars overhead, but the leaves were too thick. No way to tell how time passed. She heard no noises from the fort, now, and only wind in the trees. She stretched first one arm, then the other. It was colder. She rubbed her arms, hard, then took down her hair and rebraided it by feel. The wind picked up; it smelled like rain. She thought she heard a drum in the distance, and wondered again who the attackers were. An owl called, a long wavering *hooo-hooo-hoo hoo*. She stretched one leg at a time, and wished she had not wrapped Canna in both cloaks. It seemed much colder. Saben began to snore. Paks stretched out and touched his shoulder.

"Don't snore," she said when he jerked awake.

"Umph," he said, and rolled over. She stood and swung her arms vigorously to warm up. Better. The wind dropped, and she squatted down against the tree again, hoping it would not rain, hoping the wind would die away altogether. It didn't. Just when she thought she would be warm enough after all, a chill current of air flowed into the hollow and she started shivering. She rubbed her arms again, but it didn't help. Her teeth chattered.

"Paks," said a voice out of the dark; she nearly yelped. But it was Canna's voice. Paks scooted around to her side.

"What is it?"

"I woke up and heard your teeth—take this cloak; I don't need it."

"I don't want you to get chilled."

"I'm warm enough. Don't be silly; take the cloak." Canna heaved up and began unwrapping herself from the second cloak. Saben woke up.

"What's going on?"

"Paks is freezing, and I'm giving her back her cloak."

"It's time for me to take a turn watching anyway. Warm up, Paks; I'll wake you later."

"Th-thanks." Paks rolled into the warm cloak, and lay beside Canna, shivering for awhile. She fell asleep as soon as she was warm. She woke in a panic, with Saben's hand firmly over her mouth. Before she could move away from his hand, she heard the reason for it: horses somewhere nearby. She touched his wrist, and he moved his hand away. She looked at Canna. Canna looked back without moving. She had heard the horses too. A heavy wet fog lay between the trees; their cloaks were furred with moisture.

The horses came nearer. She could hear the jingling bits, the squeak of leather. And voices. "There won't be stragglers out here—we'd have found 'em holed up in that woodcutter's hut in this weather."

"Or else they're already far away."

"No—we hit late enough, they'll have been close in. The only thing is those brambles, the big ones, but Palleck's squad went over that yesterday."

"Shot arrows into it, you mean. Those lazy scum wouldn't pick through thorns. But I agree, that should have flushed anyone out. Still, if *he* wants us out here, here we'll be."

"Right enough. I won't argue. I wonder though—I thought we were going to lift the siege at Rotengre. What's he want to come up here and take a bunch of mercenary prisoners for?"

"I don't know. One of his schemes, I suppose. You know how he hates 'em. I don't doubt this Duke Who-ever, the Red Duke, will be angry enough at the green ones when he finds his men where they'll be. And Tollen told me the Red Duke's at the siege."

"Is he? That's a bit clearer. My lord Siniava will be up to his usual tricks, no doubt." The voices had moved past, and now faded into foggy silence.

The three in the hollow looked long at each other.

"They're taking the prisoners somewhere," said Saben softly. "I wonder where?"

"But what about the fort?" asked Paks.

"Siniava—Siniava. I should know that name. Yellow and black—and Siniava. Oh!" said Canna.

"What is it?"

"We can hope I'm wrong, but I think I know who that is: Siniava. I think it's the Honeycat. You've heard—?"

Paks shivered. "Yes. Too much. Now what are we going to do?"

"Tell the Duke. Now more than ever. I wish I knew *where* they were taking the prisoners. He'll want to know."

"And if they're trying to break the fort to get more," said Saben.

"Yes. There's a lot we need to know—where they're going, and when, and by what road—"

"We—I—could try to get close to them and find out," suggested Paks.

"First we need to get Canna outside their skirmish lines," said Saben. "She can't travel as fast. But this fog's a big help; they can't see us."

"Do you know which way is which?" asked Canna.

Saben's face fell. "No. I didn't think of that."

"I do," said Paks. "At least I'm fairly sure. Let's go south a bit more, and then cut west to the road."

She helped Canna stand; the dark woman was steadier than Paks had expected. Then she led the way from tree to tree, with a pause behind each to look and listen. The woods were silent, except for the drip-drip—of fog from every twig. They went on. It could have been hours; the light grew only slightly, and the fog was just as thick. At one pause, Saben asked, "How do you know this is south?"

"Remember the view from the wall—beyond the biggest brambles, and running south, was a belt of fir trees. I remember wondering if it had been planted there for some reason."

"Fir trees. How do you know fir trees from pines or anything else?"

"I'm from Three Firs, remember? Fir trees I know."

"Huh. And I thought you were smart or something." Saben gave her a quick grin before going on.

They had come up a long slope, and now they felt an open quality to the silence that meant a ridgetop. When they started down the far side, the firs disappeared.

"Now what?" asked Saben.

"Now we stop for a bit," said Paks, eyeing Canna, whose face was pinched with pain or cold. She found a spot below a rock ledge, and they settled their backs against it. "We can have those berries now. Do you have a tinderbox, Saben?"

"No, worse luck. But we couldn't start a fire here, could we? So close?"

"No, but later. I don't have anything. Canna?"

"I don't know. I can't remember. There was no reason to bring it out, but I'll look in my pouch. Yes. There it is."

Paks grinned at the other two. "We're in good shape, really. We've got something to make a fire, and something to cook in—"

"And nothing to cook," Saben reminded her.

"Don't ill-wish," she retorted. "We could be dead, or prisoners, and we're not. If only Canna hadn't been hit—"

"If never filled the pot," said Canna. "I'm doing well—it hurts when I move that arm, just what you'd expect." Despite her words, Paks noticed that she sagged against the rock.

"Well, I need a rest, if you don't," said Paks.

"Now I know how you knew which way was south," said Saben. "But how are you going to find west? I don't remember any convenient belts of trees in that direction?"

"This ridge runs west, more or less," said Paks, who had finally thought of that only a few minutes before, when she too wondered how she'd find west without the sun.

"Umm. You're right again. But I don't think following it will be as easy."

"No. I don't either. It would be nice to find someone's path going the right way."

"If we can find a path, so can their men."

"Yes. I should have thought of that. Well, we'll just have to try. If we do get lost, the sun will come out someday."

"Let's go on and share out the berries," said Canna. The berries seemed to have shrunk overnight, and did little to fill their empty bellies.

"The next time we do this sort of thing," said Saben, "let's be sure to carry three days' rations in our pouches, and tinderboxes, and bandages, and—let's see—how about mules and saddles, too."

Paks and Canna both chuckled. "In a pouch—of course," said Canna. "To be honest, I don't plan to do this again, if I can help it."

"Come now," said Saben. "We're going to be heroes in this tale. Escaping the villain, bringing word to our Duke, rescuing our friends—" Paks nodded; she had already imagined them freeing the prisoners on the road, and returning to the Duke in triumph. Of course, it wouldn't be easy, but—

"If we come out of this heroes," Canna said soberly, "we'll earn it. Every step of the way. You two—you've done well, so far, but you don't understand. There are too many things that can go wrong, too many miles. This is no fireside tale, no adventure for a hero out of songs: this is real. We aren't likely to make it as far as the Duke, though we'll try—"

"I know that," Saben broke in. "We aren't veteran scouts. But still—it's easier to think about if we think of it as an adventure—at least I think so. The bad will come soon enough without looking for it—beyond being careful, of course."

"As long as you don't think we'll go dancing down the

road and find the Duke as easy as finding those berries—"
Canna sounded doubtful.

Paks shook her head. "We know, Canna. A lot can go
wrong; we need you to keep us from making stupid
mistakes that will get us all killed. One of us has to get
through." She still thought they could do it; Canna was
just worried because of her wound. She took a drink
from her flask, then shook it. "I wonder how far
downslope water is. Canna, how's your water?"

"About half. We probably should look for more."

"You stay here," said Saben. "I can't get lost if I go
down and back up. I'll hoot like that owl last night
when I think I'm near again." He took their flasks and
disappeared into the fog.

"If they are marching to Rotengre," said Paks, "do
you think they'll go through Sorellin, or around it?"

"Not through, even if they control the city—it'd be
risky. I expect they'd take the fork we came up by."

"I hope so. That will be—a week on the march, at
least, and more likely eight or nine days with that
crowd. We'll have to get food somewhere. We can
march two days on water alone, but not a week. D'you
think we could buy food somewhere? I've got a silver—a
nis—and some coppers—"

"It depends. If we're seen, we can be talked about. If
we're far enough behind to be safe, we could lose them.
Probably we'd best stick to what we can find—or steal."

"Steal!" said Paks. "But we're not supposed to—"

"I know. But it's better than capture. We can tell the
Duke, when we get to Rotengre, and he'll make it
good."

Paks sighed. It was beginning to seem more complicated. "If we stay close enough to know where they are,
we'll be close enough for their scouts to find, won't
we?"

"Yes. If we knew their route, we could go ahead of
them—that would be best—but we don't." They sat in
silence awhile. Canna shifted her back against the rock.
Paks looked at her.

"Do you want to lie down?"

"Better not. Let me think—if they march like others I've seen, they'll have two waves of forward scouts, mounted, and a patrol on each flank. The flankers usually stay in sight of the column; the forward scouts may not. And a rearguard. The first day will be hardest, until we find out their order of march."

"I don't know whether to hope for rain, to slow them down, or dry weather to make it easy for us."

"Either way we'll have our problems; so will they. Best be ready to take what comes. One thing, Paks—"

"Yes?"

"We need to agree on who's in command."

Paks stared. "Why—you are, surely. You're senior."

"Yes—but I'm not even a file leader. And I'm injured; I couldn't *make* you obey, unless you—"

"*Hooo-hooo-hoo hoo.*"

"Saben's coming. *Hooo-hooo.*" Paks tried to hit the same pitch. They saw a human shape loom out of the fog.

"There's a good spring not far down," said Saben. "And I found these growing around it." He dumped out a pouchful of small shiny red berries and a few hazelnuts. "I don't know what those berries are, but they taste good."

Paks tried one. It was tart and juicy, very different from the luscious sweet bramble-berries. She and Canna ate while Saben cracked the hazelnut husks and piled the meats.

"I can take the pail down there," said Saben, "and gather more."

"I don't think so," said Canna. "Look at the fog." A light wind had come up, and the fog was beginning to blow through the trees in streamers. "We should be heading for the road. Saben, I was telling Paks that we need to agree on who's in command—"

"You're senior, Canna. Whatever you say—"

"All right. Paks agreed too. But if I'm disabled, one of you will have to take over, and—"

"Oh. Paks, of course—don't you think?" He popped a hazelnut into his mouth.

"That's what I thought." Canna sounded relieved. "I wanted to be sure you'd agree, though. I'm not a corporal or anything."

"That's all right. It's no time to worry about *that*."

"Good. Let me tell you what I think is next; if I miss anything, bring it up." They both nodded, and she went on. "We need to be close enough to know where they're going, without getting caught. That means staying out of their sight. If they head for Rotengre, we can stay together; if they don't, we'll have to separate: one goes straight to the Duke, and the others follow Siniava."

"But Canna," said Paks, "can't we do something about the prisoners? To free them, or something?"

Canna shook her head. "No—I don't think we can. The most important thing is to tell the Duke what's happened. If we try to free them and fail—and think, Paks: just the three of us, with daggers; we would fail—then we'd be caught or killed, and the Duke still wouldn't know. I don't like it either, but we won't help that way." She waited, looking from one to another. Paks finally gave a reluctant nod. Saben grunted. Canna went on. "Another thing—if one of us is caught, or killed, or—or whatever—the others must go on. Someone has to get to the Duke, no matter what, or the whole thing is wasted. Clear?"

Paks had found the other hard enough to accept; this was impossible. She and Saben spoke together. "No! We can't—" Saben stopped and Paks continued. "Canna, you're hurt now—we can't leave you. What if they found you? We're—we're friends; we've fought together, and—"

"We're warriors first," said Canna firmly. "That's what we're here for. If you accept my command, you must accept this. We're warriors, and our duty is to our Duke. He's the only one who can help the rest, anyway. I'd leave you—I wouldn't want to, but I would.

And you'll leave me, if it comes to that, rather than let the whole cohort be lost, and the Company after it."

"Well—all right. But I hope it doesn't." Paks stood up and stretched.

"So do I," said Canna. Saben gave her a hand up. "Now—remember to use hand signals as much as you can; sound carries, as we heard." They nodded. "Paks, if you think you can find the way west, lead off. Whatever you do, don't veer north."

"I'll be careful." Paks looked around. The fog had thinned; she could see a short way through the trees. At the top of the ridge she followed the crest of it west—or what she hoped was west. In the dampness the leaves underfoot made little noise. They could hear nothing nearby, but from time to time they heard a distant drum.

Chapter Fifteen

Paks tried to think where they were as they walked. They'd been south of the southeast corner of the fort—then they'd gone south, and a little east, with the firs. Now she hoped they were walking west; the road lay west of the fort. But how far west—she remembered several turns before it got to the bridge—where were the turns?

This was going to be trickier than she'd thought. Where the trees were open—on the ridge—she could see better, but so could any enemy. She heard a horn call off to the right, and froze. It came again. She looked at Saben and Canna behind her. Canna shrugged. Paks gestured to the thicker growth downslope, and Canna nodded. They eased their way into it, and rested for a few minutes. Paks explained her concern—noisy progress through the thick growth, or visible progress through the thinner woods. After some discussion, they decided to stay in the heavier downslope woods, moving more slowly for silence.

It was harder going, but Paks felt safer. They stopped

at intervals to listen, and kept a nervous eye on the rise above them. A patrol could come very close before they saw it. Suddenly she stopped. She thought she saw a lighter area ahead—a clearing, perhaps, on the road. She gestured, and the others lay down. When she looked back at them, their white faces showed clear against the dark wet leaves. She dug into the leaf-mold with her fingers and smeared it on her face, then looked back again and pointed to show what she'd done. They nodded, and began doing the same. Paks gestured again, for them to stay in place, and began to creep forward, keeping to such cover as she could find. From her position, she could see very little. After a few damp, tiring yards of creeping, she was tempted to stand and look. But when she glanced back to see how far she'd come, Canna's hand signal was emphatic: down. Stay down. Paks nodded and went on.

She was sure she was near the opening, whatever it was, when she heard the beat of many horses coming rapidly. She stared to leap up and run, but controlled herself. They were on the road, by the sound: it must be the road. They wouldn't see her unless she moved. She told herself that again and again, forcing herself to stare at the layers of leaves on the ground lest her eyes be visible. The horses came from her right: at least ten, she thought. She would have sworn that they trotted right over her. The hoofbeats passed and died away. Paks breathed again, and lifted her head. She could see a gap, and trees beyond it. She crept forward until she could see the road itself, scarred with hoofmarks and wheel ruts—the wheel ruts were fresh. If the enemy had wagons, they would slow them. She looked along the road as far as she could without getting out in the open. Nothing.

It was much harder creeping back to Saben and Canna with her back to the road. She was sure that someone was there, watching her, perhaps drawing a bow to shoot. She wanted to jump up and run forward. Her shoulders ached. The wet leafmold ticked her nose;

she wanted to sneeze. She kept crawling, muttering silently in her head, and almost bumped into Canna.

"The road," she said unnecessarily, in Canna's ear.

Canna was pale. "I was afraid you'd jump up and bolt. Those horses—"

"I almost did," said Paks. "Let's move farther back—"

They crawled back, then turned downslope again and went deeper in the hollow, squatting under a clump of cedar. "I didn't see any sentries," said Paks. "I looked both ways. I don't know where the horsemen were going."

"Did you get a good look at them?" asked Canna.

"No. I was afraid they'd see my face, so I stared at the ground. It sounded like ten or more."

"I thought about a dozen," said Canna. "They might have been going to that farm, the one where we got the ox that time."

"I suppose so. I was hoping they were going south and wouldn't be back."

"Unlikely, unless they're messengers. I expect they were after supplies, or information."

"Now that we've found the road, shouldn't one of us try to find out what's happening at the fort?" asked Saben. "At least we can find out how big the Honeycat's force is."

Canna shook her head. "No—I'd agree if we had a few more. But as it is, we can't take the chance of losing even one."

"But if they take the prisoners away by a different route—"

"How can they?" asked Paks. "North is only that track over the mountains—why would they go there? This is the only road south; they'll have to use it."

"Unless they go across country."

"With wagons? I saw fresh wheel ruts, deep ones. They'll have to stay on a road."

"How far is the crossroads?" asked Saben.

Paks looked at Canna. "Do you remember? I think it was a day's march—we got here at midafternoon, and the fork was where we halted the day before, wasn't it?"

"Yes. That's the road that goes to Merinath, east of us, and to Valdaire if you go far enough west. But they won't turn there for Rotengre. They'd stay on this road through two crossings—no—southeast at the second. The way we came, anyway. But they could go through Sorellin, or even around it to the west, for some reason."

Paks had been sketching in the dirt with a stick. "So—a crossroad here, where they could turn, and another here? Right. And then Sorellin, and then—how far is Rotengre? It's east as well as south, isn't it?"

Canna peered at the furrowed dirt. "Yes. Let me think. We're about two days from Sorellin, I think, and it's—oh, call it four days *this* way—" she pointed at the route east of the city, "—from that village we stopped at, coming up. I think it's about as far from us as Sorellin, but I'm not sure."

"Six or seven days altogether—about what I remembered. But we could go ahead of them this far," said Paks, pointing to the first crossroad. "They have to take this road that far, and they might not expect us to be ahead of them."

"But we don't know how long they're going to stay here," said Saben. "We could wait a month for them, and the Duke none the wiser."

Canna shook her head. "No. Siniava has a name for moving fast. I think he won't try the fort more than a day or so; if they don't break, he'll leave someone behind and take the rest of his force south. I can't see him tying up his whole army for one little fort."

"And I thought," said Paks, "that if we got ahead of them, we could get some food, too, before they came along to buy it up."

"Yes, but then we've been seen. They'll ask questions. If they find out that someone in Duke Phelan's colors has been buying food, they'll come looking for us."

Paks frowned. She was very conscious of her empty

belly. A few berries and hazelnuts were not going to be enough—and they wouldn't have time to gather many.

"Well, Canna," said Saben, "do we have to stay in the Duke's colors?"

"Yes—or be taken for bandits or spies. With our scars, we can't pass as farmers. But Paks has a good idea: we can move south along this road to the first crossing, and wait a day or so. If they don't come, we can decide then who will go straight to the Duke, and who will keep watch."

"Let's go then." Paks rose with the others. Although the fog had cleared, the light was already waning under an overcast sky. She led them downslope again, across a narrow trail, and up the next gentle rise. She tried to stay just close enough to the road to be aware of the gap in the trees. They saw no one, and heard nothing on the road.

Paks had just begun to wonder if they were nearing the farm when she smelled woodsmoke, and saw more light off to the right. She recalled the four or five huts and a barn, a rail-fenced enclosure for stock, and long narrow strips of plowed and fallow ground. Her mouth watered at the smell of the woodsmoke. She looked at Canna and Saben; they looked as hungry as she felt.

"I might be able to steal something," she said.

Saben nodded, but Canna shook her head. "No. Remember the horsemen." Paks had forgotten, in her hunger. "It would help, though, to find out if that's where they are. We haven't heard them on the road: I hope they aren't sweeping the woods."

"I hadn't thought of that," said Paks.

"I didn't think you had. We're not out of the net yet; we need to think of everything—because they will. Saben, why don't you slip up to the road this time. Just like Paks—stay down, no matter what."

"Right away. Oh—is my face dirty enough?"

"Not quite." Paks smeared leafmold across his cheek. "There."

"And I'll do as much for you next time," he said,

grinning. Paks and Canna sat down to watch as he crept toward the road.

"That's hard on the arms," said Paks as she watched.

"Yes. I don't think we should talk." Canna's face was grim. Paks shot her a glance and went back to watching Saben. He looked very slow, but she knew how hard it was. She thought about the chance of a mounted sweep in the woods and shivered. No fog to hide them—not enough underbrush here. We ought to be farther apart, she thought. Then they might find only one—or that might make them look harder for more. Her belly growled loudly. Canna looked at her, and Paks shrugged. No way to stop that without food.

Saben was out of sight now, among the bushes by the road. Paks slipped her knife out and looked at it. If she hadn't given her parole, she would not have a knife— would not have been out berrying, most likely. She would have been in the fort, maybe in a cell. But then, she'd have a sword by now, because the Halverics had armed the Phelani. But besieged by such a force—she shook her head, and returned to thoughts of the route south. A day to the crossroads and wait. They could do that, even without food. Her belly growled again, louder. Except for Canna, she thought. Canna's been hurt; she has to have food. And if I can find food for one, I can find it for three. She cheered up a bit. There was Saben, creeping back toward them. The smell of smoke came stronger as the wind veered a moment. Saben came nearer. When she met his eyes, he signaled them to move farther away from the road. Saben followed them. When they stopped in a thicket, Paks saw his face was pale under the leafmold.

"What is it?" asked Canna.

"They're there," he said in a strange choked voice. "I counted twelve horses tethered along that fence—you remember. They've—they've killed the farmers—and their families. The—the bodies are just—lying around. Like—like old rags, or—" His voice broke, and he stopped, choking back sobs. Paks had a sudden vision of an army in Three Firs. She had never thought of that, of armed men coming onto her father's farm—her brothers and sisters—

"Saben!" Canna shook his arm. "Saben, stop it. You've seen dead before. It's terrible, yes, but we don't want to be next—"

He looked up, eyes wet. "But we're fighters, Canna—that's what we're for. Those weren't soldiers; they didn't have a chance."

"Saben, it's only your second year—and we don't do things like that—but surely you know that some armies do."

"If only we'd come faster, we might have stopped them," he said.

"Three of us? With daggers? Remember what you said last night, Saben."

"But our people," said Paks. "What about our people? If they'd kill farmers like that, what will they do to soldiers?"

"Paks, don't think about it. All we can do is get help: tell the Duke. Whatever can be done, he'll do. You know that." Canna turned back to Saben. "Do they look like they'll be there long?"

Saben took a shaky breath, then another. "Yes. They—they were cooking. One of the cattle, I think. They're all around the fire."

"Then we can slip past, probably, and we'd better—" She broke off as a rattle of hooves rang out on the road.

"One horse," said Paks. "Messenger?"

"Could be."

"Let me look," said Saben. "I won't do anything."

"Well—"

"I'm all right, Canna. We do need to know what they're doing."

"All right. We'll stay here. Don't get caught."

"No." Saben turned away, toward the road, and disappeared. Paks found she'd slipped her dagger out again. Canna shook her head and pointed at the sheath. She slipped it back in. They waited. They heard a shout

from the distance. Another shout. Paks felt her heart
give a great leap in her chest.

"Saben?" she gasped.

"I hope not," said Canna. "Holy Gird defend him. If
that was a messenger, maybe they're shouting at each
other." Her face was paler than before.

They listened. No more shouts. Paks imagined Saben
full of arrows, his body dragged to the fire, or taken
alive for questioning. She shuddered. Canna touched
her hand. "Don't think about it. We don't know—
imagining things will make you weaker." Paks nodded
without speaking, and tried to force her thoughts elsewhere. Again the noise of hooves, this time many of
them, on the road. Was the whole troop leaving? They
waited in a silence scarcely broken by the rustle of
leaves in a slight wind. Paks gave up looking in the
direction Saben had gone, and stared at the ground.
She jumped when Canna nudged her.

Saben was coming toward them, walking almost upright. He was grinning. Paks felt a rush of relief that
made her unsteady on her feet as she rose. "I thought
you'd—"

"I know," he said. "When they yelled it scared me,
and I could see what was happening. Canna, the troop's
gone, ordered back to the fort, and they left a whole
cow on the fire. The messenger, that single horse, told
them not to wait, because they were starting south in
the morning. If we hurry, we can have meat, and
plenty of it." At once Paks's hunger returned.

"What about sentries?" asked Canna. "Surely—"

"No—all the horses are gone, and every horse had a
rider; I made sure of that. Please, Canna—it's our best
chance."

"It's risky—but you're right. It's our chance."

"We could pass the farm," said Paks. "Saben and I'll
double back if it's clear. How's that?"

"Good idea. I hope they've cut that meat; I don't
want to leave any obvious signs."

"I never thought of that," said Saben. "They were

poking at it; I saw that the first time I looked. But I
don't know about cut—"

"We'll see. Even if it hasn't, we ought to be able to
find other food there—and they may think one of theirs
took it."

They moved on, carefully. The farm clearing lay across
the road; when they had passed it, they moved to the
road edge and looked both ways. "Maybe only one of us
should cross," said Paks. "If anything happens, maybe
they'll look on that side—"

"I don't know if that matters," said Canna. "Still, any
precaution might help. Saben, you've seen the worst
already—can you go?"

"Yes, Canna." Behind the leafmold, his face was com-
posed, his blues eyes steady.

"Good. If the meat isn't marked up, haggle a corner
off; don't leave clean knife cuts. Maybe they'll think a
stray dog got it. See what else you can find, but don't
leave anything so stripped that it's obvious."

"Get some clothes for bandages, if you can," said
Paks. She thought Canna looked worse than she had
that morning.

"Yes, and another tinderbox, if you see one," added
Canna.

"I'll see what I can find." After another careful look
both ways, Saben darted across the road into the trees
on the far side. Paks could see him skirting the clearing, coming in behind one of the huts. He disappeared.
After a long wait, she saw him come back toward the
trees, then turn back to the huts again. This time he
was gone even longer. Then she could see him again,
edging along the clearing toward the road, with a pack
slung over one shoulder and a bundle in his arm.

Once across the road, he handed the bundle to Paks
and urged them back into the trees. "Wait until you see
what I found."

"Hush," said Canna. "We're too close." They walked
on until the road was completely hidden, then sat down.

Paks unrolled the bundle, Saben's cloak wrapped

around a number of things: three round loaves of brown bread, half a small cheese, six apples, a small padded sack of lumpy objects— "Careful," said Saben. "Those are eggs."—onions, a few redroots, several strips of pale linen, a small stoneware crock with a pungent smell, and a short-bladed knife.

Saben was pulling other finds from the worn leather pack he'd found: strips of half-roasted beef, another cheese, and a roll of cord. "They'd hacked the cow up with their swords," he said. "Some was bones with meat on, and some just strips of meat, so I took these. We could get more without it being noticed, I think, but I couldn't carry more, and didn't want to take too long. It must have been baking day; bread was rolling all over the hut floors. I took what had rolled under things. There was a barrel of apples; we can get more easily. Not so many cheeses, unless they're stored somewhere else. I didn't look in the barn. The eggs were under a bed; I felt them when I reached for the bread."

Canna smiled. "Saben, you found a treasure. I don't know about going back—but now we'll eat. Let's see— we'll share a half-loaf of bread, and one of those big strips of meat, and have an apple each. More than that, and we'll be slow and sleepy."

Paks and Saben sighed at that, but by the time they'd eaten what Canna allowed, Paks felt much better. Not satisfied, but better.

"Let's see your shoulder," she said, when she had swallowed the last bit of bread. "These strips will be softer than that old sack. And I think this stuff in the crock is for wounds, isn't it?"

Canna sniffed at it. "It smells like that stuff the surgeons use, yes." Paks unwound her hasty bandage of the day before, and Canna slipped off her tunic, wincing. The folded sack, blood-stained, was firmly stuck to the wound. Paks poured some of her water over it.

"Brr. That's cold," said Canna.

"I thought that would loosen it."

"It may, but it's cold." Paks worked as gently as she

could, and finally got the sack off. Underneath, Canna's shoulder was swollen, red, and warm to touch. "It's—tender," said Canna, as Paks probed it. "Is it going bad?"

"I can't tell. It's red, and it feels different. Maybe just swollen. Here—I'm going to try this stuff." Paks smeared some of the gray-green sticky gunk in the crock over the wound. "How's that?"

"It stings a little. Not bad."

"Maybe I should have washed it first. If we had hot water—"

"No. That's all right. Just tie it up, and we'll hope for the best."

Paks folded the soft linen into a pad, then bound it on as she had before, this time with the softer linen strips. "Now you can put your tunic over it," she said. "Maybe that will be more comfortable."

"I wouldn't mind," said Canna. She was pale and sweating.

"What about another trip to the farm, Canna?" asked Saben. "This won't last long, and we may not have such a good chance again."

"We've got to travel light—"

"I know, but a week's march—"

"Let's see what we've got now. Enough bread for a couple of days, with this meat. Cut it in hunks like this, Saben—" Canna showed the size. "I don't know how that cheese will travel, but we can wrap it. Those redroots will have to be cooked, but they'll keep. You're right—we could use more. But it's getting late—"

"Less likely to be seen, then. I'll be careful."

Canna looked uncertain. "I—wish I knew—"

Paks felt a vague uneasiness. "I think we should get farther away."

"You'll think differently when we're hungry the day after tomorrow," said Saben.

Canna looked from one to another. "I—I say no, Saben. We'll go on. We shouldn't take chances we don't have to; the ones we must take are bad enough."

Saben shrugged. "Whatever you say; you're the commander. Here—let me see what I can fit in this pack." The bread, cheese, onions, and redroots disappeared into the pack. They stuffed their pouches with the pieces of meat, and Paks tucked the eggs inside her tunic. Saben took the crock of ointment, and Canna stuck the knife in her boot. They filled their flasks at the little creek that flowed eastward from the farm into the woods.

"We should go as far as we can while we have light," said Canna. "I think it will be safe enough to stay near the road, but if you see anything—even a woodcutter or herder—drop and get out of sight. And be as quiet as possible."

At first Paks led the way, but Canna was clearly tiring. After the third time Paks found herself far ahead, she suggested that Canna lead. The dark woman nodded without speaking. Paks and Saben moved out to flank her, and they went on in the growing dusk.

Chapter Sixteen

The ground was gently rolling, each low ridge less steep than the one before it, as the land subsided from the mountains to the north. Darkness seemed to flow up out of the hollows as light faded from the gray sky. They had no idea how far they had come. Paks was thinking of nothing in particular when she realized that she had lost Canna in the gloom. She stopped and peered into the woods. An owl called from somewhere behind her. She shivered, listening for any sound of her friends. The owl called again, the last hoot sounding odd. It must be Saben, she thought, and hooted in reply. A short hoot answered her; she moved toward the sound quickly. She missed them in a thicket. Saben's voice nearly startled her into a scream.

"What happened?" she asked when she got her voice back.

"It's your long legs," said Saben. "You distanced us again, and Canna fell, trying to hurry."

"I'm all right," said Canna. Her voice was strained. "But it's too dark to walk safely in these trees."

"Nothing's on the road," said Paks. "Nobody travels this late—couldn't we use it for a few miles?" Out of the dark a hand squeezed her arm as Saben spoke.

"I'm legweary," he said. "We'll do better for a rest."

"Paks, I—don't think I can go farther tonight," said Canna. "Even on the road."

"Let's see if we can find a good place to sleep, then." Paks peered around, but could hardly see two trees away from the gloom.

"This will do," said Saben. The hand on her arm tightened and released. "You didn't see us."

"Mmm. You're right. Hope it doesn't rain, though." Canna, Paks saw, had already slumped to the ground. She herself, though still hungry, was too keyed up to feel tired.

"You had first watch last night, Paks," said Saben. "I'll take it; I'm sore but not sleepy."

Paks felt the same but did not argue. "Canna, are you warm enough?"

"I—can't get this cloak—wrapped, somehow."

"Let me help." Paks helped Canna sit up and untangle the cloak. "What did you hurt when you fell?"

"Nothing. It jarred me. I'm all right."

"We'll hope so." Paks doubted it, but there wasn't anything to do. "Would you rather have a back rest or front rest? I want to keep warm."

"Back, if you're giving choices."

Paks rolled herself into her cloak and lay behind Canna. "Don't eat all the bread while we sleep," she told Saben, who chuckled.

"Ha. And here I thought you'd forgotten .it." She heard a rustle and saw a shape moving in the darkness as Saben took a position between them and the road. She thought she was not sleepy, but Saben's hand on her arm woke her much later to a cold night, not so damp as the one before.

"I can't keep my eyes open," he murmured. "No trouble so far." Paks stretched and unrolled herself while Saben lay down in the warm spot she'd made.

She rubbed her face hard with her hands to wake up, and took a swallow of water from her flask. No trouble so far. How long would that last? She felt her stomach clench on nothing, and thought about the meat in her pouch. No. She drank again. Canna was right about that—they had to space the food out. She thought of her father's tale about the famine when he was a boy, the year the wolves came. *We tried to eat the grass,* he'd said. Her stomach growled. *Don't think about food. We have food, but not for now.* She looked up to see if the stars were out, but could see only blackness. In that cold, hungry darkness, for the first time she doubted that they would reach the Duke. She forced herself to think. *Tomorrow—tomorrow we'll get to the crossroad. Unless Canna—no, surely she's all right. I wish we could go on ahead. They must take the short way, if they're going to Rotengre. We could stay safely ahead if we knew.*

She hardly noticed when the light began to glow. All at once, it seemed, she could see her hands and arms, and the two dark shapes stretched out below. She yawned and stretched, wondering if she'd dozed awhile. The light gave no color yet. She nudged Saben with her toe; he gave a sort of gasping snort and sat up.

"What?"

"Dawn. We should be going soon." Canna had not wakened. They both looked at her. "Do you think she'll be all right?" asked Paks softly.

Saben frowned. "Not all right. But it wasn't a deep wound—I think—"

"We need her."

"Yes, but we're no surgeons."

"I wonder if that—Effa said St. Gird healed people. Canna's a Girdsman. Maybe he'll heal her."

"*If* he does. But if he can, why not just do it? Already?"

"I don't know. I never heard of Gird back home—"

"What about Gird?" Canna had awakened. She grimaced as she moved, then forced a smile. "Don't look so worried; I'm fine."

"We wondered if Gird would heal you," said Paks.

Canna looked surprised. "How did you know—you aren't a Girdsman! It takes a Marshal or a paladin to heal, though."

Saben looked stubborn. "If it takes a Marshal or a paladin, what has it got to do with Gird?"

"Saben, you drink water, but when you carry it from the river, you have to have a bucket to put it in. I don't know what kind of power it is that Gird wields, but it must come through a Marshal or paladin."

"So a prayer wouldn't work?" asked Paks.

"No. A prayer for courage, or strength in battle—and it can't hurt to pray for good fortune—but not healing."

"We could try," said Paks. Canna stared at her.

"What are you, a paladin in disguise? You aren't even a Girdsman."

"No, that's true. But we need you to be well and strong."

"I'm—oh, all right. If you want to. It can't do any harm."

"But I don't know how," said Paks. "You'll have to tell me what to say."

"Paks, I don't know. I'm no Marshal, and Gird knows I'm no paladin, either." She paused for breath. "Here—" She fumbled at her neck for the chain that held her medallion. "You'll need this. Hold it. Then say what you want, in the name of St. Gird."

Paks took the metal crescent and held it a moment, thinking. Then she laid it on Canna's shoulder, over the bandaged wound. She looked at Saben, who looked back, quirking an eyebrow.

"St. Gird," she began. "Please heal this wound. This is Canna, who is your follower, and she was hurt by an arrow. We are trying to escape to tell our Duke of the Honeycat's treachery, and we need Canna's help. In—in the name of Gird—I mean, St. Gird."

"Ouch!" said Canna. "What did you poke it for?"

"I didn't," said Paks. "I just laid your symbol on it; I didn't push. What happened?"

"It must have been a cramp, then. That hurt. It's easing now. It seems—I can breathe a little easier."

"But it still hurts?"

"Yes, but the sharp pain is gone—whatever it was. Don't worry, Paks. I didn't expect a cure."

"I suppose not." She handed back the medallion and turned to the pack. "What can we have for breakfast?"

"Bread. We'll try that half-cheese, too." They divided the small cheese and each took a slice of bread from the half a loaf left the night before. That took the edge off their hunger, though Paks felt she could have eaten much more. Saben managed to fit the eggs into the packs this time. "Let's go," said Canna abruptly. Paks and Saben looked at her, surprised, but rose at once.

The morning was still and gray, with a murkiness between the trees that was not quite fog. They stayed close to the road, but Canna would not let them walk in it, fearing a forward patrol. They walked in silence, three dark shadows among the black tree-trunks. Canna set a better pace than the evening before. When she finally called a halt, they moved away from the road and stretched out under a large cedar.

Saben wiggled his shoulders. "Ugh. That pack—the straps are too short. He must have been a skinny man."

"I'll take it next," offered Paks.

"You're not a skinny man."

"No, but it'll get the cramps out of your shoulders."

"I wish I'd found a weapon," he grumbled. "A bow, or a sword—"

"We're better without it," said Canna.

"How so?"

"If you'd found one, you'd be tempted to fight, wouldn't you? You'd want to kill one of their scouts to get still more weapons—then free the prisoners—" Saben was blushing, now, and Canna nodded before going on. "There's not a weapon in the world, Saben, that would let you take on that force single-handed and survive.

Our job is to get word to the Duke. For that we need wit, not blades."

"Yes, Canna. But think how much fun—"

"If we get to the Duke," said Canna grimly, "we can have all the fun we want—with weapons he'll give us." Saben subsided. Paks wondered again if it was as bad as Canna seemed to think.

"When the column does come," she asked, "how are we going to move with it without being seen? The woods don't last all the way to Rotengre."

"You would ask that. I've been trying to remember what the country is like. We can use any trees—hedges— and if it's dry, they'll raise a cloud; we can stay far off and still be sure where they are. But it's going to be hard."

"I was thinking—surely they'll take the short way, east of Sorellin. Why can't we just go straight for the Duke?"

"We can't be sure. Siniava has a name for being indirect."

"You mean he might go around in a circle, or something—?"

"Yes. Find a weak spot in the siege lines, and try to break it there."

"But then what does he want prisoners for? They'll only get in the way."

"I don't know. Some wickedness." Canna took a swallow of water. "I wish I knew how close we were to the crossroad."

"Why?" asked Paks. "We'll find it if we stay near the road."

"If I were the Honeycat," said Canna slowly, "I'd have someone posted at the crossroads."

"But we're well ahead of the forward patrol," said Saben.

"That's exactly what I'd want stragglers to think," replied Canna. "If someone got through the sweeps and patrols, they'd think they were safe, and they'd be careless. Besides, suppose the Duke sent a courier for some reason—Siniava would have to stop that. So I think we can expect trouble—at every crossroad, and every place a messenger or straggler would be tempted to use the road. Probably disguised as traders, or brigands, or something, to keep the peasants from gossiping too much."

"How do we get around them, then?" asked Paks

Canna shrugged. "They don't *know* that anyone's coming. We do. And we expect them. We'll move very quietly, and watch very carefully, and not set foot on the road."

After a scant ration of bread, they set off again. Canna forbade **any** talking until they cleared the crossroad, and they moved as quietly as they could. The road wound back and forth around low rounded hummocks; Paks found it hard to keep an even distance from it.

From far behind came a long low horn call. They stopped and looked at each other. In such cold air, a horn would carry a great distance. Three short blasts of a higher-pitched horn came from the road ahead. This sounded closer than the other, but distance was impossible to judge. Canna nodded at the other two and grinned. She gestured them still farther from the road, and forward. Paks felt her heart begin to pound, drumming in her ears so that she could hardly hear. This would be the real test, getting past the guard at the crossroad. She looked at Canna, who was still moving strongly, and stumbled over a briar. Calm down, she told herself. Saben and Canna gave her a warning glance and went on.

As the road began a curve right, Canna signaled a halt. She beckoned them close, then murmured in their ears. "I think they're on top of the rise ahead—see how open the woods look up there? They could see the road and the woods both. We'll swing around the far side of the hill. Be careful. No stumbling about." Paks blushed.

They turned left along the slope, climbing no higher. As they moved away from the road, the woods thickened, and undergrowth screened them. They could not see more than a few yards uphill. More evergreens cloaked the northern slope. It was easy to walk quietly on the fallen needles, and they moved faster. Still, several hours of tense and tedious work brought them only to the eastern end of that hill, and a low saddle between it and the next rise to the east. As they came up the saddle, the trees thinned again.

Canna waved them down, then peered upslope. Paks looked too, and saw nothing. Trees masked the higher slope and crown. For a second time, they heard the long horn call. This time it seemed closer, hardly north of the hill. At once two short blasts rang out upslope. Clearly Canna had been right about the location of the watch. They crept through the trees, keeping every possible leaf between them and the upper slope as they cleared the saddle. Now they could see, at the foot of a gentle slope, a broad rutted road running east and west. It disappeared behind a south-jutting face of the hill between them and the crossroad.

When they reached the road, Canna stopped them. "I'll cross first," she said. "If anything happens, go east another hill, then head south. Don't come back for me; go to the Duke. If nothing happens, count twenty, then Paks comes. Then twenty again, and Saben. No noise, and get to cover fast on the other side. May Gird be with us." Canna turned away, crept to the very edge of the road, and looked. Nothing. Still bent low, she scurried across and dived into bushes on the far side. Paks counted on her fingers to be sure not to skip any; when she had counted twice over, she checked the road and ran across. Once in cover, she turned to watch for Saben. He crossed the road safely, and the three of them moved to deeper cover under the trees.

Canna swung right, back toward the south road, cutting the corner. They had covered what Paks guessed to be half that distance when they began to hear shouts, the clatter of horses, and the rumble of wagons from their right. Suddenly a thrashing and crackling of undergrowth broke out behind. They dropped where they were. Thudding hooves pounded nearer; Paks could hear the jingle and creak of tack and armor. This time the mounted men were silent. They were spaced in easy sight of one another, passing on either side of the fugitives. Paks saw the hooves of one horse churning the leaves scarcely a length from her face. As the horse cantered on, she saw that the rider had a chain-mail shirt under a yellow surcoat, and a flat helmet with a brim. He had a sword at his side, and a short-thonged whip thrust into his belt behind.

When the hoofbeats died away, Canna urged them up and led them back east. "We know how far out he sends the sweeps, now," she said. "But without seeing the column, we don't know if these were the forward or the flank."

"At least we know he's going south," said Paks.

"How about one of us going in for a closer look?" asked Saben.

Canna frowned. "It'll be dangerous. I think we can do better. We'll climb the next hill on our side, and take a look from a distance. As long as we stay outside the sweeps—" They walked on, more quickly, in case another patrol was riding behind. The ground rose under their feet; again they were in the evergreens of a north slope. They toiled upward, panting. Paks felt the pack of food dragging at her shoulder, and wished they could stop and eat. They heard more noise from the road. A mounting excitement seized all three of them; they began to hurry up the slope, eager to see the enemy column at last.

Paks, shouldering her way through thick pines and cedars, thought only of how they hid her. When she broke into the cleared space of the hilltop, a pace or so ahead of Canna and Saben, she found herself face to face with one of the mounted men. He had turned toward the noise she'd made; as she came in sight he grinned and lifted his reins.

"So there is something here besides rabbits, eh?" He

turned in the saddle, taking a breath. Paks shrugged the pack off her shoulder and threw it at him. His horse shied, and he nearly fell. "Why, you—" he began, drawing his sword. Paks had her dagger out and charged the horse, which snorted and backed. He jerked the reins and spurred. She dodged to the unarmed side and jumped to grab his arm. The horse jumped sideways as he overbalanced, and he slid out of the saddle on top of her, swordarm flailing. Paks was stunned by the fall under him. With a snort, the horse clattered off into the trees. Paks struggled to catch her breath and squirm free. Canna and Saben appeared and jerked him aside; Canna had a knife in his throat before he could make a sound.

"Now we're in trouble!" Canna gave Paks a hand up. "Get that pack, Saben. Come on!" She led them down the east side of the hill as fast as they could go, slipping in the leaves. Paks was so shaken that she had trouble keeping her balance. At the foot of the hill, Canna would not let them rest, but set off southward at a brisk pace. "I should have thought," she said sometime later. "They'll have a lookout on every hill. Especially now."

"Surely they've—found him—by now," said Paks. She couldn't seem to get her breath.

"I hope not. It depends how they set it up. If they were stationed at intervals, to wait for the column to pass, they won't know until it does—or until his horse wanders back to the road."

"It won't," said Saben.

"What—"

"You didn't see. I was behind you—I caught the reins, and tied it."

Paks looked at him. "That was quick thinking."

"Very good, Saben," said Canna. "I didn't think of the horse until afterwards. You were lucky not to be trampled."

"We were all lucky," he said soberly. "Paks stopped him calling an alarm—"

"Yes. When I saw you throw that pack," said Canna, "I thought we were lost."

"You're right that we must stick together, Canna. One alone couldn't have made it through that."

They walked on in silence for a space, keeping to the low ground and swinging east of the low hills they met. Some time in the afternoon, they heard several horn signals far behind, but they did not know what it meant. They only knew they had to keep going. As light began to wane behind the clouds, Paks asked, "Do you think they'll camp for the night, or march through?"

"I think they'll camp. I wish I knew the road better. Somewhere between here and the next crossroad we come out of the trees." Canna sighed. She had slowed the pace; they were all legweary.

"I'm worried about keeping up," said Paks. "We should be faster, just the three of us, but we're having to cover more ground. Once it's open, it'll be worse. What if they distance us and take a turn we don't see?"

"We'll ask someone. I don't think they will, though."

They went on until the light was almost gone, and they were stumbling with weariness. When they finally stopped in a hazel thicket, they were all exhausted and hungry. Paks had been struggling with a sharp pain in her side where she'd fallen on rocks under the horseman. Now it was worse.

"I wish we could have a fire," she said. "Those eggs—"

"We'll eat them raw," said Canna. "We can't risk a fire." She dug into the pack. Two eggs had broken, but five remained.

"You can have my share," said Paks. The thought of raw eggs revolted her.

"They're good. Don't waste 'em."

"I'm not. You eat them." Paks took a scrap of meat from her pouch. Canna looked at her.

"Paks, I should have asked—were you hurt?"

"Just bruised, I think, from the rocks. It catches when I take a deep breath. How's your shoulder?"

"It hurts a little, but not like yesterday. I should have

remembered that the day after is worse than the day something happens. Here's some bread."

Paks took a slice. "We ought to change the bandages, and put on more ointment—"

"It's too dark," said Saben. "We can't see what we're eating."

"In the morning," said Canna. "We'll look at your bruises, too."

They settled into uneasy sleep. Saben took the first watch. When Paks woke in the early dawn, she found that Canna had taken the second. She started to sit up and bit back a groan. She was stiff from head to heel, and her right side throbbed. Canna insisted on seeing the damage.

"I thought so," she said. "A fine lot of bruises and a bad scrape—hand me that pot, Saben—and maybe a broken rib or two." Paks winced as Canna spread the ointment. It stung like nettles. "Don't move—you'll have your turn next," said Canna. But Canna's wound was clearly healing: no longer an angry red. Canna twisted her head to look. "That's much better," she said. "It's just a little sore this morning." She gave Paks a long look. "Maybe you did do something with that prayer."

Paks ducked her head. "It's not healed completely, Canna. And we put ointment on it."

Canna looked at their food. "We'll eat the cheese— and some bread. That leaves—umm. We'll be out again by day after tomorrow. Well, no help for it." After that scant meal, they were ready. Paks needed Saben's help to stand, and found walking difficult.

She was wondering how they would know if the column was still going south when they heard horsemen to their right: they could see nothing. All that morning, as a weak sun struggled through clouds, they moved with hardly a pause. Paks found it harder and harder to keep up. Near noon they reached the southern edge of the unbroken woods, and Canna waved them to a sheltered hollow.

Paks slumped onto the leaves and wished she didn't have to move. She closed her eyes for a moment and opened them to see Canna and Saben watching her. She forced a grin. "I'm just sore. It's not as bad as yours, Canna; I'll be better tomorrow."

"Let's have an apple," said Canna. Saben opened the pack and passed them around. "Paks, we need you. We need all of us. We'll slow if we have to—"

Paks shook her head. "No. You said getting to the Duke was more important than anything. I'll keep up, or you'll go on. After all, once they've passed I'll be safe enough."

"I've changed my mind," said Canna. "After yesterday—if we can possibly stay together, we should. At least for now. The column's not ahead of us."

"Speaking of the column," said Saben. "I think I'll crawl up there—" he nodded at the treeline, "—and have a look. Maybe I can spot them."

Canna nodded, and he moved away. Beyond the trees was rough pasture; they could see his head outlined against the tawny grass. Presently he came back.

"They're there," he said. "The column and sweeps both. Very impressive. They were still coming in sight when I came back. Want to take a look?"

"I will. Paks, you stay here and rest." Paks wanted to protest, but felt more like lying still. She fell into a doze while they were gone, and woke with Canna's hand on her arm.

"Paks. Wake up. They're moving south, and the prisoners are with them. We think at least sixty prisoners, both ours and Halveric's. I'm not sure how many troops, but there are ten wagons and several score horse."

"Did the whole column pass?"

"Yes. They may be trying to reach the second crossroad by nightfall. I wish I knew how far that was."

"Then we'd better go. I feel better."

"Good. Saben and I think we've found enough cover for the next stretch." Canna helped her up. Paks tried to convince herself that she would feel better moving, and they started again.

Out from under the trees, with the sun's disk showing through the clouds, it was easy to keep their heading. Luckily the fields were edged with strips of woodland or hedge, and all through the afternoon they were able to keep up with the column while staying well hidden. The mounted sweeps never came as close as they had; Canna worried more about being spotted by a herder or farmer who might tell the tale.

By late afternoon the column reached the second crossroad, where the road from Dwarfwatch crossed the great Guild League road. The three fugitives had gained on it, now even with its middle. They could see the head of the column swing left, onto the direct route for Rotengre. They could also see the mounted patrols that moved out along all the roads to screen its passage. They dared not risk moving forward before dark.

"It's not lost time, exactly," said Saben. "Now we know how many of them, and what equipment—"

"Too many," said Canna. "Over three hundred foot and a hundred horse. If the whole Company was here, it wouldn't be an easy fight."

"At least he's obvious," said Paks. "A force that size will be seen—someone's bound to tell the Duke even if we fail."

"Don't forget those farmers—he may be killing everyone he sees."

"Come on, Canna; he can't kill everyone on the road between here and Rotengre. Traders come this way, and—"

"Saben, from what I've heard of him, he'll kill anyone who stands in his way."

They had turned east across the fields, and come to the caravan road well beyond the patrol's position. Besides, they had seen the riders turn back. Even so, they took no chances. Canna scouted the road, and they crossed one by one, as before. The night was cold and clearer than the day had been; the stars gave just enough light for them to walk on open ground. They went on until they saw the fires of the encamped column.

"Here," said Canna, stopping them in a little triangular wood. "This will do. Paks, how's your side?"

Paks leaned against a tree. She felt that if she sat down she would never make it back up. "Stiff," she said finally. "A night's rest will help."

Canna handed around a meager measure of the remaining meat and bread. They had eaten it almost before they tasted it. "It has to last," said Canna. "I don't know where we can get any more—we'll do better spacing it out—" She did not sound convinced. Paks clenched her jaw to keep from asking for more. She knew Canna was right, but her belly disagreed. Saben gave a gusty sigh out of the darkness.

"My old grandmother used to tell me, when I wouldn't stop begging for sweets on market day, that someday I'd want 'em worse than I did then, and because I'd begged I wouldn't have any. What I don't understand is how the food would be here now if I hadn't begged then. Do you suppose there's some magic—?"

Paks found herself chuckling. "Only if learning not to ask meant learning not to want. It's an idea, though: things you want and don't ask for coming when you need them."

"I don't think it works like that," said Saben. "So much the worse. Canna, if we wait until this column has passed that village, can we go and buy food?"

"No. I expect Siniava will have spies there."

"What a suspicious old crow," grumbled Saben.

"If he weren't, he wouldn't be that powerful. I'll take first watch tonight, Saben; you and Paks get to sleep."

Paks was tired, but her side hurt so that she found it hard to get comfortable. She would have sworn the ground was covered with cobbles, yet Saben was snoring lightly in minutes. She tried rolling onto her back. Her legs stuck out into the cold. Her stomach growled loudly, and she found herself thinking of stew, and hot bread, and roast mutton— I'm as bad as Saben at the market, she thought. She turned on her left side. At last she fell asleep, to be wakened by Saben on a clear frosty dawn.

As they chewed their scant breakfast, trying to make it last, they watched the distant fields. The sun rose and glinted on the enemy helmets as they assembled. Thin streams of smoke from their fires rose straight into an unclouded sky, to bend southward above the trees. The column began to move. Suddenly a puff of blacker smoke billowed up, then another and another. In a minute they could see the red leaping flames.

"They're torching the village," said Canna. "I daresay they've killed the villagers, or taken them prisoners." They watched as yet another billow of smoke stained the sky. Paks thought of the friendly folk who had waved at them on their way north.

"Why burn it?" she asked.

Canna shrugged and sighed. "I don't know. To hide the murders as wildfire? Who can imagine what that filth would be thinking."

As the tail of the column disappeared, they set off across the fields, angling toward the burning village. They could see the dry grass near the huts burning, flames spreading toward stubbled fields and woods beyond. A light breeze came with the morning, moving the fire south, a pall of smoke with it. Soon they were up with the smoke, paralleling the fire. The smoke set them coughing. Paks felt a stabbing pain when she coughed. She was uneasily aware of the flames creeping along the ground or rising in crackling leaps when they found more fuel than stubble. But the wind never strengthened nor shifted direction, and soon they had passed the fire by.

All that day they dodged and darted from hedge to hedge to thicket, keeping the column in distant view. As the day wore on, they worried more about farmers. They feared that Siniava had offered a rich reward for reports of stragglers. Paks moved more easily, despite continuing pain; by late afternoon what really mattered

was the gnawing hole in her belly. They had scarcely
spoken to each other all day, but she could see the
same hunger in the others' drawn faces.

Despite the clear sky, it was still colder; Paks dreaded
the night to come. The column halted; the smoke of
their watchfires stained the evening sky. Canna kept
moving, and they edged past at a respectful distance.
Paks wondered why, but she was too breathless to ask.
At last Canna stopped, well beyond the head of the
column, and explained her reasoning.

"We're sure now where they're going, and by what
road," she said. "Now's the time to separate. We've
found no food; if one takes all we have, that's enough to
make the Duke's camp—I think three days' travel. They'll
take at least five, with those wagons. But without food,
all three of us can't make it. The Duke must know—"

"But Canna, you said yesterday we should stay together," said Saben. "One person could be stopped by
anything. And what about food for the two left behind?"

"We'd find something," said Canna.

Saben snorted. "You with an arrow wound, and Paks
with a broken rib? I suppose you meant me to go?"
Canna nodded, and Saben shook his head. "No. I won't
leave two wounded companions and take all the food—
not if there's any other way."

"Why don't we stay ahead tomorrow," suggested Paks.
"Maybe we'll find something to eat—and if there's a
chance to stay together—"

"I suppose so," said Canna, sighing. "I wish we dared
have a fire; those redroots would be good."

Paks felt her mouth water. "You ate raw eggs; why
not raw redroots?"

"Tastes awful," said Saben. "But it might fill the
holes."

They gnawed on the raw roots, bitter and dry, and
ate a slice of bread each. Paks offered to take first
watch, but the other two insisted that she sleep. By
morning the ground was frozen, white hoarfrost over
the stubble.

Chapter Seventeen

About midmorning, they were striding through a small wood when they startled a sounder of swine; the boar swung to face them with a wheezing snort. Paks froze. Beside her Canna and Saben were as still. The boar's little eyes, set in wrinkled skin, were golden hazel; the bristles up its back were rusty brown. Paks watched as the pink nose twitched in their direction. One of the sows squealed. Two others began to mince away on nimble hooves. The boar whuffled, and swung its head to watch the rest of the pigs. Now they were all moving, drifting along a thread of path.

"Roast pig?" said Saben plaintively. The boar looked at him and grunted.

"Not with daggers," said Paks, remembering the butchering at Amboi's farm. The boar grunted again, backed a few steps, and swung to follow the others. Paks relaxed and took a deep breath. "I hope we don't meet more of those," she said.

"Right," said Canna. "We'd have a—" she stopped abruptly as a boy dressed in rough shirt and trousers jogged into their view and stopped short. His eyes widened.

"Soldiers," he breathed. He backed up a step, fumbling for his dagger.

"We won't hurt you," said Paks. "Don't be afraid."

He was poised to run. "Ye—ye're a girl, an't ye?"

Paks and Canna both grinned. Paks answered. "I am. Were those your swine?"

His eyes narrowed. "Why'd ye ask—ye'll not take 'em, will ye?"

"No," said Paks. "I just wondered."

"Wheer ye be goin'?" he asked. Paks judged he was about fifteen or so, a short muscular redhead with pale eyes in a heavily freckled face. She thought of Vik with a pang, and wondered where he was now.

Paks winked at the boy. "We're just—taking a little trip, lad, you might say. Know where we could find some good ale?"

He relaxed a bit and grinned. "Is it ale ye're wantin'? Ye look more like robbers, I was thinkin', but if ye've got the coppers I know wheer ye can get ale."

"Robbers?" Paks tried to sound shocked. "Nay—we're but travel-worn and thirsty. As for coppers—" she jingled the coins in her pouch.

"Well, then," he said, "ye might do worse than my uncle's place, over on the river down yon—" he pointed south. " 'Tis not what ye'd rightly call an inn, not bein' on th' road. But serves the farmers round, ye see, with my uncle's brew and no tax to pay like that Silver Pheasant out on the road. And I'm thinkin'," he added shrewdly, "ye may not be robbers, but ye look like ye won't have to do wi' roads, eh?"

Paks grinned. "As to that, lad, if you should happen to see a sergeant, you might not remember you saw us—would you?" She had a copper ready for the hand he held out.

The boy snickered. "All I seen in these woods is swine—that's all." He turned to the path they'd taken and followed it.

"I wonder how many fugitives that lad's 'not seen,' " said Canna.

"Or turned in," said Paks. "I know it was risky, Canna, but I couldn't see killing him—"

"Of course not. We're not the Honeycat. I daresay he thinks better of us for being irregular. He won't turn us in unless the price is right."

"If we're lucky, they'll try to bully him first," said Saben. "That one won't bully easily. Do you think we can stop at uncle's for anything?"

"No—" Canna began; Paks interrupted.

"It's our one chance to get food, Canna. He may not tell on us if we go, but he'll surely gossip if we don't. And we can go straight on from there, with a good start on the column."

Canna frowned. After a minute or so she said, "Well, it's worth trying, I suppose. If it works, we'll be much better off. But—they don't need to know how many of us there are. Only one will go—"

"Me!" said Paks and Saben together.

"No. Saben will. Paks, you and I will stay under cover. If there's trouble, Saben, yell out how many. If we can, we'll take them. Don't hesitate to walk out if you sense anything wrong."

They could see a line of trees ahead, and the gleam of water beyond. A thin stream of smoke bespoke a chimney. Canna and Paks melted into the hedge along one side of the hay meadow they were crossing, and Saben walked openly beside it to the cluster of shanties on the riverbank.

The largest building had two chimneys, one smoking, and two children playing in a wattle-fenced dooryard. As Saben neared the fence, the children looked up and yelled.

"Ma! Ma! A man!" The door to the shanty opened, and a tall fat woman peered out.

"Good day, mother," called Saben. Paks could not hear if she answered. "A lad I met in the wood said I might find somewhat to eat here, a deal cheaper than the Silver Pheasant, he said." The fat woman's head moved, as if she spoke, but again Paks could not hear. Canna nudged her and pointed; Paks saw a lean figure dart from one of the huts behind the larger one. Paks slipped her knife from its sheath.

"I'll watch Saben," said Canna in her ear. "You keep an eye out for more lurkers." For several minutes Paks saw nothing. She stole a glance at Saben, now lounging against the gate of the wattle fence. She looked back at the other huts. A flicker of movement: she'd missed seeing what or how many. Beyond the buildings, a narrow trail led westward into trees; it must go to the distant road. She glanced around the margin of the clearing, and caught a movement not ten yards to their left. A tall man in rough leathers, with a heavy bow, crept to the edge of the trees; he was watching Saben intently, his mouth agape. Paks nudged Canna, whose eyes widened. With infinite care she eased back, leaving Paks on guard, and made her way behind the bowman. Paks did not shift even her eyes, lest it call attention away from Saben.

"Ye might come in whilst ye're waitin'," called the woman from the shanty door.

"Thank you, mother, but no," said Saben casually. "I'm not fit to enter anyone's house. Another time, if if pleases you."

"Please yerself. We're not fine folk here," answered the woman. "The bread'll be out directly." Pak's mouth watered at that. "Ye'll be havin' a hard journey all alone," the woman went on.

"No one's lonely, going home," said Saben.

"Oh? Well, where's yer home, if I may be s'bold?"

"Far away, mother, and worse that I have to dodge all around, going as many as a cock picking straws—why, the woods be full of sergeants, and at this rate it'll be Little-eve before I see my sweetheart again." Paks had never suspected Saben of so much imagination.

"I only wondered, ye see, because ye wanted so

much—more than fer one fellow, even such a big 'un as ye be."

"Why, mother, wait till your little lads grow taller—my own family always said I ate more than any two grown men. They were glad enough to see me leave, for all I work as well as I eat."

"And will they welcome ye?"

"Aye. I told 'em the time, ye see, and she said she'd wait so long and no longer. So when they told me I must serve more months, well—I'm no deserter, mind, nor traitor—but I've served my years, as I count 'em, and I'll not lose my sweetling for any sergeant."

The woman cackled. This time her voice was warmer. "Ye're a fine one, I can tell. And ye've been savin' yer honey all this time, eh?"

"Well—" Saben sounded doubtful. "Depends what you mean. I've sweets for my sweetling, if you mean so."

"I'll say ye have." She cackled again and withdrew inside. Paks saw two figures leaving the back door of her shanty. One flattened against the wall facing her; he had a naked sword in hand. The other disappeared around the far side. Nothing moved for several minutes. Paks wondered where Canna was, and if the bowman had drawn his bow. Then the shanty door slammed open, and the fat woman emerged with a steaming sack.

"Here, ye are, lad—hot bread, a bit of cheese, and I threw in a leg or two of fowl—ah, thank ye, lad—" as Saben dropped coins into her hand. She passed the sack over the fence. Paks saw that the man on her side had bent double and moved along the wattle fence to the corner, where he crouched in readiness. "Now, lad," said the woman. "Give me a kiss for luck, and I'll be hopin' yer girl waits fer ye." She leaned over the fence, reaching out a huge red hand to Saben's face.

Saben had stepped back, out of reach. "No, mother," he said. " 'Twould not be respectful, and me so dirty as I am, but thank you all the same for your good wish."

He backed farther from the fence, and turned toward the trees.

"Dirty thief!" screeched the woman. "Robber! Liar! Help!" Saben swung around to face the two men who rushed him from either side of the dooryard.

"Now, mother, that was unkindly said," he called, swinging the sack to hold them off as he drew his dagger. Paks hurtled out of the trees, heedless, as a thrashing commotion broke out where the bowman had been. She hoped Canna could handle it. The swordsman nearest her spoiled his stroke at Saben as she surprised him. With an oath he turned on her; she faced a notched but broad-bladed longsword. The other man had a curved blade; neither had shields.

Paks jumped back out of range of a sweeping blow, then darted forward. The backstroke nearly caught her, but she ducked it. Again her opponent lifted the sword for a two-handed swipe. This time she waited until the stroke was committed, then pivoted in to grab his elbow and throw him sideways, stabbing under the armpit. He yelled and went to his knees. Paks jerked the sword out of his hand as he slumped to the ground, and spun to help Saben. He was backing slowly toward the river, parrying the strokes of the curved blade with his dagger. Paks hesitated a moment, but the fat woman waddled forward with a hefty slab of wood. Paks aimed a powerful slash at the man's back. He screamed and dropped his sword. Saben scooped it up as Paks turned to face the woman.

"Murderers!" she yelled. "Bandits! Robbers! I'll teach ye—" She broke off with a screech as Saben poked her back with his newly acquired weapon.

"Now, mother," he said politely. "Calm down and be quiet. We didn't start this, but I'm not loathe to finish it, if you'll have it so." The fat woman stood like a stump, chest heaving.

"Drop that," said Paks. The woman glared, but dropped her stick.

Saben grinned at Paks over the woman's shoulder.

"Well met, messmate. Perhaps I do want someone to travel with. Now, mother, you'll be wise to stand still, while this lady makes sure you have no more unpleasant surprises." Paks thought the woman might explode, she was so red in the face, but she said nothing. Paks backed away and looked around the clearing. Nothing that she could see. She ran her eye along the trees and caught a quick hand-signal. She said nothing, and brought her gaze slowly back to the shanty in front of them, then to the woman's face.

"Think I'll take a look inside," she said. The woman's face lighted, then twisted in a grimace of fear.

"No! Please—my babies—don't go in there. Ye've killed my man; don't hurt my babies—"

"Your babies won't be hurt if they don't hurt us. I daresay you've a houseful of stolen bits and pieces taken from honest travelers." Again Paks surprised a fleeting look of cunning and hope on the woman's face, followed by exaggerated fear. Saben quirked an eyebrow at Paks over the woman's shoulder, and Paks, moving toward the shanty, gave the hand signal for danger. She ducked behind the wattle fence, slid around the windowless end of the building, and came to the back door before the woman realized her intent. She shot another glance at Canna, who had moved to a position covering the back door. Paks took a deep breath and slammed the door open.

As she had hoped, the remaining defenders were in the front of the shanty, one to either side of the front door. She had entered the kitchen. Grabbing a poker from the fireplace, she met the faster of her opponents in the narrow opening between the two rooms. This was a gawky youth with a club. Paks caught his hand with the glowing tip of the poker and he screamed and dropped the club, stumbling back into a heavy older man armed with two daggers. He kicked the boy aside and came at Paks through the opening. With her long arms and weapons, Paks held him off easily, until he reversed one of the daggers and threw it. A burning

pain seared her left arm; she dropped the tip of the
poker. At once he rushed her, forcing her back against
the heavy table, and aiming a thrust at her face. Paks
rolled away and slashed at his legs with the sword. He
hopped out of reach, swearing, and turned to the fire for
a weapon of his own. Paks surged forward, and thrust
the long blade between his ribs before he could turn.
He gave a gurgling groan and sank to the floor.

Silence. Paks stood breathless, sides heaving and sweat
running down her face. She felt weak and shaky. The
cut on her left arm hurt more than she expected. She
wondered about the boy, and looked into the front
room. A crude ladder led to a loft, and she heard
rustling from above. Quickly she stepped to the back
door and caught Canna's glance; she signalled and looked
back into the kitchen. Flitches of bacon, hams, strings
of onions, fowl tied by the legs—all hung from a beam.
On a shelf by the fireplace were at least a dozen loaves
of dark bread. Paks stepped onto the table and cut
down a small ham, then took six loaves of bread and
wrapped her cloak around the lot. Then she returned to
Saben.

The fat woman was as pale now as she'd been red
before. Paks shot her a hard glance before opening the
sack Saben had dropped. Three soggy loaves, dipped
in boiling water to make them steam, a cheese that
stank when she opened the sack, a string of onions.
Paks held up the onions. "Fine drumsticks your fowl
have," she said. The woman did not answer. Paks turned
the bag inside out, filled it with the food she'd taken,
and looped the string closure. "I'm thinking you should
be quiet at home this day," she said. "All that yelling
might have given someone the wrong idea." Paks flipped
the woman's headscarf off her head and folded it. She
looked at Saben. "That bit of cord?"

"Good idea," he said. "My pouch." Paks held the
woman at sword point while Saben extracted the roll of
cord and bound her hands behind her. Then they pushed

her over to the shanty wall, forced her down, and tied her ankles as well. Paks gagged her with the headscarf.

"Her babies will free her soon enough," Paks murmured, "but we'll have a short lead."

"Time to head for home, I think," said Saben, with a last look around. They re-entered the trees and worked their way to the river. There they found a convenient rock and waited for Canna. Saben had taken a cut on the knuckles of his dagger hand, and sucked at the wound. When Canna came up beside them, she was carrying a big bow.

"Nice friendly folks, uncle's family," said Saben. "I'm keeping this blade, in case we meet more cousins."

Canna nodded. "At least we got food. But now we go straight in; it's our only chance."

"I'm sorry, Canna," said Paks. She remembered that she should have waited for a command before rushing out.

Canna shrugged. "It worked—worked well, but for leaving such a trail. What was in the house besides food?"

"Two," said Paks. "Boy with a club, and a man with two daggers. He threw one."

Canna looked at the cut. "We ought to wrap that; it's still bleeding." Paks had not noticed the blood still dripping off her elbow. "We'll take off mine; we don't want to leave a blood trail."

"We forgot to change yours yesterday," said Saben. "How is it?"

"Fine. It's healing fast. Hurry; we need to cross this river and be gone." When they got the bandage off Canna's shoulder, her wound was dry and pink. Canna wound a linen strip around Paks's arm and helped her up.

They had crossed the river before on an arched stone bridge, but that bridge was on the road. Now they looked at the cold gray water and shivered. Canna sighed. "No help for it. At least it's not wide." She led the way to the bank and they took another look. Upstream, to the left, it seemed it might be shallower. An overgrown but rutted opening into the trees on either side revealed a disused ford. They took off boots and socks, and waded out into the water. It was icy; Paks's feet began to ache almost at once. The water tugged at their ankles, then their knees. They were halfway across—two thirds—and at last they were climbing the far bank, shivering. They replaced their footgear, and Canna led them away from the river into the trees before she let them stop to eat.

They started by finishing the stale bread and meat Saben had found the first day, then ate a loaf from uncle's. Paks felt strength flowing back into her; she noticed that Canna and Saben looked less pinched.

"Now," said Canna, as they finished, washing down the last crumbs, "straight south as fast as we can. If that woman sets the Honeycat on us, he'll send horses. We stay away from everyone, fill the flasks at every stream, and move."

For the rest of that day they walked steadily southward, taking care not to cross open fields where they could be seen from a distance. They drank as they marched, and stopped only once before nightfall to eat generous wedges of ham and bread. Although they crossed several narrow lanes, they saw no one but distant farmers. They could not tell if they had seen them.

By nightfall they were far south of the slower moving column, Canna was sure. They had not seen anything of a mounted pursuit, and she told them she thought they might be clear. They sheltered in a thicket for a hearty meal.

"I think we may make it," said Canna, looking truly cheerful for the first time. "But we must go on. We can see to walk in the starlight, and the more ground between us and them, the better. We might make Rotengre by the day after tomorrow, if we're lucky." Paks was stiff and sore, but able to manage another hour or so of travel. The next day they were up at first light. Again

Canna served out a husky portion of food, and they set off at a brisk walk. Paks kept a nervous eye over her shoulder for the first hour or so, but saw nothing.

In early afternoon, they saw ahead of them a large forested rise, and remembered the forest near Rotengre. They pushed on as fast as they could, hoping to be well into the trees by nightfall; these last few hours the land behind them had been open, with scanty hedges. Again and again they had to cross open ground, all too visible if the wrong eyes were looking.

Thicker than the little woodlots they'd been in for the past few days, here the trees were tall, with leaves just falling from elm and oak and hornbeam. Scattered clumps of evergreens made gloomy shadows within the forest shade. The ground was more broken, with outcrops of pitted gray rock as they climbed away from the farmland. Canna took a long look at the angle of the sun before they lost sight of it. It would be hard to keep a straight course in the forest.

It was also, they found, impossible to keep going as late. Trees dimmed the starlight; they stumbled into rocks and hollows. Finally they stopped in a clump of cedar. They ate another loaf of bread, and thick slices of ham. If they reached the Duke the next day, or even the one after, they need not worry about food. Paks took first watch, a silent space of darkness in which nothing happened, and went to sleep feeling sure that the next night would see them safely warm around the campfire of the Company.

She woke to a thin cold rain falling out of thick clouds. Canna looked gloomier than the weather. "We can't find our way in this," she said. "We need the sun for directions. Unless you have another trick, Paks—"

Paks shook her head. "No. All I know about this forest is that it's big, and the farmers near Rotengre said it was full of brigands."

"That's all we need," said Saben. "Brigands. Brrr, it's cold. And wet. We can't sit here and do nothing, Canna. We'll have to find our directions somehow."

Canna spread her hands. "And if we get lost? We could get farther from Rotengre than we are now, if we wander around."

They ate an ample but damp breakfast, huddling under their cloaks. Paks looked back the way they'd come, seeing nothing but rain-wet trees. Any brigands, she thought, would be holed up in a dry cave or fort. She shifted restlessly and a trickle of icy water ran down her back. She looked at the others. Saben, for the first time, looked sulky. Canna was staring glumly at the ground.

"Could we—" she began slowly. Canna looked up. "Could we try to find the road again and follow that? We must be far ahead of the column, and the wagons will slow in this wet. Or if you think we can't find the road by cutting through the forest, we could backtrack to the edge and go that way."

Saben smiled at her. "Good idea. Canna, we can do that, can't we?"

"I suppose. I still worry about getting lost, and if we backtrack, we'll be closer to Siniava."

"If we stay here, he's coming closer to us. At least that gives us a chance—and they can't see far in the rain."

"True. I'd be glad to be moving, myself—the Duke needs to know." Canna looked around. "Let me think. The road was off to our right, and we were headed that way—I remember that holly tree. I think we should go this way—" she pointed. "Do you agree, Paks?"

"Yes." Paks rose, and the others followed her.

The sopping undergrowth slapped against their legs; they were soon much wetter, though warmer for the walking. Rain fell out of the sky with quiet intensity: never hard enough to force a halt, but never stopping. Paks thought of her first long march, the wet days on the road south of Vérella. She glanced at Saben, wondering if he remembered; his face was thoughtful and remote.

After some time, they saw that the ground was rising

in a rocky hummock. They paused to consider which way to take. Paks was not tempted to suggest a trip to the top of it.

"If we bear right," said Canna, "we'll come to the road sooner, but closer to the column. If we bear left, we could swing too far from the road."

"Let's toss," said Saben. He pulled a copper from his pouch.

Canna took the coin and tossed it. "St. Gird, guide our way," she said as it spun over and over. Paks caught it and slapped it on her arm.

"Shears, we go right," said Saben. She uncovered it, and the shears of Sorellin were uppermost.

"Right it is," she said.

Circling the hill led them back sharply right at first, but after awhile Paks felt they were back to their original heading. She wondered how close the road was; her stomach clenched in anticipation. What if the column was already there? She looked at Canna. Canna's face was set and grim. At last they came to a gap in the trees. This time Canna moved forward while the others waited. When she came back, she was grinning.

"It's the road. And it's muddy, so they'll be slowed down."

"Are you sure it's the right road?" asked Paks.

"Yes—that's the best part. Remember that place where a pine on the bank had been struck by lightning, and a bush was growing out of the dead limb? There couldn't be two such, just alike. This must be the right road. We've a long march in this weather, but at least we can't get lost. I think—I really think we're going to make it. By Holy Gird, I think we are. Let's go."

It was now nearly noon; they ate as they marched, moving back from the road, but keeping it in sight. They stretched their legs, making the best time possible. Canna was smiling, and Saben hummed softly, his stolen blade bouncing slightly where he'd tied it atop the pack. With every stride Paks felt safer from the menace behind; she let herself think of hot food, a dry

bed, clean clothes. The hill they had circled fell away
behind them; other hummocks rose ahead. Still they
kept the rhythm of their strides, not stumbling now or
weary, with their goal so close.

Chapter Eighteen

They missed the armed band until they were face to face. Eight heavily armed brigands in scale and chain mail, with good swords at their sides, seemed to spring from the trees to surround them. Two had shields. Paks clawed for the blade slung over her shoulder. Canna had no time to string the bow; she was grabbed from behind and wrestled to the ground. Paks found herself facing three men, who circled to get behind her. Her longsword gave her a better chance than Saben's curved one, but not much. She backed a step, glancing around. Canna was heaving and pitching under two of the man, and Saben fenced frantically with three opponents. She parried thrusts of two blades at once, and dodged the third. One man tried to get behind her again; she backed quickly, unable even to look behind.

Paks heard a hoarse cry from Saben, then Canna: "By St. Girxd!" Again she retreated, and again. Canna yelled, "Paks! Run! Run for it!" just as Paks backed another step and the ground gave way beneath her. She tucked her head and tried to roll as she tumbled down a high

bank of earth and leaves into a shallow stream. Above
her was a roar of laughter, voices, and the squelch of
wet leaves as someone started to follow her down. She
forced herself up, stumbling on a loose stone, and fell
again. But her vision had cleared, and she saw the
single pursuer, picking his way carefully down the slope.
He was only halfway, and testing his footholds.

Paks gathered her legs under her, then realized she
had dropped the sword in her fall. No wonder he wasn't
in a hurry. Then she remembered Canna's words. She
looked around; above her, the ruffian chuckled at her
evident fright. That way, she decided, upstream. Taking two quick breaths, she hurled herself into a run
along the creek bed. The brigand shouted and threw
his sword at her; it missed by a foot, but she did not
stop to grab it. Behind her came other shouts. She ran
as fast as she could, watching her footing. After fifty
yards or so, the creek banks were not so steep, and she
scrambled up the south bank and set off through the
woods. She heard arrows thunking into the trees around
her, but none touched her.

After the first frantic spurt, she settled into a steady
run, wondering if the brigands had horses. She was not
sure of her direction. Darkness closed in around her.
She slowed to a jog after several falls, but kept going.
She could not stop. She swung right, back toward the
road. When she could not run any more, she slowed to
a walk, gulping for air. Wet ferns whipped her legs;
vines tripped her. Somewhere she lost her cloak, and
she was wet through. Keep moving, she thought. Keep
going.

When she came to the road at last, it surprised her.
For a moment she could not think what it was, or why
she had wanted to find it. The rain had stopped; the
road was just visible against the solid dark of the trees.
Paks turned and walked beside it, just out of the mud.
She got her breath back, and began running again.
Canna's cry rang in her head. And Saben. What had

happened to Saben? She found herself running faster, and sobbing as she ran.

After some time she realized she was no longer running beside trees: the forest was behind her. She stumbled into a brimming ditch beside the road, and scrambled out on the wrong side. It didn't matter; she settled back to a jog and went on. The fields were soft with rain; she staggered when she hit the deeper mud of plowland. Her thighs ached. She slowed to a walk; the night grew lighter. She hoped for dawn, but looked up to see the clouds blowing away and stars shining between them.

At last she saw the twinkling watchfires ahead. She forced herself into a run again, terrified that something, even now, would come upon her before she reached the Duke. By the time she hit the outer guard perimeter, she was staggering with weariness.

"Halt!" came a shout from before her. Paks stopped and stood, swaying slightly as she gasped for breath. She heard the squelch of footsteps approaching. "Who's there?" demanded the guard. "Give the password."

She could not recall what the password had been weeks ago when they left for Dwarfwatch; surely it had changed by now. Besides, she had no breath for speech. A hard hand gripped her arm and shook her.

"Speak up, there. Who are you?"

"Duke Phelan's Company," she managed. "Must see the Duke."

"At this time of night? Sober up, soldier—what'd you do, go off on a tear and get lost?" Someone brought a torch near; she could see the polished armor of the guard who held her. "Tir's gut, you're a disgrace," he said disgustedly. "Duke Phelan's Company—I don't believe that. His people don't wallow in filth."

"Is that a bandage, Sim, on the left arm?" asked another voice.

"Who can tell?" grumbled the first. "Are you hurt?" he bawled at Paks.

"Just a cut," she said. Her voice shook. "Please—I must get to the Duke now—it's important."

"You've missed rollcall, if that's what you mean," said the first guard. "That was hours ago. They won't thank you for showing up now."

"Well, but Sim—we don't want this mess in our area, either. Let the Phelani take care of it, if it's theirs."

"I don't know what it is—d'you think that was ever his uniform?"

"It might have been. We'll be in trouble if it is, and we don't—"

"All right, all right. You take it—her—over then, if it concerns you so. Tir's bones, I hate to be seen near such a ragbag. If it is the Duke's, I don't know what he's coming to."

"Please," said Paks. Her legs were trembling under her, and she was afraid she might faint. "Please, we must hurry. It is important, and the Duke must know—"

The second guard grabbed her arm and swung her ahead of him. "Don't tell me what I 'must' not when I don't know who in thunder you are. We'll go, but at my pace."

Paks found even that hard to sustain as they headed their way between tents toward the Duke's perimeter. At last they were challenged by a voice she knew. She started forward, but the guard pulled her back. "Not so fast," he said. He raised his voice. "It's me, Arvor of the Sorellin militia, with someone who claims to be one of yours. Came in on our north perimeter, dirty as a miner and no good tale to tell."

"Let's see, then." It was Barranyi holding a torch. "Who are you?"

"P-Paks," she stammered. "Barra, I've got to see the Duke. Now."

Barranyi held the torch closer. "Paks? Tir's bones, it is you! But you were with—" she flicked a glance at the Sorellin guard.

"Well now," he said. "Seeing as you know her, I suppose it's all right—"

"Yes, Arvor—thanks—" said Barranyi in a rush. "Paks. Come on. What happened?"

Paks heard the guard leave, and tried to muster her thoughts. "C-call the sergeant, Barra. I must see the Duke tonight. I—I can't explain to anyone but the Duke."

"This late? He's long abed; you can't see him now. Why do you—you're wet through!" She took Paks by the arm; Paks winced. "What's this—a wound?" Paks nodded, suddenly too tired to speak. "You might trust *me*," said Barranyi, her voice sharpening. "We trained together, after all." She paused but Paks said nothing. "Very well, then; I'll take you, but—"

"Sorry," murmured Paks. "Can—can I sit down?"

"Wait. Malek!" she called back toward camp.

"Yo."

"Mal, take over here; I have to take someone to the sergeant."

"Sure thing."

"Come on, Paks. Sergeant Vossik is by the fire; you need to warm up, I'll warrant." Paks followed Barra's stiff back to a fire some yards away. She was shivering hard now, and stumbled repeatedly. She barely heard what Barra said about her. Vossik's voice seemed to come from a great distance, and she had to puzzle out the meaning of his words before she could answer.

"But did you break your parole?" he insisted.

"She must have come all that way afoot," said another voice.

"But why? Paks, tell us—"

"The Duke—" she said again. She felt herself sagging, heard a gasp from Barra, then a grunt as Barra caught her and eased her down. Her eyes closed in spite of herself. "The Duke," she repeated. "Must see the Duke."

"She's wet through and cold," said Vossik. "Not making sense. Get warm blankets, Barra. Seli, fetch a pot of sib."

Paks tried to struggle up again; Vossik held her shoulders. "Please," she said. "Please, sir—take me to the Duke. He has to know—right away."

"Know what? And we'll get you warm and dry before we—"

Paks shook her head and tried to free herself. "No—sir—must know *now*." She felt tears burn her eyes.

"Know *what*? If it's important, tell me—"

"Honeycat," said Paks. "Tell the Duke—"

"What!" Vossik lowered his voice after the first bellow. "What about the Honeycat? Is that your message? Have you seen—?"

"Tell the Duke," repeated Paks. She felt herself hauled to her feet.

"All right," said Vossik grimly. "For that you'll see the Duke. If this is some game, Paks—"

"No, sir. Im-important." She shivered violently as Vossik supported her. He wrapped his dry cloak around her and called someone to help as he took her to the Duke's tent.

The sentries there were reluctant, but Vossik overrode them. "Either you call him now, or I'll raise a shout that'll have half the camp up." One of them ducked inside. The others stared curiously at Paks. A light flared inside the tent; dark shapes moved against the lighted walls. The sentry reappeared at the door and took up his post. One of the Duke's servants peered out the opening. "He says come in," said the man softly. Vossik pushed Paks forward into the tent's main room. Another servant was lighting oil lamps around the room, but there was already enough light to see the Duke standing by his work table with a fur-lined robe thrown about his shoulders. His hair was rumpled, and his eyes were cold.

"This had better be important, Vossik. Have you a good reason not to go through your captain?"

"Yes, my lord, I believe so." Vossik cleared his throat. "This is Paks, my lord, of Ferrault's cohort. She insisted she had to speak to you at once—and sir, she mentioned the Honeycat."

The Duke crossed the room in two strides to stare closely at Paks. "Honeycat! What do you know about the Honeycat? Why did you leave the fort? What's happened?"

Paks tried to focus on his face. "Sir—my lord Duke—he's coming. On the road. He has—he has a large force, sir, and—"

"Did Ferrault send you?" asked the Duke abruptly.

"No, sir. He—he's been taken, I think."

"Taken! Who? Not the Honeycat; the Halverics wouldn't turn prisoners over to him."

"Sir, they took—took the—we think they took the fort. They killed the Halverics, and took prisoners, and—"

"The Honeycat? How do you know? Did you see it? Did you escape?" Paks tried to nod, but felt herself starting to fall.

"Sir, we—we weren't taken—we saw—" She could not get the words out. Her legs were limp. Vossik let her down gently on the carpets that overlay the tent floor. She heard the voices above her, but could not muster the energy to answer.

"Is she wounded?" asked the Duke.

"I don't know, my lord. I know she's wet and cold and filthy, but when she said Honeycat, I brought her straight to you."

"Very well. Vossik, I want you to send the captains here at once."

"Yes, my lord."

"And alert the perimeter, but don't say why. And send the surgeon, and tell the cooks I want something hot at once."

"Yes, my lord."

"You may go."

Paks was hardly aware of it when the Duke's servants stripped off her wet and filthy tunic and wrapped her in warm furs. She roused, coughing, only when the surgeon spooned a bit of fiery liquid into her mouth.

"I hate to do this," the Duke was saying, "but we

must know what message she brings. Can you tell how badly she's hurt?"

Paks opened her eyes and tried to focus on the surgeon. He pressed a mug to her lips and she swallowed. Whatever it was, it sent warm currents through her cold arms and legs, and cleared the fog from her head.

"Exhaustion, mostly," said the surgeon. "Maybe a broken rib or two, and this cut—sword or knife wound, but not bad. Bruises and scrapes; I'd say she's fallen many times in the last day or so. She needs sleep, my lord, as soon as may be." He met Paks's eyes. "Better now? Drink the rest."

Paks swallowed again, and then again. He took the mug away and offered another, of steaming sib. When she had drunk half of that, she turned her head to see the room around her. The Duke was dressed in his usual mail, as were the captains with him.

"There, my lord," said the surgeon. "She'll be able to talk with you a short while; I hope it's enough."

"If not, we'll dose her again."

"My lord, that would be most unwise. She will need to sleep—"

"You may go," said the Duke. "And leave that stuff here."

"But my lord—"

"I've no more wish than you to harm a good soldier, Master Visanior, but I must know her message. You may go."

Paks felt the surface under her shift as the surgeon stood, and realized that she lay in a bed. The Duke's face replaced the surgeon's.

"Now, Paks," he began. "You were in the fort when the Halverics came. Your name is on the roll I received for ransom. What happened: did you break your parole?"

Paks shook her head. When she tried to speak, the words came easily. "No, my lord. We were waiting to be ransomed—most of the Halverics had left, and they let us outside a lot. We were gathering berries one day when strange troops came up the road—many of them—

and the Halveric captain rode out to meet them. Then he fell from his horse, and they started chasing those outside the walls—"

"Except you?"

"As far as I know, my lord. We—"

"Who—how many?"

"Three of us, sir. Saben and Canna and I. We were in tall brambles, and they didn't see us. We made it into the woods, and—"

"What about the fort?"

"They attacked it, sir, but the Halverics dropped the portcullis—we heard that—and we saw our men on the wall as well as theirs. So we started south to tell you—"

"You came all the way from the fort?" Paks nodded. "On foot?"

"Yes, my lord."

"How long were you? When did the attack happen?"

Paks tried to count back. "Sir, we were—seven days, coming. It was the afternoon before we started that they came."

"Were you on the road all the way?"

"No, sir; we weren't on the road at all. They had patrols, and we were nearly caught the first day, so Canna said to stay off the road, as far as we could and not get lost."

"Where is the Honeycat now?"

"I—don't know, sir. They were on the road—we watched them past the crossroads to be sure, and then we came ahead. We had—had trouble." Paks shivered at the memory of uncle's place.

"I daresay." The Duke sighed, and looked up. "Well, captains, we have trouble ahead of us, too. If he's come to relieve the siege, he'll hit the lines somewhere, and we'd best find out where." He turned back to Paks. "Where are the others, Paks? Were they killed?"

Paks had forgotten Canna and Saben in her anxiety to see the Duke. Now the memory of their last encounter returned full force. Her eyes widened. "Sir! The brigands! They attacked us in the forest, and—and Saben and Canna—I don't know what happened. Canna said to run—I had to leave them. I had to get to you, my lord, but I didn't mean to leave them to—"

"Shh. That's all right. We don't think that of you. You did well."

"But sir, you must find them—they need help—" Paks felt her strength and awareness slipping away again. She wanted to get up and find Saben and Canna, she wanted to chase the Honeycat, she wanted—she fell into sleep as dreamless as a cave.

She woke again in broad daylight, hearing voices from the next room. For awhile she lay with her eyes closed, listening idly.

"I don't want guesses, Jori; I want facts." That was the Duke, and he sounded angry.

"No, sir. But the scouts haven't found anything else."

"They'd better. Jori, go back to the Sorellin—no, wait. Take this to Vladi—"

"Sir, the Count?"

"Yes. Don't look like that, just do it. It's around the far side; take a fast horse. Wait for an answer. I'll go to the Sorellin commander myself. Go on, now."

A much younger voice. "If only they hadn't been so careless in the forest."

The Duke snorted. "What is it, Jostin, did you expect me to scold her for that?"

"Well, my lord, you've always said to us—"

"Lad, some mistakes carry their own punishment. And consider what they did—I doubt any of you squires could make such a journey. After all that, you don't scold like an old granny for things they couldn't help."

"But they should have been watching—"

The Duke's voice hardened. "When you've done as much, squire, you may offer criticism. For now, you may ready my mount. Go."

Paks opened her eyes. She was in the tent, in a small curtained room, wrapped in soft furs on a bed. Slumped on a stool nearby was a servant, who jumped up when he met her eyes.

"Are you awake? Can you speak?"

Paks yawned, swallowed, and managed to say yes.

"My lord Duke," called the servant. "She's awake." He offered Paks a mug of sib. She was warm and comfortable as long as she held still, but when she tried to lift her legs, she ached in every muscle. The Duke pushed through the curtains between the rooms.

"Paks, I know you need more sleep, but I need more information. Sim will bring you something to eat, while you answer my questions."

Paks tried to push herself up in the bed, but failed. "Yes, my lord."

"Good. Now, this force you reported—the colors were black and yellow, you said. Any other reason for thinking it was the Honeycat?"

"Yes, my lord. That first day we overheard one of the mounted men; he called his commander Lord Siniava. Canna said that was the same."

"Yes. It is. You said he took prisoners—do you know where they are?"

"With the column, sir. I don't know about the fort, but the ones outside are with the column."

"Just our men?"

"No, sir. Some Halverics, too. But he killed those who tried to run or fight."

"Just a moment; I want someone else to hear this." The Duke stepped to the curtain and returned with a man in dark green that looked like the Halveric uniform. "Cal, you'll need to hear this for yourself. Go on, Paks."

Paks looked curiously at the man before turning back to the Duke. She was not sure what he wanted to hear.

"Tell us again what happened when the Honeycat's force reached the fort: what did the Halverics do, and what did our men do?"

"Yes, sir. I think almost half our men and the Halverics were outside the gates. When the column was sighted,

the Halverics' horn blew. Then a man rode out of the
fort—we thought it was the Halveric captain. He seemed
to be talking to someone at the head of the column—"

"Had it halted?"

"Yes, my lord. Then he backed his horse a length or
so, and raised his arm, and fell from his horse. We
thought he'd been shot; they had bowmen."

The man in green stood abruptly, face pale. "Seli!
No!"

Duke Phelan shot him a glance. "Who—?"

"My lord, he—my brother Seliam—you wouldn't remember him. Seli dead, and by treachery!"

"Cal, I'm sorry. I do remember—a little lad of six or
so, perched on your father's saddle."

The other man turned his head aside. His voice
shook. "My lord, it—it was his first command." Suddenly he was at the bedside, hand fisted in the sleeping
furs at Paks's throat. "Are you sure it was Seliam? How
do you—?"

Duke Phelan reached out and removed the hand.
"Let be, Cal. 'Tis not her fault." The younger man
turned away, shoulders hunched. "You thought it was
the captain, Paks. Why?"

Paks was frightened. "He—he wore a cloak of gold at
the shoulders, my lord; it glittered. And he rode a
dapple gray with a black tail."

"It must be so," whispered the other man. "Sir, I
must go at once. By your leave—"

"Wait. You may need to know more of this."

"I know enough. Seli dead, my men prisoners, others
sieged—"

"No. Stay and hear. Not for long, Cal." The Duke
and the other matched gazes; the young man's eyes fell
first.

"Very well, my lord Duke, since you insist."

"Go on, Paks. After the captain fell, what then?"

"Then the Honeycat's men moved in squads, rounding
up those who were outside. Some of the Halverics
fought, and tried to get back to the fort or protect our

men, but they were outnumbered. Some of ours tried to escape, but we saw them fall. Then we heard the portcullis go down, and after a bit we saw ours on the walls along with the Halverics."

"Where was Captain Ferrault?"

Paks thought back. "I think, my lord—he was inside."

The Duke grunted. "And you don't know how big a force the Honeycat left at the fort?"

"No, sir. We thought of trying to sneak back and find out, but Canna had been hit. She said we should shadow the main column and come to you."

"Canna was hurt? I thought you said you weren't seen."

"We weren't, my lord, not then. But their first sweep around the fort, they shot into the brambles to scare anyone out. It was bad luck she was hit; they couldn't see us."

"I see. Now—you're sure that some of the prisoners were taken with the column?"

"Yes, sir. We couldn't see it often, because of the sweeps, but on—it must have been the third day—Canna and Saben got a clear look. They said sixty or more prisoners, both ours and the Halverics."

"And how many enemy?"

"Something over three hundred foot, and a hundred horse, and ten wagons." The Duke turned to look at the man in green. Paks watched their faces, trying to understand why the man looked so familiar—had he been at Dwarfwatch with the Halverics? Suddenly she realized that, though taller and not bald, he looked like Aliam Halveric. She looked more closely. His well-worn sword belt was tooled in a floral pattern; his cloak was fastened with an ornate silver pin. If he was a Halveric son, and the captain killed at Dwarfwatch his brother—she shivered.

"Now," said the Duke, "What time yesterday did you meet the brigands?"

"Afternoon, sir, and starting to get dark."

"And when did you last see the Honeycat's column?"

Paks thought, counting the days. "The—the fourth
day, sir. They had passed the Guild League road; there's
a village just south, and they burned it. Then we passed
the column, the next day, and that was the fourth after
we started."

"How fast were they traveling?"

"Sir, I—I don't know. Canna said when we were
three days from here that it would take them five—but
that was before the rain."

"Yes. With rain—those wagons should be slowed—
Cal, tell you father this. I'm leaving today, with the
Company, to see if I can catch them on the road. After
that, I'll go north. I'll do what I can to save his men; I'll
expect to meet him soon. I can't offer you much escort—"

"Sir, I'll be fine."

"Cal, the Honeycat is infinitely devious. Let me send
my youngest squire, at least: he's brave, if pigheaded."

"Sir, I thank you, but my own escort will suffice."

"Be careful, then. And Cal—be fast."

"I'll kill every horse I own, if I must. May I go?"

"Yes. Luck go with you." The young Halveric bowed
and withdrew. The Duke looked at Paks; she was drinking a mug of soup the servant had brought in. She
started to put it down when she saw him looking. "No,"
he said kindly. "Go on and finish it; you need that.
Paks, the first scouts I sent out last night have come
back; they found no trace of your friends or the brigands. I'm not sure they went far enough; I had told
them to be back an hour after sunrise. We'll keep
searching, you may be sure. As for you—" he sighed,
and sipped from the mug the servant had handed him.
"You heard me tell Cal I'm leading the Company out.
If we're lucky, we'll catch him on the road, unprepared.
You're not fit for this—" Paks opened her mouth to
protest, and he waved her to silence. "No. Don't argue.
You'll stay here. One of my scribes will take down
everything you recall—no matter how unimportant—
about your journey and the Honeycat. You will not talk

to anyone else about it until I give you leave. Not even the surgeon. Is that clear?"

Paks nodded. "Yes, my lord. But sir, I could—"

"No. You've had less than half the sleep you need; I'm not risking my only source of information. When the surgeon passes you as fit for duty, there'll be plenty for you to do." The Duke's sudden smile held no humor; Paks shivered. "Now. What can you tell me about their order of march, and the scouts?"

Paks explained the forward and flank sweeps as well as she could. The Duke nodded, and stood. "Very well. Remember that if anyone other than my scribe Arric tries to ask questions, you'll have a lapse of memory."

"Yes, my lord." Paks felt a wave of sleepiness rise over her. She hardly knew when the Duke left, and she slept heavily several hours. The tent was very quiet when she woke, and she fell asleep again quickly. The next time she awoke, the lamps were lit, and the surgeon was beside the bed, calling her name.

"It's partly the stimulant you were given," he explained when Paks asked why she was so sleepy. "That and the exhaustion from your journey. If you didn't sleep now—well, you must. Try to eat all Sim brings, and sleep again."

Paks had trouble working her way through the large bowl of stew and half-loaf of bread. Even swallowing was an effort. She sat up briefly, but sleep overwhelmed her again. She woke in early morning feeling much better. When she asked for clothes to put on, Sim told her she was to stay in bed.

"You'll be getting clothes when the surgeon says you can get up and not before. That's the Duke's orders, so it's no good looking at me." He left her to her meal, and Paks looked around the room. It had not registered before that she was in the Duke's tent—she noticed a carved chest bound with polished metal, a three-legged stool with a tooled leather seat, the rich sleeping furs she lay under—in the Duke's own chamber. She finished breakfast. When Sim came to take the dishes,

Arric the scribe arrived, a slender man of medium height whom Paks had often seen in the quartermaster's tents.

When he had readied his writing materials, she began to tell her story again. Arric was accustomed to the halting accounts of inexperienced soldiers, and prompted her with pointed questions when she faltered. Paks was surprised when Sim arrived with lunch for them both. After lunch they began again. Paks was beginning to tire when the surgeon came to check on her. He drove Arric off, and Paks slept for several hours. She woke with a huge appetite, ate everything Sim brought—and greeted the surgeon with a demand to be let out of bed.

"Being hungry's a good sign," he told her. "You'll come back fast now. I'll have Sim bring more food in an hour. Work with Arric a few hours tonight, and you may be able to get up tomorrow. I'll check on you before breakfast."

Paks devoured her second supper eagerly, and answered Arric's questions as fast as she could. She dared not ask if they had had word from the Duke; she thought she heard more noises in camp, and was determined to be ready if he called. She was sure she would not sleep, when Arric finally left, and thought of trying to sneak out of bed and find clothes. The bed was warm, though—and the surgeon woke her as he came in the next morning.

He had brought a bundle of clothes, as if certain she would be well enough. Everything was new, from boots to cloak. She said nothing while he looked her over. He sighed.

"It's too early, really, but you'll be well enough if you don't exhaust yourself again. Eat more than usual for several weeks, and rest when you can. Your wounds are healing cleanly, no trouble there. Dress and come out front."

When she came through the curtain, the Duke was standing in the tent entrance, talking to someone outside. The surgeon stood frowning by the work table.

"Ah, Paks," said the Duke, as he turned and saw her. "You're better, I see. Ready to ride?" The surgeon grunted, but Paks grinned.

"Yes, my lord. When?"

"At once. We ride north, to the fort; I expect to meet the Halverics there." He moved toward the table, and sat, looking up at Paks. "We hit the Honeycat on the road, with Vladi's spears and Clart Cavalry to help. He and his captains escaped, but the rest didn't."

"And our men, my lord? The prisoners?"

The Duke frowned. "Most of 'em had been killed. We saved some—by Tir, that devil-worshipper has earned a beating—I've heard how the others died." He looked so stern that Paks dared not ask who lived. "Get some food for yourself, and a sword; we'll have to catch up with the rest on the road."

Paks left the tent to find the camp almost deserted. She got sword and scabbard from the quartermaster, and filled saddlebags with food at the cooktent. Rassamir, one of the Duke's senior squires, beckoned her from the horse lines.

"Here—I've saddled for you, and you'll lead a spare. Are you ready?"

"Yes, sir." Paks slung the saddlebags over and fastened them.

"Fine. Mount and wait here." He swung himself onto a rangy bay, and took up the leadline of one of the Duke's chargers. Paks mounted, wincing at her painful ribs. One of the horseboys handed up the lead rope for a horse much like her own sturdy mount. In a few minutes the Duke and Rassamir rode up beside her; each took another horse to lead.

"If you start feeling bad, Paks," said the Duke seriously, "I want you to drop back with the wounded that'll be coming in from yesterday's battle. You won't help us any if you can't fight when we reach Dwarfwatch. The surgeon thinks you shouldn't go, but—"

"I'm fine, my lord. I'll be all right."

He smiled. "I thought you'd say that. Just remember:

you've already served me and the Company well; I won't think less of you if you can't ride and fight so soon." Paks nodded, but she was determined to find out what had happened to her friends. She knew she would make it to the fort, surgeon or no surgeon.

The surgeon, in fact, was riding north too. "Arbola's coming back with the wounded," he said. "He won't be able to catch up. You'll have plenty of work for Simmitt and me both." The Duke merely nodded and they set off.

Chapter Nineteen

Their return to the north was swift and direct. Mounted, with no pack train, they made the northern crossroad in two days. A fast unit of Clart Cavalry had rounded up the "huntsmen" camped on the hill over the crossroad; they thought no warning had been passed on. The Duke, Paks knew, hoped the Halverics were coming from the east, but they might be a day or so away. She wondered if he would wait for them.

That night she woke to the clatter of a single galloping horse, and slept again when no alarm sounded. They moved at dawn. Paks and the others who had been north before were assigned the forward and flank sweeps. Now it was her turn to ride through the cold woods, looking for enemy strays. For the first hour, they moved at a brisk trot. Paks found herself reaching for her sword again and again. Not yet, she told herself. After that, they slowed to a walk. Paks looked for the farmers' clearing. When it finally opened on her left, she felt a cold thrill down her back. Close. She waved the forward group to a halt, and looked over the clearing. The Duke rode up to them.

"Trouble?"

"No, my lord," said Paks. "But we're close now, and I know they came out this far. Do you want us to leave the road here?"

"No. Riders off the road mean trouble. Let them think we're friendly—or at least neutral—if they hear the horses. With the wind north, they shouldn't. How far to the last cover?"

Paks thought a moment. "I'm not sure, my lord, but there's a ridge just before the trees end, and a double curve in the road."

"If they've gotten sloppy, we might make the edge before they notice. I'll ride with you, Paks, and you point out that ridge." He turned to his captains. "I want the Clarts ready to split into two columns, just as we did before; I expect a force near the gate. Archers next; they've got crossbows. I want the swords and spears dismounted this time, and in the usual formation. If our friends are alive, and can make a sally, so much the better. After the first shock, unless things change, Clarts hit cavalry first, then sweep up and harry stragglers. There's a small chance still that we could meet them on the road—remember our plans, if we do." They nodded. "Very well. Let's go." He wheeled his horse and started up the road. Paks legged her horse up beside him, and the column followed.

That last stretch seemed the longest. Paks felt her heart hammering in her chest. A sour taste came into her mouth. Her horse began to jig and toss its head. She thought about what they might find. Perhaps the Honeycat's men had already taken the fort—killed the defenders—gone away. Or they held the fort—or the defenders had killed them at last— Ahead the road swung left to climb a steeper ridge. Paks recognized it, and waved to the Duke. At his signal, the rest halted while he, Paks, his squires, and two others rode ahead. They reached the ridgetop; Paks reached for her sword, but the Duke gestured: no.

Here the road swung right; through the wind-torn

foliage they could see the open meadows below. The Duke sent one man back to bring up the column. A cold wind out of the northwest roared through the trees; Paks felt her skin stiffen under it, and never heard the column come up behind her. The Clart riders had lances in hand, tossing and twirling them; the leaders grinned as they rode up. Behind them, the Duke's men were grim-faced. Paks could see nothing of Vladi's spears but the tips bristling above the riders between.

The captains came forward, and all shook hands with the Duke and each other. The Duke gestured to the standard bearers, and they unrolled the banners: his own maroon and white, with the crest of Tsaia and the fox mask; Clart Company's white horse on rose, under a spear; Vladi's black and silver, the mailed fist over the eastern rune for ice. The Duke beckoned to Paks, and she moved her horse near him.

"When we break cover," he said, "shift left at once, and let the Clarts through. Then drop back to Dorrin's cohort."

"Yes, sir." Paks found it hard to speak; her throat was tight.

"It's only a few hundred yards, right?"

"Let's go." He lifted his reins and his horse moved forward. Paks saw his hand rise to his forehead; his visor dropped in place. Without checking his horse, he drew his sword. Paks glanced at his squires; they rode on either side, swords ready, grim-faced. She looked at the road ahead. Somewhere they must have sentries. A horn cry rang out to one side of the road. There, she thought. She heard a faint shout from somewhere ahead.

"Now!" yelled the Duke, and spurred to a gallop. Behind her, the Clart riders began their shrill battle cry, and the road erupted in a thunder of hooves. Paks leaned forward, her horse fighting for its head with the excitement of running horses before and behind. She edged to the left of the road. She was sure the Clarts were riding up her backbone. She could see the end of

the trees, the open slope down to the river, the river
itself. They were out. She yanked her horse to the left,
and a stream of rose-clad riders poured past. She fought
her mount to a bouncing trot, waiting for the archers to
pass. Scattered small groups of black and yellow dotted
the meadow; a larger cluster lay against the gate of the
fort. The fort itself—she squinted to see the banners
flying from the tower. Green and gold, the Halverics,
and below, the Duke's maroon and white. From the
walls came a high, musical bugling. She looked back at
the column for Dorrin or Sejek, and swung her horse
into formation as they plunged down the road to the
bridge.

There were bodies now along the way, one and two
together, some with lance wounds, others sprouting arrows. Ahead the battle clamored, as the Clarts ran
headlong into the Honeycat's massed force by the gate.
Horses and men screamed. Dorrin yelled a halt. They
dismounted, the left file taking the horses, and formed
again, shields and swords ready. Around the southwest
corner of the fort came a cavalry unit in black and
yellow; it charged, swerving away when Vladi's spearmen, still mounted, rode between. A section of Clart
riders, still shrilling, broke from the melee in front of
the gates and rode at the cavalry.

"Forward!" yelled Dorrin; Paks stepped forward with
the rest. Directly ahead was a milling mass of horses:
their own archers, shooting into the enemy. Dorrin and
Sejek rode ahead, swearing at them. A path opened.
Now Paks could see the pikemen, trying to form in
their direction and move out from the wall. She heard
the wicked thin flick of a crossbow bolt, and the man
next to her stumbled. His shield partner moved over
and closed in.

Now she could see the faces under the strange helmets: pale or dark, they looked the same to her with
their teeth gleaming. She heard above the roar another
bugle call from the gate tower, and shrill voices from
the wall. She saw stones fall, aimed at the enemy. Then

they were too close to see anything but the faces and weapons and bodies in front of them.

"Remember your strokes!" yelled Sergeant Vossik. "Shieldwork! Shieldwork. Get under those pikes." Paks watched the pikemen thrust and jab; the chopping stroke that made the broad blade so effective against horsemen was no good once you were inside it. They couldn't jab and chop at the same time.

She thought of Canna and Saben, and felt a wash of anger erase the last nervousness. I'm going to kill you, she thought as her rank reached the pikes. She ducked under a pike to slash at the enemy. One in the second rank chopped at her; she dodged without thinking and darted between the front pikes while she was still off balance. Her sword almost took his head off. She felt without looking that her companions followed her example, felt the first quiver of yielding as the pikemen realized that these swordsmen were not held off by the bitter tips of their weapons.

A terrible crashing and booming from the gate, and a roar of "Halveric! Halveric! The Duke! The Duke!" The defenders had come out. Paks could not see them, but she could feel, as if it were her own body, the shudder that ran through the enemy ranks. The swordsmen pressed forward in response. Suddenly the enemy stiffened again, and began to fight harder. Paks felt a give, a weakening, on her own left flank. Something had happened there; she could not see what. She fought on; it didn't matter, she was going to kill these scum until she died. She felt the pressure shifting her to the right, foot by foot, cramming the leftward files against her, and her against those to her right. Again. Another bellow added to the din. She could just distinguish the deep chant of Vladi's spears, somewhere to the left. The pressure against her eased; again she was able to drive forward. The pikemen began to look aside. Through their ranks she could see Halveric green near the gate.

"Now!" bellowed Vossik. "Now! They're breaking. Hit them!" With an answering roar, Paks and the others found they could move faster, swing harder. The pikes began to melt away. Some were dropped. A few of the soldiers turned to flee. Paks drove forward. Now more dropped their pikes; they were in among the crossbowmen, who had no time to reload and fire. Many of these had drawn short curved swords, but they were no match for the angry swordsmen of the Duke. Those who did break and run were killed.

They were through. The little group of Halverics and Phelani in front of the gate met Paks and the others with hugs as they broke through the last of the pikes. Paks looked anxiously for her friends, but Vossik and Kalek were yelling at them.

"No talking now, you fools! Reform! Come on, there's still a battle going on!" Paks tore her eyes away from the few Phelani and finally obeyed the sergeants.

The fleeing enemy had turned south, away from Vladi's spears. Now the Clarts had cut them off. Vossik called his cohort away from that easy bait to the block of pikes still intact, near the north corner of the fort. These were engaged with Vladi's spears on one side, but were holding together. They fought desperately, seeing they would receive no quarter. Paks was breathless and aching all over when the last one fell. She looked around. Nothing remained of the enemy but the crumpled bodies piled in rows, and scattered across the open ground between the fort and the river. The Clarts, reunited, were riding around the perimeter of the open ground—almost to the brambles, Paks noticed.

She wiped her sword on the dry grass of the meadow, but the blood on it had hardened. Paks started toward the river, limping slightly and noticing the limp before the pain that caused it. When she thought, she could recall a pike-butt slamming into her leg. Her ribs hurt, too. She pulled a handful of grass before stepping down the rocks to the water's edge to dip it in the icy flow and scour her sword. She cupped a handful and drank. When she stood, the others were already stripping the enemy bodies and hauling them to a pile. Paks sheathed her sword and walked toward the gate. She could see the Duke's horse just inside. Vossik yelled something at her, but she shook her head and pointed inside. She didn't want to be part of that, not this time.

Inside the fort, no one had much to say. Vik was alive, hobbling toward her on bandaged legs. When they met, he hugged her fiercely.

"Was it you?" he asked.

"Yes." Paks found her eyes filling with tears. She knew his next question.

"Saben? Canna?" She shook her head, tasting salt, unable to answer. She could not say she had left them, that no one knew where they were, if they were alive. Vik hugged her again. "At least you made it—I don't know how. By all the gods, Paks, it did me good to look down and see you marching up from the bridge. We were sure you'd been killed in the woods. Pernoth— he's one of the Halverics—thought he'd seen you three in the brambles just when the trouble started, but nothing after that. You'll have some tales to tell, when we get the chance. But you'll want to see who's left, and the Duke told us to gather in the main courtyard."

Together they limped across the outer court. Vik told her how many had been inside, and how many were left; about the two abortive attempts to break the siege and send word forth. The Halverics, he said, had accepted Ferrault as commander after their captain was killed. Within minutes, the Phelani were armed, and together they withstood the shock of the Honeycat's assault.

"It's a good thing he had only scaling ladders, though," said Vik. "They outnumbered us, but couldn't get enough of them up the walls at once."

"What about water?"

"It rained the day after they came. That helped; it got slippery down below. And it made his fire-arrows useless. And the next day—that's when he pulled out. We were collecting it in everything we could find.

Then several days later it rained again for a day and a half."

As they came into the main court, Paks saw that almost everyone there was from her own cohort—perhaps twenty. She glanced at Vik. He nodded. As they came to speak to her, she realized that every one was bandaged somewhere.

"I hear you're the hero of this tale," said Rauf, a twenty-year veteran.

Paks blushed. "Not me. Canna and Saben—I'd never have made it without them." He didn't ask about them, but went on.

"But you did. Heh, you'll be working up to sergeant at this rate. We'll be calling you 'Lucky Paks,' or 'Paks Longlegs.'" Rauf displayed his wide, gap-toothed grin. Paks could think of nothing to answer; she felt a great desire to fall down and sleep somewhere warm. Hands patted her back and shoulders as they all came together for a few moments.

"Paks!" It was the youngest squire's shrill call. She looked and saw him beckon from the door to the keep. "The Duke wants you." She pushed herself away from her friends, and limped stiffly toward the door. "Are you hurt?" asked the squire, frowning.

She shook her head. "No. Not bad, anyway. Just stiff." The squire was younger than she had been when she left home. But he, if he survived his time, would be an officer—maybe a knight. She flicked an appraising glance at his thin face, still with the unformed curves of a boy despite its leanness. She felt much older than that. The squire reddened under that brief look; she wondered if he had expected her to answer with sir. Not for you, yet, she thought. Not for you yet awhile.

The room he led her to overlooked the courtyard; two narrow windows let in the cold afternoon light. Inside were the Duke, one of the surgeons, and a man in a narrow bed. Paks wrinkled her nose at the smell. The Duke looked up.

"Paks. Good. Come on in." She stepped into the

room. "Captain Ferrault would like to speak to you,"
said the Duke formally. Paks had not recognized the
captain. He was pale, his face gaunt, his usually mobile
mouth fixed in a grimace. The Duke, Paks saw, held
one slack hand. The surgeon bent over him, gently
removing bandages with a pot of sharp-smelling liquid.
Paks came to the head of the bed.

"Yes, sir," she said to the Duke. She had seen enough
to know that Ferrault was dying. She knelt beside the
bed. "Captain—? It's Paks, sir."

For a moment he seemed to stare through her, then
his eyes focussed. "Paks. You—did—well. To go. I
told—the Duke."

"Thank you, sir. I'm sorry we weren't faster, sir, for
the rest of you."

His head rolled in a slow shake. "No matter. Did
enough. I hoped—" he broke off with a gasp. Paks saw
his knuckles whiten on the Duke's hand. She heard a
curse from both the surgeon and the Duke.

"Sorry, my lord," said the surgeon. "Sorry, captain.
Just—one more—layer. There." Paks saw sweat film
the captain's face. "Umm," said the surgeon. Paks glanced
down Ferrault's body to the wound now exposed. No
doubt where the stench came from; she swallowed hard
to keep from retching. Ferrault's face was grayer now,
and wet.

"You—can't do—anything," whispered Ferrault. It
was not a question.

The surgeon sighed. "Not to cure it, no. Not so late,
with that—a pike, they said? Yes. It's gone bad, but
you knew that, with the fever. But I can—" he turned
to rummage in his bag. "I can make you more comfortable. It you drink much, you'll vomit, so—" He rose
and came to the head of the bed. Paks moved back.

"Will it be—?"

"Long? No, captain. And this should make it easier.
No wine; it'll taste bad, but drink it all." The surgeon
held a tiny flask to Ferrault's lips as he swallowed. Then
he stepped back and returned to the pile of bandages.

He took a clean one, dipped it in the pot, and laid it gently over Ferrault's wound, then gathered up the soiled bandages with his bag. "My lord, that dose should ease him for some hours. I'll be back in time to give him another, or if you have need of me I'll be with the others."

"Very well, Master Simmitt, and thank you." The surgeon left the room; the Duke turned back to Ferrault. "Captain—"

"My lord. Did I tell you—the seals—"

"Yes. You broke them."

"I'm sorry—"

"Don't be. You did the right thing. Don't worry."

"But—my lord—I lost the cohort—and then the seals—and—"

"Shh. Ferrault, it's all right. It's not your fault. You did well—you've always done well. Your St. Gird will be pleased with you, when you come to him. I don't know many captains who could have held off so many with a tiny mixed force."

"But our losses—what will you do?"

"Do?" The Duke stared at the wall a moment, then smiled at Ferrault. "Ferrault, when I'm done with him, neither Siniava nor his friends nor his followers will have a hut to live in or a stone to mark where they died. I'm going to destroy him, Ferrault, for what he did to you and the Company. We've already destroyed the army he brought north this year, and that's only the beginning."

"Can you—do all that—my lord?"

"With help. Clart Company rode with us. Vladi sent a cohort of spears. I expect Aliam Halveric to arrive any day to avenge his son. So you take your rest, Ferrault, and tell Gird we'd be glad of a little assistance."

Ferrault smiled faintly. His eyelids sagged as he whispered, "Yes, my lord."

The Duke looked up at Paks, now leaning against the wall. "And you, Paks, know nothing of my plans, is that clear?"

"Yes, my lord."

"You may go. Send my captains to me, please, and see if you can find the Halveric sergeant; I want to speak to him."

"Yes, my lord." Paks tried not to limp as she left the room, but her leg had stiffened again.

"Are you hurt?" came the Duke's voice behind her. She turned.

"No, sir; just bruised."

"Well, see the surgeon after you've given my messages. Don't forget."

"No, sir; I won't." The same squire was standing outside the room; he scowled at her and went to the door as she started for the stairs. Paks ignored him. In the courtyard she asked Vik where the Halveric sergeant might be, and he jerked his head at a group of Halveric soldiers in one corner. Paks knew a few of the faces, but was not sure of the sergeant until he stepped forward.

"I'm Sunnot," he said. "The sergeant. Were you looking for someone?"

"Yes," said Paks. "The Duke asked me to find you; he'd like to speak to you."

Sunnot grimaced. "I'll bet he would. What a mess. Where is he?"

"Up those stairs, third room on the left."

"Oh. He's with the captain, then. How is he?" Paks shook her head. Sunnot sighed. "I thought maybe your surgeon could do something. Well—I hope your Duke's not too angry—"

"He is, but not at you."

"Umm. You're the one who got through, aren't you?"

"Yes." Paks turned away. "I've got to find the captains; go on up."

"I will."

Paks limped into the outer yard, looking for the captains, and found them busy. Pont was in the barracks where the wounded had been moved. Cracolnya was preparing the pyre of enemy bodies, and Dorrin was in the enemy camp, supervising the looting. Sejek was dead, of a crossbow bolt through one eye. When Paks had finally delivered her messages, she struggled back to the fort. Erial, one of Cracolyna's sergeants, was waiting for her at the gate.

"You need to see the surgeon," she said gruffly. "The Duke's called assembly after we eat, and we want all you walking wounded there." Paks did not argue. Between her leg and her ribs, she was not sure she was still walking wounded.

Master Visanior looked up as she came into the barracks. "You again. Thought I told you to stay out of trouble." Paks said nothing. How could she fight and stay out of trouble? "Hmmph," the surgeon went on. "Stubborn as a fighter always is. Well, let's see the damage." She fumbled at the thongs fastening her greaves, and he helped draw them off, and the boot beneath. A large, hard, dark-blue swelling throbbed insistently. The surgeon poked it; Paks clenched her jaw. "Not broken, I don't think, but it's taken damage. What was it?"

"Pike butt."

"And you've that broken rib, too. Anything else?"

"No—nothing like that, anyway."

"Good. If this hasn't damaged the bone, it'll hurt for ten days or so, but it'll heal. Try not to hit it again. Stay off it as much as you can—keep your leg up. I'll tell the sergeants. Have you eaten yet?"

"No, sir." Paks had not even thought of food, or mealtimes; now she wondered how late it was.

"Then you'll stay here until you do. Just lie down over there—" he pointed. "Someone will bring you food."

Paks thought of trying to leave, but the surgeon's sharp eye was on her until she stretched out on a pallet. Her leg throbbed. She closed her eyes for a moment. Someone touched her shoulder and she jerked away. Surely she hadn't been asleep—but it was almost dark. Torches burned in the yard; lamps, in the stable itself.

A private in black and white held a steaming bowl and mug toward her. She tried to gather her wits as she reached for them; he grinned and turned away.

The stew was hot and savory. Paks ate hungrily. As she finished, she saw the surgeon making his rounds of the wounded. She had not realized before how many there were. He came to her at last.

"You're to stay down. I told the sergeants."

"But the Duke—"

"Not until morning. He's staying with Captain Ferrault for now. I'll have someone help you clean up; then sleep. We don't want a relapse."

Paks thought she should argue to be allowed up, but she truly did not want to move. She was asleep within the hour.

When the Duke's summons came the next morning, all who could walk or be moved assembled in the inner court. They formed into the original three cohorts, not near filling the space they would have crowded two weeks before. In Paks's cohort, only twenty-two were left there; all had been wounded. The other two cohorts mustered one hundred forty survivors of the two hundred eight they had had. Three of the six sergeants and four of the six corporals were dead or dying: all in Paks cohort, Juris and Kalek of Dorrin's, and Saer of Cracolnya's. And two captains were dead: Ferrault and Sejek. Paks slid her eyes from side to side, meeting other worried glances. How could the Duke go on after such a loss? His words to Ferrault seemed sheer bravado.

The Duke came out, trailed by his squires. He was bareheaded, the chill breeze ruffling his hair and lifting his cloak away from his mail. The captains greeted him. He smiled and nodded, then paced along the ranks, looking at each soldier as if it were any other inspection. At last he walked back to the front of the Company, and turned to face them. The silence had a life of its own.

"Sergeant Vossik."

"Yes, my lord."

"Close the gates, please. We don't want to be disturbed for awhile."

"Yes, my lord." Vossik beckoned to his remaining corporal, and they closed the courtyard gates, then stood in front of them.

The Duke raked the Company with his gaze. "You have all," he began softly, so softly that Paks had to listen closely, "you have all won such glory in these few days that I have no words for it: you still alive, and our friends we have lost. You have defeated an army more than twice your size—not with clever tactics, but with hard and determined fighting. Each one of you has won this victory. I knew, companions, that you were the best company in Aarenis, but even I never knew, until now, how good you were." His gesture evoked the two battles, the fort held against Siniava's men, Paks's journey. He nodded to them, and his voice warmed.

"Now you look from side to side and think how many friends are lost forever. Your ranks are thin. You know that no plunder can repay the losses we have taken. You want to avenge the treachery and the murders and the torture—and you wonder how." A long pause.

"I'll tell you," he went on. "You and I are going to destroy the Honeycat, and his cities, and his allies, and everything else he claims. When we are through, his name will be spoken—not in fear or hatred, as now, but in contempt and ridicule. He thought he could gut this Company. He thought he could scare *us*, chase *us* away—" a low growl from the Company interrupted for a moment. The Duke raised his hand, and silence returned. "No. I know he was wrong. You know it. Nothing scares you, my friends; no southern scum can chase you away. And he has not come close to destroying us—but, companions, we are going to destroy him." The Duke rocked back on his heels and surveyed each face again.

"Yes," he said firmly. "We can do that, and we will. You already know that other companies are with us: the Clarts, the Halverics, Vladi's spears. Others will join us. I pledge you, sword-brethren, that until this vengeance is complete, I will consider no other contract, and all I have will support this campaign." The Duke drew his sword and raised it in salute to the Company. "To their memory," he said. "To vengeance." And the Company growled in response: vengeance.

When he sheathed the sword, he motioned to Dorrin. She came near. He seemed more relaxed. "You are all worthy of praise," he began. "And we will raise the mound both here and on the battlefield near Rotengre for our fallen companions. Still, there are a few who deserve praise before the Company, for deeds uncommon even in this uncommon campaign. Captain—?"

Dorrin began. "My lord Duke, I have four soldiers to recognize. Simisi Kanasson, who held off three guards from the prisoners, though his horse had been cut down. Sim was wounded then, and again today when fighting the pikes. Kirwanía Fastonsdotter, who led her file against the pikes both north of Rotengre and here, and accounted for eight dead by her own sword. Teriam Selfit, who rallied his squad after Kalek was killed, and prevented a breakout. Jostin Semmeth, who accounted for two of the mounted guard, was hit by a crossbow bolt, and went on to slay three bowmen and a pikeman before falling himself."

"Come forward, then," said the Duke. As they stepped out of line, he took from a casket held by one of the squires a ring for each of them. As they went back to their places, the Duke gestured to Cracolnya. He too had several soldiers to honor, and the ceremony proceeded. When the last of Cracolnya's men had stepped back, the Duke turned to Paks's cohort.

"You have no captain to speak for you," he said. "Nor sergeants, nor corporals. Yet your deeds speak aloud without their aid. I cannot pick and choose among you; I will have made for each of you, from these spoils, a ring to commemorate your deeds. But those to whom you owe your lives, who brought me word of your peril: even among such honor, they deserve honor. Three started: Canna Arendts, Saben Kanasson, and Paksenarrion Dorthansdotter. When they were attacked by brigands near Rotengre, only Paks was able to win free. We do not know the fate of the others; be assured that search will continue until we know. But now—Paksenarrion, come forward."

Paks felt herself blushing, and could hardly tear her eyes from the ground. She limped forward.

"Here is a ring," he said, "that I think best represents your deed. Three strands, for the three who started together, braided into one: the one who succeeded, the message, for returning to the place you began. And imperishable gold, for loyalty." Paks took the gold ring he held out, and stammered her thanks. This was not the way she had dreamed of winning glory, when she was still herding sheep. It felt indecent to be praised so, when her friends were captive or dead.

When the blood quit roaring in her ears, the Duke was still speaking to her cohort. "I want you to stay together," he said. "You are still Arcolin's cohort; you'll remain so. When I bring the recruits down, you'll be brought up to strength. In the meantime, until Valdaire, you'll form a squad in Dorrin's cohort. She will recommend temporary corporals. We will stay here until we raise the mound for our friends, when the Halveric arrives." He turned to the captains. "You may dismiss your cohorts when you're ready."

"My lord." The captains bowed. The Duke gave them all a last grim smile and returned to the keep. In a few minutes, the muster was over, and Paks had limped back to the stables with Vik. She spent the day doing such chores as she could manage without standing. Someone brought a pile of swords for her to clean and sharpen; she found her own, now notched, as she worked.

Sometime in the afternoon, they were startled by a horn cry from the gate tower. Paks stiffened, her hand clenched on the hilt of the sword she was cleaning. The fort erupted into action and noise. A squad of Clarts came boiling out of the inner court, their horses striking sparks off the stone paving. Through the open gate Paks could hear shouts from outside. These ceased, and she heard the drumming of a single galloping horse coming nearer. She glanced around the stableyard, then toward the inner gate. The Duke, armed and mounted, sat his horse in the space between the walls, his squires behind him.

The hoofbeats outside slowed, then halted. The Duke raised his hand. Into Paks's view rode a mailed figure in Halveric green on a lathered chestnut horse. He pushed up his visor; Paks thought she recognized Aliam Halveric. He rode forward until his horse was beside the Duke's and they were face to face. They clasped arms.

"I have much to say to you," said the Duke.

"And I to you," replied the Halveric.

"I fear we are crowded within," said the Duke. "Though I would welcome you and your captains to the keep, we have many wounded and I have brought them all inside the walls."

"We came prepared to camp," said the Halveric. "For a long time, if need be. I am only sorry we missed the battle. I would be glad, however, to accept your generous offer of a roof for myself and my captains. Where would you prefer I place my company?"

Paks thought she saw a smile flicker across the Duke's face. "Old friend," he said, and the Halveric relaxed visibly. "I will answer what you are too courteous to ask. Your men within these walls are at your disposition, to stay or go as you direct. Between us now there can be no question of captives. Your men have acted in all ways honorably and bravely. I would suggest you leave the wounded inside the walls. Now—will you see them first, or come with me?"

The Halveric spoke in a softer voice, and Paks could not hear. The Duke nodded, and beckoned a squire forward. The Halveric spoke to him, and he rode out the gate. The other squires dismounted, one taking all the horses, and the other holding the reins for the Duke and the Halveric to dismount. The two men stood talking while the horses were led away. In a short time Sunnot, the Halveric sergeant, came from the inner court and went down on one knee before the Halveric, who raised him up at once. Some command was given; Sunnot bowed slightly and turned away, leading the Halveric toward the barracks with the worst wounded. He was grinning.

When the great burial mound was finished, all the companies assembled there for a final leave-taking. The names of the fallen were called aloud one last time. Vladi's spearmen sang "The Dance of Frostbreath" and tossed their spears over the mound. The Clarts performed a wild dance mimicking combat on horseback; the thunder of hooves, one of them had explained to Paks, would carry their fallen comrades to the endless fields of the afterworld, where horses never tire, nor riders fall. Aliam Halveric and his captains sang to his harper's playing, the old "Fair Were the Towers Whose Stones Lie Scattered" that Paks had heard even in Three Firs—but instead of the name of the Prince and his nobles, they sang the names of the Halveric dead. Then the Duke signaled his piper, and a tune Paks had never heard before seemed to drag all the sorrow and anger out of her heart with its own bitterness. It was the "Ar hi Tammarion," the lament written for the death of the Duke's lady by the half-elven harper at the Court of Tsaia, and not since then played openly. Paks did not know the history of the song, but felt its power, as the rough wind dried tears she had shed without knowing it.

Their journey back to Rotengre passed quickly and uneventfully; five days after leaving the north they were back in position. The horses they had ridden had to be returned; most had been borrowed from one or another militia. Paks led half a dozen back to the horselines of Sorellin. Coming back, she was hailed by a burly sergeant. His voice was vaguely familiar.

"Hey! Duke's sword! Aren't you the one who came across the lines that night?"

Paks looked at him, not sure of his face. "Yes. Why?"

"By the sword, you look so much better I'd not have known you but for your size and yellow hair. Why? Because we've heard about you—and I'm sorry we gave you such trouble that night."

Paks thought back to that black wet night and shivered, though it was daylight. "That's all right."

He sucked a tooth for a moment. "Well—I came close enough to tossing you in our guard cell. It was a lesson to me. Anyway, I'm glad you survived it all. I'm Sim, by the way—Sim Plarrist—and I'd be glad to stand you a tankard of ale—"

Paks shook her head. "Not until the city yields. May it be short—but until then we're to stay strictly with our Company. But thank you."

"No hard feelings, then?"

"No." He waved her on, and Paks threaded her way to her own lines in the fading light. There, in another echo of the earlier event, was Barra on guard.

"Paks, the Duke wants to see you."

"Do you know what about?" Her stomach clenched, expecting bad news.

"I think he's heard about Saben and Canna."

"Bad?"

Barra shrugged. "I don't know anything. When I asked, I was told to mind my own business and see you got the Duke's message. But if it was good news, I think we'd know."

"I suppose." Tears stung her eyes, and Barra's face seemed to waver before her. Barra squeezed her arm, and Paks went on to the Duke's tent.

The lamps inside were already lit, and a brazier warmed the room. The Duke moved to his work table; Paks glanced at it, and saw on its uncluttered surface a little red stone horse strung on a thong, and a Girdish medallion on a chain. She knew them at once, and felt the blood drain from her face.

"You recognize them." Paks looked up to meet the Duke's steady gaze. She nodded. "Paks, I'm sorry. I had hoped they would be found sooner. The surgeon says that Saben had taken a hard blow to the head, and probably never woke up. He died soon after they were found. Canna was not badly wounded in the fight, but when the brigands realized their hideout had been found, they tried to kill all their prisoners before they fled. Canna was one of five or six still alive when the militia got in. But she took a bad wound, and died several days later, here in camp. She knew you had made it, and that we'd defeated Siniava's army on the road and gone on north. The surgeon said she wanted you to have her medallion, and wanted you to know you did the right thing. She was glad you made it through; he said she died satisfied." The Duke paused. Paks was trying to blink back tears, but she could feel them trickling down her face. "Paks, are you a Girdsman?"

"No, sir."

"Hmm. Girdsmen usually want their holy symbol returned to their home grange, with an account of their deeds. I wonder why Canna wanted you to have it, if you aren't Girdish."

Paks shook her head, unable to think why or answer. She had hoped so that they would be found alive, unlikely as it had been. Even now she could scarcely believe she would never see Saben again.

"Paks—you were Saben's closest friend, as far as I know. Did he ever say what he wanted done with his things?"

Paks tried to remember. "No—sir. He had family, that he sent things to. But he—he—"

"He didn't make plans. I see. We'll be sending them word, and his pay, of course, and—do you think they'll want his sword, or were they against his choice?"

"No, my lord; they favored it. He had five brothers at home, and six sisters. They were proud of him, he said; they'd be glad of the sword."

"And this pendant—was that from his family?"

"No—my lord. It was—was—my gift, sir. It—it was a joke between us."

"Then you should take it, for his memory, as well as Canna's medallion." The Duke scooped them up from his table and held them out. Paks stared at him helplessly.

"Sir, I—I cannot—"

"You must take Canna's, at least; she wanted it so. And I think your friend Saben would be happy to know you have the other."

Paks took them from his hand, and as her hand closed around them the reality of her loss stabbed her like a sword. She fumbled at the flap of her belt-pouch and pushed them in.

"Here," said the Duke; when she looked up, he was offering a cup of wine. "Drink this. When you are calmer, you may go; I am joining the Halveric for dinner." Paks took the cup, and the Duke caught up a fur-edged cloak from its hook and went out. The wine was sweet, and eased the roughness of her throat, but she could not finish it. After wiping her face on her sleeve, she returned to her own cohort. Vik knew already, she saw, and he told her that the Duke had released word as soon as he had told her himself.

"We miss them too," said Vik fiercely, hugging her again. "But you, Paks—"

"We were so close," she whispered, as tears ran down her face. "Only a few more miles, and they—" She could not go on. Arñe got up and put an arm around her shoulders; they all sat together a long time in silence.

Chapter Twenty

The next day the regular siegework began again. The Halverics moved in beside Duke Phelan's Company, slightly narrowing the Sorellin front. This suited Sorellin, but drew catcalls from the battlements; these ceased after four men fell to the Phelani bowmen. Weapons and armor taken from the Honeycat's force were divided among the different companies; Paks had the chance to try a crossbow (at which she nearly cut off her thumb) and a short curved blade much like the one Saben had taken.

Day by day she grew to realize how much she had leaned on Canna and Saben—Saben especially. She found herself looking for his cheerful face in the meal lines, waiting for his comment when she came off watch—missing, increasingly, that steady pressure of good-will she had always felt at her side. They had been together from the beginning. When she went to the jacks, she remembered the trench they had dug together her first night as a recruit—and cried again, knowing it was silly and ridiculous, but helpless to hold back the tears. It was impossible that he was gone, and gone forever. She had thought of her own death, but never of his—now she could think of nothing else.

She could not talk about it to anyone. She knew that Vic and Arñe watched her, and almost hated them for it. She heard a Halveric ask Barra if she and Saben had been lovers, and did not know which was worse, the question or Barra's scornful negative. She and Saben had shared everything but that: the early hopes and fears, the hours of work, the laughter, that final week of danger. Everything but love and death. For the first time, she wondered what it would have been like to bed him. It was something he had always wanted, and now there was no chance. But if she had—if it hurt more, to lose a lover—she shook her head, and went doggedly on with work she hardly noticed. Better not. She had never wanted to, and surely it would be worse to lose a lover. It was bad enough now.

For awhile she felt cool and remote, as if she were watching herself from a hilltop. Never care, came a whisper in her mind. Never care, never fear. But in the firelight that night, the concern in Vik's eyes and Arñe's roused a sudden rush of caring for them. With it came the pain again, but she felt it as a good pain: as wrenching as the surgeon scouring a wound, but necessary. Fear came, too: fear for them. She looked at her own hands, broad and strong, skilled—she could still protect, with those hands. She said nothing, and the tears came again, but somewhere inside a tightness eased.

The city had been silent now for more than a week. No more taunts over the wall, no pots of hot oil, no stones. Heads showed above the battlements occasionally, and the gates were barred, but the enthusiasm of the defenders had gone. Paks wondered if they were going to surrender.

Late one afternoon, a trio of Sorellin militia rode into the siege lines from the north; in minutes messengers came to the Duke. Soon everyone knew that they had found a tunnel from the brigands' hideout, where Canna and Saben had been found, into Rotengre. A small group of Rotengre soldiers had come out in their midst; now Sorellin controlled the forest end of the passage.

"That must be how the Honeycat meant to relieve the siege," said Vik.

"And why he wanted live prisoners," said Paks. "Once he had them in the city—"

"Yes. Ugh. I wonder where the Rotengre end is. If only we could use it."

"With an attack on the walls at the same time. Yes—or if they're all trying to escape that way, we could just sit there and take them as they come."

"I'd rather go in," Arñe looked eager.

Paks grinned. "So would I. I never heard of a tunnel that long; I wonder who dug it and when."

"The reputation this city's got," said Vik, "it may have been there since the walls were built. It would explain a lot of things about Rotengre."

As dusk fell, the entire camp bubbled with speculation. They mustered after supper, and the Duke explained their plans. The Phelani would assault the wall, while the Halverics tried their ram on the north gate. Vladi had taken a couple of spear cohorts and joined the Sorellin militia for an assault through the tunnel. The remaining Sorellin militia would attack with their catapult and ladder teams. Cracolnya's cohort would lead the Phelani assault, followed by Dorrin's. These instructions were followed by a breathless wait in the dark.

Suddenly the Halveric's ram battered at the north gate, and an outcry came from the gate tower above. Torches flared along the walls. As heads showed, the Duke's bowmen fired. Soon arrows were flying in both directions. Paks heard not only the regular crash of the battering ram, but the occasional stunning crack of the Sorellin catapult's stone balls slamming into the wall itself. Horn calls and shouts from inside the city redoubled, loudest from the gate tower. Then Paks heard

more distant signals, from the south side. She realized
that the south gate, too, must be under attack.

Now, with others of Dorrin's cohort, she stood at the
base of the ladders as the specialists of the mixed cohort
led the climbing teams up. These made it to the top
before being seen, and secured the ladders as the first
fighting teams came up. Paks, below, heard the scream
of the Rotengre guard who first saw them, then a body
slammed into the ground nearby. Those on the ladder
surged upward. As soon as they could get footspace on
the rungs, others followed.

"Keep your shields *up*," yelled Captain Pont. "Cover
your heads until you're up."

Paks found the ladder harder than she remembered,
as she tried to balance with her shield arched over her.
By the time she reached the top, the Duke's men
formed two lines across the wall, protecting access for
those still climbing. She was surprised to see green-clad
Halverics coming off the ladders behind her companions, but had no time to think about it. She jogged up
to join the line moving toward the gate tower.

Facing them were two lines of Rotengre guards in
blue, and more ran from the direction of the gate
tower. The Phelani advanced; the Rotengre lines retreated, even before making contact. When they pursued and engaged, the enemy still retreated, though
their swordwork was excellent.

"Keep pressing 'em!" yelled Vossik. "They'll break.
Keep at 'em." Even as he spoke, those on the inside of
the wall tried to slip down a stair to the city below.
Bowstrings twanged behind Paks; at least two fell from
the stairs. Vossik told a party to hold the stairs against
an assault.

Now they were close to the gate tower; the rear ranks
of defenders turned and raced for the tower doors as a
heavy fire of arrows struck the Duke's men from an
upper level. Several fell. Paks and the others threw up
their shields and charged, trying to make the tower
door before it was slammed against them. The remain-

ing defenders went down under the charge; Paks raced
through a gap to hit the closing door with all her
strength. Instantly several of her companions were there
to help, and together they forced the door open, battling past the defenders. More of the Duke's men poured
into the opening.

They were in a small chamber that ran along the west
side of the gate tower; two doors opened into a larger
room where Paks caught a glimpse of the gate ma-
chinery before the door slammed.

"We'll need to get those doors down," said Vossik.
He had come limping in after the others, having taken a
crossbow bolt in the leg. "And those plaguey bowmen
are somewhere overhead, too." They looked around,
but saw no access to the upper level. They could feel
the concussion when the Halveric ram hit the gates.

"How about that door we just took?" asked Vik.

"Good," said Vossik. "Take it apart and see if it won't
make us some rams." With four stout lengths of oak
from the first door, they began smashing at the inner
doors, a squad for each. All at once one of them splin-
tered between the bars that held it, and they smashed
the rest of the wood free and poured through. They
were met by a line of crossbowmen, as they expected;
the first flight bristled in their shields. Before the bowmen could reload, the Duke's men were on them, and
they fell in a welter of blood that made the floor slippery. The remaining defenders, some two score, had no
chance. As they darted toward the stair that led to
ground level, the attackers cut them down. Vossik
stopped them from following the few survivors downstairs.

"Wait. We need to get these gates open."

"Here, sir." It was a mixed-cohort man. "Just let me
get to those pulleys."

"Need any help?"

"Just a moment. Yes—here. Two of you do this—" he
demonstrated. "And two over here, on this one." They
pushed on the windlass spokes; chains tightened and
slid through great pulleys above and below. Beneath

them, the heavy gate creaked open; they heard wild cheers from the Halverics. Meanwhile someone had identified the portcullis mechanism, the several were at work to raise the massive grate. Paks looked out the window that looked into the city. She could see torches in the street below and gleams of steel.

"Paks." It was Artfiel, one of the new corporals Dorrin had named. She turned. "Take a squad and make sure the gate tower is secure on the east. I expect they've all fled into the city, but I'd hate to be surprised."

Paks collected a tensquad and found a long narrow room on the east side: twin to the one they'd broken into on the west, except that in this room a narrow ladder led through a hole in the ceiling to the higher level. One of the bowmen scampered up this, to report no enemy above, and no one visible on the wall. Paks went back to Artfiel and he assigned a squad of archers to keep watch from the upper level; she took her own squad out onto the east wall.

From the streets below rose a confused clamor, and the deep chant of the Halveric foot. She found a stair going down, and positioned her squad to guard it. They could see very little, and Paks was not tempted to light a torch. They peered into darkness, with its confusing patches of wavering torchlight, and tried to interpret the noise.

Coming out from under the gate tower now were mounted troops, the horses' hooves ringing on stone, and behind that the Sorellin foot. Far across the city Paks saw a bright blue of flame atop a tower. Now they heard shrieks from below, and again the clash and clang of weapons. Paks yearned to go down the stair and be part of it, but she knew Artfiel was right: a desperate or cunning enemy might try to climb the wall and retake the gate tower—or escape.

Gradually the noise receded toward the center of the city. There it intensified, a harsh uneven roar punctuated by occasional high-pitched outbursts. It was cold on the wall. Paks huddled into her cloak, cursing the orders that kept her idle and cold when a good fight was raging. The tower door opened. Paks glanced toward it to see a tall figure stepping out on the wall. She stood, stamping her feet, as the Duke came up.

"Any trouble?"

"No, my lord."

"Good. Foss Council militia are going to take over the wall. Bring your squad—I daresay you'd like to be in at the finish."

"Yes, my lord."

"Very well. We'll go back through the tower." The Duke led them, nodding at the Foss Council captain as they passed into the tower. At the foot of the stairs, a squire held the Duke's charger; the others who had been in the tower bunched nearby. He mounted and rode slowly up the wide street toward the battle. Paks and her squad marched on his left; two squires rode in front with torches. The street was ominously silent. Paks feared that hidden archers might shoot the Duke, but nothing happened.

As they came to the center of the city, they could see more torchlight and fires set against the walls of the old keep. This keep, the Duke had said, formed an interior defense completely separate from the outer walls. The Halveric ram was at work on this inner gate. Defenders were thick on the wall. Fire arrows flew in both directions. Something inside the keep was burning; heavy smoke blew away on the north wind.

They had just reached the rear of the attacking lines when shrill screams broke out inside, and the men on the wall turned away. At once the attackers flung up ladders and swarmed up the wall. Paks, waiting beside the Duke, found herself dancing from foot to foot. The gates opened, and the ram crew surged forward, followed by everyone who could cram into that narrow space. The Duke rode on, forcing a passage with his horse; Paks shoved her way alongside.

Within the gates all was confusion. Several small buildings were on fire, lighting the court with dancing yellow that glinted off weapons and armor. It was hard to tell defenders from attackers, Rotengre blue from Halveric green or Foss Council gray. Paks started yelling the Phelani battlecry after nearly being spitted by one of Vladi's spearmen.

The fight raged until every defender lay dead in the court or passages of the keep. Even then the noise and confusion kept on, for the attackers began competing for plunder. Paks had never seen anything like this, or imagined it. She expected the captains to call them all to order, but instead they urged on their troops or ignored them.

Fights broke out between militia and mercenaries over bales of silk, caskets of jewels, kegs of wine and ale—only then did the officers step in to restore peace. At first, Paks stayed out of the way, carrying water to some of the Duke's wounded until wagons came to take them back to camp. But when Vossik found her standing in an angle of the inner wall, he took her arm and led her upstairs.

"This is where we make our stakes," he said laughing. "Don't worry—the Duke said we could sack the keep. Try not to get in fights, is all. Look—here's a good place to start." He shoved open the door of a small room that had been a study. Scrolls littered the floor around an overturned desk, its drawers scattered. "These things always have secret compartments," said Vossik. "And militia are hasty. Watch—" He wrenched a leg off a chair and smashed the desk apart. Suddenly a handful of loose jewels rolled across the floor. "That's what I meant," he said. "Go on. Take 'em."

Paks scooped up the little chips of blue, red, and yellow: the first jewels she had ever held. Vossik looked at them critically.

"I'll take this—" he picked out a red one and a blue one, "as my share for showing you how. Get busy now, or these damned lazy militia will get all the good stuff." He left Paks alone in the room. She put the stones in her pouch, and looked at the smashed desk. Was there another compartment? She picked up the chair leg.

By dawn, Paks had prowled through most of the rooms in the keep, and her pouch was stuffed with coins and jewels. She had a strip of embroidered silk wrapped around her neck, and a jewel-hilted dagger thrust into one boot. She could not bring herself to destroy furniture, so most of her finds were bits and pieces that had rolled out of sight of earlier plunderers. She headed downstairs, hoping to find something to eat. Along the way she passed drunken, sleeping fighters snoring beside the dead. Paks wrinkled her nose at the stench of blood, sour wine, vomit, and smoke. In the courtyard, a circle of soldiers were cooking food over the remnants of a burning shed. Everyone seemed to be draped in stolen finery: velvet and fur cloaks, bits of lace and silk that might have been shawls, gold and silver chains and bracelets. Paks looked around for someone she knew. These were all militiamen from Sorellin and Vonja.

"Where's Duke Phelan's Company?" she asked one of them.

His mouth was full of sausage, but he pointed toward the keep gates. Paks made her way out into the streets.

"There you are," said Vik. He had a green velvet cap with a feather atop his helmet. "Have you had breakfast yet?"

"No." Paks yawned. "Have you? I wish I could sleep."

"Here—" Vik handed her a roll and hunk of cheese. "I tried some of the stuff from their kitchen, but this is better. What'd you find in there—anything good?"

Paks nodded, her mouth full of bread.

"We're supposed to clear the northwest quadrant today, but what we find goes to the common store, worse luck. Though I've as much as I can carry now."

Paks swallowed noisily. "I've got some jewels, and money, and this—" she indicated the strips of silk. "Did you see those militia?"

"Furs and things? Yes—well, they have baggage wagons to go home in. How do you like my new hat?"

"Ummm." Paks thought it was as silly as a lace shawl, but didn't want to say so.

"It'll travel well, rolled up," he said seriously. "Except for the feather, and any barnyard cock will give me a new one."

"Yes—well—it's nice, Vik." Paks yawned again and ate the cheese. She emptied her water flask. A haze of smoke hung over the city; the wind had dropped. "When do we start—?"

"When the captain gets back. Gah—I'm sleepy too." Vik settled against the wall and put his head on his knees. After a moment Paks squatted beside him. She looked around. Maybe a third of the Company was visible along this stretch of wall; most slumped against it or each other, and looked asleep. Some were chatting quietly. Bundles wrapped in a variety of unlikely things—curtains, bed linen—lay among them. Paks had not thought of that.

She did not realize she'd fallen asleep until Captain Dorrin's voice woke her. She yawned again as she pushed herself up. She was stiff and cold; others looked worse than she felt. She was glad she hadn't been drinking all that ale and wine.

Unlike the chaos of the night before, the day's sack was systematic and careful. Paks found herself one of a squad of ten, assigned to go through buildings along one street. They began with a house, smashing its locked door, and opening every door of every room from cellar to garret. When they knew what it contained, they reported to a sergeant, who told them what to load in which order.

Paks carried out one load after another. Bed linens, cook pots, clothes from clothes presses, a roll of fine wool from a room with a loom in it. Her companions brought the loom, a sackful of scrolls, dishes and spoons, shoes and boots and hats, a patterned carpet, a trunkful of uncut velvet—everything they could move. As the rooms emptied, they thumped the walls, listening for any sign of a secret hideaway. Paks felt strange, rummaging around in someone else's clothespress, carrying away a stranger's empty garments. In a small room under the eaves, Paks found the string of tiny bells under the short bed; when she shook them, they gave a faint musical chime. A child's toy. She looked out the window, across the street, and saw a bolt of blue cloth unwinding as it fell. Erial shouted from below, angry. Paks turned away. She felt a vague pain in her head, and wondered if it came from the smoke still hazing the city.

Down in the cellar someone found a hollow-sounding panel and smashed that. Behind was a row of winecasks, and a little iron-bound coffer. With much grunting and heaving they got these up the stairs. Erial ducked into the house to check it and come out nodding. They passed to the next building, and the next. Not all were as rich as the first, but by midday they had piled two wagons full of loot. Other companies were clearing their assigned sections, and wagons were lined up coming and going from the different camps.

The rest of that day was much the same. Houses, shops, and warehouses, with a few craftshops. Paks found a secret passage in one shop, following it to a vault full of fancy leathers and fabrics. In the next house along, Paks heard a thin wail behind a wall on the third floor. For a moment she thought of saying nothing about it, but her squad leader had heard it too. Behind the false wall a thin girl of perhaps fourteen clung to an infant less than two months old; she wore only a rough shift, and an iron ring circled her neck. Her eyes were blank with fear.

"Just a slave," said Aris, the squad leader in disgust. "Come on out, we won't hurt you." The girl shivered, but did not move. "Come on." He reached for her arm, and the girl threw herself at Paks, holding up the baby, who began to cry. Aris gave Paks a wry grin. "Your problem now, Paks. Take her to the captain." He turned away. Paks reached gingerly toward the baby, and the girl let go so fast that Paks almost dropped the child. It screamed louder, and the girl cried out in a strange language and fell to her knees.

"It's all right," said Paks, convinced that it wasn't. "I won't hurt your baby. Here, you take—" she tried to hand the baby back, but the girl was kneeling, and would not look up until Paks touched her shoulder. Even then, she would not stand, and Paks had to fold the girl's arms around the child before she would take it. "Now come," said Paks softly, and tugged her shoulder; the girl started crying. "Look," said Paks, "I won't hurt you or your baby, but you must come." The girl kept crying, and made no move to reply. Paks straightened to ease a cramp in her back, and glanced around. By just so much the crossbow bolt missed her as it passed over the kneeling slave to stick quivering in the wall. A crack showed in the back of the recess. Paks started a split second as it widened, then yelled as she swept out her sword and charged.

Behind her she heard the girl shriek, and the clatter of boots as her squad came to her aid. Her sword smashed the half-open panel, and she grabbed the crossbow lefthanded, jerked it away from the dark-robed man who stood in a second recess. She freed her sword from the shattered panel as he reached to his belt for his dagger. Huddled beside him was a woman in a silk gown, and behind were a youth and a girl, both richly dressed.

"Come out of there," said Paks grimly. The man shook his head, and said something she could not make out. He had the dagger out, and held it as if he knew how to fight. Paks did not like the cramped space; she started to step back. The man spoke again, and a blow from behind knocked her off balance as a thin arm crooked around her neck. At once the man struck. Paks deflected the blow with her sword, feeling a sting on her knuckles, as the four of them rushed her. She heard a shout from behind, then a scream. The weight fell from her back; the arm no longer choked her. She half stumbled backwards; two of her squad were beside her, swords drawn.

"What happened?" asked Aris.

"Crossbow, from a concealed panel behind the first recess," said Paks, gasping a little. She did not take her eyes from the man in front of her. "Just missed me, while I was trying to get that slave to move. I saw the opening, and found those behind it. She jumped me from behind—I think he told her to, but I don't know the language—and they all tried to spit me."

"Damned northern war crows!" the man burst out. "May you all die strung from the walls like the carrion you are."

"Come out, or I'll call pikes," said Aris calmly. The man muttered in the unknown tongue. "Now," said Aris. The man stood still, as if considering, and the girl behind him began to cry. For some reason this made Paks angry.

"Stop that noise," she said roughly, and the girl looked at her and was still, tears still running down her face. The man glared at Paks.

"I should have killed you. Two times, you great cow, and you still live." He spat at Paks, but it fell short. She felt her companions stiffen, and Aris's voice roughened.

"Drop that knife and come out, or we'll kill you all."

The man looked at the knife in his hand, then reversed it and threw it spinning at Paks's chest. She jerked her shoulder aside, and it bounced off her corselet, but again the four rushed forward. She thrust her sword into the man's robe. His weight bore her back; when she tried to step back, she tripped over the slave's body. The silk-clad woman had pulled out a dagger to slash at the soldier before her; she too was cut down. The youth had a short sword, which he had held hidden behind the man, and fought the soldier on Paks's left with surprising skill. The girl, no longer crying, had a slim stiletto with which she attacked the soldier fighting the boy. Paks grabbed her arm, and the girl struck at her face. Almost in reflex, Paks thrust in her sword, and the girl folded over with a cry. At the same time, the soldier got past the youth's guard and sank his sword into him. The boy's weapon fell with a clatter. Paks took a breath and looked around. Aris met her eyes.

"That was a new one. Sorry, Paks; I didn't know—"

Paks shook her head. "I shouldn't have gone between them, not after the crossbow. Is the slave—?"

"Dead. Sim stuck her when she was choking you."

"It wasn't her fault." Paks looked for the baby, but it too was dead, having caught a stray bladestroke. No one knew whose, and no one cared to guess. They wiped their blades on the man's robes, and examined the inner recess, but found nothing more.

"They'll have something somewhere," said Aris. "Let's check 'em over." The man was dead, but the woman and the two younger ones were still barely alive. At Aris's nod, the other soldiers gave each the death-stroke, and began to search the bodies. Paks, suddenly shaky about the knees, leaned on the wall. She could not get out of her mind the frightened face of the slave, kneeling at her feet. Her knuckles burned; she looked at the shallow cut—from the man's dagger, she supposed. She glanced at the window. Nearly dark, now—no, that can't be right—we couldn't see in here— She realized she was sliding down the wall.

"Paks. Paks, what's wrong?" Aris had her arm. She felt very strange.

"I think this dagger's poisoned," said someone from a distance, and someone else added, "So's this sword, if the junk on the blade means anything."

"Paks—did that dagger cut you?" Aris seemed to be yelling very softly. She held up her hand, and felt it taken and turned. Someone cursed; boots clattered over the floor and into the passage. Paks opened her eyes again, and found that everything seemed a strange shade of green. She blinked, tasting something vile, and tried to think what had happened. Someone pushed the edge of a flask against her lips and said "Swallow." She did. For an instant or so she thought a whirling wind was loose inside her, and then her vision cleared. Sim held the daggers, stiletto, and sword; Captain Dorrin peered at their blades.

"This sticky orange stuff is almost certainly some kind of poison—either weak or slow-acting, to judge by its effect on Paks. Put these aside, carefully, and we'll let the surgeons see them." Dorrin glanced at Paks. "You better?" When Paks nodded, her face relaxed, and she offered a hand up. "You keep pushing your luck, Paks, and you won't have any left."

"Sorry—captain." Paks still felt remote, but that sensation cleared quickly. The others had found several small pouches in the dead family's clothes, and the man's belt had a long packet sewn in, which bulged suggestively. Under his outer robes he wore a massive silver chain with a curious medallion. As Kir slid it out, the captain swore. Paks peered at it, wondering what was wrong. As big as a man's palm, it looked like a silver spider, legs outstretched on a web.

"Drop that," said Dorrin harshly, as Kir started to touch the medallion itself. Startled, he obeyed. The captain drew her sword and slipped it beneath the chain. The chain and medallion let off a pale green glow and slithered away from the sword point, which was also glowing. "By all the gods and Falk's oath," said Dorrin. "It's a real one."

"Isn't that the—the Webmistress's sign?" asked Sim nervously.

"Yes. Don't any of you touch it. It's the right size for one of her priest's symbols, and they're dangerous." Dorrin touched the point of her sword to the medallion. Green light flared upward, and a rotten stench filled the room. The sword's glow was clearly visible now, blue and steady against the pulsing green. Dorrin pulled the sword back, and both glows faded. "Well, that's that. We can hardly leave it there. We need a cleric to counter it. Paks—" Paks jerked her eyes away from the medallion: was it moving slowly? The captain nodded when their eyes met. "Go find the Duke, and tell him we need a cleric. Don't tell anyone else. Wait—do you have Canna's Girdish medallion?"

"Yes, captain."

"You're wearing it?"

"Yes, captain. Isn't that all right—?"

Dorrin gave her a long look. "Seeing it probably saved your life, I would say it's all right. It's well known St. Gird has no love for Achrya Webmistress. But let's see—take it out,"

Paks fished the medallion out of her tunic. Dorrin took it and let the chain slip through her fingers until it hung above the silver spider on the floor. Again the green glow rose from the spider, but the crescent above did not change. Dorrin handed it back to Paks.

"Yours is the weaker one, or at least it doesn't reveal any power. Still, you're alive and he isn't." She nudged the dead man with her boot. "Go on—find the Duke. And the rest of you search these bodies carefully. We might find more mischief."

Paks tucked Canna's medallion back into her tunic as she jogged down the stairs. By the time she had found the Duke, and carried his message to a tall man in black armor in Vladi's camp, a Blademaster of Tir, it was dark. She was both eager and afraid to see what he would do, but Dorrin met her on the stairs and sent her back to camp.

"It's priestwork now, and none of ours," she said firmly. "We've much to do tomorrow, and much to guard tonight. You're on second watch; get some food into you and rest before you're called."

The next day brought no such excitements, but more work, as they cleared the rest of their sector. Paks could not begin to guess how many bales of cloth, rolls of carpet, boxes, bags, and trunks of moveable treasure, copper, bronze, and iron pots, dresses, gowns, robes, tunics, shirts, shoes, boots, buckles, combs, scrolls, daggers, swords, shields, bows, bowstrings, arrows, war hammers and wood hammers, battle axes and felling axes, reels of yarn and fine thread, needles, knives, forks, spoons of wood and pewter and silver and gold, figurines carved of wood and ivory and stone, harps and horns and pipes of all sizes they had taken and packed in wagons. The very thought of all those things made her tired. What could people use it all for? A well-stocked larder or armory made sense, but not all the rest. In one house she had seen shelves of little carvings: horses, men, women, fish, leaves of different shapes, birds—what could anyone do with those but look at them? No one worshipped that many gods. She had run her hands over fine silks and velvets, furs of all colors, and handled lace so fine she feared it would tear in her fingers. And these were beautiful. But—Paks thought again of the militia around the bonfire in their stolen finery—they weren't for her. Not now.

More to her mind was the captain's sword and its blue glow. She wanted to ask about it, but she was with a different squad, and she did not know Dorrin's people that well anyway. Had she imagined it? Could it be a magical weapon, like those of old tales and songs? Paks remembered Dorrin's scars—those any soldier her age might carry—and thought not. Yet she worried the question, in the back of her mind. She had heard of Webmistress, Achrya, though around Three Firs they called her Dark Tangler, or the Dark One. But she had never seen any evidence that Achrya was real until that spider medallion reacted to Dorrin's sword. She had thought of Achrya as another name out of old stories—something in her grandfather's time, perhaps, when orcs attacked Three Firs—but not a present danger. Now she had the uneasy feeling that she might not know as much as she'd thought. She pushed that thought aside and asked her new squad leader about the plunder they were packing.

"What do we—what does the Duke—do with chairs and tables and old clothes? The gold I can understand, but—"

"He sells 'em; either down here, or back north. There's a good market for good things—even partly worn things. You'll see."

They built another mound north of the city, and with the Halverics held another memorial celebration to honor those who had died as Siniava's prisoners or in taking Rotengre. The Guild League cities each sent a representative, but their militias stayed away; Paks was glad. After that, the heavily laden wagons of plunder followed the Company north and west to Valdaire along the Guild League route. It was later than usual, already winter, as Aarenis knew winter: cold and unpleasant enough. Their elation at breaking Rotengre drained away the closer they came to their winter quarters, for every day on the road they marched with the ghosts of the slain.

Chapter Twenty-one

When they reached Valdaire, Arcolin took the remnant of his cohort and assigned them the same quarters as the year before. Paks almost wished he had left them with the others; alone in a barracks meant for a hundred or more, they were achingly aware of their losses. Even the winter routine of training and work could not distract them. Every night Paks faced the rows of empty bunks, and looked aside to meet eyes as unhappy as her own. They had been told the Duke would replace the missing—he had already ridden north—but this was no comfort. Who could replace Donag, thought Paks, or Bosk? She would not let herself think of Saben and Canna. Day by day she and the others grew even more silent and grim.

Then Arcolin announced a feast for them at the White Dragon. This was no ordinary dinner; though they came unwillingly, the splendor Arcolin had ordered had its effect. The table was loaded with roast stuffed fowl, a great crown roast with candied fruit for jewels on the crown, roast suckling pig in a nest of mushrooms, a pastry construction of the city of Rotengre, with little figures assaulting the walls and gate, and colored sugar flames rising from the roofs. Dishes Paks had never seen before: steamed grain with bits of mushroom, nuts, and spices in it, vegetables stuffed with cheese or meat or another vegetable or nuts. Thick soups and thin soups, sliced cheeses in every shade from white to deep orange, sweet cakes and pies of every kind. They ate until they were full, and overfull, washing it down with their choice of wines and ales. Paks drank more than she ever had, and felt, for the first time since seeing Siniava's army come out of the trees, truly relaxed.

At the end of the meal, when the food was cleared away, and the servants had left, Arcolin passed around the rings which the Duke had made for them. Paks looked at hers before slipping it on her finger: a plain gold band with a tiny foxhead stamped on the outer surface, and the word "Dwarfwatch" and a rune that Arcolin told them stood for loyalty engraved on the inside. She ran her thumb lightly over the foxhead, and glanced aside to see Arñe doing the same thing.

Arcolin waited for them all to look up before speaking. "I wish," he said quietly, "that I had been with you, to fight beside you. Not that you could have done better. Tir knows what I—what everyone—thinks of your fighting. But you have shared something now, bitter as it is, that will bind you heart to heart for the rest of your lives." He stopped and looked around, gathering every eye that had dropped, before going on. "Very shortly," he said, "the new recruits will be down; we'll be back to size, or near it. You know, and I know, that they cannot take the place of those we have lost— but they can help avenge our friends. The Duke has sworn vengeance on Siniava. So has the Halveric. Let us, then, swear our own oath, for the memory of our friends and the destruction of our enemies." He read out again the names of those who had died; they gave a great shout after each. Paks was crying; she saw tears glisten on most faces. Hand felt for hand around the table. Then Arcolin said, "Death to the Honeycat!" and the responsive roar shook the room. Paks felt a surge of rage, felt the anger in the others that made them one. She wished they could march at once.

But it was some weeks before the new recruits arrived. After the banquet, Paks felt more at ease; she and the others began looking forward to the new campaign almost as much as backward to the past one. They drilled with every weapon they had or had captured. Paks spent more time with the longsword. She enjoyed the great advantage her height and reach gave her with the longer weapon. But not all her time was spent in practice.

That winter the Vale of Valdaire seemed even fuller than usual of wintering troops. Paks met more of the Golden Company, commanded by Aesil M'dierra, a dark hawk-faced woman from the west. She saw Kalek Minderisnir, a scarfaced, bandy-legged little man who commanded the Blue Riders, and Sobanai Company, whose dapper commander looked, to Paks, too dressy to be a good fighter. The talk was of war: battles and encounters, siege and assault, tactics for polearms and blades. It was not long before they all knew of Paks's journey. The Guild League militia had the tale from Sorellin, and the Halverics had not failed to spread it either. She found she was accepted by graying veterans as well as by eager young warriors her own age. And ever and ever again the talk turned to the Honeycat, and what could be done against him. Golden Company had fought him more than once; they argued fiercely with the Halverics about strategy. Paks listened carefully, trying to picture the coastal cities fair on their cliffs, and the grim forest where Alured the Black took toll of every passerby.

At last a runner brought them warning, and in an hour or so they saw a column approaching, with the Duke's banner flying ahead. Paks watched the marchers critically. Was it only two years ago that she had come that way? Had she looked so young? She saw the whites

of their eyes as they glanced from side to side. They
were hardly more than children, she thought—then
spotted a gray-headed man, and another, in the midst.
Stammel led the second unit, and Devlin was behind
him. The column halted. Paks tensed, waiting.

When Arcolin yelled, the Company formed, falling
into place with the startling speed that never failed to
impress the newcomers. Paks suppressed a grin, remembering her own reaction and seeing its mirror on
the recruits' faces. The Duke rode forward and looked
them over. He turned to Arcolin.

"Well, they look fit enough. Are they ready?"

"They'd march today, my lord," said Arcolin.

The Duke smiled. "Not quite today, captains. Captain Valichi will break the column for you."

"Yes, my lord." The Duke rode away, and Valichi
dismounted, coming to stand by Arcolin. Paks wondered why he had come. Who would captain the year's
recruits?

"Well, Val, what'd you bring us?" asked Dorrin.

"About the usual, plus veterans the Duke asked back
in. He's hired a captain, too, but he'll tell you about
that—should be here within the week. Arcolin, you'll
have Stammel and Kefer for sergeants, and Devlin and
Seli for corporals. The Duke suggested that you take
most of the veterans for your cohort, since it was worst
hit; you'll also have almost half the recruits."

Arcolin stretched, shaking his head. "Well, then,
we'd best settle the troops. Go ahead, Val."

Valichi sent two files from Kefer's unit and all of
Stammel's unit to Arcolin's cohort, where they moved
up behind the survivors. The rest of Kefer's unit and
two files of Vona's went to Dorrin; the remainder to
Cracolnya. The sergeants relocated themselves; Stammel gave the cohort a long, appraising look. When he
met Paks's eyes, one eyelid drooped in the merest
suggestion of a wink.

Two hours later, the newcomers had distributed their
gear in the barracks, and the bustle of sixty two addi-

tional members gave the feeling of a full cohort again. Paks had been assigned four recruits to introduce to their new life. Her group included three men and one woman. As she told them where to store things, and where they would eat and sleep, she was reminded of her first night with the regular Company. But then there had been many more veterans than recruits.

She could tell they were full of questions, but she kept them busy. She didn't want to talk about it yet with these people she did not know. Stammel came around to check, before supper, and gave her a grin.

"Well, Paks, I heard about you—you've had quite a year."

Paks nodded. "It's been—difficult."

"Sounds like it. I've heard the Duke's version; I'd like to hear yours. How about a mug at the White Dragon after supper?"

Paks frowned. "I've got second watch tonight—"

"That was before we came. Arcolin said to work in the recruits at once; they'll start tonight. What about it?"

"Yes, sir; I'd like that."

"Good. We're not eating in formation; just make sure your group gets over there and back. I'll be around somewhere." Stammel moved on, and Paks surprised an expression on the recruits' faces that made her uncomfortable.

"Come along," she said brusquely. "Time to eat." She led them to the serving lines, then to a table. Vik was there with three recruits. He rolled his eyes at her. Paks grinned.

"Paks, these are Mikel, Suri, and—and Saben." Paks felt her face freeze. The recruit flinched; she realized she must be glaring. She swallowed and nodded at them, trying to smile. "This is Paks," said Vik to them. The new Saben was thin and dark, with green eyes. Paks looked away, swallowed again, and introduced her own recruits, pointing a finger at each in turn.

"Volya, Keri, Jenits, and Sim; and this is Vik. Don't dice with him; he'll win."

"If you're going to tell tales, Paks, I'll start on you," threatened Vik.

"Huh. There's nought to tell."

"Is there not? Well, I'll let them find out for themselves. Did you hear that Stammel's changed the watch lists?"

Paks nodded, her mouth full of food.

"We're off for two days, all the old ones. Want to come in to Valdaire with us tonight?"

Paks shook her head, spit out a piece of gristle, and said, "Not tonight. Stammel wanted to talk."

"About——?" Vik jerked his head to the northeast.

"I expect so." Paks went on eating, aware of the recruits' interest.

Rauf sat down across the table from Paks with an older man and two recruits. "Paks, Vik—this is Hama, and Jursi, and Piter, who thought he'd retired." Piter laughed at this; he had none of the recruits' nervousness. He grinned at Paks.

"Are you the Paks that went seven days across country to bring the Duke word?" he asked.

"That's right," said Vik before Paks could answer. "Paks Longlegs—" Paks put an elbow in his ribs and he broke off.

"I'm impressed," said Piter. "What did you do for supplies?"

"The first day we scavenged some food from a farm near the fort; the farmers had been killed. We tried to space it out—but we were short until—I think it was the fifth day. We tried to buy food at a little settlement, and they tried to rob us, and—we came away with enough to finish the trip."

Piter nodded as he ate his stew. Then he frowned. "You say 'we'—I heard it was you alone that brought the message."

"Three of us started. Two died." Paks looked away, avoiding the recruits' eyes.

"Umph. I remember trying to shadow a column once, just for a day and night, and that was in summer. I could see their dust. Even so, I lost them twice and was nearly taken."

"I remember that," said Rauf. "It was my second—no, third—year, and you were in—was it Simintha's cohort?"

"No, that was the year Sim had that bad fall; Follyn had just taken it. That was Graifel Company I was following, you remember; they disbanded some ten years ago, but they had a very good light foot."

Paks listened to their remembrances, well pleased to have the conversation turned. She finished her meal, and saw that her recruits were finished too. Vik turned to her as he climbed over the bench. "Paks, I'll see you at weapons drill tomorrow, if you're not up when we get back."

"If you're coming back that late, all you'll see at drill is the ground or sky." The recruits looked shocked. Paks and Vic grinned at each other, and Paks climbed up too.

"Glad to have met you, Paks," said Piter, saluting her with a hunk of bread.

"And you," she said. Her group was up, and waiting for orders. "Let's get back," she told them, and led the way out.

"Paks—" It was Volya, the single woman of her group. "Yes."

"Will you tell us, someday, about what you did?"

Paks shrugged. "There's not much to tell."

"But surely—" began Jenits. Paks cut him off.

"Not now. Some other time, maybe, if you haven't heard enough from the others." She led them to the barracks at a fast pace.

Captain Arcolin was standing with Stammel just inside the door; the recruits shied around them. Stammel beckoned to Paks, and she came to stand nearby.

"—and that's all I know," said Arcolin. "We've two months' training to make up in as many weeks. The veterans—" he nodded at Paks— "will all be instructors. I understand you've put the recruits on guard duty—"

"Yes, sir. For a few nights anyway."

"Good. Oh—by the way—the Duke was talking of taking a section for drill himself."

Stammel grunted. "It won't be the first time, sir, but thank you for the warning."

Arcolin glanced at Paks again. "You're going in to Valdaire?"

"The White Dragon," answered Stammel. "I'll be back by second watch."

"No problem. I'll be checking the guard posts as usual. Take care." Arcolin went out. Stammel looked after him a moment, then turned to Paks and smiled.

"I've already told Kefer I'm going; are you ready?" Paks nodded. "Good." He started out the door. "Have you done much drilling with polearms?"

"Some. We drilled with Vladi's spears before the siege ended, but not so much since we've come back."

"Hmm. The Duke wants us to be able to use 'em. I was hoping some of you could help teach—"

"I think we could use them. I don't like 'em though, nearly as well as swords; they're too clumsy in close."

"We'll have to try." They were in the lane that led to the White Dragon; in the light spilling from open doors and windows Paks saw that Stammel was watching her from the corner of his eye. "Paks—these recruits, they're greener than you were: they've had two months less training. You heard the captain. We have to work them into the Company in a hurry. I don't know when the Duke plans to march, but I doubt he'll wait until summer. Now, the Duke's told them some of what's happened, and what you did. They're all excited—I thought you should know what he'd said, so when they ask—"

"Do I have to talk about it?"

Stammel took a great breath and blew it out, a pale frosty plume against the sky. "No. No, you don't. Not even to me, if you don't want to. But you may find it hard: they'll be asking, you see. I know what you mean.

Some things you don't want to make light of, by too much talk. But they'll be looking to you, Paks, whether you tell them or not. I thought you should know."

"I wish they wouldn't," muttered Paks. She could feel her ears glowing.

"You would have yourself," said Stammel reasonably. "I remember you with Kolya, and Canna: it's natural. The youngsters always want to hear the stories and dream. And it will help get them ready fast, for them to think of all you veterans as heroes: song fodder." Paks was glad they still had a distance to go; she knew she was red. "We have some old veterans back, too," Stammel went on. "They'll have their own problems—may be a bit touchy at first. Don't pay any mind if they go on about how things have changed. Once we're fighting, they'll be a big help."

"I met one tonight," said Paks. "Piter—?"

"Yes, old Piter. He's a good man. We started together, but he took a bad wound and fever, one year, and decided to retire. He joined one of his brothers running barges on the Honnorgat. Claims he's kept his sword skill against river pirates: I don't know about that, but he's kept it. He's good with a curved blade, too; knows every trick. How did you get along?"

"Fine. He wanted to know—but it was more like one of us. He asked what we'd done about food—it seemed natural, talking to him."

"Good. Oh! I nearly forgot. Kolya sent you her greetings and a bag of apples. It's somewhere in the baggage; I'll find it tomorrow."

"That was nice of her."

"She had a good harvest this year. She wanted to come, but the Duke had other plans."

"Is it true the Duke left the stronghold empty?"

"How did you know that?"

"I heard the captains say something—"

"Well, don't you say anything. Gods above! I hope no one else mentions it. It's true—except for those in the villages—and I hope the Regency Council doesn't hear about it."

"But what if something breaks out in the north?"

"We'll just hope it doesn't. Nothing's happened for years." Stammel sighed and changed the subject. "What did you get from the sack of Rotengre? Wasn't that your first?"

"Yes," said Paks slowly. "It was."

"Didn't like it, eh? What about it?"

"It was—everyone shoving and yelling and breaking things. I—I can't see breaking up good furniture for the fun of it, and tearing things and spilling wine all over."

Stammel chuckled. "No—I suppose you wouldn't. But surely you found something for yourself."

"Oh, yes. Some unset jewels, coins, a jeweled dagger, and a length of embroidered silk. I'm keeping that for my mother. I was thinking of keeping the dagger, but it looks silly with these clothes."

"Couldn't you have found some finery to go with it?"

Paks snorted, then laughed, remembering the militia primped up in velvets and laces. "Well, sir—I looked at some of the others—and it just looked silly. And besides, where would I keep the things?"

"It's not impossible. You're a veteran now; you're entitled to some space in the Company wagons and stores."

"I suppose. I didn't think of that then." They were nearly at the inn, and Stammel led the way to the door. Once inside they found the usual assortment of customers: mercenaries of half a dozen companies, a scattering of merchants, and a few professional gamblers (or thieves) who tossed their ivory dice whenever conversation and business lagged. Stammel looked at the crowded common room and crooked his finger at the landlord.

"Yes?" Rumor said the landlord was a veteran of Sobanai Company.

"A quiet corner anywhere?" asked Stammel.

"Sergeant Stammel, isn't it? Yes, I think we can find you a quiet spot. Just follow me." He led the way down a passage to a tiny room which had a bench built against either wall and a table close between them; it might have been possible to squeeze in four people. It was lit by two fat candles in a wall sconce. Stammel took the bench on one side, and Paks took the other.

"Bring us some ale," said Stammel, and the landlord withdrew. Paks threw her cloak back and pushed up her sleeves. Stammel looked at her critically.

"You've been keeping fit, I can see that. You may have strengthened that left arm even since last year. How's your unarmed combat coming?"

"Better. At least, when I needed it on the way, it worked."

"Ah. Now that's what I'd like to—" The door opened, and the landlord put a jug and two mugs on the table, then waited while Stammel fished out some coins. When he was gone, Stammel poured a mug of ale before speaking. "Go on," he said to Paks. "I won't drink all of this myself. Now—if you don't mind telling me about it, I'd like to hear it from you."

Paks sipped the ale before replying. "I don't mind telling you, sir. In fact, I wished you were there, right after, to talk to. But—but it still—" her voice faltered.

"You still feel it when you tell it," said Stammel. "No wonder."

Paks nodded, staring at the scarred tabletop. When she began to speak again the story came out in fits and starts. Stammel did not interrupt, and asked few questions. By the time she came to the incident with the mounted sentry, the story seemed to be rolling out of her, almost as if she were telling a tale that had happened to someone else. Then she came to that last afternoon, and the memory bit deep. She stopped, drained her mug, and started to pour another; her hands shook.

Stammel took the jug and poured for her. "Take it easy," he said. "Do you want something to eat?" Paks shook her head. "It's amazing you made it so far without losing someone," he went on. "You took more

precautions than I would have. I'm not sure I would
have thought of a sentry at the first crossroad. With
food so short—I might have tried a village; hunger's
hard to ignore. You knew that place was risky; you got
out of it with the food you needed. And on the last day,
so close to the Duke, so far ahead of the enemy—I'd
have felt fairly safe myself."

Paks wrapped her hands around the mug and stared
into it. "I heard one of the squires talking to the
Duke. He said we should have been more careful."

"The Duke?"

"No—the squire."

Stammel snorted. "As if he'd ever done anything like
that! I'll warrant the Duke didn't back him up."

"Well—no. He didn't. But—"

"Then don't pay any attention to a squire. Which was
it, anyway?"

"The youngest one. Jostin, I think his name was. I
haven't seen him—"

"You won't. The Duke sent him home; I'd wondered
why. He's got Selfer, Jori, and Kessim now."

"What about Rassamir?"

"Oh, he went back to Vladi. He's a nephew, or
something like that. Well, then: what happened in the
forest?"

Paks had relaxed; now she hunched her shoulders
again. "We were moving fast; the light was fading . . ."
She told it as it lived in her mind: the brigands suddenly around them, Canna down before she could string
the bow, Saben fending off three, her own fall into the
stream, the grinning man who came down after her,
sword in hand. "So—so I turned and—and ran." Paks
was trembling as she finished.

"Best thing you could have done," said Stammel
firmly. "Did they come after you?"

Paks nodded. "For awhile. They had bows—they
shot. But the trees were thick, and it was getting dark—"
There wasn't much to tell about that long wet run in
the dark, no way to describe what she'd felt, leaving

her friends behind. "It took a long time, with the mud and all," she said. "The sentry I ran into didn't believe I was in the Duke's Company at first. No wonder, really, as dirty as I was. But Canna and Saben—" Paks could not go on.

"If you'd stayed," said Stammel, "there'd have been three dead right there, besides all the prisoners, and those in Dwarfwatch as well. You didn't kill them, Paks; the brigands did. Save your anger for them." He leaned back against the wall and gave her a long look. "Do you really think their shades are angry with you? Canna left you her Girdish medallion, didn't she?"

"How did you know that?"

"The Duke, of course. He was curious about that—asked me about you two. But think, Paks—if she'd been angry, she wouldn't have left it for you."

"I—I suppose not."

"Of course not." Stammel reached across the table and laid his hand on hers. "Paks, the Duke thinks you did well—and by Tir, he should! So did Canna. So does everyone I've heard speak of it. It was a hard choice; you chose well. Sometimes there's no way—"

"I know that!" interrupted Paks, fighting tears. "But—"

Stammel sighed. "They were your best friends—and after that—Paks—you may hate me for this, but—did you ever bed Saben?"

Paks shook her head, unable to speak.

"That's part of it, then." He held up a hand as she looked up, angry. "No, hear me out. I'm not arguing about whether you did or didn't: that's your choice. But you two were closer than friends; it's natural in friends to want to have given everything. I'd wager part of your sorrow now is that you didn't give him that, when he wanted it. Isn't it?"

Paks nodded, staring at the table. "Yes," she whispered. "And yet, I—"

"You truly don't want to—that's obvious. You know, Paks, you really have chosen the most difficult way—or it's chosen you, I'm not sure which. Remember, though, that Saben respected your choice. I know, because he told me that back when you were a recruit, in that trouble with Korryn."

Paks felt herself blushing. She had never imagined Saben and Stammel discussing her that way.

Stammel chuckled. "Maybe I shouldn't have told you. Anyway, if it's not your nature—and I think it's not—you have nothing to reproach yourself for. Saben liked you, and respected you, and even loved you. Grieve for him, of course—but don't hamper yourself with guilt."

Paks shook her head. She felt hollow inside, as if she had cried for a long time; yet she felt eased, too. She realized how silly it was to think of Saben's shade hanging around unsatisfied because of her. Such a man, after such a death, would surely have gone straight to the Afterfields, to ride one of the Windsteed's foals forever. She let a last few tears leak past her eyelids, look a long breath, and sipped her ale.

"Better?" asked Stammel. She nodded. "Good. Now," he said briskly, "I'm still curious about that Girdish medallion. You never listened to Effa—had Canna been talking to you? Had you handled it?"

Paks leaned back, staring at her mug. "Well—I did handle it, once."

"Well?" prompted Stammel.

"It was just—well, I don't know. It was strange."

"So you didn't tell the Duke's scribe about it?" suggested Stammel.

"No. No, I didn't. It wasn't anything that concerned the Company, like the rest of it. And I don't know what happened. If anything happened."

"Were you thinking of becoming a Girdsman?"

"No. Nothing like that. I suppose it started the first night, when Cana asked us to pray with her. She knew we weren't Girdsmen, but said it would be all right. The next day we could tell that she was having a lot of trouble with her wound. It was swollen and hot, very red. When Saben and I woke up the next morning, I remembered hearing that St. Gird healed warriors sometimes. Canna was a Girdsman; I thought he might heal her." Paks paused for a sip of ale. Stammel watched her, brows furrowed.

"I asked her; she said it had to be a Marshal or paladin. But I thought if we could pray to Gird to help our friends, why not for healing?" Stammel made a noncommital sound, and Paks hurried on. "Canna said to hold the medallion, and then ask for what I wanted. I put it on her shoulder, where the wound was, and asked for it to be healed."

"Then?"

"It didn't work. It just hurt her; she said it felt like a cramp. It didn't get worse, and she could walk fast all that day, and from then on. But we found that pot of ointment, too. I don't know—"

Stammel heaved a gusty sigh. "That's—quite a story, Paks. Have you told anyone else?"

"No, sir. I don't truly think I did anything. But it might be why Canna left the medallion to me. Maybe she hoped I'd become a Girdsman."

"Maybe. They encourage converts. But that healing, now—"

"But it didn't work," said Paks. "Not like that magical healing, my first year. Some the mage touched, and some got a potion, but it didn't hurt, and the wounds were healed right away."

"Yes, but that was a wizard, someone whose job it was. You aren't a Marshal or paladin; I wouldn't have expected anything at all to happen. Or if it angered Gird, or the High Lord, it should have hurt you, not Canna. Did you feel anything?"

"No. Nothing."

"And she did get better, well enough to draw a bow only five days later."

"That might have been the ointment," said Paks.

"Yes. It could have been. Or else—Tir's bones, Paks, this makes my hair crawl. If you did do something— maybe you ought to find a Gird's Marshal, and tell him about it." Paks shook her head, and Stammel sighed again. "Well. Has anything strange happened since you've been wearing it? You are wearing it, aren't you?"

"Yes. And nothing's happened—really."

"No mysterious cramps that healed anyone, or saved lives?"

"No. Well—it's not the same thing at all, but—it was a cramp in my back that saved me from a crossbow bolt in Rotengre."

"What!"

"But it's nothing to do with the medallion, Stammel. I'm sure of it. We'd been loading plunder all day; we were all tired. I was stooping over this slave we'd found, trying to talk her into getting up and coming along—she was so frightened, I didn't want to drag her—and I got a kind of cramp in my back, and had to straighten up."

"Yes?"

"And the crossbow bolt went where I'd been. There was a second concealed room behind the niche where we'd found the slave, and Captain Dorrin said the man in it was a priest of the Webmistress, Achrya."

Stammel made a warding sign Paks knew. "One of *her* priests! And you just happened to get a cramp. What did Dorrin say?"

"That I was pushing my luck."

"She would. Well, Paks, I can see why you haven't talked about this. I think you're right, unless you decide to find a Marshal. Just in case something is going on, you might like to find out what."

Paks frowned. "But I don't think anything is going on. And I'm not a Girdsman."

"Whatever you say. You're either damned lucky or gods-gifted, or you wouldn't be here today. What a year you've had!" Stammel stretched, arching his back. "Well, it's getting on toward second watch—" He took a final swallow of ale, and nodded for Paks to finish hers. "Now these recruits, Paks, have had their basic training in swords, and they can go through the pair exercises without spitting each other. But they need weapons drill in formation, and a lot of two and three on one. Their shieldwork is as bad as yours was—or worse. Tomorrow I want you to take your four and work on the basics. Be tough with 'em, but try not to scare them so they can't work. All right?"

Paks relaxed, draining her mug. "Yes, sir."

"You heard the captain say the Duke might join us. If he does—he'd rather take a fall than have one of us do something stupid."

"Yes, sir. I'll remember."

"Come on, then." They unfolded themselves from either side of the table, passed through the noisy common room, and went out into the frosty night.

Chapter Twenty-two

Siger, the Duke's old armsmaster, had come south since, as he said, the Duke had left him nothing to do at home.

"You must be some quicker," he greeted Paks. "Or by what I hear you wouldn't be alive. Here—take these bandas for your recruits. Who've you got?" Paks told him. "Volya's quick, but not strong enough yet," he said. "Her shieldwork's wretched. Keri forgets things. Keep after him. Jenits is the best of those—just needs practice and seasoning. Sim's very strong, but slow. Not clumsy, exactly—just slow. I'll check on you later."

Paks collected her little group in one corner of a yard that grew more crowded every minute. With swords alone, they looked fairly good. Sim was a fractional beat behind the count, but it hardly showed. She had them pick up shields. Now the drill grew ragged. Sim slowed more, and Keri kept shoving his shield too far to one side. Volya couldn't seem to get hers high enough. Paks had them pair off, still working on the counted drill. With this stimulus, Volya improved her shieldwork, but

Sim stayed slow. Keri made touches he should not have, and Sim failed to take advantage of Keri's bad shieldwork. Jenits still looked good. Paks moved around them, watching carefully at every stroke, and talking herself hoarse. Finally she stopped them for a water break.

"I suppose," she said, after a drink had restored her voice, "that Siger told you, Sim, that you are too slow?" He nodded. "And Volya—if your shield is down around your ankles, it won't do any good, right?" Volya blushed. "And you, Jenits," she went on. "You may be the best of this group, but you have a long way to go."

"Siger said I was coming well," said Jenits. Paks grinned. She'd hoped for a challenge; it would be a welcome change from talking.

"Well, let's see. Maybe I was fooled by watching you with another recruit. The rest of you: don't sit; you'll stiffen in the cold." Paks drew her sword, took Volya's shield, and faced Jenits. He did not look as confident as the moment before. "Come on," said Paks. "Get that shield up where it'll do you some good. Now start at the beginning."

Jenits began the drill cautiously, as if he thought his sword would break on contact. She countered the strokes easily, without any flourishes, murmuring the numbers as a reminder. He put more bite in the strokes, and Paks responded by stepping up the pace, and strengthening her own. She did not deviate from the drill, but in a few minutes Jenits was sweating and puffing, and she had tapped his banda half a dozen times. She stopped him.

"Jenits, you have the chance to be very good. But right now you're about half as fast as you should be— and half as fit. Your speed will come with practice; the way we're going to drill will take care of the fitness, too. Now walk around and catch your breath while I try the others." Paks was pleased to see that Jenits no longer looked sulky, just thoughtful. She beckoned to Volya, handed back her shield, and took another. Volya was very quick, and her strokes were firm, but she could not keep her shield high enough.

"Is that arm just weak, or did something happen to it?"

"It was broken once, Paks, by a cow. I've tried to strengthen it."

"You'll have to do better. If you can't keep that shield up, you won't survive your first battle. What have you tried?"

"Siger suggested some exercises. I do those—when I remember them."

"You'll remember them," said Paks grimly, "unless you like the idea of dying very young. Right now, while you're resting, raise and lower your shield fifty times— and go this high—" She pushed the shield until it was as high as she wanted it. "Go on, now. Sim, come here."

Sim, a ruddy young boy with a husky build, moved flat-footed. Paks pointed this out, and he tried to stand on his toes instead, moving even more stiffly and slowly. "No, Sim. Not standing on your toes. Just lift your heels a little. Did you ever skip?" She knew as she asked that he had never skipped in his life, and he shook his round head. "Let's try again, then." Sim had a powerful stroke, but so slow that Paks could easily hit twice for each of his. Nothing she said or did made him faster, and she gave up in a few minutes. As least he was strong and tireless.

Keri was the last, and his main problems were sloppy shieldwork and a very short memory. At least, he kept getting the sequence of drill wrong. Several times Paks had to pull her stroke to keep from hurting him badly; he moved exactly the wrong way. She led him through the tricky parts again and again, then turned him over to Jenits. "No variations," she said. "He's got to do this right first." Paks returned to Volya and Sim, and had them pair up without shields. When they started, she began her own exercises while watching them. All around her she heard the clatter of blades and shields, the busy voices of instructors.

"What do you think of them, Paks?" It was Siger, buckling on a sword belt. "Planning to take my job?"

Paks grinned. "I didn't know it was so hard to teach—my voice gave out. But they're about what you said. Sim's impossibly slow; he's dead if he doesn't improve."

"True. Want to go a round?"

"Gladly," said Paks. "Swords only, or shields?"

"Both. Clear your group and give us room." Paks told her recruits to break, and they stepped away.

"Ready?" asked Siger.

Paks nodded. They began with the same drill the recruits knew, but they picked up the tempo smoothly, until it was much faster. Siger began hitting harder; Paks followed suit. Then Siger left the drill sequence, skipping in for a thrust, but Paks countered it, and drove him back. Paks circled, looking for an opening. She tried to force Siger's shield, and took a smart blow on the shoulder. In the next exchange, she tapped his chest. They circled and reversed like a pair of dancers.

"You are quicker," said Siger. "You're doing well. But do you know *this*—" and with a peculiar stroke Paks had never seen he trapped her blade and flicked it away. Someone laughed. Their encounter had attracted more watchers than her recruits. Paks glared at Siger, who was bouncing toward her again. She had her dagger out now, and the watchers were very quiet. With good shieldwork and her long reach, she kept him from touching her, but she couldn't reach him. She thought hard, catching stroke after stroke on her shield until she remembered something she'd seen a Blue Rider do. Suddenly she pivoted to his shield side, jammed the edge of her shield behind his, and threw her weight towards him. Siger staggered to the side, and her dagger stroke was square in the back of his banda.

"Ha!" he cried. "Enough! And where did you learn that little trick?"

Paks grinned at him. "Here and there, you might say." She was breathless and glad for the rest.

"Here's your sword, Paks," said Rauf. She looked at the respectful faces around them and took the sword, checking it for damage. Siger drove the others away and came back, patting her arm.

"That was good. Very good. Show me slowly, please." He stood in front of her, and Paks demonstrated the pivot again. She did not explain that she had seen it used on horseback, and had coaxed the Blue Rider to show her on foot.

"It works best if you have the reach of your opponent," she said. "You have to get your shield up above his shoulder, and then as the pivot continues, you've got it here—" she locked the shields together, "—and your right hand is free for the backstroke. And it's hard for him to strike over the shields."

"Is there a counter?"

"Yes—it's easy. Just step back; don't follow the pivot. Thing is, it works best against someone who thinks he's got more weapon. The start of the turn looks like a retreat; if he follows it, you've got him. But if he stays back, you can't lock shields."

"Very good. Very good. Come this afternoon and I'll show you that little twist that cost you your blade. A favor for a favor."

"Thank you," said Paks. She turned to her recruits as Siger moved away. They looked at her with more awe than before.

"Do we have to be that fast?" asked Jenits.

"It helps," said Paks. "Suppose your opponent is. You need every scrap of speed and strength you can build. I'm faster than I was, and I hope I'll keep improving."

"I'll never do it," said Sim. "I'm strong. I know I'm strong, and I thought that would be enough. I could beat up anyone in my village. But I never was fast."

"You'll get faster," said Paks firmly. "When I was a recruit, Siger thumped my ribs and yelled 'faster, faster' at me every day—and finally I got faster. You will too, unless your ribs are tougher than mine were." They laughed, a little nervously.

From across the yard came a shout: "Hey—Saben. Come here." Paks stiffened, her head swinging automatically to look before she caught herself. She felt tears sting her eyes, and blinked fiercely. Saben was a common enough name; she'd have to get used to it.

"Paks?" They all looked concerned. Volya went on. "Did you know him before? Saben, I mean?"

Paks shook her head, and took a deep steadying breath. "No. A different Saben—a good friend. We'd been together since we came in, and he was with me on—on the trip you heard about. But he died."

"Oh."

"Well, it happens. We're soldiers, after all. It's just—there's not another Saben in the Company, so when I hear the name, I think— I'll get used to it. I suppose. Now, let's get back to work. Sim, you and Jenits this time, and Keri and Volya." They started again and Paks kept after them until time for the midday meal.

Within a week, Paks lost Sim to Cracolnya's cohort. She was glad; a slow archer might live longer than a slow swordsman. Less welcome was the change in cohort position resulting from the number of recruits. Normally, recruits were kept to the rear, except for a few who had showed promise. But Arcolin decided that they should be close to their veteran instructors, which meant that Paks ended up as file sixth. She understood the reasons, but didn't like it even so.

There were other changes. Horse-faced Pont was now Arcolin's junior captain, and Valichi took Pont's place with Cracolnya. The Duke had hired a captain to replace Sejek: Peska, a dark, dour man who had been a watch captain at court in Pargun. He spoke Common with a curious accent that Paks had never heard; she was glad her cohort had Pont instead, though Barra had no complaints about him.

This year Paks could not ask Donag for advance

information—and no one in the cohort seemed to know what the Duke planned, except trouble for Siniava. When they marched out of Valdaire on the southern road, the one to Czardas that Paks remembered, she expected to see Halverics—but instead they met the Golden Company a few miles from the city. Aesil M'dierra, mounted on a chestnut horse and armored in gold-washed mail, rode beside the Duke; her company fell in behind. Paks eyed her: the only woman in Aarenis to command her own mercenary company. What would that be like? What could she be like?

But the next day they turned aside, through Baron Kodaly's lands, and Golden Company stayed on the road south. Through a steady rain they marched easily, guided by a wiry dark man who had come with the Baron. Paks thought he looked like a juggler, but Stammel laughed when she said it.

"Juggler! Tir, no. I'll admit the jugglers you see in Valdaire are his subjects, more than likely. That's one of the woods tribes—their king, or prince, or whatever."

"But why—?"

Stammel shrugged. "I don't know. They have a lot of power in the forests of Aarenis, I've heard. The Duke's always made friends with them. Maybe he wants safe passage through some forest."

Whatever he was, he led them by ways that avoided all hazards of bog and mud. Three days he was gone, but they marched easily beside a larger stream with a village in sight.

They were met, in the fields above the village, by an old man in a long robe and a fat man in helmet and breastplate commanding ten unarmored youths with scythes and pikes. Paks could not hear what the Duke said to them, but the youths suddenly trailed their weapons in the mud and turned away. The village had a cobbled square, and a group of taller buildings around it. Paks looked for an inn, hoping for ale. She saw a battered sign with a picture of a tower by a river; the sign read Inzing Paksnor. The inn yard was large, but part of the building had been torn down to build a stable. They marched through, to camp on the far side where one stream joined another.

Across the stream was a rising slope of farmland, and on the southern horizon a long stony escarpment running roughly west to east. It reminded Paks of the high moors behind Three Firs, and looked like nothing else she had seen in the south.

"That's the Middle Marches," said Devlin to a curious recruit. "Once you're up on those heights, it's sheepfarming land. And downstream maybe a day's march from here is Ifoss."

"Who claims the Middle Marches?" asked someone else.

"Whoever can." Devlin turned to look at the fire. "There's petty barons enough, near the river—like Kodaly. Ifoss claims some of it. More barons downstream until Vonja. Up on the high ground it's hard to say. There was a count Somebody, when I first came south, but he died. I heard he left no heir of the body—a nephew or something in Pliuni. The Honeycat tries to claim it, as he claims everything else. I think—I think when he took Pliuni, he captured the nephew, or married him to a daughter or niece. Or maybe that was another place."

"What's beyond it?" asked Paks.

"Straight south?" She nodded. "Well, Andressat. That's ruled by a count, if I remember. An old family, anyway, and very powerful. I think the Duke hired to Andressat once, before I joined. They've got only one city: Cortes Andres. They say its inner fortifications have never been broken."

"Does the Honeycat control Andressat?"

"Tir, no! The count—Jeddrin, I think his name is—he hates him. Then south of Andressat are the South Marches. The Honeycat claims that, and for all I know he may have a right to it. He also claims the cities along the Chaloquay, and the Horn Bay ports on the Immerhoft. That's Sibili and Cha, on the river, and Confaer, Korran, and Sul, on the coast."

"How did he ever claim Pliuni?" asked Paks.

"Just took it. Waited until the Sier of Westland was fighting up in the western mountains, and marched up and took it. Pliuni was a free city, but had always looked to the Sier for protection."

"What about the rest of the port cities?" asked Arñe.

"I don't know. I've heard the names, but I don't know exactly where they are or who controls them. Seafang, that's a pirate city, and Immerdzan, at the mouth of the Immer. Let's see: Zith, Aliuna, Sur-vret, Anzal, and Immer-something. No, Ka-Immer. Some are pirate cities, and some are legitimate traders—so they say."

Ifoss, when they came to it the next day, seemed small and dingy after Valdaire. A walled city of no more than eight or nine thousand, surrounded by plowland and orchards, it was bleak in winter. They camped outside the city on a long field sloping to the river, and wagons rolled out with provisions. With the wagons came Guildmasters to confer with the Duke; recruits and veterans alike gaped at their distinctive dress, the short-pointed, fur-edged hats, long pointed sleeves, and oddly cut jackets trimmed in elaborate braid.

They stayed at Ifoss several days. On the second night, Paks took advantage of her seniority to enter the city. Stammel had told them of a good new inn near the east gate, the Laughing Fox, so they ignored the Falcon, the Golden Ladder, and the Juggler to work their way across town to Stammel's choice.

It was new, clean, and the landlord seemed friendly. The ale was good, too, and not expensive. Paks ordered a fried fruit pie, and Vik decided on a slab of spicebread; soon they were enjoying an impromptu party. When Paks decided to leave, two of the group weren't ready to come and stayed behind—"just to finish the jug," they said.

"Don't come back too late," teased Vik, "and expect us to take your slot on guard, because I'm going to get my beauty sleep."

"Beauty sleep, or sleep with a beauty?" asked a townsmen at the next table, emboldened by his flask of wine as he eyed Paks.

"Sleep," replied Vik cheerfully. "She's on guard before I am." Which was not true, but made a good exit. Paks had already turned away, trusting Vik to find a good answer. He always did, with everyone. They got back to camp shortly before the watch change; Stammel was not pleased to find that two had stayed behind.

"Do you think they'll be back on time, or had I better go roust 'em out."

"Sif's not on until late watch," said Paks. "He's got a strong head, and I don't think he'll be late. I don't know Tam that well—he's Dorrin's—but surely Sif will keep an eye on him."

"I hope. It seems a clean enough place, but it is on the far side of town. If they're not back by midwatch, let me know; I'll want to find 'em."

The guard assignment had Paks partnered with Jenits; they had a short stretch on the east side of camp, from the horse lines to the entrance. It was nearly midwatch when she heard a wavering song from the lane that led to Ifoss. As the noise came closer, she could hear two voices. The guards at the camp entrance snickered. Paks hoped it was Sif and Tam, but they did sound drunk.

"Like the bee-e-e, so swift to anger . . . but her honey's . . . rich and swee-eet—" one of the two stopped to cough, then picked up the song again. "I don't fe-ear her painful stinger . . . but the honey-y . . . I will—"

"Quiet, there!" Dorrin, the watch captain, had heard the noise. Paks heard a hiccup and indistinct mutters from the pair. "Come up to the light," said Dorrin, "and give the password." Paks saw two shadowy figures approach the torches at the camp entrance, and heard them stumble over the password.

"You're a disgrace," snapped Dorrin. "Veterans who don't know their limit—why do you think we didn't let the others into town, eh? This is no campaign for getting drunk and blabbing in taverns. And what happened to your cloak, Tam?" Paks could not hear the answer, if he made any. Dorrin cleared her throat and spat. "Your sergeants will see to you," she said. "Wait here." She strode off.

"Is it that bad to get drunk?" asked Jenits softly. "I used to—"

"It depends," said Paks. They turned back toward the horse lines. "Anything you say in a tavern will travel. If you get drunk and talk about the Company, where we're marching, or when—that's bad."

"I see," said Jenits.

"And then if you're drunk," said Paks, "you're more likely to be taken by slavers, or attacked by thieves. Or if it makes you mean, you might brawl, and that makes trouble for the Company. Of course if it's a cohort or Company banquet, that's different."

Next day Paks saw Sif grooming mules under the sarcastic guidance of the muleskinner. She was sure that Dorrin's sergeant had found something equally unpleasant for Tam.

When they left Ifoss, it was to march across pastures towards the Middle Marches. By nightfall they were camped under the ridge. Sheep trails led up it. The next day they spent climbing, winding back and forth along the face of the slope. To the north their view broadened: they could see Ifoss with its wall, and downstream another wall and tower that Stammel said was Foss Fort. A cold wind scoured the height. They passed outcrops of gray stone splashed with orange and brown lichens. The outcrops grew rougher, formed into long lines like low walls. They passed through a gap in one, shoulder high on either side; it ran along the slope as far as Paks could see. Above it, the rocks disappeared once more under thick turf, still winter-tawny. The slope eased. They camped that night near that natural stone wall.

They reached the broad top of the ridge in less than

an hour of marching the next morning. Paks looked at the vast and empty land to the south. The great ridge seemed to fall slightly to the southwest, cleft here and there by steep watercourses furred with trees. The sky was almost clear; they could see for miles—could see, for instance, a galloping horseman far ahead. None of the officers seemed concerned, so Paks thought it must be one of their own messengers.

Although they crossed many winding sheep trails, they saw neither sheep nor shepherds. Paks realized that they were more visible than a flock of stone-gray sheep—of course any shepherd would move out of their path. That afternoon they camped where a pool had formed below several springs; a small clear stream ran away from the low end of the pool and dropped into a narrow cleft in the rock.

It was just after lunch on the next day when Paks heard horns blowing in the south; the sound trembled in the still air. She peered south, trying to see something. Far down the slope was a knot of horsemen, but the horn calls had come from farther away than that. The thunder of hooves began to shake the ground. Stammel called them into fighting formation; other sergeants were yelling. They unslung shields and drew their swords. Paks watched her recruits. Volya looked pale, but eager. Keri was frowning, and waggling his blade a little as if reminding himself of the drill. The back of Jenit's neck was red. She eased her own shoulders and took a deep breath as the riders neared. They wore brown and gray tunics, oddly loose and flapping, and carried lances with no decoration.

The leading horses slowed, and the foremost rider hailed the Duke. Arcolin rode forward with him. Once more, Paks could not hear what was said. She looked at her recruits again; they were too stiff.

"Easy," she said. "Breathe slowly." Keri's eyes slid toward hers, and he drew a shaky breath. Arcolin turned to the column and signalled the sergeants.

"Sheathe your blades," said Stammel; Paks eased her

sword back in place. Some of the recruits were so tense it took them two tries. They waited. Paks glanced down and saw a fresh green blade poking up through the mat of frost-burned turf. Ahead, almost under Jenits' left foot, was a flat rosette of leaves with two tiny white flowers on top. Almost spring, thought Paks. She looked around for other flowers, but saw none. The riders were turning their horses away. The captains came back to their commands, but the Duke and his squires moved up beside the leading rider.

"We've a fast march to make," said Arcolin, "with a fight to the end of it. Take a drink now, and re-sling your shields but be ready to shift position at any time." No one had much to say as they started south again at a faster pace. An arc of riders went before them, and others rode on their flanks. Paks looked hard at the drab tunics; when one rider bent to untwist a rein, she caught a glimpse of rose through the loose sleeve. So. They were Clarts after all.

As they went they heard horns again: deep and high, long note and sharp staccato signals. It was hard to keep the pace even; the horns and the steepening downhill slope pulled them forward, ever faster. Paks could see, now, that they were coming to a broad saddle between the high ground behind them and a similar rise ahead. To left and right the land fell steeply into deep gorges. Beyond the saddle, shining in the late afternoon sun, rose a tower; around it writhed a dark mass that Paks realized must be an army. They marched on; Paks wondered if they would make that distance by dark. And whose side were they on?

As they started across the saddle, more drab-clad riders came up from the broken ground to either side. The slope rose under their feet toward the tower. Paks could not see, now, for the riders ahead, but the crash and roar of battle came clearly. Rising excitement swamped the fatigue of the day's march. The riders pulled their baggy tunics over their heads, and Clart Cavalry rose and white glowed in the slanting sun.

Arcolin leaned to speak to Stammel. He nodded, turning to the cohort. "Shields," he said; Paks took her own shield, and made sure her recruits had theirs secure. They drew swords. As they advanced, shifting from marching column to battle order, Cracolnya's cohort moved off to their right flank.

"Slow advance—keep in line, there!" yelled Stammel. Paks heard the Clarts yipping as they spurred to the attack. Dust rose in clouds. A great yell from before them; more horn signals. The Duke appeared out of the dust to ride beside them. His squires clustered around him; Paks wondered if they could see any better from the saddle.

The Duke pointed ahead; one of the squires took off at a gallop. Arcolin jogged up from the rear of the cohort, and rode beside the Duke. Paks could hear nothing but battle sounds. Arcolin dropped back, and in a few moments Dorrin's cohort came along side on their left. Paks saw the Duke's head turn. She looked ahead. Through the swirling dust she could see struggling figures—even the colors. Green, there—black and yellow—and more green. The tower loomed higher as they neared it; its parapet was above the dust, and Paks saw blue-clad archers.

The Duke put a light hunting horn to his lips and blew a rapid five-note signal. At once it was answered by a call that Paks recognized as Halveric; the battle surged toward them as the green-clad soldiers retreated. Their opponents roared in triumph—a sound that stopped abruptly as they saw behind the fleeing Halverics the solid ranks of Phelani. Another horn-call, and the Halverics slipped left. The enemy fighters crashed into the Phelan's lines. Arcolin's cohort, nearly in the center of the arc formed by Clarts, Phelani, and Halverics, took the brunt of that charge. Paks had no time for a last encouraging word to her recruits; she was tightly engaged.

Despite the hours of practice, Paks found the curved blade strokes of the enemy hard to counter. She took several minor cuts before killing her first opponent, and was just in time to help Keri with the one who had shattered his shield. She fought on, trying to keep an eye on her recruits when she could. The cohort had nearly halted under the enemy rush, but they had not faltered, and the front ranks still held a good line.

"Arcolin's cohort! Drive em!" It was the Duke's voice, from behind them; the cohort surged forward, flattening the arc as they came. The enemy softened, rolling left away from their pressure. Still the fighting raged; Paks had no time to wonder how the battle was going. Jenits went down in front of her; she lunged across him to strike the enemy who was about to kill him. Jenits screamed as she stepped on his arm; she shifted a pace and hoped someone would get him away safely. His attacker fought wildly; she finally dropped him with a thrust to the neck. She spared a glance for Jenits and didn't see him. Good, she thought, and thrust at the oncoming soldiers.

The enemy in front melted away, though by the noise the left flank was busy enough. Paks looked around and spotted Volya and Keri. Volya was bleeding from a bad slash to her right arm; Keri's shield had fallen apart, though he still clutched the grip.

"Keri! Pick up the good shield—drop that—" He looked at her in surprise, then at his arm; she watched until he stripped off the broken one and picked up an enemy shield nearby. "Volya, get that wound tied up—drop back—one of the sergeants will tell you where to go." Other wounded were shifting to the rear, and those still sound drew together.

Paks looked for Arcolin or the Duke; she spotted Arcolin on their left front. Stammel was with him. Arcolin waved a signal to Cracolnya, who sent his cohort forward. The Clarts, having rearmed, rode up on the far right, and the right wing wheeled, compressing the enemy against Dorrin's cohort and the Halverics. Paks still could not tell how many they faced. They fought on; the enemy lines, though wavering, hardly

seemed to diminish. The sun was down; as light faded
out of the sky, the enemy made one more frantic attempt to break through. Favored by the downward
slope, they penetrated between the Halverics and
Dorrin's cohort, pouring away downhill in the darkness.
Paks heard curses from the Clarts, who spurred after
them recklessly. Paks hoped the Duke would not command a foot pursuit. She was suddenly almost too tired
to move.

Arcolin rode back to them, talking to a Clart captain.
Then he turned to Stammel. "Take them to the enemy
camp; the Clarts hold it. Set up a strong perimeter. I
think Dorrin's cohort is pursuing, but some of them
may circle back. I'll be near the tower entrance if you
need me." He rode toward the tower; light spilled from
its narrow windows. Paks wondered who held it.

The enemy camp was full of supplies. The Clarts had
overridden some of the tents, but most were still standing. Cattle roasted over a long trenchfire. Paks's mouth
watered. She and the other veterans stood guard while
uninjured recruits helped the surgeons and set up camp.
She wished she knew how her recruits were, and her
friends. She had seen Vik and Arñe only at a distance.

It seemed long before Stammel returned to the perimeter. Paks cleaned her sword and sheathed it, then
slipped off her shield and stretched. Her shoulders
were stiff where the pack straps had dug in; she hadn't
fought in a pack except in drill. Reluctantly she picked
up the shield, yawning. Now she could feel every cut
and bruise. The wind blew the smell of roasting meat
past her nose, and her stomach knotted. At last a recruit came, grease still streaking his chin, to relieve her
post. Stammel met her as she turned away.

"Here." He handed her a slab of beef on a split loaf.
"I meant to get to you earlier. You'll want to see Jenits;
his arm's broken. Volya needed stitching, but she's up
and around. Keri's fine; hardly scratched." Paks mum-
bled her thanks past a mouthful of food.

"Whose tower?" she asked, after swallowing a huge lump of beef.

"Andressat's. Their colors are blue and gold. You'll see tomorrow."

"Why didn't they come out? I thought they hated Siniava."

"They do. But they've only got forty or fifty in there. They don't want to lose the tower to anyone: not even us."

Paks nodded as she ate, and walked on to the surgeons' tent. It had evidently belonged to an enemy officer; it was large and divided by yellow hanging panels into several rooms. Jenits lay on a straw pallet with his shoulder propped up on a frame; his left arm was bound in splints. Volya sat beside him with a flask; they both looked pale, but well enough.

"Have you had any food yet?" asked Paks. They both nodded. "Good. I'll finish my supper." She squatted beside Jenits. "Did they give you numbwine?"

"Yes—they did." His voice was slightly blurred.

"I'm sorry I stepped on you," said Paks. "But that—"

"That's all right. It was—broken already. That's why—I fell."

"It's a good thing it was your shield arm," said Paks. "You won't be fighting for weeks, but it won't be as hard to retrain. You did well, Jenits. I suppose Stammel told you that—"

"Yes. But I—I forgot which strokes, after awhile—and it was so fast—"

"I forgot too, in my first battle; that's when I got the big scar on my leg. As Stammel said to me, we'll just drill you more until you can't forget." Jenits managed a shaky grin. Paks turned to Volya. "Volya, you did well too. What I could see of your shieldwork was much better. Now—did the surgeons tell you to stay with Jenits?"

"Yes. They said give him more numbwine if he needed it."

"I can do that, and let you get some sleep. We'll all

be pulling watch tonight, and fighting again tomorrow, I expect."

"Oh, I couldn't sleep. I'm still too excited." Volya's eyes were very bright.

Paks sighed. "Volya, you're tired, whether you know it or not. Go roll up in your cloak, and if you aren't asleep in a half glass, you can come back and take over for me." Volya got up reluctantly, and handed Paks the flask of numbwine. "And don't start talking to anyone; that *will* keep you awake." Volya nodded and went out. The surgeon came through from another part of the tent and looked at Paks.

"Is that your blood, or theirs?"

Paks looked at her arm. "Both, I think. Nothing serious, though."

"But you've been on guard, and haven't had time to clean them. I know the story. Let me see." With painful thoroughness the surgeon scrubbed the various cuts she'd taken, grumbling the while. "If I could just convince you heroes that cleaning these things out does as much good—no, *more* good—than a healing spell. It's cheap. It's easy. They don't fester and give you fever if they're *clean*—"

"Ouch!" said Paks, as the cleaning solution stung in a slice across her hand.

"Hold still. I have to see if that got into the joint—no—lucky. Maybe we need thicker gloves."

"I didn't have mine on," muttered Paks. The surgeon snorted and went on.

"Are you sure you aren't hiding something else?" he asked when he had finished wrapping bandages around her hand.

"Nothing else." She looked down and found that Jenits had followed the whole proceeding with interest. So had others in the room.

"Are you staying with him?" asked the surgeon.

"Do you need me to? I can."

"Yes. Please. We've got Clart and Halveric wounded coming in, and there'll be more later. You can give him enough numbwine to make him sleep. Three or four swallows more should do it. Same for the others—call if anything goes wrong." The surgeon passed on to the next room, and Paks lifted Jenits' head so he could drink more easily. In a few minutes, he was snoring. She glanced around at the others; they all seemed to be dozing. Paks propped the flask nearby and took off her pack to get her cloak. She wrapped it around her shoulders. From the other end of the tent came a sudden flurry that subsided after a few minutes.

When she opened her eyes next, she was stiff as a board and the surgeon was laughing at her in the lamplight. "Some watcher," he said. "If you were going to sleep, you should have found a pallet and stretched out."

Paks yawned and tried to focus her eyes. "I didn't know I was going to sleep. Sorry." She looked at Jenits, but he slept peacefully.

"No sign of fever," said the surgeon. "This time get comfortable before you go back to sleep."

Paks pushed herself up, shaking her head. "I won't sleep. What watch is it, anyway?"

"Don't worry. Stammel came by to tell you he wouldn't need you—"

"And found me asleep." Paks blushed.

"Well," said the surgeon, "he didn't wake you, and told me to let you sleep till dawn. That's another four hours."

Paks yawned again. "It's tempting—" The surgeon turned away. Three years' experience told her to take sleep when she could find it—but now she was awake, and curiosity kept her so. With a last look at Jenits, she left the tent and headed for the area assigned to her cohort.

Kefer was snoring by the watchfire, but roused when she spoke to the sentry. He confirmed what the surgeon had said, and told her to get what sleep she could.

"We'll march tomorrow, and if we catch them, we'll

fight." Kefer yawned. "Clarts got many of 'em, but six hundred or so are loose."

Paks held her hands to the fire; the night was cold after the surgeons' tent. "Stammel said our losses weren't bad—?"

"No—not in our cohort. Three returned veterans. One recruit. Dorrin's was harder hit—but still not bad, considering. Go on, Paks, get some sleep." He pointed to a nearby tent; Paks edged in, found an empty space, and slept until day.

Despite Kefer's prediction, they did not march the next day; instead they dismantled the enemy camp. Several squads went to the battlefield, returning with salvageable weapons and armor. Others cleared the camp itself of supplies: bags of grain and beans, great jars of wine and barrels of ale, and so on. One tent held all the gear for a smith's shop: anvils, hammers, tongs, bellows, and bars and disks of rough iron.

Most of this they carried into the storage cellars of the tower, each load tallied by a scribe from each company. Siger and Hofrin chose weapons to replace those damaged, and reserve supplies to take along. The enemy's mules were distributed to each company too, along with the feed for them.

From the talk she heard while working, Paks gathered that Siniava's army had come from the west. Before reaching this tower, they had taken those along the western border, and these were now garrisoned by Siniava's troops. But a survivor had escaped to warn the commander of the north watch, the Count of Andressat's son-in-law; when the enemy force arrived, it found this tower sealed and well defended. Clart scouts, riding ahead of the Halverics, had discovered the siege in progress, and the Halverics attacked the besiegers. Though heavily outnumbered, they had held the enemy close under the tower walls, where the Andressat archery could do its worst, until the rest of the Clarts and the Phelani arrived in force.

"They should have got out of here," said a Halveric

corporal as he and Paks dragged sacks of grain across the tower court. "Only they thought they could break us and get rid of us—the fools—and we kept 'em busy enough they didn't think of anyone else."

"You had a rough time, then," said Paks.

"Oh—we fight close order, same as you. We just drew in and let 'em pound. We knew you was comin'. And we had some Clarts, to mess 'em about on the flanks."

"It's too bad they broke loose," muttered a Halveric private. "After what they did last year—"

"Too many of 'em," said the corporal. "We mauled 'em enough, they'll be wary of us awhile. Besides, let 'em go tell their master they were beat again. Enough times running away like that, and they won't be good for anything—nor the ones they tell the story to, neither."

By that night, they enemy camp was dismantled. Everything else was piled and burned, a great fire that leapt into the dark and told everyone for miles around that the enemy's camp was gone. Paks had a share marked to her in the account books. Her recruits were recruits no longer; they had all been promoted.

When they marched the next morning, Paks found herself moved up in the column; she was sorry about those whose death and injuries gave her the place, but she liked seeing ahead. All along the way the evidence of the enemy's flight: broken weapons, blood-stained clothing and armor, and bodies. Not all had been killed by Clarts or Halverics, as the wounds showed.

By midafternoon they reached the next tower to the west. A black and yellow banner flew from its peak, and a hail of arrows met them when they ventured closer. Their assault failed, and the two companies camped around the walls. The Clarts had ridden afar ahead, to scout the tower beyond, and returned with the news that it too was held by an enemy force.

At dawn the next day, Paks was on guard on the north side when she saw about fifty black-clad fighters come over the wall, barely visible in the dim light. She

yelled an alarm and darted forward; an arrow glanced
off her helmet. The archers were awake in the tower.
She threw up her shield and plunged on with the rest
of the sentries, as the camp came awake behind her.
For a few desperate minutes, the sentries were outnumbered and hard pressed.

Simultaneously, the enemy troops tried a sally from
the south entrance, where the Halverics were just taking their positions for an assault. In minutes a howling
mass of fighters swayed back and forth in front of the
gate. More and more of Siniava's troops poured from
the gate, as Paks heard later from one of the Halveric
soldiers.

"We had to give back; they had us outnumbered, but
then your Duke brought two of your cohorts around,
and it was stand and stick. That went on all morning,
near enough. They couldn't break out, and we couldn't
get in. Then they backed in a step at a time, and got
that portcullis down—I'll say this for Andressat: they
know how to build a fort."

Paks had been on the fringe of that battle, as one of
the sentry ring on the other side. She met Barranyi in
the cook tent.

"I'll tell you what, Paks," said Barra. "He's no fool,
their captain. They came near breaking through more
than once, and if they pick the right time, they might
yet."

Paks mopped up the last of her beans with a crust of
bread. "Not with the Halveric and the Duke. He won't
surprise them. What I wonder about is how many more
there are—at the next tower, and the next. We can
hold these—but more?"

"Andressat has troops somewhere—"

"What—sixty or so in the first tower, and maybe as
many in the next one or two? And they won't leave the
towers unguarded."

"No, more than that. I heard Dorrin say something
to Val about it this morning. Troops on the way, she
said, and could be here this afternoon or tomorrow."

"I'll believe that, Barra, when I see it. Did you hear whether the Honeycat was in there?" She cocked her head at the tower.

"No. They all say not. And I haven't seen the banner his bodyguard carried last fall."

"I hope we don't waste too much time here, then. I wonder where that scum is."

"And what troops he has. All we can do is hope the Clarts don't miss anything."

"If he's clear off east—back toward Sorellin or those others cities—we could wander around here all season and never catch him."

Barra shrugged. "That's the Duke's business. Not yours." Paks stood up, and Barra eyed her. "Are you upset about anything in particular? More than Canna and Saben?"

"That and—Barra, you know what he did to some of the prisoners last year—?" Barra nodded. "We found a set of tools in one of the tents. I just want to be sure we do kill him."

"But his army'd still be—"

Paks shook her head. "No, I don't think they'll be the same, even if there's much army left. I think it's his doing."

"Maybe." Barra turned to greet Natzlin, coming from the serving line, and Paks waved and went back to her station.

The rest of the day the two forces did not change their positions. The Andressat troops arrived midmorning the next day. Paks thought they looked much more professional than the city militia she'd seen. They numbered just over a thousand, organized into four cohorts, each with two hundred foot and fifty horse. Paks watched as the Duke and the Halveric rode out to meet them. The Andressat troops moved into siege positions, and the mercenaries withdrew a space.

"I heard we march in the morning," said Vik, as he and Paks lugged tent poles from one camp to another.

"I hope so," said Paks. "That group can handle the tower without us."

"They do look good," conceded Vik. "But why d'you suppose they make their cohorts so big? They can't be flexible."

"Huh. If we had that many men, we might find four units easier to move than—" Paks wrinkled her brows, trying to think how many it would be.

"Ten," said Vik smugly. "I wish we had—then nobody could stand against us."

"Nobody's going to." Paks grunted as they heaved the poles up in their new holes. "I hope we don't have to raise all the tents for only one night."

"I don't think so." Vik rubbed his sunburnt nose. "I'd like to know how many troops Siniava has—altogether."

"Not enough to stop us," said Paks grimly.

"I hope not. But look, Paks—if he could send eight hundred or a thousand up here—and he's not with them—he must have another army someplace. And his cities garrisoned. He could have a much bigger army than the Duke's put together."

"That's true." Paks frowned. "Well—if it is—"

"We'll do like the man with the barrel of ale," said Vik with a grin.

"What's that?"

"Don't tell me you never heard that! It's old, Paks."

"I never did. Tell me."

"Well, there was a man famous for what he could down at one swallow. At a market fair, he won lots of free ale by betting that he could drink this jug or that, or a skin of wine, at one draught. Soon he was famous for miles around, and no one would bet. Then he went a journey with a brother of his, and they stopped at an inn. His brother started bragging on what he could do, and the long and the short of it is that the innkeeper asked him to wager. Well, he looked around the room, and saw no pot or jug he couldn't drain. He agreed to take but one swallow to empty any alepot in the room, or give up all his silver.

"But the innkeeper had his own tricks, and pulled aside a curtain by the bar, and there was a barrel half full of ale. Of course the man said it was no pot, but the others around said it was, and there were more of them, and they were armed.

"The man knew he was trapped, and he was angry besides. So he walked over and tried to lift it, and of course it was too heavy. The innkeeper told him to kneel down and drink from the bunghole—actually he said worse than that—laughing all the while, and the man was so angry he could nearly fly. So: No, he said, and I drink my ale standing, as any man may, he said, and he rammed a hole in the bottom and let the ale run out until he could lift it and drink the rest—in one swallow. His brother held the innkeeper off in the meantime with a sword off the wall. And when he had finished, he said: A pot's what you can lift in your hand, innkeeper, and any fool who can't tell a pot from a barrel might sell a barrel of ale for the price of a pot. Then the townsmen laughed, and not just because of his strong arm, and made the innkeeper pay up. And he and his brother made their way on the road alive and no poorer. So now, where I grew up, if anyone takes on too much, we say he must be like the man with the barrel of ale: cut the trouble down to his size before swallowing it."

Paks nodded, laughing, and Vik went on. "This is letting some of the ale out of Siniava's barrel—he lost more than six hundred men last fall, and he'll lose these, and the rest in Andressat—say eight hundred or more. You can't pull that many well-trained troops out of a hat, you know. However many he's got, this will hurt."

"I hope so," said Paks.

Chapter Twenty-three

For the next three days, the Halverics and the Duke's Company marched south to Cortes Andres. They were slowed by rain and rugged country; the road zigzagged into steep valleys and back up to the sheep pastures. Paks saw carefully terraced slopes set with precise rows of dark sticks.

"Are those young fruit trees?" she asked Stammel.

"Tir, no! Those are grape vines. This is wine country, Paks."

"Oh. They don't look like any grape vines I've seen." Paks thought of the little black grapes of the north, that sprawled over bushes and walls in an untidy tangle.

"They are. Expensive ones, too. If we break off a single twig, the Count'd have our hides."

They passed through villages nestled in the sides of valleys: stone houses built so close together that the roof of one was the first story of another. Down in the narrow valleys, little plots of spring grain showed green, and a few fruit trees were just starting to bloom. The streams ran clean and clear in rocky beds. Paks saw no

cattle, and noticed that the sheep and goats were often
spotted in bold patterns of brown and black and white.

The rain which had slowed them covered their approach to Cortes Andres. Clart Cavalry slipped between Siniava's pickets and the city, and the retreating
enemy ran straight into the front of the Duke's column.

Seen from the high ground on the northern road,
Cortes Andres gave Paks the impression of great strength
and stubbornness. Its outer walls were built of immense blocks of gray stone, while above the wall all the
towers and battlements were white. Two inner walls
circled the city as well. The innermost, like the citadel
which rose inside it, was built of pale gold stone. Of the
buildings within the walls nothing could be seen but
red-tiled roofs, which gave color to the stone around
them. Paks could well believe that this citadel had
never been taken by assault. She could not see anything of the rivers that came together just south of the
city wall; she had been told they formed a deep gorge,
and cliffs protected the city on that side.

They marched nearer. The rain stopped, and the sky
lightened. Aliam Halveric rode up beside the Duke;
both had their standard bearers display their colors. As
they neared the gates, a blue and gold banner rose
above it. Arcolin halted the column. After a short wait,
a man rode from a narrow postern to meet the Halveric
and the Duke. The Duke turned and waved; Arcolin
started them moving again. They marched nearer. Paks
noticed that the portcullis did not rise, nor the gates
open. She glanced up. Bowmen were visible on the
wall. The column had marched past the commanders in
conference, but now the man from Cortes Andres rode
forward and shouted up to the gate tower windows.
Arcolin halted them again. Paks squinted up at the
arrowslits and caught a glint of light. She felt sweat
spring out on her neck, and fought the desire to swing
her shield up. Suppose these were not Andressat's men,
but Siniava's? The Duke rode up beside them. With a
terrible screech the portcullis lifted from its bed. It

moved more slowly than any Paks had seen, crawling up its tracks. Then the gates folded inward.

The gatehouse tower was uncommonly deep; Paks saw the tracks of three portcullises. Between them, when she looked up, were convenient holes for bowmen, and she thought she saw eyes gleaming behind each hole. They came out of the tower into a stone paved area between the first and second walls, bare of cover and easily commanded by either. Part of this was fenced off for sheep pens, but all of it, Paks realized, would make a fine trap for an army that managed to take the outer gate.

The second wall was higher than the first, and its gate was some distance to the west. They threaded their way past pens of sheep to halt outside the second gate tower. These gates were also closed, but a cluster of figures in blue and gold waited for them. Paks, marching in the first cohort, could see the deference with which the Duke and Aliam Halveric dismounted and walked up to the gray-haired man in the middle. It startled her to hear them addressed as "Aliam" and "young Phelan." She expected the Duke to do something, but he answered courteously, calling the man "my lord Count." The captains were introduced, and after more conversation the Count strolled down their column. Paks wished they were not rain-wet and muddy. When he returned, he was chatting with the Duke about border towers and the condition of the vineyards. Paks could not see how they were related.

"Well, then," he said. "We haven't enough stabling within the inner walls for all those cavalry—your mount, of course, Phelan, and Aliam's, and your captains', will be in the citadel. Your troops can have barracks space in the second ring. Fersin, my aide, will direct them." One of his retinue bowed. "You'll dine with me in the citadel, and your captains as well. I expect they'll want to be housed with their cohorts, yes?" The Duke nodded. "I've arranged a suite for you and Aliam, convenient to my quarters; we have much to confer about."

The Count glanced at the column again. "Do you—do you need separate barracks space for the women?"

"No, my lord Count."

"I see." He sounded doubtful. "We don't—meaning no disparagement to your troops, Phelan, but we have not seen so many women active in warfare. A paladin here or there, an occasional knight—but—well, no matter."

"I assure you, my lord, that they are quite capable." The Duke's voice was dry, and Paks suppressed a grin.

"Oh, quite—quite, I'm sure. Meant no disparagement. But one thing, Phelan, your troops can't wander about armed in the city—"

"Certainly not, my lord. They will stack their arms in barracks, and I had not planned to permit any wandering anyway."

"I didn't mean to sound inhospitable—"

"Not at all. No one wants strange troops straying loose. These won't."

"No harm if they go to the fountains—or if you need more supplies—but it might be better if they stayed close."

"Certainly."

"Very well, then. Fersin will direct my quartermaster to stand ready with any assistance. I know you brought your own surgeons, but if your wounded need special care, you have only to ask. Hobben—" he spoke to one of the gate guards. "Open this thing and let our guests through. Come along, Phelan, and tell me what you found." He turned away; the Duke and Aliam Halveric followed him through the opening gate.

The column followed Fersin, who turned left inside the gate and led them beside the wall to two-story stone barracks built against it.

"This and the next are empty," he told Arcolin. "If you need more bedding, just tell me. The baths—" he glanced back at the column, "are in the far end of this one, and the near end of the next; there's a kitchen in each cellar. By the Count's order, water's been heating since noon, for your convenience. If you need food, we can supply it, but it will take a little time, since I must speak to the quartermaster. I'd appreciate a squad of your men—uh, troops—helping me bring it—"

"We're well supplied," said Arcolin. "We have what we took from Siniava's army. But we appreciate the offer. Where shall we take the baggage mules?"

"I'll have stable boys come help you. Just a moment—" He looked up and caught the eye of one of the soldiers on the wall, then whistled a complicated phrase. The man saluted and turned away.

"We'll take the far building," said Arcolin. "The Halverics are behind us, and the Clarts behind them; we don't want any more confusion than necessary. Now, where are the fountains?"

"Just down that street," said Fersin, pointing. "There are full waterbutts in each barracks, but if you need more, feel free to get some."

"Thank you, Fersin. Stammel, two squads for the mules; sent the rest in. I'll check back."

The Count's barracks were much like the Duke's: long clean rooms with wooden bunks. Each room would hold two cohorts if some slept on the floor, and there were plenty of pallets to make that comfortable. Soon the upper room was organized for the night. Paks caught Stammel's eyes when he came upstairs to look.

"Why didn't that man call the Duke by his title?"

"The Count?" Paks nodded. Stammel shook his head. "Oh, he's what they call an aristocrat—one of the old kind."

"So?"

"Well, he doesn't think the Duke is really a Duke— from what I hear, the only duke he thinks *is* real is the Duke of Fall, over near the Copper Hills."

Paks frowned. "Is he like those bravos, then that you told me about my first year?"

"Tir, no! Nothing like. He really is a count, the sixteenth in his line, I think."

"But you told me nobody disputed the Duke's title."

"The Count doesn't dispute it; the Duke doesn't ask him to acknowledge it. That's different. Courtesy among allies. And if it doesn't bother the Duke, why should it bother you?"

"I don't understand." Paks felt that it ought to bother the Duke.

Stammel shrugged. "Remember what I told you about Aare—the old country across the sea?" Paks nodded. "Well, these southern nobles trace their title back to it. They hardly allow that the throne of Tsaia has a king—or a crown prince, as he is—and they don't recognize Pargun and Kostandan and Dzordanya at all. You can see if they don't recognize the crown of Tsaia, they wouldn't acknowledge titles granted by it."

"I see." Paks laid out another blanket. "Well, is the Honeycat one of their kind of nobles, or our kind, or just made up?"

"I don't know. If anyone does, it'll be this count. They say he's so proud of his family that he can recite his fathers and mothers and aunts and cousins all the way back to the beginnings, and say who married whom two hundred years ago."

Paks thought about that, shaking her head. In her own family—she mused over it, coming up blank past grandparents, aunts, uncles, and near cousins. How could the count keep up with more? When she looked up, Stammel had gone on to something else.

Paks drew first shift for a bath, and came to the basement dining hall dry, warm, and comfortable. It would be strange to sleep indoors again. She wondered what it would be like to live in those barracks all the time—then remembered the count's comments on women, and chuckled to herself. Southerners had strange ideas. She wondered if southern women who wanted to be warriors went north.

The next morning they marched at first light, carrying only their weapons, to attack the besieging force that held the south road. They made their way around the city between the outer and second walls. On the south, the city seemed to tip itself over the edge of high cliffs. Before Paks could see what lay below, they dove into an echoing torchlit passage, steeply pitched, and came out on one landing of a zigzag stair winding down from wall to wall, and ending in a huge gatehouse still some way above the rivers. Here they were joined by some five hundred Andressat troops who had come by a different way. As the gates opened, Paks could see nothing at first but distant slopes, dim in the early light.

Once through the gates, the road ran steeply down to a platform above the confluence of the two branches of the Chaloquay: a wild, tossing whirlpool at this season. Upstream, on the right, a narrow road led down to a high arched stone bridge, guarded by towers at either end. These towers were held by the enemy.

With the roaring rivers close below, it was hard to hear the captains' commands, but their gestures were clear enough. Paks yawned, clearing her ears, and shifted her shield a bit as she marched forward with the others. Spray from the rivers drifted up, cold on her legs. As they dropped to the level of the bridge approaches, arrows began skipping along the stones in front of them to shatter on the wall to their right. Archers from the bridge towers: Paks knew how bad that could be as they came closer. But a flight of arrows passed over them from the wall of Cortes Andres. Paks saw several enemy bowmen throw up their arms and fall from the nearer tower. Fewer and fewer archers cared to expose themselves to Andressat's fire; the arrows stopped. Then as the road made an abrupt left turn to the bridge, Paks caught a glimpse of fleeing men on the road south. She hoped that meant the bridge was not defended. A battle was one thing, but she didn't like the thought of fighting over water, or being swept away in the Chaloquay's fierce currents.

The bridge gates, a lattice of heavy timbers rather like a folding portcullis, were closed; their own bowmen sent a volly of shafts through the lattice onto the bridge itself. The enemy retreated to the far tower. Doubling shields, the front rank of archers made it to the gates and unhooked the bar that held them closed. Another rank stepped forward to pull the gates open; soon they gaped wide. The archers ran for the tower stairs. Paks's cohort went forward onto the bridge. Nothing barred their way at the far tower; against the light that came through from the open air beyond she could see a dark mass: the enemy.

As they charged, Paks heard the whirr of a few arrows, but saw no one fall. The enemy fell back before them; the rear ranks were already turning to run. By the time the first two ranks were engaged, Siniava's men had retreated from the bridge approach, giving them room to spread out. Paks found herself an opponent. She pressed forward, fending off his blade easily until he left an opening, then she plunged her sword into his body. Another, and another, and the enemy was fleeing, breaking away from the fight in ones and twos and clumps to run gasping up the road away from the bridge. Paks and her cohort pursued, trying to keep their formation while pressing the attack. As they moved farther from the river, Paks could hear Arcolin shouting, urging them on.

Suddenly a thunder of hooves rose from behind them, and a company of cavalry in Andressat blue and gold rolled by, lances poised. Paks had a stitch in her side, and slowed her stride. With cavalry after them, they wouldn't get far. She looked around for her recruits. Keri and Volya were both grinning—she grinned back and took a deep breath as the stitch eased. Not as hard as she'd expected, not at all. Arcolin called them to a halt, and Stammel and Kefer checked the lines. No one seemed to be hurt badly. Paks could hear other troops coming up behind them. The Duke rode past, and the Count, and Aliam Halveric and his captains. They were all talking and laughing. A cohort of Clarts trotted by, yipping and tossing their lances. Paks looked up the slope. Sunlight gilded the top of it, and she watched as it crept toward them, lighting on the way the lance-tips of the horsemen.

After awhile the Clarts rode back at a walk; the leader laid his hand edgewise on his throat. Arcolin grinned. The commanders returned. The Duke reined in beside Arcolin, glancing over the Company with a broad smile before speaking a few words to his captain and riding on. Arcolin turned in his saddle, looking back down the slope.

"We march south today," he said. "My cohort will stay here. The others will go back to pick up all the gear. You did the fighting; no reason for you to climb all those stairs again." Paks grinned to herself, thinking of Barra and Natzlin having to go back. "Stammel," said Arcolin, breaking into her thoughts. "Take 'em to the head of that slope, and keep a guard posted in case the cavalry missed a few of those southerners." He turned his horse and rode back toward the bridge.

The road from the bridge angled toward the main stream of the Chaloquay before turning south in the river's gorge. Instead of this, Stammel led them upslope, until they were well above both road and river. Here an ambush would be impossible. From this vantage point, Paks could see how Cortes Andres had been built on and into a natural cliff. From the rough gray native stone at the river to the pale golden towers of the inner citadel, the city's southern face offered no weakness to an attacker. Paks could not see how anyone could hope to break such a wall: too high to scale, no cover for sappers, the foundation stones three or four times the length of a man, and man-high. If this was how cities were built in the far south, they would have trouble.

Andressat troops—five hundred foot and a hundred horse—marched on the lower road, while the mercenary companies traveled across the rough pasture of the upper slopes. It was pleasant weather, Paks thought, and the spring turf was a welcome change from a muddy road. The next day the valley along the river widened;

Paks looked down gentler slopes to see plowland and the pink and white of fruit trees in bloom. It was almost too warm for cloaks. About midday, they moved down to join the Andressat troops on the road. That afternoon they passed through several little villages. Peasants fled, scrambling over the low field walls, and dragging away sheep, goats, and even a pig from its sty. Paks noticed that the Count permitted no straggling or looting. When she looked back, she saw the villagers sneaking back toward their homes. By nightfall, she could see that the slope west of them curved around to the south, blocking their way. She wondered if the river entered another gorge.

The next morning a rumor ran through the camp that a courier had come in with news of Golden Company. "I don't know anything about it," Stammel kept saying. "A rider came from Andressat. But it could just as likely have been word from the Viscount. More likely." But when they were ready to march, the Duke rode up, smiling.

"Just to make sure you get it straight," he said, "Pliuni rebelled against Siniava's regents and yielded to the Golden Company—" He paused while a delighted roar went up. "Aesil M'dierra is on her way south, with Pliuni and Westland troops as well as her own. If the Honeycat is in his own cities, we'll have him in a few days. If not—well, he won't have a warm hearth to come home to."

Ahead of them, the Chaloquay swung sharply away to their left. The Duke led them away from the road, up across the rising ground ahead. As they climbed, they could see banks of cloud coming up from the south. Soon a thin steady rain began. Paks was glad to be walking on turf. She could not see far, through the curtains of rain, but by late afternoon they were moving downslope again, along a sheep track. Ahead was a river.

"It's the same," Stammel said. "We cut across a loop of it. Now we follow it west to Cha." That night they camped within sight of the river, and the next day they marched beside it again. Here there were low terraced hills planted to grapevines and a scrubby tree Paks had never seen before. Near the river all was cultivated, in little stone-walled plots: early grain, now a hand tall, fruit trees, neat rows of vegetables. The villages were built of stone, with tile roofs on most houses and walled yards beside the larger ones. They passed a small inn, its windows crowded with staring faces. At the edge of that village, the Clarts were holding a prisoner, a man who had tried to escape west on horseback.

"And too good a horse, my lord," one of the riders was explaining to the Duke as Paks marched by. "He'll be an agent of Siniava's." Paks caught a glimpse of the man's white, frightened face, and his stout brown horse. She never saw him again.

The rain stopped in late afternoon. The next day was cloudy but rainless, and they marched through a widening belt of rich farmland. Beyond one village, the road was paved with great stone slabs, amply wide for the column. In the ditches on either side Paks saw the purple and yellow stars of early flowers. They looked like nothing she had ever seen. She saw more orchards of the scrubby trees. At one of the rest halts, she found an older veteran who knew what they were.

"Oilberry," he said. "That's what makes the best lampfuel, unless you believe the seafolk—they say some kind of a sea monster's gizzard, but I never saw any. Down here they eat the berries, or press them for oil—cook with it, and all. They ship some of it north, but it's for rich folks there."

"But why don't we grow it in the north, if it's so good?"

He shrugged. "Why don't they grow apples down here? I don't know—maybe they just won't grow."

The river curved south again. Paks wondered how far away Cha could be seen. All she knew of it was that it lay north of the river; no one in the Company had been there. About midafternoon, she heard an alarm from the Clart forward scouts. Several riders galloped back to confer with the commanders. The column armed. Paks hoped the Andressat troops would fight as well as they looked. They marched on. Suddenly Paks spotted the enemy: a small force forming a line behind an improvised palisade at the edge of a village.

Paks's cohort had been marching left of the road. Now they wheeled and shifted farther left, allowing Andressat troops to take the middle, between the Phelani and the Halverics. Arrows flew from behind the palisade, answered by archers on both flanks. Paks heard cries from behind the piled brush and stakes. Cracolnya's cohort sent a flight of fire arrows; almost flickered out. Two seemed to catch, and wisps of smoke rose, thickening.

Now they were close. Paks could see bobbing helmets behind the barricade. No more arrows. She wondered why not. Arrows from their own men whirred overhead and came down behind the brush. More yells from the enemy. Only a few yards more. She could see the helmets in retreat. The front ranks broke into a run, eager to fight. Stammel bellowed at them to halt, but several had already hit the brush and tumbled forward.

The barricade rolled into the pit behind it, and Paks could see the sharpened stakes set into the bottom just as three people fell in. Stammel cursed explosively. The rest of the front rank managed to balance on the brink. Riders leaped the pit to harry the retreating army while they lifted out the wounded. Paks was furious. Jori, the only casualty in their cohort, was lucky; he'd live, though he wouldn't be fighting for some days. But the thought of the trap made her stomach roil. She wished the enemy had not run. She ached to hit someone.

None of them slept well that night. The camp simmered, a low rolling murmur of anger and anticipation. The next day they marched warily, eager for a confrontation, but the villages they passed seemed deserted, and they arrived before the walls of Cha without any more contact with the enemy. Paks eyed the walls with

professional interest. They were nothing like Cortes
Andres, for this city stood on a wide plain beside the
river, just above its confluence with the Chaloqueel.
Sapping would work here, she thought.

Chapter Twenty-four

Their first test of the city gates proved them to be well-defended; the army pulled back to encircle the city and organize the siege. By the next afternoon, they had constructed portable shelters to protect the sapping teams, and had them in place. Several sapping crews were at work, spaced around the wall. Paks spent the time helping to set up the Duke's camp. Like the other experienced veterans, she had been assigned a night guard slot.

Just before sunset, a rider galloped toward them from the west. Clart Cavalry intercepted, then escorted the rider to the Duke's tent. Paks recognized a Golden Company courier. With several friends she edged close to the Duke's tent to pick up what news she could. The rider's horse was lathered; one of the Clarts walked it out. Suddenly the Duke looked out of his tent and glanced around at the loiterers.

"Ah—Paks."

"Yes, my lord."

"Find Arcolin and Cracolnya, and send them here.

Then take this—" he handed her a scroll, "—to Aliam Halveric."

"Yes, my lord." Paks was glad to run his errands, but wished the Duke had not found her idling; she had heard his opinion of nosy soldiers before. She knew where Arcolin was, looking over wood for a catapult with one of the Halveric's sons, but she had to ask Arcolin where to find Cracolnya.

"He's around the city, with that other sapping crew. You'd best take a horse." He looked around, and waved to someone leading two horses. "Take my spare; he's not been ridden today."

"Thank you, sir," said Paks. "And where would I find the—the Halveric?" She was not sure this was the correct form to use to his son.

"My father?" asked the young Halveric.

"Yes, sir. The Duke gave me a message for him." She thought the younger man might offer to take it himself, but he simply nodded.

"He's to the south, about a quarter of the way around; the sentries will guide you to the tent."

"Thank you, sir." The boy leading the horses had come near, and Arcolin took the reins of the black and handed them over. Paks mounted, finding the captain's saddle very different from the ones she'd ridden before. But the horse answered heel and rein easily, and she made good time to the opposite side of the city. By the time she had given her message there and ridden on to the Halveric's camp, it was full dark; she was careful to call her name and unit clearly when challenged. Aliam Halveric was eating supper in his tent, along with his eldest son. Paks recalled them clearly from the previous season. The Halveric smiled as she handed over the scroll.

"Ah—I remember you. I was afraid you weren't going to give your parole, and then you made that remarkable journey—yes. Sit down; I may want to send a reply."

Paks sat where she was bidden, on a low stool, while the Halveric read the scroll and handed it to his son.

While his son read, he finished the dish of stew before him. He cocked his head at the younger man when he finished.

"Well, Cal? I think I'd best go myself, don't you?"

"Certainly, sir. Have you any orders in the meantime?"

"No—I expect to be back in a few hours, or I'll send word. Get me a horse, please." The younger man nodded and withdrew. The Halveric looked at Paks. "Well—what was your name again. My memory has failed me—"

"Paksenarrion, sir, but I'm called Paks."

"That's right. Paks. Do you have a horse?"

"Yes, sir."

"Good. Then I won't need another escort." Paks flushed at the implied compliment. The younger man returned, and the Halveric stood, reaching for his helmet. Paks rose and held the tent flap aside as he walked out. She mounted and took the torch she was offered by a guard. All around the city was a circle of watchfires and torches; she scarcely needed the one in her hand. At the Duke's tent, one of his squires, Kessim, was waiting to take the Halveric's. He raised an eyebrow at Paks when he recognized Arcolin's horse, but refrained from comment. She grinned at him as she rode off to the horse lines.

The next three days were simple siegework in support of the sapping teams. No one knew what the Golden Company courier had brought. The captains discouraged questions. For Paks, it was an alternation of camp chores and stretches of guard duty—a routine that dulled very quickly. But her recruits thought it was exciting. They asked her dozens of questions about the techniques of sieges, sapping, siege engines—the same questions she had asked the year before. She told them what she knew, then sent them to older veterans.

On the night of the third day, Paks had just gone off-watch and was enjoying a hot drink by one of the watchfires before going to bed when an excited Volya appeared at her elbow.

"Paks—come here!" Paks rose reluctantly and stepped away from the fire. Volya was dancing with impatience.

"What is it?"

"Paks, someone came over the wall and wanted to talk to the Count. Someone from inside the city—what does that mean?"

Paks thought a moment before answering. "It could mean they want to surrender—or some of them do. Or maybe the Count has an agent in the city, a spy, and he came out to report. I don't think you should be talking about it—"

Volya nodded. "I know. That's what Sergeant Kefer told me, and I won't. I just—"

"You mean the sergeant told you to keep shut about it, and you came straight to me to tell?" Paks was suddenly angry; Volya flinched.

"But Paks, he wouldn't mind about you. You wouldn't tell anyone else, and—"

Paks glared at her. "Volya, an order's an order. When you're told to keep quiet, you do—you don't tell anyone, friend, lover, or whoever. I didn't get the reputation I've got by blabbing off to people or hanging around loosetongues. You say you trust me—fine, but how d'you know there's not someone else near enough to hear, eh?"

Volya sounded near tears. "Paks, I'm sorry—I won't do it again. I—I thought it was all right to tell *you* anything."

"Well, now you know it's not," said Paks shortly. Then she sighed. "Volya, there's more to being a mercenary than fighting and camp work. This thing of talking—you haven't been to a city yet, so Stammel hasn't given you his speech on it. But we don't talk to anyone about Company business, or anything that could be Company business. Even in an ordinary year, every tavern is full of spies. If someone knows who hired us, and what road we're marching on, and when—d'you see?" Volya nodded. "And this year—we can't afford any loose talk. We're almost certainly outnumbered.

Our Duke will be trying to move us to the best field for battle without alerting Siniava."

"Yes, Paks. But—the Company is safe, isn't it? We're all loyal to the Duke—aren't we?"

"I hope so. Yes. But even so—you never know who might be listening. And some can't keep shut if they've been drinking. Loyal as a stone when they're sober, but everyone's friend when they've got a load of ale or wine. So when you're told to keep something quiet, you do. From everyone. Clear?"

"Yes, Paks. Should I tell the sergeant—?"

"No. You've had your scolding. Just remember." Volya nodded, and Paks waved her away. She was no longer sleepy, however, and spent the rest of that night wondering about the man who had come over the wall.

The next morning it became clear that something was happening inside the city. There were fights on the walls, and bodies thrown over. Sentries close to the walls heard shouts and the clash of arms. Older veterans reminded the younger that most sieges fell by treachery and dissension. Late in the afternoon, a small party offered to parley with the Count of Andressat. Paks watched as they filed out the postern: two men in long gowns and three in armor. The Count and all three mercenary captains went to meet them. They talked for some time, then bowed and separated. As the party started back to the city, the two men in gowns fell with crossbow bolts bristling from their bodies. The armored men spun around and ran for the besiegers' lines, while a great cry rose from the walls.

Just as that disturbance quieted, a column of smoke rose from across the city, followed by more outcry.

"The sappers," said Stammel. "They've fired their supports, and in a little we'll find out whether they breached the wall."

"Will we go in?"

"Not around there. Halveric troops are over there; they'll go." They listened closely until Arcolin called them into formation. Paks noticed that her recruits did not look nervous any more. She herself felt an anxiety she did her best to conceal. This was one of the Honeycat's own cities—what sort of traps and powers might be here? But no word came for an attack; as the red glare of sunset faded from the walls, they were dismissed again. Assault in the morning, the rumors ran.

With morning came riders of the Golden Company, and Aesil M'dierra's senior captain. He had not finished talking to the Duke when the word ran through camp: M'dierra was at Sibili, already in position with Golden Company and the Pliuni volunteers. Westland troops were at Sibili as well. Paks felt a rising excitement. She did not doubt Cha would fall, and after it the Honeycat's home city, Sibili. Paks thought of him looking from his palace windows to see the banners of his enemies.

She squinted against the early sun and saw the city wall crowded with men. Smoke rolled up from the sapper's work near the northwest corner of the city. Paks saw archers lean to shoot into the roofed shelter; their own archers replied. An outcry rose from the main gate tower: Siniava's black and yellow banner sagged from its pole, and slipped back toward the wall. Someone up there waved a smaller flag; Paks could not see the colors. The Count's herald blew a long blast. It was answered from the tower, and followed by even more noise from within the walls.

By the time they entered the city, Paks had heard that a faction favoring Andressat had opened the gates. Siniava's men still fought, but they were hampered by the factions opposing them. Despite the warning, Paks had not imagined how chaotic this could be. She soon found out. Just as they came to the first side street, a body of armed men rushed out to form a line across it. These were Siniava's, armed with pikes. They had scarcely engaged the enemy when another band— bowmen in plain leather with a twist of blue and gold on their helmets—charged out of a building behind the enemy line and fired into the back of the pikemen.

Fifteen or so fell at once, hit squarely in the back at close range. One arrow hit Paks's shield with enough force to drive the head through; another struck someone behind her. She heard the yell, half pain, half fury. The enemy fighters whirled to meet this attack, and the front ranks of Paks's cohort charged, trying to run them over before the archers made another dangerous shot.

Several more fights interrupted their progress to the city's center. Twice they fought their way out of attempted ambushes. Bodies littered the streets: men, women, children, animals, caught in the street fighting and left behind when the flood of violence passed. At last, beyond a mass of frightened people crammed into a large square, Paks caught sight of the Halveric banner.

As her cohort spread around its side of the square, a small boy broke away and darted toward the street they had left. Rauf made a grab at him and missed; Paks swung her shield across his path. He ran into it headlong, and slipped to the ground, crying. Paks sheathed her sword and reached down to help him up. She heard a cry from the crowd as the terrified boy tried to twist away from her.

"Here now, I won't hurt you," she said. The boy screamed, flailing at her with pudgy fists. "Stop that," she added. He froze in her grip, staring at her with wide eyes. "Now—what did you run for? Don't you know you should have stayed with—your sister, was it?"

"I'll take 'im, Paks," said Rauf. "His sis is all upset—" But as Rauf reached out, the child started fighting again.

"I'd better—" said Paks. "Now, lad—be quiet—you're not hurt, and you won't be." He calmed again, and Paks glanced around for the girl. She was standing only a few yards away, held there by a serious-faced Keri. "Let's go back to her now, lad—and you stay with her, you hear?"

"But—but my puppy!" He choked on the words and started to cry.

"Your puppy? You lost your dog?" His accent was thick, but Paks thought she understood.

He nodded. "He was mine—my very own—and he's not here. He got lost."

Paks thought of the dogs she'd seen, dead in the gutters. "Lad—you stay with your sister. Find your puppy later—not now."

"But he's got lost. He—he'll be frightened without me." Paks thought it was the other way around, but knew it would do no good to argue.

"Even so— What's your name?"

"Seri. Seriast, really."

"Well, Seri, even though your puppy may be frightened, you stay with your sister. She'll help you find your puppy later. Now promise you'll stay with her—" The boy nodded finally. Paks thought he was the same age as her youngest brother, the year she'd left home. She put a hand on his shoulder and steered him toward the girl. "Come along now." The girl grabbed him and held him close.

"I tried to tell her, Paks, that you wouldn't hurt him," said Keri, sounding worried. "I don't know why she thought—" Paks waved him to silence. The girl looked up, her eyes blurred by tears.

"I think he'll stay with you now," said Paks. "But keep a close grip on him for a few hours." The girl nodded, tightening her grasp until the boy squealed.

"Please don't take 'im," she begged. "Please don't—he won't harm ye none."

"We won't take him. What would we want with a child that size?" But the panic on the girl's face made Paks uneasy for days. What were these people used to, to fear intentional harm to so small a child?

The next day, as Halveric Company rode away to Sibili, Paks found herself hard at work in a warehouse, cataloging plunder for the Duke's Company. This time, at least, she did not have to drag it out, but counting sacks of wool and goat hair, and barrels of wine, beer, oilberries in brine and oil was a hot, dusty, boring job.

They finished this chore in one day; the next was spent loading supplies for Sibili and repairing damaged equipment. Paks got a new shield, as did Keri, and Volya had snapped a sword tip against a wall. Jenits came up while Paks was helping Volya wrap the grip of her sword; he had a lumpy bundle of shiny yellow silk.

"Wait until you see this," he said, dropping it on the ground. It clinked. He worked at the knot one-handed. Keri reached to help. "Thanks. There: look at that." They looked at a miscellaneous collection of bracelets, rings, coins, and little carved disks of ivory or shell. Jenits grinned. "That's what I get for being one-armed right now—not strong enough for the heavy stuff. Kefer had me working through the goldsmithies and jewelers' shops with him, and he said to take this much—and to share it with my friends, if I wanted to keep any. I knew that you, Paks, were stuck in those warehouses, and Keri and Volya hadn't found anything better than a stray silver, so here I am. Take your pick."

"Is it really gold?" asked Volya doubtfully.

"I think so. It's soft, like gold, and it doesn't look like copper. It's heavy."

Keri reached over and picked up a ring with a pale green stone. "I wonder what this is."

"I don't know. But let's split it up, before I lose my generous impulses. Paks, you choose first; you're the veteran."

Paks looked over the small pile. "I could take this bracelet for my sister," she said tentatively. It was made in a pattern of linked leaves, with tiny blue stones between them. "We'll take turns," she went on.

"Go on, then. Keri?"

"I'll take this ring."

"I'd like this," said Volya. She had found a little gold fish, arched as if it were leaping, with a loop formed by the dorsal fin to hold a chain.

Jenits held out his left hand, with a heavy gold ring set with onyx on the first finger. "I cheated," he said. "I took my favorite out first." They laughed and went on choosing. When they'd finished, Jenits folded the square of silk and tucked it into his tunic. "I feel much safer now," he said. "I was afraid I'd have a greedy fit, and you've done all the fighting. By the way, Paks—"

"Hmm?"

"My arm doesn't hurt any more—when can I come back to regular duty?"

"What did the surgeons tell you?"

"Oh—well—six weeks altogether. But it's been three, and it doesn't hurt. I don't want to miss Sibili, and I feel well enough. I thought you could say something to the sergeants."

Paks looked up from Volya's sword and shook her head. "Jenits, it's up to the surgeons. You won't do us any good if you try to fight and it's not healed. Likely it'd come apart at the first stroke, and you'd be worse off than ever. You can ask the surgeon—"

Jenits scowled. "The last time I asked him, he said to quit pestering. Bones heal at their speed, he said, and not for wishing."

"That sounds like Master Simmitt. He's the sharp-tongued one. You won't miss Sibili anyway. We're all marching—"

"But I'll miss the fighting. And if Siniava's there—"

"You wouldn't have a chance at him anyway. You'll see enough fighting, if you stay whole."

"I hope so. To break an arm, my very first—" Jenits broke off as Stammel came up; he squatted beside them with a sigh.

"Well, Jenits, is your arm holding up?"

"Yes, sir. I was just wondering—"

"No, you can't fight with us at Sibili. Not unless we're longer taking that city than I expect. Paks, the Duke's enrolled a few men from Cha—Andressat's faction, of course—and we'll have six of 'em in our cohort. You've gotten these well broken in. I'd like you to take on one of the new men."

Paks thought of several questions, but when she met

Stammel's brown eyes she was guided by their wary expression. "Yes, sir. When?"

"Now." Paks rose when he did, and left the rest where they were. When they were out of earshot, Stammel had more to say. "This is new, Paks, taking new men during a campaign. The captain said it's because he wants us at full strength. I suppose that means he'll be recruiting all season. These men, now—the Count vouched for them, and they look like fighters, but of course we don't know anything about them. If you start having doubts, let me know at once." He shot her a hard glance, and waited until she nodded. "Another thing—down here they don't have many women fighters. You heard what the Count said. Well, I thought if we take these men, they'll have to get used to our ways. That's one reason I wanted you to help. Clear enough?"

Paks nodded, though she still felt confused. It was hard to imagine strangers—outsiders—*southerners* as part of the Company. But she could see that Stammel had no answers, and possibly even more questions, so she asked nothing. He sighed again and led her to a group of about twenty men standing with the captains. Three of them had mail shirts, and four had bronze breastplates. The rest wore leather armor. They were all muscular and looked fit enough. Several of Paks's friends stood nearby: Barra, Vik, and Arñe. Vik raised his expressive eyebrow but said nothing. Stammel turned away, and came back in a few minutes with three more of Paks's cohort. He spoke to Arcolin, who pointed out six of the strangers. They followed Stammel.

"Paks, this is Halek," Stammel said. Halek was several fingers shorter than Paks, with sandy hair and mustache, and pale eyes. Stammel went on. "Halek, she'll show you where to eat and sleep, and what you're expected to do—"

"She?" Halek's tone was derisive. Paks felt a prickle of anger. "What do you think I am, a little boy to take orders from a nursemaid?" Paks clamped her jaw shut. Stammel gave the man a cold stare.

"Either you follow orders, Halek, or you explain to the captain that you don't want to join us—and why." The man opened his mouth, but Stammel gave him no chance to speak. "No argument. Obey, or leave."

Halek glanced sideways at Paks and flushed. "Yes—sir."

"Come along," said Paks, and walked off without looking at him. She felt his resistance, then a slackening as he gave in and followed her. She was glad she was taller. When they had walked some strides she spoke over her shoulder.

"Our cohort—Arcolin's our captain—is loading today. When did you eat last?"

"This morning. Early." He sounded grumpy.

"Then we'll eat now." Paks angled toward the cooks' tent. "What weapons do you use?"

"Sword," he said. "Not like yours—longer, and not so wide. Or the curved blade Siniava's men carry."

"Are you used to formation fighting? Can you use polearms?"

"No. Where would I learn that? The only organized units around here are Siniava's, and I wouldn't fight for that." The man spat, then lengthened his stride to come up with her. "Listen—are you really a soldier, not a cook or something?"

Paks glared down at him and he reddened. "Yes, I'm a soldier—as you'll find out soon enough. More of one than you, I daresay, if all you've done is play around with a dueller's weapon. I hope you can learn formation fighting, or you won't be any use to us at all."

"Your tongue's sharp, anyway," he said.

"You can test my blade later," said Paks. She led Halek through the serving line, then to a loading crew. He was strong and willing to work; Paks tried to think better of him. By midafternoon the loading was done; they went in search of the armsmasters. Siger was already working with two of the other newcomers, these assigned to Dorrin's cohort. A number of the Duke's men stood around watching. It was always a treat to see the wizened little armsmaster drive a much bigger opponent around the practice ring. Finally he called a halt, and the two men, puffing and sweating, moved out of the ring.

"Not enough marching," grumbled Siger to their backs. "More wind's what you want, and then an old man like me couldn't make you lose breath." He turned to the circle of watchers. "Enjoying yourselves, eh? Well, you all need a workout. Suppose you, there—and you—" he pointed, "get busy with swords, and you four with pikes—" The crowds melted away. Paks and the others with new men stayed. "Ah yes," said Siger when he saw them. "What have we here? Let's see your paces." He beckoned to Halek, who stepped into the ring. "Sword?" asked Siger. "Polearms?"

"Sword," said Halek. "But not that short one. I've used a longer one, or the curved—"

Siger grinned at him. "You'll learn. That's what I'm for, and Paks will teach you a lot." He handed Halek a blade. "Now—are you used to a shield?"

"I've used one."

"We'll start without. Go slowly until you get used to the length." They crossed blades and Siger began his usual commentary. "Hmm. I see you've done more fencing than military—that stroke won't work with this blade. You don't have the length. No, and you can't dance about like that in formation, either." He tapped Halek's ribs when an opening came. "When you don't have a shield, your blade must do its work. A little faster now—yes." The clatter of blades speeded up. "No, you're still jigging around too much. Stop now—" As Halek lowered his blade, Siger looked around and motioned to Paks and several others. "Form a line with him," he said. "Paks, come over here and take my shield side. Now—what's your name?"

"Halek."

"Halek, good. Now you'll see what I mean about staying in formation—these on either side will protect your flanks, as you protect theirs. If you stay in line with them, you'll be fine. Clear?"

"Yes. But there's three of us, and only two of you—"

Siger glanced at Paks and smiled slightly. "That's no problem to *us*. Paks, put a banda on; we don't want you stiff at Sibili." Paks stepped to the pile of bandas and returned to Siger's side. Facing her was Sif, of Dorrin's cohort, with Halek in the middle and Vik on the far end. She found she could hold her own against him easily, with strokes to spare for Halek. Siger, despite Vik's aggressive attack, had breath and arm to spare, as usual. He continued his commentary on Halek's swordsmanship and found time to correct the rest of them.

Halek kept trying to shift to one side or the other, but found himself locked between his companions and his opponents' swords. Finally he seemed to get the idea, and began working with Vik and Sif. Sif, now that Halek was doing better, pressed harder. Paks was acutely aware of her unprotected shield arm. She found herself countering strokes rather than pressing her own attack. Halek almost made a touch on her. He grinned. That, thought Paks, is a mistake. She slipped the leash on her anger, forcing a startled Sif back, and back again, and giving Halek two good thumps with her blade. Siger moved with her, stroke for stroke, and they pushed the others to the edge of the ring.

"Hold," said Siger. As they lowered their blades, he said, "Halek, you'll need to practice this way every day. Your bladework is fair, considering your experience, but your cross-body strokes are weak; that's why you shift so. Come back here in a half-glass with a shield, and we'll start again." He turned to Paks. "Tell Stammel that Halek needs the time with me, and see if they'll release you, too." Paks nodded.

"Come on, Halek," she said. "We'll get you a shield from the quartermaster."

"What about a sword?"

"Not until I say you're ready," said Siger.

Paks and Halek walked back toward the quartermaster's wagon. Halek was silent for a few yards, then said gruffly. "You're—you're good with a sword."

"I ought to be," said Paks cheerfully. "Siger spent enough yelling and bruises on me." She felt good.

"Mmph. Well—I didn't think you would be. I've never seen women fighters before."

"Siniava doesn't use them at all?"

"Oh, I hear he's got a few girls—they duel, and that, at banquets and the like. And of course there's women with his army, but not for fighting." He chuckled. Paks felt herself getting hot again.

"Things are different in this Company," she said firmly.

"I can see that." He walked on a few paces in silence. "But—I don't see how—why—a woman would want to be a fighter. It's hard work—dirty—you can get killed—" He sounded genuinely puzzled.

Paks found herself suppressing a laugh. "Hard work? Were you ever on a farm? Working? No, I thought not. This is no harder than farmwork I was doing at home, and it's no dirtier than butchering sheep. As for getting killed—women die having babies, if it comes to that." She glanced at him to see his reaction; his face was furrowed in a frown. "Besides," she went on, "I like fighting. I'm good at it, and I enjoy it, and I get paid for it. I'd make a very bad farmer's wife."

"Well, but—aren't you going to marry someday?"

Paks shook her head. "No. Some do, but not me. I never wanted to."

"I just can't—are there many women like you in the north?"

Paks shrugged. "I don't know. Some. You saw Captain Dorrin, and Arñe at lunch. Maybe a fourth of us in this Company are women."

"I see." He still looked puzzled.

Chapter Twenty-five

Early the next morning they set out for Sibili, marching along the north bank of the Chaloqueel on a wide stone road. Those three days came back to Paks later as a kind of dream—the rich valley farmlands, with fruit trees in full bloom, clouds of pale pink flowers that strewed their petals on every gust of wind, leaving the hollows of the road drifted with delicate color. On the slopes, the grapevines were tufted with furry greenish-white leaflets. Rows of vegetables, plots of grain like green velvet—but all empty and quiet.

The sun had just set on the third day when they came in sight of Sibili; it loomed against the glowing sky. They camped near the Halverics, on good ground some distance from the walls. Rain began again that night; the next day they moved their camp closer to the walls, and picked up what news they could. Sapping teams had been at work since the Halverics arrived. Cracolnya's cohort went to work helping a small group of men in rust-colored tunics build siege towers and catapults.

"Who's that?" asked Keri. Paks shrugged.

"I don't know. I never saw them before." She stopped Devlin and asked him.

"That's Plas Group—Marki Plas. They're a special company—all they do is siege machines. A section of them came down with Aesil M'dierra."

Despite the heavier rain the following day, the assault began. Andressat and Westland troops struck first; the mercenary archers scoured the wall. Paks could not see much through the rain. She watched Plas Group specialists operating the two catapults, winding down the arm, loading stones into the cup. They had to adjust the ropes with each shot, to compensate for dampness. But although the attackers made the top of the wall several times, they were driven back onto their towers and away.

During the night the rain stopped. The Phelani and Halverics struggled to move a third siege tower to the walls under cover of darkness. It bogged down in the mud, and at dawn they were still some distance from the walls, in easy range of enemy bowmen. They withdrew for a time, and Paks had a chance to look the city over. It appeared to be shaped something like Rotengre, longer than it was wide, with a gate on the narrow east end, and another larger one off-center of the long north side. It was built on a hump of ground near the river. Above the outer wall was another that enclosed the inner citadel, itself as large as some towns. The walls were well built of buff colored stone, and while the city did not look as formidable as Cortes Andres, it looked worse than Cha.

Both sides tried fire weapons. The defenders poured oil on one of the siege towers and lit it, just as a cohort of Pliuni were halfway up. The Pliuni fled. Plas Group started lobbing stones smeared with burning pitch over the walls. After some hours, smoke rose from within. The defenders fired the second tower; Andressat and Phelani troops rushed to drag it away from the walls and managed to keep the fire from burning the lower framework.

That night Paks helped drag the remaining siege tower into place while the saps were fired. She heard a deep rumble off to her right, and shrill cries from the walls.

"Don't stop!" said Captain Pont. "Move this thing!" They kept pulling; over the pounding of blood in her ears, Paks heard horn signals and the clamor of combat. At last the tower was in place. A body of men they could not see jingled past and started up the tower stairs.

"Get armed and ready," said Devlin. Paks wiped the sweat from her face and stretched before slipping her arm into her shield grip. It promised to be a long night. They moved into the base of the tower.

Suddenly a crash from the top of the tower and a cry from the wall signalled the start of their own assault. The troops on the stairs surged upward. Pont held them back until the first group was halfway to the next level, then sent them on. It was pitchblack. Paks fell up the first two steps; someone else stumbled into her, cursing. She found her balance and went on. As she neared the top, dim light filtered in. She saw torches on the wall, and fires in the city itself. As she crossed the bridge to the wall, she tried not to think of the many feet of empty air below.

Once on the wall, Paks turned right to support the line clearing the wall in that direction. The troops in front of her were Halveric; she caught a glimpse of green as they passed a torch. In front of them, black and yellow troops with pikes withdrew slowly. Both sides fought hard. A pike thrust past the Halveric line to Paks. She knocked it aside. The man in front of her went down, and she leaped forward over him, facing a serried row of pikes.

It was hard to see thrusts in the dancing torchlight; at least the enemy could see no better. Paks ducked under one pike and slashed at a man in their front line.

She got a hit, then another, then something—what she didn't know—hit her helmet and almost knocked her down. The enemy yelled, as she staggered, and Halverics closed around her. Then she was up, and fighting again. Someone yelled in her ear, and she shook her head, trying to understand. What did they mean, "almost there"?

Then a horrible howling noise stunned her, followed by a blinding blue flash that lit up the entire city. For just an instant, Paks could see the breach in the wall, just behind the enemy she faced—only six ranks or so deep. Then came blackness, utter and thick. All around were screams and bellows. The lines crashed together; Paks was crushed in a welter of bodies, all struggling. Something raked her sword arm. She could not get free for a swing, but drove the tip of her sword into what she hoped was an enemy. Someone fell into her. She lost her balance and fell sprawling under a pile of men and weapons, the stink of blood and sweat strong in her nostrils.

All at once light returned: not torchlight, but a mellow golden light over the city itself. In an instant the pile of fighters separated into warring factions, struggling to kill and get free. Paks felt a stabbing pain in her leg, as she wrenched her shield free of a wounded man's shoulder and parried an enemy thrust. She made it to one knee. Someone grabbed her shield arm and pulled. She tried to pivot, but a man on the wall thrust up at her; she had to counter that. The pull steadied her; she got her legs under her again, and whoever had grabbed her let go. She was in a ragged line with several Halverics and some from her own cohort. Most of the enemy were down, and some were crawling away. They waded into the rest, and cleared the wall as far as the breach before the golden light faded. Paks looked for the source, but could not see it.

"Are you all right?" It was a Halveric private beside her.

Paks nodded; pain shot through her head. "Yes—just winded, I think."

"Your arm's bleeding a lot. Sorry I grabbed you like that—"

"Was that you? It helped. I thought you were one of them, at first."

"I know. You seemed dazed, and those scum were moving—"

"Paks." Devlin had come along the wall. "What besides this arm?"

Paks shifted her weight as Devlin took her arm, and the pain in her leg reminded her. "Left leg—something, I haven't looked. And something hit my head hard; it feels like the helmet's too tight."

"You'd better go back—"

"No, I'm fine. Now that I've got my breath—"

"Go back. This isn't over yet. Get that arm tied up, at least. We'll need you later."

As Paks edged her way past those who had just come up, she felt the day's fatigue like a smothering sack of wool. One of the surgeons was stationed near the bridge from the siege tower. He motioned her down next to a group of wounded. Paks sank down and tried to ease her helmet off. It wouldn't come; she felt a dint in the front.

"Wait," said the surgeon. "Just sit there a minute while I—" he turned to one of the others. "We'll need more torches here." The man nodded and moved off, and the surgeon tightened the bandage he was applying. "There. Yes. Now let me see that helmet—yes. Quite a dint. Do you know what hit you?" Paks shook her head. "Did you fall down?"

"Not then. Not quite."

"Let me get it off." He pulled it off and touched her head. Paks winced. "Tender, eh? I'm not surprised, with that lump." Several men came up with torches. "Good," he told them. "Hold one here. Now look at it," he told Paks. She squinted at the bright glare. "Not too bad. Let's see that arm—anything else?"

"Something stuck my leg." Paks moved her left leg a little. Someone—not the surgeon—took off her boot. It hurt. She tried to see what it looked like.

"Hold still," scolded the surgeon. "This arm just needs cleaning and wrapping; I'll see the leg in a moment." Paks smelled the pungent cleansing solution and braced herself for the sting. It felt cold, then burned. Her head throbbed, and she closed her eyes. She felt the surgeon start probing the wound in her leg. She heard him mutter to someone else, and hands steadied her leg as the pain sharpened. She wanted to argue with him, but it was too late. She thought he must be sewing up the hole, whatever it was, but it felt much worse. She wanted to throw up.

"It's the head, mostly," said the surgeon; Paks opened her eyes. Kefer was there, staring at her, and Arcolin stood by the tent flap. Tent?

"I thought we were on the wall," she said. The surgeon turned to her.

"You were. You'd been hit on the head, and you passed out while I was working on your leg."

"Oh." She couldn't remember anything of that, just being on the wall, and fighting, and strange lights.

"Was there a blue light?" she asked doubtfully. "And a yellow one later?"

"Yes." Arcolin stepped nearer. He was scowling. "That was clerics—theirs first, then ours."

"Clerics?" Paks felt even more confused. She had never seen any priest or Marshal like strange lights.

"Never mind that now." He turned to the surgeon. "How long?"

The surgeon shrugged. "A good night's sleep, I expect. Maybe a day." He brought Paks a mug. As her vision blurred with numbwine, she saw the surgeon follow Arcolin and Kefer from the tent.

She woke to broad daylight. The surgeon, busy with others, saw her test the tender lump on her head.

"How is it?"

"Fine."

"Try moving around." Paks sat up and winced as her bandaged arm and leg twinged. But these were minor pains; she was able to move easily. "Go on and stand." She had no trouble with that, either, and he sent her out. "Get a new helmet—size or so too large, and use extra padding for a day or so. If you get dizzy, or your eyes blur, come back at once. And eat before you go back to duty."

Outside, the camp was in turmoil. Paks could see more troops—Westland men—marching into Sibili through the breached wall. She wondered why they weren't using the gates. Smoke rose over the city walls. As she headed for the quartermaster, she saw Dorrin's cohort returning from the city, faces black with soot and grime.

Her new helmet felt unwieldy, even after she wrapped a cloth around her head. She tried again. Still odd-feeling. When she got to the cooks' tent, she found Barra and Natzlin.

"We heard you were hurt," said Barra, dishing up stew.

"Something hit my head."

"Are you going back in?" Paks wondered if she imagined the edge in that tone.

"Of course. Where's Arcolin—or Pont?"

"They're inside. It's a mess in there, too."

"What about it?"

"They've got some kind of wizard or priest—just when you think you've got a group on the run, there'll be a stinking black cloud all around; you can blunder into anything. Walls, a fire, their fighters—you can't see your own nose."

"And look out for the ones that don't look armed," added Natzlin. "They dress like rich folk, but they carry throwing knives." She gestured to a cut on her cheekbone. "They're good with them, too. You could lose an eye."

"Who've we lost?" asked Paks.

"In Arcolin's? I heard that Suri fell from the tower

last night, and someone—who was it, Natz?—took a
crossbow bolt in the eye."

"Gan, that was—Gannarrion. And Halek—"

"Halek? What happened to him?"

"Sword thrust in the gut, on the wall."

Paks finished her stew in silence. She had not liked
Halek, not at all. But she wished she knew it had not
been her sword, there in the darkness. By the end of
that day, the gate tower had fallen, and the attacking
troops moved freely through the twisting streets of the
lower city. Paks hardly noticed; she marched with the
others back to camp, aware only of great weariness.

She woke early, just at daybreak, feeling rested. She
was startled to find Volya beside her.

"You were acting strange, yesterday," said Volya.
"We thought someone should keep an eye on you."

"I was?" Paks had only the haziest memory of the
previous day. There'd been fighting on a wall or a gate
or something like that. "I'm fine, now."

"That's what you told Barra yesterday." Volya looked
stubborn.

"It's true now, anyway." Paks combed her hair and
rebraided it. She was very hungry and wondered if
she'd eaten the night before.

Although the outer part of the city had fallen, the
central inner citadel still resisted. Sapping teams were
busy at those walls, now, and the partially burnt siege
tower, repaired, was ready to move up. Paks was helping to drag the siege tower when a shout made her look
up. A black cloud rolled over the citadel wall and
flowed down toward the sapper's shelter. A man in
glittering mail spurred his horse toward that part of the
wall, raising a mailed fist over his head. Light streaked
from his fist to form a web between the cloud and the
sappers. When the blackness reached it, green flames
sprang up and the cloud disappeared.

Vik nudged her in the ribs. "I heard that's a paladin
of Gird."

Paks stared. "That?" She had never believed she would see one.

"Yes. There's a High Marshal here too, and two Swordmasters of Tir, and more—I don't know what— from Pliuni and Westland."

"What have they got inside?"

"I heard it's a temple to the Master of Torments— some southern god, I suppose. But their priest or whatever they call him has power enough. That's what that blue flash and darkness was, the night we broke the wall. And these black clouds."

Paks watched as the mailed figure rode away from the wall. Paladin or not, she had never seen such a striking-looking warrior. Every bit of metal glittered like polished jewels, and the horse—it moved lightly as wind-blown down, yet gave the impression of strength and power. For an instant she pictured herself in that mail—on that horse—but that was ridiculous. She leaned her weight on the rope.

By the next afternoon, they were fighting their way through the citadel streets, upward and inward toward Siniava's palace. At last Paks could see behind the defenders an open space. Foot by foot they pushed Siniava's men back to what was now clearly a broad paved court or square. Directly across from them was a high arched doorway in a tall building ornamented with balconies and turrets. To the left was a massive edifice with a pillared porch above the wide flight of steps. More enemy troops poured out of the doorway across the square; others surged up from another street entering the square. She had no more time to look. Her arms ached as the hours of fighting dragged on her.

Then their own reserves managed to force themselves to the front, and Paks and the others in front edged back. She leaned on a wall and caught her breath, watching. More reserves passed her. With them were two Swordmasters of Tir, in their black armor, and the High Marshal in chainmail under a blue mantle. Beside the Marshal was a man in glittering chainmail under a

flaming red surcoat embroidered with the crescent of
Gird. The paladin, thought Paks. She had not seen him
so close before. Without thinking, she pushed herself
away from the wall to follow him.

They had advanced across the square toward the
battle still going on before the palace doors when an
ill-armed rabble poured out of the pillared porch on
their left. They looked terrified, and were dangerous
only in their numbers. The unengaged rear ranks swung
to meet them. Paks saw a small group of mailed figures
poised at the top of the steps behind the rabble. Even
as she parried the unskilled blows, and killed the first of
those attacking, a strange sound shook the air, and sent
a tremor through her. The sunlight dimmed. Someone
beside her shrieked and dropped his sword, scrambling
backwards. The attackers screamed too, flailing their
way forward with even less skill.

From somewhere behind a loud voice shouted a word
Paks had never heard and could not afterwards remember. A crackling bolt of light shot past her head toward
the group on the porch. She gaped, a cold chill rippling
down her spine, and nearly fell when something slammed
into her leg. She looked back at the attackers barely in
time to dodge a sword thrust at her neck. Light flickered over her in blues and yellows, but she paid it no
mind. The frantic crowd in front of her demanded all
her attention.

Then they were gone—dead, wounded, or runaway—
and she looked around quickly. A knot of struggling
fighters contended in front of the palace. Some of her
own cohort stood near, watching her. She realized they
were waiting for her to tell them where to go next. The
Swordmasters, High Marshal, and paladin stood just
behind the battle; they seemed intent on the group on
the stairs, but Paks could not tell what they were doing.
She started to lead her companions toward the fight. As
they circled behind the clerics, she glanced again at the
enemy on the stairs, and stopped, fascinated.

The tallest one wore a blood-red surcoat over dead-black mail. The surcoat had a device in black that Paks could not distinguish. On its head was a horned and spiked helmet; the visor was beaked. It carried an immense curved jagged blade with one hand, and a many-thonged whip in the other. Its red cloak was clasped with a length of black chain, and chain belted the surcoat and scabbard. The others also wore black armor, and tunics of red and black plaid. All their weapons were spiked or jagged. Paks shivered. She wondered if she should offer to guard the clerics.

Suddenly the black-armored figures moved, racing down the steps and screaming strange words. Paks felt a sting on her chest, and thought at once of Canna's medallion. The light dimmed again; the enemy fighters brought a cloud of darkness with them. One of the clerics spoke, and a golden light lay over them all, bright enough for Paks to see the glitter of eyes within the visored helmets. Then the two groups crashed together. Eerie howls, blasts of wind both hot and cold, sizzlings, cracklings, flashing lights—she fought to keep her attention on the fight.

At first both sides ignored her, and they were so closely engaged that she could not find a good opening. Then she saw that the paladin was fending off two: one with both sword and whip, and the other with an axe. The spikes on the whip were catching in the paladin's mail, little jerks that might catch him off balance. Paks shifted that way. Just as she reached the paladin's side, the whip fouled his shield-arm, and the axeman aimed a sweeping stroke at it. Paks threw herself forward, trying to block it with her sword.

When the blades met, a flare of blinding light sprang up, and her blade shattered. The hilts were red-hot, burning through her glove before she could drop the broken blade. She staggered into the axemen, seeing nothing but spots from the flash. Pain shot up her arm. She couldn't seem to draw her dagger. She blinked furiously to clear her vision, and felt herself being hoisted by shoulder and hip. She kicked out strongly, and hit something. Then she fell, hard, onto the stone, and had just time to see a black-booted foot swing back before the kick landed.

She woke to the muted light in the surgeons' tent. She had no idea why she was there until she tried to move her right arm. Her hand and wrist throbbed. When she looked, a bulky bandage swathed her arm to the elbow. She was thirsty. She looked around, and saw only other wounded on pallets. A low murmur of voices came from the next room. The curtain between the rooms billowed and the surgeon came through, the High Marshal at his heels.

"Ah—Paks," said the surgeon softly, coming to her. "You did wake up finally. How do you feel?"

"Thirsty," she said.

"No wonder." He poured a mug from the tall jug in the corner, and offered it. Paks reached, but when she lifted her head to drink pain stabbed her head and darkened her vision. The surgeon moved quickly to help her. "Blast it. I hoped you would be over that. Go on, now—drink as much as you can." She managed five or six swallows. "Is it just your head?"

"Yes—that is, my sword hand hurts some. What happened?"

"You don't remember?"

"No. The last I remember is—is pulling a siege tower. And there was a cloud coming over the wall, and someone stopped it."

"Hmm. You've lost some time. You got a knock on your head some days ago, and then another one that left you flat out. And you've got a burned hand, though it will heal. You can thank High Marshal Kereth that it's no worse."

Paks looked at the Girdsman, now squatting on his heels beside her pallet. She had never been so close to any cleric. He had thick dark hair cropped below his ears, and the short-trimmed beard of one who fought in a visored helmet. Even out of armor and relaxed, he conveyed power and authority.

"They tell me," he began, "that you are not a follower of St. Gird. Is that so?"

Paks started to nod, but the pain lanced through her head again. "Yes, sir; it's true."

"But you wear his holy symbol. It was given to you, I understand, by a Girdsman?"

"Yes, sir. A friend—Canna."

"Ah. Did she tell you why she gave it to you? Had she been trying to convert you?"

"No, sir. I—I wasn't there when she died. The Duke told me she had left it to me. He—he said it would be right to keep it."

"It's unusual. Most Girdsmen, if they die in battle or from wounds, want their symbols returned to the barton or grange where they joined. A friend might be asked to take it there, to tell the story of a brave death. Sometimes it's left to a family member. But to give it to a non-believer, out of the Fellowship of Gird—that's not common at all."

"Should I give it to you, then? To give to the—the barton?"

"Now, you mean?"

"Yes, sir."

"No. I don't think so. A dying friend's wish deserves respect; if she said you were to keep it, I think you should. But tell me, what do you know about St. Gird and his followers?"

Paks thought a long moment. "Well—Canna and Effa both said that Gird was a fighter. So good a fighter that he turned into a god or something, and now fighters can pray to him for courage and victory. And his clerics—Marshals—can heal wounds. Girdsmen are supposed to be honest and brave and never refuse to fight—but not cruel or unfair."

"Hmm." The Marshal's mouth twitched in a brief smile. "And this doesn't appeal to you?"

"Well—sir—" Paks tried to think how to say it politely. "I don't quite see how a fighter could become a god."

"Anything else?"

"Effa—when I was a recruit, and she tried to convert all of us. She told us about Gird's power and protection and all. But it seemed to me that if Gird favored fighting, he wouldn't be protecting much. And Effa got a broken back in her first battle, and died a week later. Gird didn't heal her." Paks paused and looked at the Marshal, but he said nothing, only nodded for her to go on. "And Canna—nobody could have been braver than Canna; if Gird cared about his followers at all, he should have saved her. She—she said it takes a Marshal to heal wounds, but if Gird is so powerful, I don't see why he can't go on and do it, without any fuss." Paks found she was glaring at the Marshal, furious. Her head pounded.

The Marshal's expression was serious, but held no rancor. "Let me explain a few things you may not have heard. Our histories indicate that Gird was a farmer—the sort of big, powerful farmer you see all over Fintha and Tsaia. Tall, strong, hot-headed—" Paks thought of her father. "The rulers in his day were cruel and unjust; Gird found himself leading a rebellion after they harassed his village. Now these were just ordinary farmers—they had no weapons. They made clubs of firewood, and took scythes and plowhandles, and trained in the walled bartons of the village. And with these weapons, and these rough farmers, Gird managed to defeat the rulers with their fine army and its swords and spears. That's why we call our meeting places bartons, and the larger ones granges—because from the beginning, that's where Gird's followers met, in farmyard and barn.

"His friends, after the final victory, wanted him to be king, but Gird refused. Someday maybe you'll read what he said. What he did accept was military command; he made the army into something new—the protector of the helpless and innocent, rather than the tool of the rich. His followers were sworn to honesty, justice, and the care of the poor. We have records, in our archives, of the peaceful years when Gird was chief among guardians.

"Then came a new threat. Powers of evil, supernatural beings: gods and demons. Many folk feared them too much to resist, and fled far away. But Gird went out to face them with his old cudgel. No one saw that battle, but the dark powers fled the land for many years, and Gird was not seen on earth again. Gird's best friend, who had been away on a journey, had a dream in which he saw Gird ascending to the Court of the High Lord—saw him honored there, and given a cudgel of light to wield. It was after that, when he told his dream, that the priests of the High Lord recognized Gird as a saint. We don't claim Gird is a god. We say he is a favored servant of the High Lord; he has been given powers to aid his followers and the cause of right."

Paks nodded slowly. This made more sense than Effa's explanations. "He sounds like a good man—and a good fighter."

"So are you, from what I saw yesterday, and have heard," said the High Marshal. "Your friend who gave you her symbol must have thought well of you. If you ever do become a Girdsman, you'd be a good one."

Paks could not think what to say to this. She wished she could remember just what she'd done the day before.

"You don't remember yesterday at all?" he asked.

"No, sir."

He sighed. "I wish you did. I'd like to know why it didn't kill you."

"What?"

"You crossed blades with a priest of Liart, child. That should have been the death of you, I'd have thought. It shattered your blade, burned your hand—Fenith could scarcely believe it when he saw you kick at the priest after that. It was bravely done, but foolish, to take on such a foe—and amazing that you survived it."

As he spoke, Paks saw a shadowy version of these things in her mind—not yet a memory, but the stirrings of what might become one. "Was there—someone in a red and black tunic, and a helmet with spikes—?"

"Yes. Are you remembering?"

"Not exactly. It's not clear at all. And why should their blades burn my hand? Or—or kill me?"

"Because his weapon was no ordinary axe."

"You mean magical?"

"If you call a curse magic." The High Marshal frowned. "The Master of Torments, or Liart as he was called in Old Aare, is not worshipped openly in Tsaia or Fintha; he is evil. He desires power and the fear of those he controls. He delights in causing strife, in murders and massacres, in bloodlust and torture. His weapons cause pain as well as death, and slavery thrives in his dominion. And his priests—especially those of high rank, as the one you fought—carry weapons of great power. Evil power. No ordinary weapon can turn their strokes; unless a warrior has uncommon aid or protection he dies." He smiled at her for a moment. "So you see why I am so interested in your symbol of Gird. I would not expect such a symbol alone to protect an ordinary wearer—even a Girdsman—from certain death. But I cannot think what else saved you—something surely did. Are you under another deity's protection?"

"No, sir. Not that I know of. I—we—where I grew up, we followed the High Lord—the old gods. I'd never heard of Gird until I joined the Company."

"I see. Was that in the north?"

"Yes, sir. Far north—a village called Three Firs."

"Which kingdom is it in?"

"I don't know, exactly—it's some way north and west of the Duke's stronghold."

"Fintha, or the borders of it. If you never heard of Gird, you heard heroes' tales enough, I'll warrant."

"Yes, sir. Many of them: Torre's Ride, and the Song of Seliast, and the Deed of Cullen Long-arm."

"Ah, yes. Was it those songs made you decide to be a warrior?"

Paks blushed and looked away. "Well—in a way—

when I was very small. I—I did dream about it, the magic swords and winged horses, and all. But then my cousin became a soldier. When he came back he had tales to tell, and he told me the best way would be to join the mercenaries, the good ones. He told me what to look for—not to join any wild band, but an honorable company. The others, he said, were full of thieves and bullies, and cared only for gold."

"And that mattered to you? That your companions should be honest and fair?"

"Of course." Paks stared at him in surprise.

"And have you found them so, in this company?"

"Yes, sir. It wasn't exactly what I expected, but— surely no one could ask better companions. And it is an honorable company; the Duke keeps it so."

"How was it not what you expected?"

"Oh—" Paks grinned sheepishly. "I hadn't known about the camp work—cooking, cleaning, digging, all that. Jornoth left that out. Then I had thought I'd be fighting robbers and evil things—even orcs, maybe—as in the tales. But most of our fighting is against other mercenaries or militia—whoever we're hired to fight. This year's different, of course."

The Marshal nodded. "And would you feel better if you were fighting for such a purpose all the time?"

Paks thought about it. "I don't know. I like to fight— the Duke is very good, and fair. I'm glad to serve him. It's hard to imagine anything else. And this year, we're fighting a great evil. I like that. He killed my friends last year, and tortured, too."

"Yes, this campaign is clearly one of good against evil, and that suits you. But ordinarily—?"

She frowned, choosing her words. "Sir, I—I serve our Duke. That was my oath, when I joined. He is worthy of my service; he has never asked any dishonorable thing. I have no right to question—judge—the contracts he takes."

The High Marshal looked at her thoughtfully. "I see. Yes, your Duke is a good man; I won't argue with that.

And you are loyal, which is good. But something is moving you, which I do not understand, and I think you hardly realize. You may be called to leave your Duke, at least for a time. If so, I hope you will understand the need. Now I can see that you are tiring, and need your rest. Would you like anything to eat, or just more water?"

Paks was puzzling her way through what the High Marshal said; his final question caught her by surprise. "No sir," she said. "Just—just water, if it's near."

He chuckled. "Your surgeon left a bottle here. Can you manage?" He passed it, and this time nothing happened when she lifted her head to drink. The water was cold; she shivered as she drank. The Marshal rose and brought another blanket from the pile. "Rest now," he said. "I would like to speak to you again, if you don't mind—" She shook her head. "Good. May Gird's care be with you." He moved away; Paks stared, still confused.

Chapter Twenty-six

When the sentry ushered the High Marshal into the tent, Duke Phelan and his senior captains were seated around his map table in conference. They looked up. Dorrin smiled, but the rest looked wary.

"I wanted to thank you, my lord, for permission to talk with Paksenarrion."

"Have a seat," offered the Duke. "Did you find out what you wanted?"

The High Marshal gathered his robes and sat down. "Not precisely, my lord. She is still dazed, and does not remember anything of the fighting. I did not wish to tire her. But what I learned confirmed my opinion that something is happening to her—and now I am reassured that it is more likely good than evil."

"Evil!" Arcolin straightened and looked angry. "Were you thinking that Paks was evil? Why, she's the best—"

"Enough." The Duke's voice was calm, but his eyes were flinty. "The High Marshal will no doubt explain himself."

"Gladly. I had no wish to anger you, captain, or to

419

insult your soldier. All I had heard of Paksenarrion by the time I saw her was good. But one reason why a blow from such a weapon held by a priest of that rank might not kill is that the person hit is a servant of that same deity. If—"

"Not Paksenarrion!" interrupted Arcolin.

"No. I agree. But I had to be sure; I had to see her myself. Even with what you and others had said of her service last year. There have been a few cases of Gird's symbol being worn as a mockery by those who hate him. And there are more cases of evil pretending to be good, for a long purpose."

"I'd have thought," said the Duke, pouring another mug of wine, and passing it to the High Marshal, "that you could have told that yesterday, when you found the medallion. Or—what's his name? Fenith?—the paladin. Don't paladins claim to know good from evil?"

"Yes, my lord, but only if the being is aware, which she was not." He took sip of wine and sighed. "And I'll say again—we did not think it likely that she served evil knowingly, not in this Company, not when a Girdsman had left her the medallion. But we had to know. That leaves us, however, with the same puzzle. If she were Girdish, and we assume his symbol saved her life, it would mean she had received special aid from Gird. We would consider that such a fighter might have a call from Gird himself—should go to Fin Panir, say, and train as a Marshal or paladin. But she is not Girdish; she has never considered becoming Girdish." He paused, and a smile moved his face. "In fact, she had quite—primitive, I suppose I'd say—ideas about Gird. The recruit she met—Effa, I think she said—who told her about Gird, seems to have been highly enthusiastic and quite ignorant."

Arcolin glanced at him. "Effa—yes. She was. She was crippled in her first battle, and died soon after."

"So Paksenarrion said. She considers that reason enough for doubting either Gird's power or his interest, I'm not sure which. But back to my point: since

Paksenarrion is not Girdish, it's hard to see why—or even how—the symbol could have saved her. I asked her about other deities, but as far as she's aware, she's under no special protection."

"Did you consider Falk or Camwyn?" asked Dorrin. The High Marshal smiled and nodded.

"Indeed yes, captain. But she's from the northwest— Fintha or its borders—and had never heard of Gird before she joined your Company. Falk and Camwyn are better known to the south and east." He shook his head. "I cannot say who or what saved Paksenarrion, but something most assuredly did." He took a sip of wine; the others nodded slowly. "My lord Duke," he began again. "I know you have no love for the Fellowship of Gird, but you are known to be a fair and just leader. Paksenarrion has told me that she cannot imagine following anyone else. But consider, my lord: some force is moving in her life, something which may call her away from this Company. Not me," he added quickly, to the scowls around him. "I did not even suggest to her that she should join our granges or leave you. I would not dare, not knowing what the High Lord may have planned for her—"

"What do you think?" asked the Duke abruptly.

"Think?" The High Marshal leaned back in his chair. "I think you have as fine a young warrior as I've seen. That's what I hear, as well, from all who have mentioned her. Too impulsive, perhaps, like most young fighters, but that comes as much from generosity as anything else. I think she'll go beyond a hired fighter in the ranks, if nothing breaks that will or that honesty." He sipped again at his mug. Arcolin frowned at his hands locked together on the table. Dorrin fiddled with a link of the fine chain that clasped her cloak. Cracolnya, head cocked on one side, traced a river on the map. Only the Duke locked eyes with the High Marshal.

"You think this Company would do that—would harm that?"

"No, my lord. If she is what she may be, she could

not have found a better training ground than your Company. But she may grow beyond it, and if she does, she may not want to leave, being loyal. She will grow cramped, my lord, like a hawk always caged."

"All companies are cages," said the Duke.

"True. I wish, though—I hope that if she seems to be—if she needs freeing, that you will free her."

"I'm no slavemaster!" growled the Duke. "By—by Tir, you know me better than that! She's served her first enlistment; she can go when she will. But I'll not, High Marshal of Gird, toss her out for no good reason except that you worthy people and interpreters of the gods' will think she's trapped here. You'll not get what you want that way!"

"What we want?"

"Aye, what you always want. Every good fighter should be Girdish, to fight at your Marshal-General's command. Ha! You'll find, High Marshal, that there are worthy battles never sanctioned by your fellowship— helpless victims you never see that depend on others for rescue—fighters just as honest and kind and brave as your paladins who don't get the glory of it—" The Duke paused, breathing hard, his face pale. The High Marshal did not move, and the two men stared at each other in silence. At last the High Marshal set his mug on the table.

"My lord, you know we have never claimed that only in our service is a warrior warring well. There are other saints than Gird, and gods above saints. And you know I did not lie to you: I would be glad to see that girl a Girdsman, but I did not and will not try to talk her into it."

"She could surprise you and end up a loyal servant of Tir," said Arcolin.

"That may be. As long as she serves good—and not my good, my lord, or yours—I wish her all joy. We are not quite so narrow as you think us, Duke Phelan."

"Perhaps." The Duke shifted in his seat. "I hope not. And, after all, in this campaign we are allies once more." He poured more wine in his own mug and offered the jug to the High Marshal, who refused it. "I told the captains to let the Girdsmen in their cohorts know you'd be in camp this afternoon—have you seen them?"

"Yes, my lord; most of them I've seen, and all the wounded. I appreciate the chance to meet with them."

"I," said the Duke brusquely, "don't try to influence my troops."

"No? I'd have thought you influenced them daily with your example of courage and fairness."

"Don't flatter me, High Marshal, if you want something."

"I'm not flattering. You command a fine, well-disciplined body of troops; everyone knows it. You don't get that without the other. Look at Siniava's, for example—or Sofi Ganarrion's, though the cause is different." The High Marshal shifted his weight and set his hands on his knees. "My lord, it's late, and you have much to do. I will not trespass further on your time. But if you would allow me to speak to Paksenarrion again, when her memory has returned, I would like it."

The Duke gave him a long look. "It's not my decision to prevent you—but we march in the morning."

"Can she?"

"I leave no wounded behind for that scum or his agents to capture, High Marshal. Those who can't march will ride in the wagons. If you're going our way, you can talk to her again."

"Do you expect to have need of clerical aid, where you're going?"

The Duke laughed. "Delicately phrased, High Marshal. I appreciate your delicacy. No, I think not. This city, and perhaps others on the coast, were the strongholds of those deities who cannot be fought by sword alone. I expect hard battles, but straightforward ones. Your aid in healing would be welcome, but, after all, there are other sources of healing."

"I would like to be there when you take Siniava,"

mused the Marshal. "But my own command lies elsewhere. We might meet again this season, should our ways to the same end cross. I must go to Vonja, among others."

The Duke's eyes twinkled. "We might be near Vonja ourselves, though I cannot say how soon. If you would ride with us, you may."

"It's a thought—"

"But if you start with us, High Marshal, you must stay. Whatever I think of your fellowship as a whole, I trust its clerics' discretion. But Siniava has agents all over the south, and torture—as you saw, in there—is one of his pastimes. I will not risk my Company."

"No, I understand. If I decide to go with you, I will tell you in the morning, early." The High Marshal stood. "I thank you, my lord, for your courtesy. And, if you'll allow, I'll pray Gird's blessing on your ventures."

The Duke had also risen. "Blessings, High Marshal, we always accept, with thanks." The High Marshal bowed slightly and withdrew. The Duke stood, looking after him with a faint frown, before turning back to his captains.

"Well. What do you think of that?" He looked around at them.

Arcolin snorted. "Anyone stupid enough to even consider that Paks could be evil, after what she's done—" He didn't finish.

"I wonder—" began Dorrin. "I don't know if I mentioned it, my lord, but there was an incident in Rotengre last fall—"

The Duke threw himself into his seat again. "No. I don't recall. About Paks?"

"Yes, my lord. Remember that we found a priest of Achrya?"

"Oh—yes, I do. Was she involved in that?"

Dorrin nodded. "I wondered at the time if Canna's medallion had saved her. She came near being hit by a crossbow, and then the priest cut her with a poisoned dagger. Luckily I was nearby with a standard potion for traps."

"But you're wondering if it was all luck," suggested Arcolin.

"Yes. Perhaps I look at it differently, as a Falkian." Dorrin gave each of them a long look. "But I must agree with the High Marshal that far: something has protected her, and now more than once."

"She takes wounds like anyone else," said Arcolin.

"Yes—it's not that kind of protection, obviously. But when you think of it, as much as she's in the front ranks, she has fewer scars than most."

"And she's a better fighter." The Duke shifted in his seat. "So, then—you think something protects her, at least from some kinds of injury. Do you see her leaving the Company?"

Dorrin frowned, and paused before answering. "My lord, I don't know. Once, I would have said no, but the Company has changed. If she's being guided by—by something, perhaps she will need to leave."

"She could grow in the Company," offered the Duke. "She needn't stay in the ranks, if it comes to that. Sergeant—even captain someday." They all thought that over. "I know it's unusual," the Duke went on. "But so is she—and if she's got the potential you and the High Marshal think she has, I would be open to the suggestion later."

Dorrin smiled. "I'd rather her than Peska, to tell the truth, my lord."

The Duke laughed. "Dorrin, I promise you he'll be gone after this campaign. And you must admit he's a good field commander."

Dorrin grimaced. "In a way. If you like that sort."

"I agree," said Arcolin, with a sideways look at Dorrin. "He's not what we want to keep in the Company, my lord. But about Paks—I'd thought she would make a good sergeant, when she's had more experience. I hadn't thought of more."

"We don't have to," said the Duke, "until later. And

I can't see encouraging her to leave the Company any time soon. She hasn't the experience yet to be a free lance. But I'll do this, Dorrin—with Arcolin's agreement—I'll see the armsmasters encourage her to pick up solo skills. And if anything else happens with her and that blasted medallion, be sure to let me know. All right?" Dorrin nodded, and Arcolin, and they returned to the maps.

Chapter Twenty-seven

For some days of the journey away from Sibili, Paks rode in the wagons, unable to stand without help. Between the pain in her head, the rain, and the swaying and lurching of the wagons, she was miserable enough not to regret having missed the sack of Sibili. From Volya, who came every evening to check on her, she learned some of what she'd forgotten: which night they'd assaulted the wall, which day the paladin had repelled a black cloud near them, which day the citadel had been taken. Volya's tale was incredible—it didn't seem possible that she could have forgotten such fighting, just from a knock on the head. She worried at her mind, trying to force the memories to return, but nothing worked. She had fought beside a paladin—he had come later and tried to heal her—and she could not remember.

Volya's reports of the city's sack were almost as strange, but not as disturbing; it bothered Paks less to have missed something completely than to have been there and forgotten. Volya told of rich treasure in the palace: "Gold," she said. "I never imagined so much. Even a gold mirror. And most of the rooms had pictures on the floor, made of little bits of rock laid in patterns: all colors. And in one room, the walls and floor were all white stone, carved in patterns of vines and leaves. When the light came in the window, it glowed. We just stood and stared; it was wonderful. But underneath—" Volya paused, and went on to describe the horrors that Sibili had concealed. Both Siniava's palace and the temple of Liart overlay dungeons and torture chambers. They had found victims still alive, but hopelessly crippled, and on the high altar in Liart's temple a child's body, still warm. Paks thought at once of the girl in Cha who had feared for her little brother—was that what she'd expected?

"How many days did I miss?" Paks finally asked, when Volya had run down.

"You were out for more than a day—but from what you say, you don't remember much from the day or so before that."

"Huh. Not doing the Company much good."

"No, the fighting was almost over when you went down. Oh, and Paks—you should have seen the servants in the palace—"

"Why?"

"They all had marks on their faces—tattoos, Stammel said. Seems Siniava marks all his own household—his personal bodyguard, too: blue or black tattoos all over the face. It should make them easy to recognize."

Paks nodded. "It should indeed. Makes it hard for them to run away, too."

Volya grinned. "I hadn't thought of that." After she left Paks realized that she'd have to quit thinking of Volya as a recruit: she and the others had come a long way since the winter. Already they had more combat experience than Paks had had in her entire first year.

By the time they passed Cha again, retracing their earlier route, Paks was walking part of the day. Her burned hand was too tender yet to hold a weapon, but the surgeons had showed her how to exercise it. She knew that the Halverics and Clarts were traveling with them, that Golden Company had taken a contract with Andressat to govern and control Sibili and Cha; the Count of Andressat had laid claim to the South Marches and those cities.

"That's why he was so angry with the Westland and Pliuni troops for destroying the orchards and vineyards." Jenits, eating lunch with Paks and Volya, took a pull at his flask. "They made a mess—hacking down trees for cooking fires—"

"They cut down orchards?" Paks was shocked. Jenits and Volya nodded. "But we don't do things like that. What about the crops?"

"Those troops from Pliuni," said Jenits, "want to destroy everything the Honeycat ever owned. We've got some of 'em marching with us now." He made a sour face. "Huh—it's all the Duke and the Halveric can do to keep them from torching everything we pass."

"Then why are they with us?"

"Well—they can fight. They want to fight Siniava. That's it, I suppose. We've had losses—if they'll fight, that's what the Duke wants. But they're not much like us, I can tell you that."

"Are they spread through the Company, or what?" Paks glanced around, trying to distinguish them.

"No. They're in their own formation, under their own captain." Jenits craned his neck to look. "You can't see them from here; they wear green and purple."

After marching east from Cha, along the river, they took the same shortcut across the loop, this time moving northeast. But when they rejoined the river, they forded it instead of turning toward Cortes Andres. Atop the rising ground to the east was a thick forest. Paks had heard of this—the haunt of Alured the Black, the sea pirate turned brigand.

Paks was still unarmed, for the skin of her hand was not tough enough, the surgeons insisted. She hated marching in back with the other wounded, where she could do nothing. As they neared the trees she felt grumpy and nervous at once. Once in that cool shade, undergrowth screened the view to either side; the sunlight almost seemed green. Paks had relaxed a little when the horn call for danger rang out ahead. She felt her heart thudding; her hand dropped automatically to the sword that wasn't there. Halveric fighters moved up from the rear to screen the wounded. Once they were in place, it was quiet but for the rustling leaves overhead. Paks looked at the broad back of the Halveric nearest her. He looked strong, but she still wanted her own sword.

Her first sight of Alured the Black confused her. He looked nothing like the pirate or brigand she had pictured in her mind. The Duke and the other captains escorted him along the column, introducing him to the troops. He had long black hair in a braid, and a black beard; his face was darkly tanned. Strong bones, strong arched eyebrows, snapping black eyes. He sat his black horse easily, his broad shoulders square and erect, his hands quiet on the reins. As he and the others rode on down the column, she saw that his glossy black braid was bound with green leather and decorated with several bright-colored feathers. Paks thought this looked a little silly, but his longbow and sword were workmanlike enough.

They spent almost four days crossing the forest, camping each night in clearings Alured designated, and closely watched by his men. These wore mottled, drab clothing well-suited for forest work, with a badge on the left breast: a gray tower on a green field. Paks wondered what it meant. Alured's men provided fresh meat each night: rabbits and other small game, for they would not hunt the red deer in spring.

On the afternoon of the fourth day, they reached the forest edge. On their left, the land dropped steeply to a river they could see but not hear—the eastern branch of the Chaloquay. Ahead were the pastures and fields of Cilwan—three days ahead was Cortes Cilwan, the city. Scattered groves and patches of forest extended some distance from Alured's domain; they marched to one of these before camping for the night. Paks thought of the band of men she had seen watching the column as it left the forest. She wished she knew what they were thinking.

By this time Jenits's arm was out of splints; he carried a shield as he marched to strengthen it. Paks had been cleared to return to her cohort. The lump on her head was much smaller, and her hand healed with little scarring. She had to rub and stretch the scars with oil every day, and wear a glove all the time, but she had a sword at her side again.

Cilwan was much lusher country than Andressat or the South Marches. Never a stone showed in the dark soil; flowers edged the garden plots on the farms they passed. Most buildings were well-kept, shutters and doors brightly painted. But the people shunned them, hiding in the fields until the column had passed.

Near noon a day or so later, they passed through a small village. Paks was shocked to see the Pliuni troops in front of her slip from the column to enter houses, emerging with arms full of food and clothing. Hooves pounded up from behind. Arcolin yelled at the Pliunis. They shambled to a halt. Paks could see the resentment in their hunched shoulders as Arcolin argued with their captain. A loose shutter creaked in the breeze.

"No raiding!" Arcolin was still shouting. "These aren't enemies—we aren't robbers; we're soldiers. You have enough food. You don't need to do this."

The Pliuni captain had pale red hair; his skin flushed to the same color. "This is silly. Siniava robbed us often enough—these are only peasants—"

"They aren't even Siniava's peasants! No. No raiding. You wanted to come with the Duke, and you agreed to obey him—"

"The Duke, yes," growled the Pliuni captain. "Not a bunch of damned nursemaids!" Paks heard a mutter of agreement from the Pliuni troops near her. Her hand slipped toward her sword; she saw Arcolin's hand move toward his. The Pliunis seemed to draw together. Paks

looked for the sergeants. They both nodded slightly as
they moved, one on either side of the column, to the
head of the cohort. From the rear came another clatter
of hooves. Pont and Dorrin rode up beside Arcolin.

"Problems?" asked Dorrin.

"They were raiding," said Arcolin, with a nod toward
the Pliunis.

The Pliuni captain's face was now beet-red. "And we
will raid, Duke's man, when I say so. Your Duke isn't
paying us anything for our help, after all." Again a
mutter of agreement from the Pliuni troops. Dorrin
frowned.

"If you march with us, you follow our rules," said
Arcolin.

"Not *yours*," sneered the Pliuni. "Your Duke's
maybe—if it suits us."

Arcolin was white with rage. Dorrin spoke before he
could say anything. "Are you not aware of the Duke's
policy on raiding?"

The captain glowered at her. "Oh, he says there's to
be none—and that keeps the peasants quiet—but of
course he knows we must do *some*."

"Perhaps you'd like to hear the Duke's opinion in
person?" Arcolin's voice was cold.

"Perhaps I'd like you to mind your own business!"
The Pliuni captain glanced back at his men. "You think
you're so special, captain—just because you mercenaries fight for money instead of honor—" At the word,
Arcolin's hand signal passed to the sergeants. Every
blade in the cohort slipped from its sheath. Paks saw
the Pliuni captain's eyes slide sideways to see what had
happened. Arcolin's eyes never moved.

"Captain Pont, ask the Duke to attend us, please,"
said Arcolin. Pont nodded, and legged his horse to a
hand gallop toward the front of the column. Paks grinned
as she saw the Pliuni captain's shoulders twitch. Men in
the rear Pliuni ranks glanced back at Arcolin's cohort,
paling as they saw the naked blades. Their own hands

twitched; those who had taken bundles from the houses dropped them.

"You can't attack us," began the Pliuni captain. "We're your allies. You shouldn't draw sword against us—"

"Against you?" asked Dorrin. "The captain has not moved his troops an inch—are you afraid to see swords inspected?"

"Inspected! It's not—he was—"

"You," said Arcolin firmly, "were insulting us. I saw a dozen hands on sword among your troops. So I thought we'd best be sure ours were clean—ready for any—difficulty." He looked at Stammel. "They are, aren't they?"

Stammel grinned broadly. "Certainly, captain. Any time."

The Pliuni captain turned even paler. "It's—it's treason—a trap—you're looking for some excuse to kill us all." His men shifted in their ranks, murmuring.

"Tir's gut, Captain, if we'd wanted to kill you, you'd be dead by now. Don't be ridiculous." Dorrin's scornful voice caught all their attention. "We—and you, I hope—want to kill the Honeycat. That's why we're here. That's why you asked to march with us. Isn't that right—that you hate Siniava?"

"Yes." Most of the Pliuni troops were looking at her now.

"Then concentrate on that, and not on making trouble. Plunder Siniava's camp, not some poor peasants who hardly have a spare tunic."

The Pliuni captain was still disgruntled, and looked ready to argue, but they heard the beat of many galloping hooves. Duke Phelan, Aliam Halveric, Captain Pont, and the senior Halveric captain halted beside Arcolin and Dorrin.

"Do I understand, captain, that you have a problem?" Duke Phelan was angry, his voice icy. The Pliuni captain looked around but found no support.

"My lord Duke, we—we were but—"

"Plundering," said the Duke. "Stealing. And from peasants we hope are still loyal to their count, who is our ally."

"No one's paying *us*," said the Pliuni, unwisely. "We have to have something—"

"No one's paying me, either," said the Duke. "I have no contract to defeat Siniava, only the vow I made to our dead. If you want plunder, captain, you can wait until you take it from Siniava—or you can march alone. I won't have thieves under my protection." The captain flushed again, but the Duke went on before he could speak. "Either you control your men, and obey my commands as given through my captains, or you march away, right now, and stay clear. And if you leave, you'd best not use my name, or that of my allies: we'll consider you as any other band of brigands. Is that clear?"

The man turned to the Halverics, but both of them gave him a tight-lipped stare that promised no softening of the Duke's position. His shoulders sagged.

"Yes—it's clear."

"Well, then?"

"Well—" He looked around at his men. "We'll march with you."

"And obey? That means at once, without question."

"Yes—my lord."

"Good." The Duke swept his eyes over the Pliuni contingent. "Have your men return whatever they took to the correct houses, at once." The captain turned to his sergeants and gave the orders. Those who had taken bundles picked them up and moved reluctantly toward the houses. "Hurry up!" called the Duke sharply. "We've wasted enough time on this nonsense."

In a few minutes the men were back in formation and the march resumed. Paks wondered how good the Pliuni troops would be in a fight—and how loyal.

The next morning they met Vladi's Company in a narrow wood. They were grim and weathered-looking; soon the stories were trickling through the troops. Vladi's men had reached Cortes Cilwan before Siniava, but had found the city divided in allegiance. The city militia, so the tavern gossip ran, was half for Siniava already. The Count of Cilwan would not risk rebellion on the eve of war, and refused to arrest even known traitors—some said because his dead wife's brother was chief among them. Although it had been planned otherwise, the Vonja militia had not joined Vladi's men, wanting to be sure which way trouble was coming before moving. So although messages were sent as soon as Siniava's presence in the Immer valley was known, the Vonja troops were several days' march away.

"And that left us," said the burly sergeant talking to Stammel. "We marched out to meet his whole army. Just us. Those damned militia wouldn't leave the city walls, and Vladi refused to take the Count's Guard—said they were loyal, and he had too few who were." He hawked and spat. "You can imagine—outnumbered about five to one—all we could do was slow 'em."

"Did you get the Count out?" asked Stammel, as he offered the other man a skin of wine.

"Mmm. That's good; we haven't had anything but water these last weeks. No, their fool Count wouldn't come. He said he was Count of Cilwan, and he was staying where he belonged." He swallowed again. "They killed him when they broke in, a couple of days later. Hung his corpse on the gate, and that. He did let us get his heir out. Boy of eleven or so. Nice lad. I suppose now, with the news you brought about the south, they'll send him to Andressat. The old Count's daughter is the Viscount of Andressat's wife; he'll be safe enough there."

"I imagine so. We don't need a child with us on this campaign." Stammel shook his head. "Well, did they pursue you when you came here?"

"Pursue! Ha! We tried to attack their rear, before they broke the citadel, and they drove us back—pretty bad, that time; we lost too many. Then we moved south, toward Immervale, and harried their supply line. We kept hoping those Vonja militia would show up in time to save the citadel. Finally Vladi took us around north of the city. We finally found 'em, a day's march out, and after the citadel fell. We were all well chewed up by this time, and Vladi gave their captains a few choice words. About took the bark off the trees, he did, and so they said they'd get Siniava themselves if we'd guard the Andressat approaches. That's when we moved over this way and tried to get back in shape. But you can imagine what they did."

"No, what?"

"Well, our spies said Siniava had garrisoned Cortes Cilwan and was moving toward Koury. We thought even Vonja should be able to trap him there, with Ambela and Sorellin coming down from the north. But that fell apart. Siniava's factions in Cortes Vonja and Pler Vonja revolted, and as soon as the militia heard, they hared off home to join in the fight. Sorellin never moved, so Koury fell easily, and Siniava had fresh troops. He went for Ambela next, and held off the Sorellin militia long enough to breach the wall and loot. In fact, I hear he routed both the Sorellin militia and a group from Pler Vonja. The last I heard, he was actually marching on Pler Vonja, and Foss Council had finally decided to send someone like they promised. Of course, they're on the road somewhere, and Tir knows if they'll come up in time to fight. Or if they'll fight. Militia!"

Stammel nodded his agreement. "Has it been quiet over here, then?"

"Not really. You'll find out. He must have a small army of agents in Cilwan; they can take out sentries without a sound. You'll lose a man or so every night if you don't double your guardposts. And all you ever get back is pieces—hands and feet lying in the trail, or an arm tacked up on a barn."

"And you've never caught them at it?"

"No, not since we left the city. We lost three men in Cortes Cilwan, but we caught those bastards who did it in the same house with the bodies. Out here, no."

A shout from the captains ended this conversation, and the army was soon marching again, enlarged by Vladi's Company. The rest of that day and the next they marched north and west, angling toward Cortes Vonja. By nightfall the first day, they had reached the south bank of the Immerest, the great western arm of the Immer River. They passed no bridges, and the river was too deep to ford, so the commanders decided to march upstream another day rather than risk a boat crossing. The Halverics thought they remembered a ford somewhere south of Cortes Vonja.

It was on this day, in broad daylight, that Siniava's agents struck at the column. The first Paks knew about it was in forming up again after a rest break at mid-morning. Three people were missing; a search of the riverbank and woods along it yielded nothing. The Pliuni smirked, and Paks heard one mutter something about "typical mercenaries—deserters—." After a half-glass spent searching and calling, the column moved on. Paks knew that old Harek, a veteran, would never have deserted.

Perhaps an hour later, Aliam Halveric rode up beside her cohort and asked Stammel if he'd seen the senior Halveric captain. When Stammel said no, he rode on up the column. Stammel looked worried. Paks wondered if the Halveric captain had disappeared. She felt a cramp of cold fear. Could he have been captured? In daylight? When the column halted at midday, orders were given that no one move out of sight of the column. Paks saw the Duke and Aliam Halveric ride down the column together, talking quietly. She had never seen the Halveric like that, gray-faced and drawn; it must be that the Halveric captain—his oldest living son, she'd heard—was gone. She thought of what might be happening to him, and felt cold again.

Shortly after dark that night, Stammel told Paks to report to the Duke's tent. When she found her way across the darkened camp to his tent, she found the Duke and the captains and several other soldiers. She had just greeted them when three more soldiers came in.

"That should do it," said the Duke. "Now—I have a very dangerous and difficult mission for you. If any of you are not fit—if you think you're coming down with a

fever, or a wound's bothering you—or if you don't want
to risk yourself away from the Company—tell me now,
and I'll release you. You've all been recommended by
your captains, both for bravery and woodscraft. But this
is no ordinary soldiering I'm asking of you; I want only
those who are willing." Paks thought of what he might
want them to do. Sneak into Siniava's camp and kill
him? One of the others sneezed explosively. "Now that,"
said the Duke, "is what we can't have—you may be
excused."

"But my lord," said the man. "This just come on since
we ate—I can pinch my nose. I wouldn't make that
noise, my lord; I know I wouldn't."

The Duke smiled. "I know you'd try not to—but you
can't pinch your nose if you're carrying something. This
is too important to chance. Go on, now. I don't think
the worse of you." The man looked at his captain,
Dorrin, who nodded toward the entrance. He shuffled
out, shamefaced. The Duke glanced around. "I take it
the rest of you are willing?" They nodded. "Good.
Some of you may have guessed that the Halveric's
eldest son has disappeared. We are fairly sure he was
captured. I think they will not kill him at once; he's too
valuable as a prisoner." Paks felt a thrill; the Duke must
be planning to get him out. She could not imagine how
they could get into Siniava's camp, find the Halveric,
and escape, but it was a worthy endeavor.

"You will not be going into Siniava's camp yourselves," said the Duke, breaking into her thoughts.
"We have agents who can move there openly. You
don't need to know about that, but they are trying to
find and free Cal—the captain—and move him out of
camp. If he's already dead, they'll bring his body out.
You'll meet them beside the river, on the far side, and
bring him back; they cannot be seen near us. Now—
several of you can handle a boat, right?"

"Yes, my lord." Tam and Amisi from Cracolnya's
cohort, and Piter from Arcolin's stepped forward.

"Good. The rest of you, listen to these three when it

comes to crossing the river. Come and look at this map." They all gathered around the map table. "Here we are," said the Duke. "Take this lane, west of camp, then look for a big stone barn. Cut across here—there's an orchard and two fields—and you'll come to the river. There's a big willow with a limb hanging out over the water—the only tree that size for a half-mile along here, so you should find it even in the dark. There'll be a boat there, big enough for you and Cal. Across the river is a stone ledge, three men high. Upstream of that is where you'll wait for them to bring him. Remember that sound carries more over water than on land. Whatever you do, don't separate. They'll cut you up if you do, and you're more likely to be captured. The password on the far side, to the men who'll be bringing Cal, is a question: Where lies Havensford? Their answer is: Across the mountains. Anyone else will tell tell you it's four days march upstream. Siniava's watchword is a challenge of apricot, and the answer is brambles. Don't confuse them." No one asked how the Duke knew the enemy watchwords. With the rest, Paks repeated them several times. The Duke nodded finally.

"Good. You'll go armed, but without shields. Make sure you don't show anything shiny. You should be back by dawn or a little after. If you have trouble on this side of the river, make as much noise as you can. I don't want to move troops around tonight, or his agents might figure out what we're doing, but I'll have them ready to move fast if you call. If they do get Cal to you alive, don't let him be captured again—whatever you have to do. Give him the death-stroke before you're disabled, if it comes to that. Are you ready?"

Paks's throat felt like dust. She hardly heard the boat specialists giving them a few advance instructions: sit still, don't move around, don't stand up, don't trail your hands in the water, don't talk or spit. In a few minutes they were clear of the camp, walking quickly down the lane the Duke had shown them on the map. After some minutes of walking, Paks could hear something besides the blood pounding in her ears. The night was clear; brilliant stars gave some shape to the land and trees. A vast dark shape loomed up before them: the stone barn. They turned aside. Starlight glimmered on the blossoms left on the fruit trees in the orchard; their scent was stronger in the damp night air. The first field beyond was plowed, and their boots rasped on rough furrows and clods. The next was in grass; once more they moved quietly, slipping along the margin of the field by a hedge as fragrant as a flower garden.

Trees loomed before them and starlight danced on the river. They slowed, looking for the willow tree they were to find. Suddenly Paks felt a hand-grip signal passed back: there. She edged forward, alert for stones that could roll beneath her feet, or sticks that could crack. Once in the willow's shadow it was even harder to see. Paks stumbled on a rock, lurching forward and biting her tongue against any sound. Someone grabbed her arm and steadied her. She did the same for another who stumbled into her a moment later. They found the limb, wide enough to walk on, and then the boat.

The boat experts urged everyone into a huddle, then loaded the boat, guiding them with nudges and hand-grips. It had looked a large dark shape to Paks when she saw it empty, but once aboard it felt too small. Not crowded—but the sides were too low, and she felt too close to the water. And the boat tipped and shifted with every motion of its passengers. She tried to keep from moving in response, fearing to tip the whole thing over.

With a rower at each end, and one in the middle, they moved quietly across the current. Paks did not know how the rowers could tell where they were going. When they landed on the far side, just where they had been told to wait, she was glad to crawl from the boat to solid ground again. She crouched silently in the dark, waiting for someone to arrive. It seemed a long time.

They heard the hoofbeats coming from upstream for some time before the riders were close enough to challenge. Amisi, in a southern accent, asked "Where lies Havensford?"

"Across the mountains," came the soft reply. The horses had stopped, and Paks could just see two cloaked and hooded shapes swing off their mounts and move to help a third.

"You've got him alive?" asked Amisi.

"Aye." Paks and the others moved toward the voice, and helped to steady the man they were supporting.

Chapter Twenty-eight

"How careless of you, Captain, to be riding alone so far from your troops." The voice was soft and gentle. The bonds on his arms and legs were not. Cal Halveric said nothing. "You might have met with some fatal accident, you know. It is fortunate for you that my servants are not quick to kill. We do not entertain guests of your distinguished rank often, Captain." Cal could see nothing through the hood that covered his head but the glint of light between dark threads. Captain they could have guessed from his clothes and his horse; he hoped very much that they did not know which captain. "I hope," the voice went on, sharpening a little, "that you are attending to me——" Something, it could have been boot or pike-butt, prodded his ribs. When he said nothing, a much harder blow slammed into the same spot. He felt one rib crack, and caught his breath in a gasp of pain.

Before he could recover, rough hands dragged him up from the ground and tightened the hood around his neck until he could barely draw a breath. A hand felt over his face, applied pressure to the eyeballs, the angle of his jaw. When he tried to twist away, the cloth around his throat tightened. He tried not to react, but at last air hunger overcame his control and he choked, fighting the halter and the merciless hands. Instead of release, he got hard blows to the belly. When he was reeling, the tightness eased slightly, and he gasped for breath, unaware of anything else. When he could hear again, the soft voice was speaking.

"You see, Captain, I must be sure I have your attention for our very important conference—do I?" When Cal did not answer, the cloth at his throat tightened again, slowly. His throat moved convulsively and he choked. "Was that a 'yes,' Captain?" the voice went on. "You must speak clearly, so that we do not mistake one another." Cal fought back a desire to speak all too clearly to this scum, and thought instead of Seliam, dead in his first command. This time the choking continued until he passed out completely.

Someone was calling his name. "Cal—Cal—" the voice went on. A soft voice. He couldn't think who it was. "Cal—wake up." He stirred and took a long breath. Pain stabbed his ribs; his throat was sore—it was dark. He started to reach for his dagger, as always when he woke, and realized that his arms were bound. And his legs. He was flat on his back, and cold. He shifted his head, trying to remember, to think.

"Caliam Halveric," the voice mused. "Oldest living son of Aliam Halveric—his second in command—his heir, I understand. Cal, they call you, don't they?" A hand brushed his body and he realized he was naked—then remembered the hood—and what had come before. The hand traced some of his old scars, slowly. He shivered, telling himself it was from the cold. The voice began again, brisker. "Caliam Halveric. What are you worth to your father—" the hand touched his manhood, "—whole? What would he give for you? Anything? Or—would you fetch a better price elsewhere? As a gelding, perhaps. Or perhaps his enemies would pay for you—" the hand touched here and there, "—piece-meal, so to speak. Eh?"

Cal smiled grimly under the hood. He knew his worth to his father well enough, and the price someone would pay for his death. "I have sired sons enough," he said, answering that oblique threat.

"Ah yes." The voice carried amusement. "You are married, are you not, to—now what is her name?" Cal did not answer. "Five sons and three—no, four—daughters, as I recall. But Cal—what makes you think I have no agents over the mountains. Are five sons enough, if you cannot get more?"

He had not thought of that. Surely they were safe, so far away—young Aliam, only fifteen but furious at being left behind, Berrol the stubborn twelve-year-old, Malek and Kieri and baby Seli, born just a month after his uncle's death. And the girls: tall Tamar, wild as Aliam, and Zuli, and Volya and Amis. Surely they were safe. But his breath came quicker. How did they know this? Were some of his own men traitors?

After a long pause, the voice went on. "Your father, Cal—he has made a very unfortunate alliance with that crazy dukeling, Phelan." Cal suppressed a snort. Phelan was as crazy as his nickname of fox. "But perhaps, if he values you, he might be persuaded to—to forget that alliance, at least for awhile."

"He will not be likely to forgive your murdering one of his sons because of your threats to another," said Cal calmly.

"Murder? You aren't even harmed—yet—barring a rib you might have bruised falling off your horse."

"You mean your spy system does not extend to know-ing all his captains? How incompetent."

"But when did—oh. Was that your brother, last fall? I had been told a hireling captained that troop. Then is that why—?" Cal was silent, willing enough to let him think his brother's death was the only reason for the Halveric-Phelan alliance. That reason might be public knowledge; the rest were secrets he did not care to have probed. The voice went on.

"The loss of one son should not harden a man to the loss of others, surely? You must be even more dear to him—or your sons must be. We must convince him, Cal, that his desire for vengeance will condemn you, too. And to no such quick death as your brother. I do wish I'd known who he was. Even so, he would be alive had he released his prisoners to me, as any sensible person would have done. That nonsense you mercenaries spout about honor—ridiculous!" With no warning, scalding liquid splashed Cal's chest. "Oh—" the voice said archly. "How clumsy of me!"

Cal was suddenly disgusted by the tone as much as the pain, so angry that it swamped his fear. "South coast scum," he began. "You're not just clumsy, you're stupid and incompetent as well. You couldn't captain a mercenary company, because the only way you can get fighters to follow you is to threaten their families—coward as you are. And you don't have the guts to stay and fight with 'em, when you lead 'em into a mess—" The blows began soon after his words, but he kept on until he passed out once more. "Stupid—cowardly—scum— that's what you are, and furthermore—"

This time pain woke him. He was wedged into a space so small that he could move nothing but his head, and that only slightly. His arms had been rebound behind him, tightly; he could not feel his hands at all. His bruised cheek rested on his knees. Everything ached and throbbed, and he had a cramp in one shoulder. With every breath his broken ribs grated and stabbed. He had had bruises and broken ribs often enough before—but not the other pain, growing fire that gnawed between his thighs, leaving him no doubt about one irreplaceable loss. Perhaps, he thought grimly, I will bleed to death from this. If only I had been able to taunt him longer, he might have killed me at once. He felt contempt for his captor, who could so easily be moved by a rough tongue. But Halverics are not bred to despair or suicide, and his mind returned to his children. If he died, they would avenge him: but he was not dead, not yet. His mind wandered to his own childhood, when Kieri Phelan was his father's squire, and he had seen Kieri's scars. "Don't ever ask," his father had said, "and never complain, Cal, until you've borne the like."

He woke, not knowing he had dozed, at the touch of a hand on his leg. A voice—not the soft voice, but one with a northern flavor—whispered nearby. "Are you th'Halveric, are ye?" He froze, afraid to answer. It must be a trap. The hand, hard and horny, slid along his thigh to his buttocks. A whispered curse, then a comment: "Holy Falk, he's been—" Another whisper, silencing the first. He worked his tongue around in his mouth, as the hand found his ankles and a cold thin thing—blade?—slipped under the thongs that bound them. He heard the thongs snap. The blade slid up and cut the thongs at his knees. He tried to whisper, but it came out as a grunt, unintelligible even to him. "Quiet," the voice commanded, itself very soft. "Are you the Halveric?" He nodded, then realized it was dark and managed a shaky yes. "Don't make a noise," the voice said. "We'll pull—don't fight us."

The hard hand grasped his feet and pulled them to one side. The wrench of pain that followed almost drew a sound from him, but he clamped his jaws on it. He felt his legs scrape past an edge of some sort, and smelled fresher air, cold air. The hand reached up past his thighs to his body, felt around toward his arms. Again the blade, still on his upper arm, slicing the bonds at elbow and wrist. His elbows rolled out, catching on the sides of whatever held him with a little thump. Again a muffled curse. The hand reached and pulled first one arm forward, then the other. Something soft bound his forearms loosely together. He leaned now against the side of the container, trying to yield to the hands without making any sound. One set grasped his legs below the knees, and the other reached in and lifted his hips slightly. He choked back a scream at that, and tried to arch his back against the surface behind him. They pulled, and his body eased out, his head sliding down the wall. He tipped his head forward so it would not thump on the floor of the container. He could feel hot blood seeping from reopened wounds. At last, inch by careful inch, the unknown hands drew him free of his prison, and he lay at full length on a flat surface.

"Be very quiet," a voice murmured in his ear. "Not out yet. Talk later." Meanwhile the hands were busy, running along his arms and legs feeling for broken bones. His hands began to come to life again, with the throbbing pain of returning circulation. He flexed them, glad to have control over something. "Need cloth," murmured the voice. "Blood trail if we don't."

"Here," said the other voice. He was lifted and a pad of cloth wrapped against his back—then he could feel them dragging a tunic over his head. A flask pressed against his lips and he swallowed. While he was dreaming, he thought, he might as well dream numbwine— but it was water, cold and clean. He realized that his mouth was full of some foul taste, blood or vomit, and swallowed again. Very quickly they had him ready to move, with loose trousers drawn up to his waist, and stockings pulled over his feet. "Will hurt," said the voice in his ear. "No sound." A hand lay along his face for a moment, and he nodded.

He felt himself slung over a shoulder, but in the pain of that jolting movement, he passed out again. He came to with a hand hard across his mouth. "Quiet," the voice said. He nodded, and the hand released its pressure. It was dark, but now he could see. Yellow blurs in the distance—torches, he thought—and a vague sense of darker nearby shapes looming over him. "Horse lines," murmured the voice. "Got to ride—too far on foot." Cal shuddered at the thought of straddling a horse.

"C-can't," he croaked.

"Quiet. You must. That or the deathstroke. You've no bones broke but ribs—we'll help you." Cal was shaking now, shaking too hard to help as they urged him up.

"By St. Falk, we'll never—" The second voice sounded scared.

"We will. The numbwine, Jori." Cal felt a flask against his lips again. This time it was numbwine, strong and bitter with the pain-killing herb. He swallowed twice, three times, before the flask was taken away. "No more," said the voice. "You must be awake for the sentry." In a few moments the pain eased, though the thought of mounting was terrible. The hands pulled at him, lifted. He could just stand, half-supported by one of his rescuers while the other shoved a horse over to him; he smelled the pungent sweaty hide. "Stirrup's low," murmured his supporter. "You can reach it—I'll help. Jori's on the other side."

Cal raised his foot, surprised that he could, and slid it into the stirrup he felt. He leaned into the horse as the man behind him shoved him up; his right leg swung to clear the saddle out of habit. He stood, leaning forward on the beast's neck, while Jori fitted his foot into the off stirrup. Then the man on the near side vaulted up behind him, and he heard Jori mount another horse. "Lean on me," said the man behind him. He sank back. The pain was impossible; sweat sprang cold on his whole body—but he did not faint. The horse began to move.

"When we reach the sentry lines," the man said in his ear, "you'll have to ride alone—maybe fifty yards—no more. Jori's got a horse for me to go through the lines with." He was fitting a hooded cloak around Cal as he spoke. "We're Vonja militia, remember that. Going back to Vonja. I'm sergeant; you're just a private. Don't say anything. If they ask your name, say Sim. They won't ask unless their sergeant is there—if they stay bought. At worst we'll see to you. You won't be caught again. Now—when I slide off, sit up straight. Just a few yards, remember?"

"Yes—I will." Cal spoke softly. "Who are you?"

"Right now, I'm a sergeant of Vonja militia, a turncoat. We'll talk later. Almost there—I've got to change horses before we get to the torches. All right?" Cal nodded. As the man behind him slid from the horse, Cal sagged and almost fell. He managed to pull himself upright, and tried to tuck the cloak snugly around himself. The horses hardly paused before moving on. He could see, against the torches ahead, the third horse now in the lead.

A sentry hailed them. He heard the voice ahead, bantering now in a southern accent. He looked forward. It was hard to follow the conversation. Laughter. A face upturned to his, whites of eyes glinting in the light. The horses moved on, into darkness. Cal concentrated on his balance. He dared not look back to see how far they had come. It seemed forever before the voices spoke to him again. "Can you ride alone?" one asked. "We can make better time if you can—we need to get to the river."

"I—think—so," Cal managed to say. "But not—not trotting—"

"No. Of course not."

"Should we tie him to the saddle?" asked the other. "If he falls—"

"If you think you can't make it," said the first voice, "tell us. Don't fall."

"No," said Cal. "I won't fall." He began to believe it might be real. They rode on. Just when he was sure he would faint, strong arms lifted him from the saddle. There were more voices now. Again he thought of a trap, and tried to sit up, but firm hands pressed his shoulders down.

"Take it easy, sir," said one of the new voices. "We've got to get you across the river. Just lie still as you can."

"But who—" His voice was harsh and unsteady; he

swallowed and tried again. "Who are you? Who got me out?"

"No names this side of the river, sir," came the reply. Cal felt the grip of many hands as he was lifted, then laid on a hard surface that seemed to dip and sway. A hand touched his face, gently.

"Good luck to you, sir," came the voice he'd heard first. "We hope to see you someday, me and Jori."

"But—aren't you coming?"

"Nay—we've to get back to Vonja and act our part."

"Tir's gut!" exclaimed someone else. "That's a dangerous game—what if you're caught?"

"We won't be," said Jori. "We've daggers and the wit to use them. And by Holy Falk and Gird, we'll meet you all in a tavern not too long from now."

"I wish," Cal interrupted. "I wish I had something for you—after all this."

"You gave us your silence," said the first voice. "That was gift enough, considering. Don't worry, Captain— Jori and me are weasels for cunning." Cal heard the horses moving away. He felt the surface he lay on tip sharply, and the muffled thuds of other bodies settling onto boards. Of course, he thought: river, a boat. He closed his eyes as the boat moved out onto the river. It fetched up on the far back with a bump that jounced him into pain again. He was lifted from the boat to the bank, and given another swallow of numbwine and as much water as he could drink. Then he was carried, on a blanket slung between poles, for a long distance: or long it seemed, when every footfall waked another twinge in his battered body.

For the most part he kept his eyes closed, but once when he opened them he noticed the sky above was paling. It must be nearly dawn. The soldiers carrying him were no longer dark blurs against the sky; he could see the shape of their helmets, and the faces beneath. The light grew. He could not distinguish color yet; their tunics were dark, and could have been any dark color. But the helmet shape—the cut—he thought it must be— One of them looked at him.

"Nearly there, captain. You're safe now."

"You're—"

"The Duke's men, sir. We're nearly back to camp. Sorry it's taken so long."

Cal felt a ridiculous desire to laugh. He was hardly likely to complain about how far they'd had to carry him. "My father?" he asked. "Does he know?"

The man shook his head. "Don't know, Captain. The Duke will have told him, I'd think, or maybe he's waiting until you come in." Cal let his eyes sag shut. He had no idea how long he'd been in the enemy camp, and he didn't really care to know. Not yet. Enough to know he was out, and safe. As safe in Phelan's camp as in his own. He heard the challenge of sentries, and his escort's reply. A voice he knew, one of the Duke's captains, he thought, said: "Duke's tent." He thought he should open his eyes again, but it was too much trouble.

At last all motion ceased. He lay on something soft, and smelled the pungent reek of surgeons' gear. Feet stirred on the floor nearby; something rustled. He struggled to open his eyes. Sunlight bled through the tent walls. The Duke stood by the bed he lay in, staring at the floor. Cal swallowed and tried to speak. The Duke glanced at his face with the first sound.

"Cal. You're safe now. Your father will be here soon. My surgeons are ready—"

"My lord—I—thank you."

The Duke made an impatient gesture. "None needed. I'm glad you're no worse."

"It was Siniava's camp, wasn't it?" The Duke nodded, and sat abruptly on a stool beside the bed. Cal rolled his head sideways, and felt his hand lifted and held. A surgeon moved to the bed. Cal swallowed. "Sir—my lord—"

"Yes, Cal?"

"Please—don't stay. Go—wait for my father."

"What? Cal, I've seen wounds before; I won't faint."
Cal shook his head. "Please—don't stay—"

"Cal—what is it?" He could not answer. The Duke
met his eyes in a long silent look, and suddenly he saw
the sense of what he could not say looking back at him.
He saw tears fill the Duke's eyes, saw them blinked
back, saw the rage he had seen last fall return. When
the Duke spoke, his voice held nothing of that, nothing
but calm. "As you wish, Cal. If you want me, I'll be in
the front room." He sighed, and released Cal's hand;
sighed again, and stood.

"My lord—"

"Yes?"

"If I could bear anyone—it would be you—"

The Duke nodded and withdrew. The surgeons un-
wrapped the cloak around him and went to work.
Numbwine masked the physical pain for the next hour,
but not the mental. Now that he was safe, now that he
might have thought all was well—he told himself he
should be glad of the children he already had, the
campaigns he had already fought, the rank he had already won. But what he had lost intruded. How could
he command a company, once it was known? He knew
too well the ways of rumor to doubt that it would be
known, and known widely.

He was still thinking this, gloomily, when his father
arrived, bursting past the Duke with hardly a word and
into the bedchamber. He saw at once that his father
knew. The dark eyes were snapping, the beard bristling
in all directions. Cal stared back at him.

"Well," said his father gruffly. "Thank the gods they
took the only thing you *don't* need to be a commander—
or my heir." Cal wondered if he'd heard rightly; he
knew his face must show his shock. A grim smile parted
his father's beard. "Hadn't thought of it that way, had
you? Arms and legs, Cal: brains, eyes, ears—oh, and a
strong voice—that's what you need. That you've got.
Ask Aesil M'dierra if she ever needed balls to run a
company—ask with a mile's head start, and the fastest

horse in my stable—you might make it home." He sat down on the stool by the bed. "And thank the gods we didn't give in to young Ali about coming this year. That would have been a real mess." His face softened. "How much numbwine have you had?"

"Enough, sir." Cal still felt faintly affronted.

"Good. Cal, I'm not ignoring your loss. I know—I *do* know—what it means. But I know what it doesn't mean. You've got heirs of the body—more than our friend Kieri has. You've got everything else I need. I'm not going to lose a son, Cal, because you lost a few lumps of flesh—even those lumps."

"I—I thought you would mind—"

"Mind! Of course I mind; I'll serve you that bastard's balls on toast, if you don't get 'em first. But you're a Halveric. My son. My commander and heir. You still have everything else, and it's enough."

"Yes, sir." Cal felt better. A little better. "He—he said, sir, that he had agents north of the mountains. He said five sons might not be enough."

Aliam Halveric snorted. "You must have been dazed, Cal, to worry about that. Didn't you think I'd take precautions? And better, told your mother about it." He chuckled, and Cal relaxed enough to smile. "I'd like to see anyone sneak past your mother—your wife, now, she's a handful too, but Estil—" Cal thought of his tall mother, still hunting at her age with a bow many men could not bend. "Now. Did the surgeons say how long you'd be down?"

"No—not yet."

"Hmmph. I need you up, and you need to be up. Did they try a potion?"

"No—I don't think so. But—"

"Then I'll ask. Cal, think of his face when he hears you're back in command again. He'll get no joy of his doings then! I'll be back." He rose.

"Sir?"

"What?"

"How did you—who told you?" His father grimaced.

"Oh, that. Well, that scum sent them. With the badge off your cloak, incidentally. Good gold, that. It's as well he did, Cal: he has nothing to do magicks with, except some blood, and you've spilled blood all over the south. Now rest, and I'll see what the surgeons say." His father left; Cal found himself smiling.

From the front room came a murmur of voices. The surgeons would have no chance, Cal realized. Soon enough they came trooping back in, along with his father, a Captain of Falk, and the Duke's mage.

"I don't care," his father was saying, "which of you does what, or in what order—but I want him up this day."

"But, my lord—"

"Impossible. If he—"

"I can't be expected to—"

"Silence!" That roar was the Duke, just inside the chamber. "Aliam, my surgeons are at your command. My mage has some constraints I don't understand—but, Master Vetrifuge, I expect you'll do what you can. I do suggest, Aliam, that as he got no sleep last night, you might let him rest today."

"Kieri, he'll sleep better when he's healed—"

"Very well, then. As you will." The Duke withdrew. The surgeons looked at each other and at the mage and cleric. The mage stared at the floor, and the cleric looked at his father.

"Get on with it," snapped Aliam Halveric.

He woke, hungry and rested, in the long spring evening. His father sat beside him, and the Duke was sprawled in a seat at the end of the bed. They were talking strategy, low-voiced, until the Duke noticed his open eyes, and nodded to Aliam. Cal gave them a smile.

"I'm hungry."

"Good. They said you would be." The Duke sent his servant for food.

"I've got your clothes," said his father. He gestured

to them, hanging over a rack. "I brought mail, too—
your old set. Come out when you're dressed."

"You ought to tell him," said the Duke, "that while
he slept the day away, we moved camp." He grinned at
Cal. "We loaded you in one of Vladi's wagons, and you
didn't even murmur. The teamster said you didn't rouse
all day. We'd begun to wonder just how much numbwine
you'd had." He turned and went through the curtain
into the front room.

"Come on," said his father. "Don't take forever."
And he, too, left Cal to stand and dress alone.

Chapter Twenty-nine

Paks snatched a few hours of sleep before they set off again, upstream along the river. She was still tired and sleepy, and concentrated on putting one foot in front of the other. No one asked her any questions. They came to a shallow stony ford just as the Clart scouts discovered an enemy party guarding it, but the skirmish ended quickly.

"Well," said Piter generally, "now we know we're going the right way—"

"If those lights we saw last night were Siniava's fires, we'll have to turn back east," said Vik.

"I'd like to find the Vonja militia," said Devlin. "At least to know which side they're on." But they found nothing that day.

The next morning they found traces of a large camp. While looking for a clue to which army had used it, they found a refuse pit half-full of bodies. Here were the missing men: young Juris, and Sim, of Dorrin's cohort, and old Harek. Harek was still alive, missing both hands, now, and with a festering wound in his

457

belly. The other bodies bore evidence of the same bitter torment. Paks helped dig the graves; as they buried Sim and Juris, she glanced over at the Pliunis, massed across the clearing. They had said no more about deserters. Nothing could be done for Harek, but numbwine to ease his pain and a friend's hand for comfort. When he died, they laid him in the grave they'd dug. Paks heard from Piter about his family.

"It was his last year," he said. "He got his little bit of land two years ago, and he was going to retire last year, only this came up. It's a shame—" Piter spat. "His oldest boy is old enough to farm that land, but he's always been wild to join the Company. Effa, that's his wife, is a hard-working woman. Those scum—one more year, and he'd have been home, working his own bit of land."

Paks felt a pang of guilt—they had come so close, to help Cal Halveric, and had done nothing for their own companions. The rest of that day she marched with deepening anger, anger reflected in the eyes around her.

The next day they found the Vonja and Foss Council militia at last, drawn up facing Siniava's lines. In the hours of daylight that remained, Paks looked over their allies. Units from all three Foss Council cities were there, distinguished by the color of their trousers and the trim on their gray tunics: red for Foss, green for Ifoss, and yellow for Fossnir. Like the Vonjans, they wore trousers tucked into soft-topped boots in the field, though at home they went bare-legged. Vonjan militia wore russet-orange tunics over black trousers. Those from Cortes Vonja had orange helmet-plumes as well, and a leaping cat in black on their tunics. In comparison, those who had come with the Duke looked shabby and travel-worn—but, Paks noted, equally ready to fight.

Across a shallow valley, Siniava's camp was set on rising ground. In the late slanting sunlight, Paks could see troops in the familiar black and yellow, and other colors: light green, blue, and many in rough brown leather. She wondered if they would attack that afternoon; her heart leaped to think how soon Siniava might be dead, and the war over.

But overnight Siniava slipped away eastward, eluding the militia scouts who should have alerted them. The Duke came back from the council of commanders in tight-lipped fury; the militia commanders were arguing about the order of march. It was some hours before the army moved at all. They finally caught up with Siniava again at nightfall. His position was even stronger than before: rising ground sheltered from flank assaults by hummocks of broken rock.

"He'll have bowmen in there, I don't doubt," said Stammel, frowning. "We can't see 'em, and they'll have a lovely field of fire. Sun behind 'em, too. Blast those militia! Why wouldn't they *move*?"

"For that matter, why didn't they notice when he moved in the night? They said they had their scouts out and didn't need ours." Kefer glared across the space as if his gaze could strike a blow.

"Militia—" began Paks and stopped short. What she knew of some Vonja militia was not to be talked about.

"Well—" Stammel stretched and sighed. "The Duke won't let 'em slip away again. We'll have a day's work tomorrow. Paks, make sure everyone in your file has rechecked their weapons. Vik, the same for you. And tell the other file leaders. We don't want any more surprises than *he* gives us."

By first light they were arrayed in battle formation, watching the sky lighten behind the slope Siniava held. Paks flexed her hand on the shield grip, tested one more time the balance of her sword. She glanced down the line. At the far end, barely visible in the dimness, were the Pliunis and two cohorts of Vladi's spears. Next was a solid block of Foss Council militia—a thousand pikemen—then the Vonja militia, half pikes and half swords. The right flank was Arcolin's and Dorrin's cohorts, and beyond them two cohorts of Halverics. Vonja archers stood behind the left flank, and Cracolnya's

cohort and Halveric archers behind the right. Clart
Cavalry, the rest of Vladi's spears, and some five hundred mixed militia were held in reserve.

When their advance began, Paks wanted to run,
wanted to charge into the enemy lines like an arrow in
flight.

"Steady now!" bellowed Stammel. "Keep the lines,
Tir blast you! You'll need that strength later." Paks
forced herself to slow, shortening stride slightly and
keeping the drum cadence. She willed the strength she
saved to flow into her sword arm. She could feel
Canna's medallion and Saben's stone horse on her chest.
Soon, she told them. Soon. They were halfway to the
enemy lines where lowered pikes awaited them. She
heard the whirr of a crossbow bolt. Someone yelped,
behind her. Directly ahead, the enemy wore dark blue
tunics bordered in scarlet. Paks wondered where they
were from. Then she heard screams from the rocks to
her right, and a roar of sound as Siniava sent his army
forward. The men in blue charged, keeping no formation; the lines crashed together into chaos. Paks thrust
her sword into the first blue-clad body, blocked another's slash with her shield, and drove forward.

The rest of that day was a mixture of confusion and
exhaustion: the armies struggled on, hour after hour,
unable to win or withdraw. The lines swayed back and
forth, dissolved, reformed squad by squad. Dust choked
the fighters and hid the action from their commanders—
and the noise drowned out their commands. At times
allies who could hardly see each other for the dust
fought desperately for some minutes before the error
was known. Paks fought pikemen in blue, pikemen in
black and yellow, swordsmen in brown—and nearly
found herself battling a squad of green-clad swordsmen
until they cried "Halverics!" She fought until she could
hardly lift her sword, and still fought on, with the
memory of Harek and Canna and Saben filling her
mind.

At last both armies faltered. Fighters stepped back

when they could, and quit driving forward. A gap opened between them; the dust settled slowly. When Paks looked up, she saw it was long past noon. She was thirsty and hungry and ached in every bone. She tried to gather her wits and help reform the cohort, but she could not see them at first. She heard the Duke's horn call and looked around—there. Still alert and wary, she picked her way across the battlefield, littered as it was with dead and wounded fighters, to join them. Stammel was checking over her cohort as she came up. Their faces were gray with dust, sweat-streaked, with eyes like dark pits of exhaustion.

"There you are," said Stammel, as she found her place. "Seli's with the surgeons; he'll be out some time. Take over for him, junior to Devlin."

"Yes, sir." Paks was too tired to feel any elation at the promotion.

"Take whoever you need—we'll need water up here, and bandages—food if you can find it."

"Yes, sir." In the next hour, she had supplied the cohort with water and food. Other companies began to regroup; the Halverics looked almost ready to fight again. But the militia seemed to be wandering around in confusion. She could not see the Pliunis at all, and wondered if they'd deserted. Across the field, the enemy army slowly condensed into formation. Paks's bones ached as she thought about another battle. But it was late afternoon before the field was cleared, and neither army moved from its position. As the sun slipped westward, Paks began to feel chilled in her sweat-damp tunic. Her nose itched; she rubbed it on the rim of her shield. She saw Arcolin ride to meet and speak with a messenger in Foss Council gray, then he rode back. The trees behind them threw long shadows that crept across the field; their own shadows loomed tall as giants. Still nothing happened, and it was dusk.

That night Paks wondered if corporals and sergeants ever got to sleep; she was busy until her turn on guard with things she had never noticed corporals doing. An endless list of chores awaited her. That night, too, assassins slipped through the lines, trying to kill both the Duke and the Halveric. They succeeded with the captain-general of the Foss Council militia. Paks and Jenits captured an enemy trying to sneak through the lines in the confusion of the assassins' attack.

Morning dawned cloudy and damp. A thin rain began just as the army formed. Battle that day was even more confused and exhausting than the day before, as the hazards of mud were added to the battle itself. When heavier rain fell in curtains after some hours of fighting, Siniava's troops gave back slowly. The Phelani and Halverics pushed forward, but the militia in the center could not advance. Paks slogged on through the slippery mud, with rain beating in her face, but she could not keep up with the retreating army, which had melted into the woods. At last the Duke halted them. As far as Paks could tell, Siniava's army was in full retreat.

Back in camp, rumors flew that Siniava was on the run and his army dissolving. Paks had her doubts. Siniava had regrouped before. She splashed through the rain, checking on the wounded, bringing food to those who could eat, and making sure that no one was missing. When she went back to the cooks' tent at last for her own meal, Stammel, Kefer, and Haben of Dorrin's cohort were inside talking.

"You can't blame the Clarts," Kefer was saying. "They've taken losses all along, and this heavy rain is hard on 'em."

"Aye—but those Blue Riders needn't have been larking about with Sorellin's militia. Not that they could have done it alone—Vonja and Foss Council just wouldn't move." Stammel turned to Paks and grinned. "Got 'em taken care of? Good. Eat hearty; we'll be marching early."

"And late," added Haben. He was Dorrin's senior sergeant. "By Zudthyi's Spear, I hope they don't slip us and get away somewhere to regroup."

"What I heard is the Blue Riders are keeping contact."

"But can we keep contact with the Blue Riders?" Haben took his bowl back for another helping. "And even if we can, would you wager those militia could?" He gulped down several mouthfuls. "I tell you, Stammel, if they set foot out of camp by noon tomorrow, I'll buy you a jug of the White Dragon's best ale."

"No bet," said Stammel gloomily. "They won't. I've heard that a good third of the Vonjans are actually Siniava's anyway."

"After today?" asked Kefer, grinning.

"Maybe not, after today. Tir's bones, I'm tired. Paks, you're watch-second to Kefer tonight. If you need me before the change, Kef, I'll be asleep near the middle post." Stammel yawned, waved, and went out. Paks finished her meal while Kefer waited. When they left the tent, Haben turned toward Dorrin's area, and Paks and Kefer walked the perimeter posts together. This was her first experience as watch second; she was very aware of her responsibility as she went from post to post during the watch.

Morning looked no better; rain had continued all night. The mercenary companies were soon ready to march, but as Haben had predicted the militia were only then struggling out of their tents to look around. When the march finally began, about noon, the mercenaries went alone, though the militia were pulling down their tents slowly.

The Clarts had found a village, mostly burned but with several large barns intact, along the line Siniava had taken. They reached this village by nightfall; all the wounded, and most of the others, slept in shelter. Paks tried to ignore the stains where the villagers' bodies had been dragged away for burial by the Clarts. Rain continued all that night, slow and steady. In the morning light, the wreck of the village was even uglier. Paks found a body the Clarts had missed: a young girl or woman who had been trapped in a burning sheepfold. She stared at it for a time before she called someone to help carry it away for burial.

For three wet days they marched on in the mud, along crooked lanes that led from village to village. Paks heard from Stammel that the militia was finally on the move behind them. But they could not match Siniava's army, and one day the Blue Riders reported that it had split. They were not sure which part of it Siniava was in. Finally the Duke turned them south, toward Cortes Cilwan.

"He thinks Siniava might have kept troops in reserve there," said Kefer. "The Blue Riders are still trying to find out which remnant he's with, but if the Duke is right, we could cut him off."

Several days later they came in sight of the high walls of Cortes Cilwan, the inner keep standing far above the main city. They marched closer, in battle order. Paks could see sentries on the walls, and hear horns cry the alarm.

"Hmmph. I don't see his standard," said Arcolin. "I wonder if they've changed sides already."

The Duke had ridden to the front of the column with Vladi and Aliam Halveric. "They'll wish they had, if they haven't," he said. "But I expect they're waiting to see who we are before they decide who they're for. Let 'em see our colors, Arcolin, and we'll find out." Arcolin signalled the standard bearers, who unfurled the Duke's banner to the light breeze.

"Nothing yet," said the Halveric. "Coy, aren't they?"

"Merchanters," growled Vladi. "No courage, no honor—bah! Tir take all such to the black realms!" Paks glanced cautiously at him; she'd never been so close to him before. He looked like someone who would be called the Cold Count: a pale narrow face with cold blue eyes and a pointed gray beard.

The Duke lifted his reins and rode a little forward; the others went with him. A bellow came from the walls. Paks could not understand the words, and the Duke made no reply, advancing farther. He was close under the walls when he stopped. After a few minutes, someone came from a postern gate to speak with him.

The discussion went on some time. Paks counted the sentries on the wall, and tried to see if there were archers up there too. It was hotter; standing in the sun she felt sweat trickling through her hair under the helmet. It itched. She resisted the urge to scratch her nose. Sun glared on the city walls. She looked past the city to the river. A bath in the river—Stammel cleared his throat and she jerked her attention back to the Duke. He and the others were riding back.

"Siniava isn't here," he told them. "They're having riots inside, it sounds like, but they all swear Siniava isn't here, and hasn't been since he marched for Koury and Ambella. They won't open the gates to us, and I won't waste time taking the city when Siniava isn't there. We'll stay here until our scouts can tell us where he is."

Paks had her bath in the river, as refreshing as she'd hoped; the camp was festooned with drying socks and tunics. By the time the couriers came in, rest, hot food, and baths had revived enthusiasm for the chase—among the mercenaries. They heard without surprise that the Vonja and Foss Council militia would not go farther east.

"I suppose we can't complain," said Devlin. "With all these bandits running loose in the confusion, and their own cities and lands at risk, I can see they'd want to stay closer to home."

"I heard the trouble with Foss Council is that they're still arguing about who's in command since their captain-general was killed," said Paks.

"Probably. Their chain of command, with units from different cities, is tangled as briars. I wish the Sorellin militia would show up. Just because they were beaten once is no reason to hang back now. Siniava's lost a lot, and not just on the battlefield."

Seli limped heavily to their fire and eased himself down.

"Are you supposed to be here?" asked Devlin.

Seli grinned. "The surgeon said to try walking a few

steps." Devlin looked at the distance from the surgeons' tents and shook his head. Seli ignored him. "Well, Paks," he said. "How do you like being corporal?"

Paks blushed. "I'm not, really. Just until you're well."

"You're doing the work. You're as much of one as I am. If you weren't doing it right, Kef and Stammel would have replaced you by now. Or so they told me, when I was worrying about it a few weeks after my promotion. I remember I was scared stiff. Did you feel like that, Devlin? I thought my friends would think I'd gotten conceited, and wondered if anyone would obey my orders."

Devlin nodded. "Yes—I think everyone feels like that at first. I'd been bedding a woman in Cracolnya's cohort, and she kept teasing me about it. So I quit, and she said my new rank had made me proud. And we had a big old fellow in this cohort then—as tall as you, Paks, and immensely strong. He wasn't too bright, but he had years on me. He'd grumbled before when someone a year junior to him made corporal, and I was sure he'd cause me trouble." Devlin paused to drink.

"Well? Did he?"

"He started to. He talked—claimed I'd done gods know what all for my promotion—things like that. I was young and brash in those days—" Seli laughed, and Devlin grinned. "Brasher, then. And a quick tongue, that I've always had. So I went to him, and we had a little talk—I asked him how he thought a little runt as ugly as I was—for that's what he'd called me—could sell his favors to anyone. And then I suggested that since he was bigger, stronger and smarter—which he claimed to be—that if I'd been chosen, it must have been with divine guidance. That was in the days when no one in this company would have considered evil influence. He hadn't thought of that, he said, and had I any proof. The proof, I said, was in the promotion— surely he knew the captains and the Duke could recognize the gods' will—but if he wanted proof, to wait until nightfall."

"What did you do," asked Seli, "coat yourself with one of those glowing mushrooms?"

"No. Better than that, I thought. We'd had a rich haul of treasure from the last campaign, and I'd noticed something—or thought I had. The quartermaster then was a friend of mine, and as corporal I could go through the stuff. I told him what I wanted, and he laughed and agreed, as long as I brought it back by morning. I'd told my troublemaker to meet me at midwatch of the second. This was late summer, and what would be rising?"

"Torre's Necklace—by all the gods, Dev, what did you do?"

"Don't be hasty, Seli; it's not good for your wound. Well, he was there, and I was, and I'd told the watch to leave us be. I think they thought that if we wanted to fight on the walls they'd rather not know. I told the old boy that my proof was this: as I saluted the Necklace of Torre, her grace would give light to my blade—only briefly, of course, unless he was one of the evil ones."

"It's a wonder you weren't blasted out of the sky."

"The gods love the brave." Devlin stretched and went on. "When the whole Necklace was above the hills and clear to see, I drew the blade I'd borrowed, and made some kind of invocation. Sure enough, it flared as blue as could be, and my—friend—nearly fell onto his knees. I sheathed it quickly, before the glow died, and had a time keeping still. The thing stung my hand when it lit up, and left blisters that lasted two weeks."

"I thought something would happen," said Seli. "The gods may love the brave, but some of them wouldn't like your jest. I assume the man gave you no more trouble?"

"Right, he didn't. But there was trouble nonetheless— one of the captains was up for some reason, and saw the flash. Next thing I knew I was explaining it to her—"

"Dorrin's sword!" exclaimed Paks.

"Yes. It wasn't hers at the time; she took it in the captain's draw a few days later. She did about chew my hide off for mocking the gods. When I showed her my hand, though, she said they'd taken their revenge, and all she wanted was the sword."

"It is a magic sword, then?" asked Paks. "I thought I saw it glowing last year in Rotengre, when we'd killed the webspinner's cleric."

"Yes, it's magic. Good magic, too. She doesn't show it off—swords like that attract thieves like honey brings bees."

"Why doesn't it glow all the time?"

Devlin shrugged. "I don't know—I suppose it was made that way."

Chapter Thirty

Early the next morning they were marching again. All around the rich farmland showed scars of war: fields unsown, orchards hacked and burned, bloated corpses of cattle and sheep. Now and again they saw little bands of ragged peasants who fled into the woods and hedges at their approach. On the third day of the march, the Duke turned sharp south, and told them why.

"Our scouts report that Siniava's holed up in a ruined city between Koury and Immervale on the river. They've seen his personal banner and troops in his colors. The Sorellin militia should be coming south to meet us. I'm telling them to come ahead. We'll assault if we can, or siege until they arrive—but I don't want to let him get loose again."

By afternoon of the next day, they were in sight of the old city. From a distance it looked more like a low hill of broken stone than a fortification, but as they drew closer, they saw that the city wall still held its shape around most of the mound. Where it had been breached, fresh piles of earth and brush blocked entry. Above the highest half-crumbled tower Siniava's banner waved in the afternoon sun. Paks could not see any sentries; she had an uneasy feeling about the whole thing.

While the commanders positioned their companies on the north and west of the ruins, archers tried to ignite the brush with fire arrows, but it was still too green. No arrows returned, and nothing showed on the walls.

"They want us to charge up there carelessly," said Vik. Paks paused beside him for a moment.

"Yes—I think so too. The Duke's smarter than that."

"I hope Siniava doesn't have something like that priest at Sibili. Or a wizard."

"If he had something that powerful, surely he'd have used it before now."

"Yes—unless it was here. Something lurking in the ruins that he knew about."

Paks shivered. "Don't say that, Vik. It's enough to spook anyone."

"Surely not you?"

"Huh. I don't think I'll answer that." Paks waved and went on. Nothing happened that night, and in the morning they prepared to assault the walls. Halveric Company would try the southern wall; Vladi's spears, the west; and the Duke's Company, a breach in the northwest angle of the wall. East of Phelan's forces, the old ruins ran apparently unbroken to the river, some distance away.

After several attempts at climbing the earthworks filling the broken wall, they were still unsuccessful; the outer face was slippery and sticky. An assault force could not climb that unstable slope while being pelted with stones and harried with arrows. While the main attack group stayed visible at the foot of the slope, Paks and Dorrin's junior corporal, Malek, each took a squad and found a climbable place on the walls out of sight, around a square jutting corner.

This was easier than it might have been. Over the years stones had shifted, giving hand and foot holds;

bushes had grown in the gaps. At the top of the wall, Paks peeked over cautiously. She saw the backs of a small group at the edge of the earthworks, some yards to her left, and nothing else. She passed a hand signal to those following, and eased up onto the wall. She heard the rasp and scrape of others coming over the rim as she drew her sword. Another quick glance showed few enemy soldiers anywhere: some on the far side of the earthworks, but equally intent on the action below. As soon as her squad was on the wall, Paks gave a last look to Bossik, below with reserves, and waved. He returned the gesture. She headed toward the enemy, counting on surprise to make up for numbers.

One of the soldiers across the earthwork gap saw them just before she reached the rear of those on her side and yelled a warning. As the first soldiers turned, Paks drove her sword into the back of the rearmost. They had not had their swords out; she killed another before facing a useful weapon. Across the gap an archer let fly. Paks heard a yelp and a curse behind her. She drove on; in minutes they had killed those on their side of the gap. Paks looked down and across. Crude steps had been cut into the fill, leading to a walkway a few feet below the rim; similar steps led up to the wall on the far side.

"Let's get across that," she said to Malek. He glanced back; Vossik was on the wall with their reserves.

"Good idea."

Paks waved to her squad and started down the steps as fast as she could. She heard bowstrings twang both before and behind as Vossik's archers tried to drive the enemy away, and the enemy tried to shoot her. An arrow sank into wet clay near her foot. Another. She held her shield before her face as she ran across the walkway. She could hear her squad coming close behind. At the foot of the steps, she took a deep breath and surged upward, yelling encouragement to those following.

When she topped the steps, no one was there. Four

crumpled bodies sprawled on the wall; the rest of the enemy were many strides away, running as fast as they could. She started to pursue, then looked back at Vossik. His hand signal was emphatic: wait. She looked back at her squad. Only Arñe was missing; she had taken an arrow in her arm, and Vossik had held her back. Paks looked down at the outer face of the wall. Some were already climbing the wall, and others followed Volya, who was cutting steps in the clay earthwork.

No enemy soldiers showed on the wall, now. Paks explored eastward, finding a narrow break with a worn footpath climbing tumbled stones from inside the wall, then winding down the slope of broken rock below the gap on the outside. Stammel posted a guard there, and another at the river end of the wall. Then they moved into the ruins themselves.

It was hard to tell what the ruins had been. Both walls and buildings had crumbled into mounds of stone that angled into other mounds. Grass, bushes, and even twisted trees grew over all. Old streets were now ravines, partly blocked by fallen stone and tangles of vines and brambles; it was impossible to see more than a few yards. They found no direct route to the tower where Siniava's banner still flew. As the afternoon drew on towards evening, the intricate maze was even more confusing. Paks hated the thought of prowling there in the dark. Despite herself, she could not forget Vik's remarks about demons or wizards.

Before dark, the mercenaries linked into a protected perimeter. Although the guard posts were closely set, the brooding ruins and Siniava's presence nearby made everyone edgy. And the night had its troubles: poisoned arrows killed two in Vladi's Company, rocks heaved out of darkness bruised several sentries.

As dawnlight spread through the ruins, the companies began to move, drawing their ring tighter about the central tower. Paks looked for Siniava's banner. She could not see it. Almost at once others noticed that it was gone, and a shout rose. Then they heard the staccato alarm call from the northern wall.

As quickly as they could, they made for the north wall, boots clattering through the twisting, cluttered streets. Paks could hear the noise of other companies behind them. More horn signals ahead. She dodged blocks of stone, and crashed through bushes, went over a place she remembered as a direct line to another street. The wall should be close. She caught a glimpse of black and yellow darting through a gap ahead of her, and yelled. Something hit her helmet hard, and she staggered. Vik grabbed her arm and steadied her. She shook her head to clear it. A shower of rocks came from the gap. Paks looked back and saw a squad of Cracolnya's archers moving into position behind her. They poured arrows into the gap; all heard the sharp cry from within. Paks jogged forward and stuck her head cautiously around the corner. Then she led her squad past a body bristling with arrows.

Now only an open space lay between them and the outer wall. A little to one side was the narrow breach where Stammel had posted a guard. The guards were gone. Clearly some force had come this way and overwhelmed them. Paks could not understand how they'd gotten through the closely guarded perimeter. She clambered up the steep path over the broken stone until she could see out. There they were—marching rapidly away along the river toward the forest that lay a few miles upstream. She turned to call Stammel or Kefer, and saw the Duke himself climbing the path, his squires behind him.

"Do you see them?" he called.

"Yes, my lord. They're retreating to the forest."

"I wish I knew how in blazes they got through our lines," he said. "Not that it'll help them. We'll harry them now—they don't have a chance." He squinted at the retreating force. "Hmm. Looks like no more than five hundred or so. What do you think, Selfer?"

"The same, my lord. Do you think the rest of his army has just fallen apart?"

The Duke grunted. "I don't know. I wish I did. But we'll be after them, Kessim!"

"Yes, my lord." The Duke's junior squire, lean and dark, seemed afire with eagerness.

"Get back to the outer camp. Make sure the quartermaster gets everyone moving in a hurry, and knows where to go. He's to stay far enough back that the wounded are safe, but not out of touch. And Jori—"

"Yes, my lord."

"Bring all the horses we'll need—Kessim can help—for the captains, too."

Kessim and Jori scrambled down the outer face of the breach and jogged toward the camp. Paks could see mounted men approaching; the Duke smiled.

"That's a smart man," he commented. "He saw something going on, and knew I'd need mounts. Paks, tell the captains I want them to form the cohorts below the wall, and wait for me."

"Yes, my lord." The Duke turned and started down the path, followed by Selfer. Paks watched them go. Then she saw a flicker of movement, of yellow, among the tumbled rocks to one side of the path. She yelled just as a man rose from the rocks and leaped toward the Duke. Selfer dove between them, clawing at his sword. Paks charged recklessly down the path. Another enemy, this one in black, leaped from cover on the opposite side of the path to strike at the Duke, who had his sword out by this time, and was fencing with the first attacker. Selfer was down, but struggling to rise.

The Duke parried the strokes of both attackers for a moment. Then Paks was beside him, thrusting at the man in black. When he turned to meet her attack, she saw a face dark with tattoos. He had a long, narrow sword and a long dagger; the tips of both were stained brown. Paks took a slash of the dagger on her shield. She could not reach him with her short blade, but she could make sure he didn't touch the Duke. She heard yells from above, and the clatter of many boots on stone. Beside her was the almost musical jingling of the Duke's mail, and the clang of blades. Her own opponent kept trying to force her to one side, exposing the Duke, but she kept her place despite the attack of both blades. She heard a yelp from the Duke's opponent, then a grunt as the Duke lunged.

Suddenly the man in black dropped his dagger, leaped forward, and grabbed her shield with one hand, fending off her thrust with his other blade. As his weight jerked forward on the shield, Paks staggered and fell. She saw his sword dart past her, and tried desperately to deflect it with her own. The blades scraped together. She heard him gasp, then he rolled onto her, and she felt hard hands gripping her throat. She couldn't free her shield arm.

"You—you northern bitch—" he growled, then his hands went slack, and many arms pulled his heavy body off her. Stammel, grim-faced, offered a hand, and Paks pulled herself up. Volya helped her reset her shield. The Duke stood cleaning his sword. Selfer lay propped against Arcolin, his shoulder soaked in blood. Both attackers were dead.

"My lord—" Stammel held out the blades Paks had faced.

"Yes?" The Duke glanced at the weapons; his face froze. "Poison!"

"I thought so, my lord. Did these touch you, my lord, or your squire?"

"No. That one—" The Duke pointed to the sword dropped by the first attacker, and Arcolin reached out to examine it. "But Paks—is she—"

"I'm not hurt, my lord," she said quickly.

Stammel looked closely at her. "Are you sure? The least scratch—"

Paks shook her head. "No, sir. He came close, but he didn't touch. I couldn't disarm him—"

The Duke snorted. "You did well enough to hold him

off with that short sword. Arcolin, what about that one?"

"I don't think so, my lord. Selfer, how is it?"

"It—hurts." Selfer was breathing in short gasps. "But—it feels—much like any wound."

The Duke knelt beside him. "Selfer, that was well done; without you, I'd have had no chance. Let's see now—" He drew his dagger and widened the slit in Selfer's tunic. "Ahhh—you'll need stitching, and some quiet days with the surgeons, but it's not as bad as I'd feared. Any other injury?"

"I think not, my lord."

"Good. The surgeons are coming." The Duke opened a pouch at his belt and wadded up the length of cloth in it to press against the wound. "Arcolin, stay with him until he's settled. I must speak to the Count and Aliam."

"Yes, my lord."

"Dorrin, get everyone in marching order below the wall."

"Yes, my lord."

"Paksenarrion." He turned to look at her.

"My lord?"

"My thanks for your warning and assistance. You have a quick eye; I hope it will be as quick to find Siniava." He grinned at her, suddenly relaxing. "You're better than a shield; I wasn't even worried."

Paks felt herself blushing. "Thank you, my lord." As the Duke turned away, Paks looked to the north. The fight seemed to have taken a long time, but she could still see the dust of the retreating force.

All that day they trailed Siniava's army, first along across the plain and then in thick forest. This close to the great river, it was damp as well as hot. Little air moved under the trees. Their scouts reported that they were gaining, but they had not closed the gap by night. Very early the next day they went on again. It was even hotter, a heavy breathless heat, but Paks had no desire to slow down. The scouts had reported the enemy to be close ahead, and moving slowly.

After a brief stop for food, they moved on, swords drawn. A scout rode to meet them. "They're set up across the road, around the next turn and on a little rise." The Duke, riding just in front of Paks, nodded and turned to the Company. Every eye was on him. Paks noticed that the air had become very still; it seemed darker. Almost as she thought, a mutter of thunder troubled the air. She felt the hairs rise on her skin. Canna's medallion hung heavy as stone around her neck. They marched faster; she heard the horses' hooves crashing in the leaves on either side of the track. She glanced sideways to see them, then beyond.

The gleam of weapons in the underbrush beyond the Clart riders shocked her so she nearly stumbled. She could not say anything, for a horrified instant, then blurted "Trap! Left flank!"

"What!" Stammel swung left and peered past the riders. "Halt!" he bellowed. From the corner of her eye, Paks saw the Duke jerk his horse to a halt and turn. "Company square!" Arcolin was yelling. The Clarts slowed, looking first at the column and then at their own flanks. The Duke spun his horse on its hocks. "Both sides!" he called. "Dorrin! Square 'em!" Now the Clarts had found the enemy, and spun to face them, lances lowered. The enemy charged, roaring.

"Get in the square!" Stammel yelled at Paks. She realized she'd been standing frozen. She'd never been in square as a corporal. She backed into the lines. "On the corner," said Stammel. "Right—there, yes. Tighten it up!" he yelled to the cohort as a whole. "Link with Dorrin's and tighten it."

As the enemy charged, the Clarts spurred toward them. They slowed but could not stop, the onslaught. Horses and men went down, screaming. The enemy pikemen slammed into the square, hacking over the first rank and the second, while their second rank jabbed at the first. Paks, on the corner, could have used four arms. She could barely fend off the enemy pikes; she had no chance to dart under the shafts. Surrounded as they were, their only chance was the tight formation. She had no time even to wonder where the Duke was, or whether the other companies had been trapped as well.

A flash of nearby lightning lit the scene with a blue glare as the storm broke over their heads. Rain blasted down on them; wind lashed the trees overhead. Paks squinted, blinking rain out of her eyes. The enemy pikemen were not withdrawing, but they pressed a little less. Between reverberations of thunder that trembled in the ground, Paks heard the Duke shouting, then Arcolin. She could not distinguish the words. Then Stammel, close behind her.

"Left flank—right by half—slow—march." With the others Paks shifted a pace forward and right, as the second rank came up into the gaps, lengthening their line. The pike in front of her wavered; she took a chance, ducking under it for one quick thrust at the pikeman. He fell, clutching his belly. "Don't charge yet," admonished Stammel. "Steady." Another long roll of thunder and gust of rain. Paks could hardly see the soldiers a pike-length away. A ripping sound, like cloth tearing overhead, and a blinding blue-white flash, followed by thunder that jarred the teeth in her head—she fought the desire to flatten herself on the ground. When a gust of wind lifted the rain like a curtain, she saw the enemy: a dark wavering mass, just out of reach. The rain came back, blinding. The enemy force wasn't attacking, but it wasn't running, either.

So the situation stayed until dark and after. In the confusion of the storm, the mercenaries could do no better than hold their formation. The enemy, though clearly outnumbering them, was curiously unwilling to press the attack. Paks, like the others, was wet, chilled, and tired. It was going to be a long night. The only good news came after dark, when word was passed that the Halverics, escorting supplies and wounded, were outside the enemy ring and still intact.

Morning was bleak. It had rained—though less

heavily—all night. All were wet; even though the worst wounded had been covered with cloaks, in the protected center of the square, they were damp and miserable. The last of their rations had gone the previous day; they were all hungry. Paks, stamping her feet to warm up, glared through the last drizzle at the enemy lines. She could see they stretched all around the Company in the woods.

Despite this, morale was higher than Paks expected. She heard someone wonder whether they would move forward, toward Sorellin, or back, to link with the Halverics. No one answered. In the center of the square, the Duke conferred with his captains and Vladi. She turned to face the enemy. Those lines stirred, as men in mail, with long cloaks, went up and down. She heard a bowstring twang, and one of them staggered. Good. Cracolnya's archers had kept their strings dry. A ragged yell came from the enemy, and a section of their line moved forward.

"Steady," said Stammel. "Wait—" The enemy advance wavered to a halt. Paks opened her mouth to lead a derisive yell, and decided to save her breath. She'd have a chance later.

In a few moments, a ragged flight of crossbow bolts thudded into the soft ground between the lines. Paks heard Stammel laugh, behind her. "Rain's a lot harder on those than on longbows," he said. "They'll have to come closer to do damage, and I don't see any eagerness—"

"Good," said Arcolin. "It was a neat trap; I'm as glad they haven't the stomach to profit by it. In fact, I wouldn't mind if they decided to back out of here when we advance."

Stammel grunted. "I could stand to know where the Sorellin militia is."

"Keeping warm and dry somewhere," said Kefer. "Like all militia."

Arcolin laughed shortly. "Probably. Now: we're going to advance west, away from the river. We think that'll pull those on the river side after us, and then Vladi's spears will hit their flank. Vladi says they've weakened the ones between them and the river."

"What about our rear?"

"Dorrin and Cracolnya will shift when we do. We'll have to string it a bit more open while the shift is going on—listen for me."

"Yes, captain."

"Pont'll be directing the archers on this flank. If I fall, Stammel, take over until Dorrin can."

"Yes, sir."

As they moved, Paks was glad to be on the forward side of the square. Stammel moved them slowly, so the right flank could stay together. Paks saw the pikes lower ahead of her. The enemy started yelling, a raucous blast of noise. Horns blared behind their lines. The enemy lines moved as slowly as their own. Mist lay along the ground; they all seemed to be wading. Paks stumbled over something she could not see, and cursed as she caught her balance. Foot by slow foot they went on. Part of the enemy lines to her left broke toward them; Paks heard the crash of weapons. Directly in front of her, the foremost rank of pikemen suddenly lifted their pikes and heaved them like lances. Paks yelled and threw up her shield. The pikes were ill-balanced for throwing; most fell short. Those soldiers drew curved blades and ran forward.

Shieldless, the enemy swordsmen could not stand against the Duke's men, who cut their way forward. Paks heard shouts and cries from behind but spared no glance for that. The troops in front gave back slowly. The third rank still had their pikes, and showed no inclination to throw these effective weapons away. A deeper roar from the rear: the cry of Vladi's spearmen charging the enemy flank. Paks found herself grinning. Despite the numbers facing her, she began to think they'd get out of this mess alive.

Suddenly the ground trembled. Another storm? Paks spared an instant's look at the sky, but saw nothing.

The noise grew, was joined by high-pitched trumpet calls. Now she could hear the rolling rhythm of hoof-beats. If Siniava had cavalry—she set her jaw and lunged at the man before her, catching him in the throat.

Horsemen erupted into sight on the right: in blue, in red and black—the Blue Riders and Sobanai Company. They were in the enemy rear, busy with lance and sword, before the enemy realized who and what they were. The lines wavered.

"Now!" yelled Arcolin. "Forward on the left!"

"Go on!" bellowed Stammel and Kefer almost together. Paks was already yelling joyously, leaping at the enemy lines. She could feel the others with her. The enemy stiffened a moment, as the first impetus of the cavalry charge dissipated, but fell back before the Phelani charge. Then Paks heard, on the right, the battle cry of the Sorellin militia, as they came around the bend and ran forward. The enemy lines disintegrated, turning almost in an instant into clumps and individuals in headlong flight. She could see horses and riders twisting among the trees, foot soldiers dodging, fallen men and horses on the ground. She pursued, fighting fiercely for a short time, until she and her friends found themselves grinning at each other over a pile of bodies.

But that was the end of fighting for them. Vik was pale and unsteady on his feet; he fainted as she watched. When Paks turned back to find help, she found it an effort to walk; her legs felt like they had an extra joint. Kefer was not as worried about poisoned blades as she had been.

"It's fighting without food," he said. "That and cold. They'll be all right." And some hours later, fed and rested, they were. Arñe was ready to return to the cohort, and Seli was already back.

"I'm not limping," he said. "And if I can fight beside the wagons—which I was—then I can fight here."

"What did the surgeons say?" asked Arcolin.

"Turned up their noses like they do. By Tir, captain, you can leave Paks as corporal, but I'm staying here."

But Paks was more than willing to return to her place as file leader. What she wanted more than anything else was sleep.

They heard from the Sorellin militia—disgustingly smug at having rescued mercenaries—that the remnants of Siniava's army had fled south, and were trying to cross the Immer at a ford. Fewer than a thousand were left to him.

"So they say," said Arñe sourly. "I thought he was supposed to be down to five hundred two days ago."

"True." Paks yawned. "How I could sleep! But they've scoured the woods, Arñe—no more of them there. And surely he'd have used all he had in that trap."

"I hope so. We were afraid you'd all be cut to pieces up here."

Paks yawned again. "We could have been. It was near enough."

That night the talk around the camp was how the Sobanai Company horse had linked with Sorellin's foot to reach them in time. A long lanky Sobanai hirstar was more than willing to explain.

"We'd been in the Eastmarches," he said. "Keeping an eye on the trouble in Semnath and Falsith—just in case you wondered why Siniava got no reinforcements from the east. Then Sorellin came to Sir Seti, and asked for cavalry aid: they were marching to meet you, and the Blue Riders were out of touch. Sir Seti spared a cohort to come, and when we met with Sorellin's troops, above Koury, we heard such that we thought haste wise. Only Sorellin was on foot and slow. We kept after them, and wouldn't let them stop to celebrate their restday, or whatever it was. Then we met the Blue Riders, but came on anyway. Yesterday, came a big storm after midday; they wanted to halt. So did we— the horses were jumpy. But after the worst had passed, we saw riders ahead—Clarts. So then we heard of the trap, and they led us here, a hard march. We stopped last night only when no one could see, and moved again at first light."

Paks realized she'd hardly seen a Clart rider all day. "How many of the Clarts got through?"

"I don't know myself. Not many, I think. They were hit hard, they said, and those who could stayed to harry the rear of Siniava's lines."

"What's going on in the east?" asked Stammel. "Does Siniava have guild support as in Cilwan?"

"Some. Cloth merchants, and such. He had strong factions in the east, even in Falsith. Probably a thousand to fifteen hundred left the Eastmarches to fight with him. There aren't that many left, of course." He grinned around the circle of listeners.

"And where's Sofi Gannarrion in all this?" asked Kefer. "I thought he was supposed to help."

The Sobanai rider laughed. "Surely you know——? No? He's in Fallo, with the Duke. The Duke of Fall's second son, Amade, is betrothed to Ganarrion's eldest daughter. He's not about to stir out of there and risk his bride-gift being damaged."

"Well, I'll be——"

"Besides, he wants the Duke's support when he makes his bid for the throne."

"Sofi? He's serious about that?"

"So I hear. You know he's always claimed to be a prince. Allied with the Duke of Fall, he's planning to take his throne back."

"Huh. I'd always thought it was just talk. He's no use to us then——"

"Unless Siniava tried to march in Fallo. I daresay old Sofi will come out of the keep then."

"I hope so. What's it like over there? And what about crossing the Immer?"

"Rich land, good open farmland. Hardly any forest: Siniava can't hide that way. Mud's your main concern. The roads are soup when it rains. As for crossing the Immer, the nearest bridge is Koury; otherwise, ford it."

Chapter Thirty-one

The next day they crossed the Immer at the same ford Siniava had used. The Duke's column spent two days crossing, but started the pursuit well-fed and rested. Siniava's trace was clear, bearing almost due east: discarded equipment and dying men littered the way. For three days they followed the trampled trail, but saw no enemy. The Sobanai riders returned to the northeast; the Clarts and a half-cohort of Blue Riders stayed with them.

On the fourth day, they sighted a large mass of troops moving slowly northeast, and followed them for several days until they found what they'd begun to suspect: these were the Falsith and Semnath reinforcements, already headed home. The Duke turned them south, toward Fallo. The next day they intercepted a courier; within an hour the news ran through the column. Fallo had closed its gates to the Honeycat, and Ganarrion was chasing him down the Imefal. He had fewer than seven hundred men left, and those were lean and travelworn.

"He'll cut through the forest," said Vik, "and head for the coast. What else can he do?"

"Try to get to the Immer and go downriver; that might work."

"Does he have any troops left at Immervale?" asked Paks.

"He won't have any troops anywhere after they hear about the last few weeks."

They were marching as they talked, angling south and west to block any move to Immervale.

"But what if he crosses the Imefal and gets into the forest?" Paks did not want to trail Siniava into another forest trap.

Arcolin, riding beside them, grinned down. "He won't."

"But—"

"You remember Alured?" said Arcolin. Heads nodded. "He's why Siniava can't cut through the forest. He'd need Alured's permission and guidance. And Alured—well, he's finding it profitable to oppose Siniava."

"But sir, he's a pirate," objected Rauf. "He could be playing both sides."

"He could. But he's smart. He can see that Siniava's beaten—he'll choose the winning side, I expect. Especially since our Duke offered something he wants."

"What's that, sir?"

Arcolin laughed. "I can't tell you that now. But it's what he left the sea for, and he thinks we have it to give. Perhaps we do."

Day after day they marched toward Immervale as their couriers kept contact with Ganarrion's horsemen. Two days running rain slowed them—the Sobanai hirstar had been right about the roads—and finally they gave up and traveled the fields and pastures. Paks felt she had a permanent crick in her neck from staring off to the south all the time.

Paks had lost track of the days they'd marched when they came over a rise to see a small, straggling body of troops off to their left. And ahead, on top of a low ridge in front of them, were the banners of Vonja and Foss Council. They were squarely between the enemy and

Immervale. The enemy army turned sharp south, and drew together.

"Now where's he going?" asked Paks.

"The river. There's nothing down there, but—" Stammel stopped and looked thoughtful.

"What?"

"I'll ask the captain—I thought I remembered something."

By nightfall it was obvious what Siniava had been making for: an old and partly ruined citadel reminiscent of Cortes Andres, built high on a rock bluff where the Imefal met the Immer. A great stone bridge spanned the Imefal below the citadel walls. Siniava had posted a rear guard here, but as the combined mercenary and militia forces came nearer, they withdrew before the archers were in range. Arcolin led his cohort across the bridge first, and swung right around the citadel, up a slope of broken rock to the forest that lay beyond its massive walls on the south side.

There they found their advance scouts talking to a company of archers in russet leather. Alured the Black, teeth flashing in his dark face as he grinned at Arcolin, waved the captain over.

"So—he's well in the trap, eh? Where's your Duke?"

"Coming," said Arcolin. "How has it gone here?"

"Easily. He wanted nothing but to put a wall between himself and trouble."

"You could not keep him out?"

"Out? But captain, your Duke wants him alive. I'd have had to kill him to hold him—if I could."

"I see." Arcolin looked up at the walls. "Well, he's caught now, and if we have a stiff fight to get in, still—"

"It is about that, captain, that I must speak to your Duke."

Paks heard no more before Stammel moved them farther around the citadel, to meet the troops coming the other way. Soon a solid line circled the walls, and camps were laid out at a little distance.

Paks was waiting in line to eat when she caught sight
of a tall man in Marshal's robes coming along the lines
from the Vonja position. With him was another in bright
red over shining mail—the paladin, thought Paks. They
were chatting with different soldiers as they moved
along. Paks didn't know if she wanted to talk with them
or not. What little she remembered about her conversation with the High Marshal was unsettling. She saw
Stammel smile as they spoke to him and looked away.

"Ah—Paksenarrion." They were in front of her. It
would be rude to ignore them. Paks met the High
Marshal's eyes.

"Yes, sir."

"Sir Fenith here wanted to meet you—awake, that
is. He is the paladin you fought beside in Sibili."

Fenith had dark hair and wide brown eyes. He grinned
at Paks. "I've been wanting to thank you. Your help
came at the right time."

Paks felt herself blushing. She wished she could remember what had happened. Without the memory, she
could not *feel* she had done anything.

"But tell us," Fenith went on, "how has the fighting
been, where you were?"

They listened closely, and encouraged her to continue when she faltered, as she told about the weeks of
pursuit and fighting. Not until then, telling it, did Paks
realize how short the time had been. She felt they'd
been marching forever, yet the spring green of the
trees was just darkening. She had seen newborn calves
even this past week. Paks wondered where the High
Marshal and paladin had been. She did not dare to ask.

"I'll be glad to see the end of this," said Fenith,
when she had finished. "It was necessary, but these
realms will suffer for it."

"Yes." The High Marshal's face settled into grim
lines. "Evil has been wakened that will take much work
to lay. And not only by Siniava." Paks felt a threat she
did not understand. He looked at her, and smiled.

"Does it seem strange to you that a High Marshal of Gird and a paladin should be regretting a war?"

"A little—yes—and this—"

"Remember what I told you, in Sibili. Gird fought as a protector, to ward his people against evil, both natural and supernatural. Not for plunder or pay—" Paks felt a flicker of anger. "No, I'm not insulting your Duke or you; I know his cause in this. But you've seen the ruined farms and homeless wandering folk. That's what will take long years to heal, that and the breach of law and trust that lets brigands roam as they will. That's what we want to see an end of." Paks slid her gaze to the paladin; he smiled at her.

"High Marshal, Paksenarrion is our ally—not a novice yeoman in the barton. She fights for honor in this—as do we." Paks relaxed a little. The paladin, she thought, was much friendlier than the High Marshal. "Tell me," he asked, "have you had any help from the medallion you carry? Do you still wear it?"

"Yes, sir; I do wear it. I'm uncertain what the help would be like. I remember the High Marshal telling me it saved my life, but I don't remember that day at all."

"Do you ever feel anything—warmth, or cold, or such?"

Paks considered telling him about the first time she'd handled it, when Canna was wounded, but decided against it. Not in front of the High Marshal. Nothing had happened recently. She forced down the memory of that weight on her chest before the ambush—she'd been very tired. She shook her head.

"If it does—if anything strange happens, if you feel anything—you'd be wise to let one of us know. It could be important, to you and to all of us." With a casual wave, the paladin turned away, and the High Marshal followed. Paks stared after them, her appetite gone.

"What was that about?" asked Jenits.

Paks shook her head. "I'm—not sure."

Jenits stared after the paladin with open admiration. "I'd like to have mail like that. I wonder how he keeps it so shiny. It makes even the Duke's look dull. Do you suppose I'll end up a paladin, Paks?" He grinned at his own joke, and thumped her arm. Paks laughed, easing her tension.

"About as soon as I will."

Shortly after dark, all those in Arcolin's cohort who wore the Dwarfwatch ring were called to his tent. There they found the mercenary commanders, Alured the Black, and a group of Halveric soldiers that Paks recognized from Dwarfwatch.

"I have a special mission for you," the Duke began. "You have known the treachery of the Honeycat longest; I assume you want him dead the most." A murmur of anger and assent followed. "Good. Our ally Alured tells me there's a secret passage between the citadel and the outside. He knows where it begins, in the dungeons under the inner keep, and where it comes out, in the forest." Paks felt a surge of excitement. She imagined them breaking in, finding Siniava in his chamber—

"He'll know of it, surely," Alured said, his rough accent breaking into her fantasy. "I sent a man to his army, when your Duke said, and he'll have told them the secret, as if he found it himself. I've used the passage a few times myself. It's narrow, but sound. You can wait at the outer end, for him to try an escape, or you can go in. If he's barred the opening, on the inside, you'd have trouble breaking in. And if he's got a wizard, you'd need a wizard to break the lock."

"Has he a wizard, Alured?" asked the Duke. Alured was silent a moment before answering.

"He's got someone in a long fancy gown. Might be a merchant or banker—a high guildsman. Or it could be a wizard. I don't know."

"Mmm. We'll wait, and let his well-known selfishness lead him out the bolthole." The Duke looked around at the soldiers. "I want you to keep watch over the forest end of the passage. You will not leave it unguarded, even for an instant. If he has a wizard—a mage—he may come out in disguise, even shapechanged. And he will certainly come out with his bodyguard and as much wealth as they can carry. Remember: their weapons may be poisoned, and the bodyguard is marked, dark tattoos all over the face. Siniava himself, if not in disguise, is a little taller than Aliam, here, and dark-haired. Harek told us, before he died, that Siniava has a small tattoo himself, between the eyebrows: the horned chain of Liart. I doubt you'll see it; he'll be in armor, most likely. But I want to be sure nothing escapes that way. Nothing. And when he comes, I want him alive. Can I trust you for this?"

"Yes, my lord!" came the response. The Duke smiled at them.

"I thought so. Now—you must go by night, so his sentries on the wall see nothing. You'll have to camp there—but no fires; they'll see light or smoke. One of us or our squires will be always near, within hail. When someone comes out, try to be sure they're all out before you attack. Set up your watch schedules so that some from both companies are always on. Paksenarrion—"

"Yes, my lord."

"I heard good things of you when you took over from Seli. You'll command our unit and work with the Halveric—sergeant, is it, Aliam?"

"Sergeant Sunnot." The Halveric looked at her. "You should remember him from last fall."

"Yes, my lord." Paks caught Sunnot's eye; he smiled.

Not long after, they were facing the black-in-black maw of the passage, an irregular hole in a rocky outcrop south of the citadel. Paks would not have noticed it, in the darkness, if Alured had not pointed it out. The next morning Paks and Sunnot examined the situation more closely.

The passage entrance faced south; above it was a steep rockface, thickly forested on top, that blocked their view of the citadel a half-hour's walk to the north.

Below, a gentle slope dipped more west than south, to the Immer; a small clearing gave them a good view of the passage and its surroundings. Paks poked cautiously into the near end of the passage. It crooked sharply left, then right, its rough walls looking like a natural fissure in the stone, but beyond the second turn Paks found smoothly hewn walls and floor, with torch brackets set into the walls. The passage ran straight from there, dipping gently. She backed out and told Sunnot what she'd seen. They decided to pile dry leaves just inside the entrance to give warning of Siniava's approach. Then they rearranged the guardposts, and decided on the signals to use when something happened.

That evening the Duke came to inspect their arrangements. "How long do you think he'll wait?" asked Paks.

"He can see us cutting timber for siege towers. I think he'll go soon, before his own men decide to turn on him. Tonight—tomorrow—tomorrow night. I doubt he'll wait much longer than that. And I'd say at night—it's how he's left every other position this campaign."

"Yes, my lord."

"But don't count on it. If he realizes his pattern, he'll change it. And remember, Paks: take him alive."

"Yes, my lord."

Paks and Sunnot walked the posts that night, but nothing happened. No sounds came to them from the citadel. In the dark Paks had time to think back over the campaign. It seemed that nothing could go wrong this time: Siniava was well in the trap. But they had thought the same before, only to face another long march and battle. She sighed, louder than she'd meant to, and Arñe spoke her name softly.

"Paks? What's wrong?"

Paks moved to Arñe's post and leaned on a tree. "Nothing—it seems strange not to be marching somewhere, that's all. I keep thinking we've got him, but I thought that before."

"I know. For awhile it seemed we'd been marching a year, and would go on forever, but—"

"It hasn't been that long. We did start early—"

Now Arñe sighed. "We did indeed. I tell you, Paks, I don't feel the same. It's only our third year, but I feel older—I feel there's been more than a year between this campaign and last spring. Do you remember when we came t Rotengre?"

"Yes. I know what you mean. We were so glad to be second-years—but we knew we weren't really veterans. And then Dwarfwatch—"

"Yes. Dwarfwatch. Then Rotengre. Then this." Arñe sighed again.

Paks pushed herself away from the tree. "Well—it'll be over soon. We'll feel different when he's dead, and when we've had some rest."

"I hope so," said Arñe soberly. Paks walked on, still thinking.

The next day was as quiet as the first. No one grumbled about missing the action at the citadel, but Paks knew many shared her fears: what if he doesn't come this way? What if others make the capture? By nightfall they were edgy and watchful. Paks and Sunnot had both slept during the day, so they'd be on together.

Night chill made Paks shiver suddenly between guardposts. She looked at the tunnel mouth and saw nothing. It was distinctly colder; she wondered if a weather change was coming. She pulled her cloak closer around her, and leaned into a tree trunk. She felt a breath of cold air drift down the slope, chilling her face. The cloak was warm. She yawned, suddenly sleepy despite the cold. Her mind wandered.

All at once a sharp prick, like a thorn, stung her chest. She jerked her eyes open, realizing in that instant that she'd been almost asleep. She looked quickly around and saw nothing. She started to relax, and realized that she should have seen at least one guard, even in the gloom. She pushed herself up. The nearest guard was slumped to the ground. Paks felt a trickle of fear, like icewater, down her spine. The hairs rose on her arms. She shook the guard—it was a Halveric, she remembered—and the woman grunted.

Paks pinched her arm and muttered, "Wake up! Trouble." The woman stiffened, grabbed Paks's arm, and started to rise.

"What happened?"

"Magic, I think." Paks drew her sword as she spoke. "Pray we're not too late. Draw your blade."

"The others?"

"Wait—we'll have to wake them, but—" She peered toward the tunnel mouth again. A dark shadow seemed to flow out of it. "There—see?"

"Falk's oath in gold! But what do we—?"

"Wake the others on this side; I'll go across. If they think we're all asleep, maybe they'll be careless. Watch—don't sit down—be sure the torchlighters are ready."

A glimmer of starlight lit the rockface, as Paks edged around in the trees to find the other guards. She could see another shadow, and another, emerge from the tunnel. She found a pair of guards and woke them, then another pair. Where was Sunnot? More shadows emerged, to cluster a few yards from the entrance. Paks had most of the guards awake; she could only hope they would stay so. She wished she knew which of those shadows was the wizard, and which the Honeycat.

The shadows took up a blunt arrowhead formation, and Paks tensed. Which way would they move? Her left hand fumbled for Canna's medallion without her thought, and it seemed to twitch left. She moved from the trees along the rockface, where she could cut off a retreat to the tunnel.

A last cloaked figure emerged, and the entire group moved slowly westward toward the trees. Paks took a deep breath and yelled, a wordless cry of mingled anger and triumph. Torches flared around the perimeter; guards stepped forward. She spared a thought of relief, that the guards had stayed awake, as she charged the group of fugitives. They turned, forming a hollow ring, blades whistling in the air as they drew them.

These were the Honeycat's bodyguards: faces tattooed in garish patterns, blades tipped with poison visible even in dancing torchlight. In seconds the woods rang with the clash of swords, and the cries of the fighters. Paks swept her blade in joyful strokes across the enemy blades, exultant. Trick *me*, will you, she thought. Ha! She glanced past her opponents to those sheltered by the ring. One as a man with a narrow dark beard— surely a wizard. The other must be Siniava. Except— Paks nearly missed a parry—except that it was a woman. Very obviously a woman, in a thin silk gown. Shape-change, thought Paks, astonished, and pressed her attack.

The fighter in front of her went down: one of the guards had gotten a lateral stroke. More were down. The mercenaries surged forward, overrunning the rest, to grapple with the two in the center. They went down in a heap of bodies, each eager to grab hold. Paks was an instant too late, and stood panting beside them. She rubbed her corselet absently; her chest itched. A tingle ran down her left arm, as if someone had jabbed her elbow. She whirled, searching the shadows, and stiffened as she caught a movement along the base of the rockface. She relaxed: it was only an animal. An instant later she charged, sword high. What animal would be out in the open with all that noise and light?

As her sword came down toward a furry back, the animal shape rippled, and she faced a man in black armor inlaid with gold. The first blow of his broadsword snapped the tip of her blade. Paks yelled a warning to the others, yanking her dagger from its sheath, as she tried to parry another of his strokes. This time her sword shattered in her hand.

"Phelan's bitch!" snarled the man. "This time you've gone too far—touch *me* with a blade, will you!" He lunged; Paks jerked aside. The thrust barely missed her. She tried to stab with her dagger, but it was too short. His blade sliced into her corselet; the force of the blow staggered her, though she felt no cut. He whirled and ran for the trees. Paks launched herself after him and managed to grapple his legs. They fell sprawling together. Before she could get loose, she felt him heave up and start to swing his sword.

The next instant he gave a loud screech, and writhed away.

"Hang onto him!" said a brisk voice. Paks clung to the kicking, squirming legs, and tried to see who had spoken. Against the light of the torches, her helper was only a dark shape. She heard boots running toward them. In moments, six or eight soldiers were holding the black-armored man down. Paks pushed herself up, panting. Her elbows hurt, where she'd fallen, and she had a stitch in her side.

The Duke strode into the light. "Got him, have we?"

"I think so, my lord." Now Paks recognized the paladin's voice. "We'll get his helmet off—"

"Allow me." The Duke knelt beside the man and slipped the tip of his dagger into the visor to lift it. Paks stared. The face inside was pale and angry. Dark eyes, a lock of dark hair showing, and a small tattoo between thick eyebrows.

"Well," said the Duke cheerfully. "It is Siniava. What a surprise, Lord Siniava, to find the commander of a besieged citadel wandering the woods at night." Paks could not hear what Siniava said in answer, but the Duke's shoulders stiffened. The paladin growled. Paks looked around, suddenly remembering the other man and woman. What had they been, and who were they? She saw a circle of mercenaries, and walked over to see two captives, bound hand and foot.

"Kieri!" No mistaking that call; the Halverics had arrived, both bareheaded.

"It's Siniava," said the Duke. "We'll have to get his armor off before you can have what you're looking for."

"We can manage that, can't we Cal?" The Halveric looked eager.

Cal was grinning too. "How badly is he hurt?"

"Nothing much," said Fenith. "Paksenarrion caught him, and I disarmed him. He's got a slashed wrist; that's all." He paused a moment. "What are you planning?"

"Don't be silly," snapped the Duke. "We're going to kill him."

"I know that," said the paladin, equally shortly. "Go on and do it."

The Duke gave him a long stare. Paks felt her belly clench. "Do you know," he asked softly, "what he did to my men? And to Aliam's sons?" Fenith nodded. "Then don't ask mercy for him," the Duke growled.

"You're a warrior," said Fenith implacably. "A warrior, not a torturer. Don't cheapen yourself."

"Cheapen myself?" Paks had never seen the Duke so angry, not even the day he'd held Ferrault's dying hand. "Sir paladin, you're the one with divine guidance. You're the one who can walk away when the battle's over. I do the dirty work, paladin, and I would more than cheapen myself, I would *beggar* myself for the honor of my men." All around the clearing the Duke's soldiers were frozen, listening; the Halverics hardly knew where to look. Paks felt choked with horror. The Duke's face was strange, utterly unlike himself. She was more frightened than she'd been facing the Honeycat with a broken sword.

She hardly knew it when she moved. The Duke's head swung to her. She could feel the stares of the paladin and the Halverics.

"Ask her, paladin," the Duke said more quietly. "Ask her, if she has forgotten her dead friends and how they died. Ask her if Siniava deserves a clean and easy death."

"And then?" asked the paladin, equally quietly.

The Duke shrugged. "She captured him, you say. I'll abide by her word on it." The Halverics stirred, but said nothing.

Paks felt a wave of horror and panic even before the paladin asked, "Well, Paksenarrion—how should this man die?" She met the Duke's angry gaze, and that of the Halverics: Aliam's dark, enigmatic; his son's bleak with remembered pain. The shades of her friends seemed to crowd the air—Saben, Canna— Tears choked her throat; she fought for speech.

"My lord, I have not—I cannot—forget those friends. And he had them killed, and hurt—I want him dead, my lord—" The Duke nodded, looking more like the Duke she knew, and he gathered courage. "But we don't—we are not like him, my lord. That's why we fought. Afterwards—but if it were me, my lord, I'd kill him now. But I have no right to say." The Duke gave her a look she could not read.

"So be it. Aliam?"

The Halveric sighed. "She's probably right, Kieri, gods blast it. I'll abide. But I was looking forward to it."

"It was my agreement. You can give the stroke." The Duke heaved himself up from beside Siniava.

"My thanks." Aliam Halveric drew his sword. "Cal, take that helmet off." Cal wrestled the helmet from Siniava's head, and tossed it aside. With a quick powerful stroke the Halveric buried his sword in Siniava's neck. The watching soldiers cheered, and in a few minutes the armor and body were hacked into many pieces. Paks watched silently, thinking of the many bodies she'd seen in the past year.

It had happened so fast at the end. She could scarcely believe it was over, and turned away, still frightened and sick. She did not realize she had fallen until a hand touched her shoulder. She flinched, fighting nausea.

"Paks?" Vik sounded worried. She nodded, unable to speak. "What's wrong? Were you hurt? Let me see." Approaching torchlight glared through her closed eyelids. She felt his hands touching her, heard the hiss when he found the gash in her armor. Other hands were about her now, supporting her. Voices. Someone swearing as he worked at the fastenings of her corselet.

She forced her eyes open, squinting against the torch-light. She saw someone walking away with Siniava's head on a pole. Then the paladin's face filled her vision.

"Paksenarrion. We think it is poison. Be still." She felt an emptiness as others moved away. The paladin's hands on her were hard. A glow seemed to rise around them. She felt a streak of pain across her chest, then a wave of comfort, palpable as a handful of clover. She took a breath and it came easy. Her vision cleared.

"My apologies," said Fenith. "You moved so well I did not think to be sure you weren't hurt. How is it now?"

Paks had not felt so well for days—even months, she thought. "I'm fine, sir; thank you." She started to sit up. Around them was a circle of her friends, looking worried.

"Here," said Vik. "Have a cloak."

"I'm fine." Paks took the cloak away. The paladin helped her stand. She felt steady and secure.

"Paksenarrion." That was Aliam Halveric. Watching her with a puzzled frown.

"Yes, my lord."

"Do you know where Sunnot is? Did he go to bring us word?"

Memory of the mysterious cold and sleep came back to her. "No, my lord. I think he must have been overcome by the sleep—"

"Sleep! What was he—?"

A clamor of voices broke out, explaining.

"We were all asleep—"

"Magic or something—"

"—and Paks woke me up, and they—"

"Silence!" Paks had not noticed the Duke still standing nearby. "Vik, look for him. Paks, tell us about this sleep—how were you awake?"

"My lord, I don't know. Sunnot and I had doubled the guards; we had just met and parted over there—" Paks pointed "—when it seemed cold suddenly. I remember a cold breeze, and wrapping my cloak. Then I woke, and I was on the ground, beside a tree—"

"What woke you?" asked the paladin. The Duke shot him a look.

"I don't know exactly—it felt like a thorn pricking my chest—"

"Where your holy symbol rests?" Paks nodded. "May I see it again, please?" Paks slipped the chain over her head and handed it to him. As he took it, it flared to a blue glow, instantly extinguished. He held the surface to the torchlight, examining it minutely.

"Then what?" asked the Duke gruffly. Paks looked at him warily, remembering his rage.

"Well, my lord, I looked around, but saw nothing. Then I found the next guard asleep, and thought of magic. I woke her; we saw the first of them coming out. She woke the guards on this side, and I went to the other. I didn't see Sunnot, but I was going by feel, to the posts we'd set. I could have missed—" A shout from Vik interrupted her. In a moment he reappeared, leading a bewildered Sunnot, who went down on one knee to the Halveric.

"My lord, I—I don't know what happened—" The Halveric smiled and gestured him up.

"You were magicked, Sunnot; not your fault. I'm sorry you missed it—"

"Did he escape, sir?" Sunnot looked ready to cry.

"No. He's dead. It's over." Sunnot looked around, still worried. Vik spoke softly to him, and he shook his head.

"Go on, Paks," said the Duke.

She was so glad to see Sunnot alive and well that she'd lost the thread of her story.

"You woke the guards," the Duke prompted.

"Yes, my lord. More of them had come out by then. When the last one came out I yelled and we attacked."

"Where was Siniava then?"

"I don't know. The bodyguard had made a ring, with two inside it—" Paks pointed to the bound prisoners. "I thought the man was a wizard, and the woman was Siniava, shapechanged."

"A good thought—"

"But it wasn't. The others had them down; I was watching. Then I had a strange feeling, like an itch—I turned around and saw an animal moving along here—" She looked at the paladin, then the Duke. They nodded. "Then I thought, what animal would be there, with the fight and all—so I went to kill it, and it changed. Into Siniava. Then we started fighting, and my sword broke. When he turned to run, I jumped and caught his legs—"

"I saw her jump," said the paladin. "He was turning to strike at her, and I was just in time to stop him. Here, Paksenarrion, take back your medallion. The rest you know."

The Duke shook his head thoughtfully. "I hardly feel I know anything. What woke her up? Was it the medallion—when she's not a Girdsman?"

"What else would you suggest? I know it's unusual—but what else?"

The Duke shook his head again. "I don't know." He sighed. "More mysteries, when I thought we'd be rid of them. Paksenarrion—"

"Yes, my lord?"

"Post a guard on this end of the passage, and come back to camp. How many wounded have we?" Paks looked around.

"My men took them back," said the Halveric. "With my wounded. Things seemed—busy—around here."

"My lord, if any are poisoned, I'd be glad to try a healing."

"Thank you, sir paladin," said Aliam before the Duke could answer. "You know the way to my surgeons' tents?"

"Certainly, my lord." The paladin turned and was gone.

Paks had organized the remaining soldiers and told them to keep close watch until they were relieved.

"Can we have a fire?" asked Rauf. She looked at the Duke.

"Certainly," he said. "As big as you like. We'll send a relief down when we get back, and then you can sleep. You've earned it. Come along, Paks." He turned to go, and Paks followed, pausing to pick up the shards of her sword. She could hear the quartermaster now: sword and corselet both.

The Duke and Aliam Halveric walked side by side back to camp, the Duke's squires before them, and Paks bringing up the rear. They said nothing to her, and she could not hear what they were saying. She didn't try. She had too much to think about. She rubbed her thumb across the medallion she held—she had not put it back on. She did not understand—did not want to understand. The Duke was angry enough; she did not want him more angry with her than he was already. She thought of Canna and Saben—would they have wanted it this way? Siniava dead so easily? Saben would have—she turned away from his memory to something else. Canna had never told her the medallion had such powers. Was that its function, to warn? And if so, why hadn't it warned Canna of the brigands?

When they reached the camp, the Duke turned to Paks. "I think you should be the one to tell your cohort that Siniava is dead, and how he died." His voice was neutral; Paks could not tell if he was still angry.

"Yes, my lord."

"You have my thanks for a duty faithfully—even more than faithfully—performed."

"And our thanks also," said Aliam Halveric. His smile was as open as ever, the corners of his eyes crinkled. "Whatever power enabled you to resist the spell, it is clear that without you that scum might have escaped." He looked at the Duke. "That power, too, must have our thanks and praise."

The Duke's shoulders shifted. "We can speak of that later. As for now, Aliam, you and I must arrange the taking of that citadel. Paksenarrion has more immediate duties, as well."

The Halveric was no longer smiling. "Later, perhaps, Kieri—but after this night's work, we can no longer ignore it."

The Duke sighed. "No, I suppose not. Go on, Paks, and tell the rest. And get some sleep. If it comes to fighting, we'll want your blade as well."

If Stammel had not been awake by one of the watchfires, Paks might have fallen asleep without telling her news. But in telling him, the excitement woke her again, and soon she was the center of a breathless crowd.

"And you're sure he's dead," said someone into the silence that followed her recital.

"They brought his head back on a pole," said Paks. "I didn't see it as we came—it must be in the Halveric camp now."

"But you caught him," said another voice. "It should be our trophy."

"The Halveric killed him. And the paladin—Sir Fenith—helped catch him. I didn't do it alone—"

"Still—" Paks recognized Barranyi's voice, this time.

"Hush, Barra," said Natzlin. "It doesn't bother Paks, and she did it."

"How did they kill him?" asked Vossik, who had not heard the first of the story. Paks tensed.

"The Halveric killed him," she said again. "With a sword."

"Huh. Slowly, I'll bet, after what he did to his sons."

"No." Paks wished she were far away, as she felt the pressure of surprise and curiosity. She stared into the fire. "One stroke," she said finally. "In the neck."

Stammel whistled. "That's—something. To show mercy like that—" He was clearly impressed. Some of the others were frowning, but Paks saw many of the older veterans relax, as if they had feared worse. Barranyi's voice broke a brief silence.

"But why? After all he'd done—I'd think the Duke

would do something! It's not right, that he should die so easy." Paks felt almost sick at the venom in Barra's voice. Before she could gather her words, Vossik interrupted Barra.

"No! That's what makes us different. Such leaders as that—that you can trust to do the right thing even under pressure. By—" he paused and looked at Stammel. "By Gird and Falk and the High Lord himself, I'm proud we've got such men to lead our companies." Vossik turned to Paks, grinning. "I daresay *you* weren't eager for torture, were you now?"

Paks felt herself blushing. "No," she muttered. She hoped no one would ask what the Duke had actually said.

"I thought not." Vossik sounded relaxed and happy. "This is an honorable company, and always has been, and always will be. Remember that, Barra." She made no answer.

Stammel was smiling too. "Well now. Just let us get this citadel taken care of, and we'll be back to normal. And a lot richer, I don't doubt. You too, Paks—you'll have a bonus for this night's work." He stood, reaching a hand to Paks. "Come on, warrior. Even you need sleep before the assault." Paks clambered up, meeting the admiring glances of her friends as she moved away. What she had left unsaid cluttered her throat.

No one woke her in the morning; the sun was high when she finally opened her eyes. The tent was almost empty; two others slept at the far end. Paks stretched and yawned. She didn't want to move. She heard voices outside and got up reluctantly. Outside, the day was fair and warm; it would be hot by noon. She headed for the cooks' tent.

"There you are." Stammel came up behind her. "You'll be glad to know that the troops in the citadel want to surrender."

Paks pulled her mind back to the present. "Oh. Good."

"They're afraid to open the gates, they say. I don't

blame them. They would expect the worst from us." He waited to say more until no one was near. "Paks—the others are back now. I spoke to Arñe and Vik. There's a lot you didn't say last night."

Paks blushed. She was afraid of his next question. Instead of asking, he went on.

"I'm glad you didn't. The Duke's a good man; you know that. I've known him a long time; I know why he might lose his temper. But you were right, Paks, however angry he was, or may be still: he's not the kind to torture. Only he wasn't himself for a bit." He went on more briskly. "I don't think the others will talk about it—I had to pull the truth out of Vik with a rope, nearly. He feared I'd be angry with you."

Paks found herself grinning at Stammel's tone. When she looked up, his brown eyes were twinkling.

"You'd best watch yourself, though," he said. "If things keep happening around you, and you keep siding with paladins, it'll rub off, and we'll only see you from far away, as you ride past on your fancy charger." His tone was only half joking.

For an instant the thought made Paks's heart leap, but she forced the image away. "No," she said firmly. "I'm staying here, in the Company, with my friends. If the Duke isn't too angry—" For she remembered the icy glare he'd given her.

"He's fair; he won't hold it against you. But Paks, it's not that bad an idea," said Stammel more earnestly. "If you have the chance, I'd say take it. You've got the fighting skills, and you care about the right and wrong of things. You'd make friends elsewhere—" Paks shook her head. Stammel sighed. "Have you thought," he asked, "that your two years is up these many months? You're due a leave—you could go north and see your family—look around—"

Paks was startled. She had forgotten all about the "two years beyond training" in her first contract. "I hadn't thought," she said. As she mused on it, the sights and smells of Three Firs came back to her. The baker's shop, the well, the striped awnings that hung out on market day. And beyond the town the great rolling lift of the moors, and the first sight of the dark slate roof of her father's house. Tears stung her eyes. "I could—I could take my dowry back—" she said.

"So you could. Your share this campaign should do it. Think about it. The Duke will be granting us all leave unless he takes us back north."

"And I wouldn't be leaving the Company."

"No. Not unless you wanted to."

"I'll think about it," she said, and Stammel nodded and left her.

Siniava's troops surrendered that day, but not to the Duke: to the combined city militia. Paks did not even see the prisoners; she heard that they'd been taken away toward Vonja. The Duke's Company entered the citadel only for plunder; they found the only treasure at the inside opening of the secret passage. Several chests of gold, Stammel said, would pay for the entire campaign, leaving aside their share of Cha and Sibili. Paks heard from Arñe that Siniava's bodyguards had all been carrying jewels and gold. "That's what slowed them down in the fight," she joked.

"Did you find out who the others were?"

"Yes. The man's some high rank in the moneylender's guild. He's got a bad wound; he may not live. The woman's his sister or niece or something." Arñe stopped and looked at Paks. "Do you know what happened with Canna's medallion? Was it really St. Gird who woke you?"

"I don't know. I don't understand." Paks could hardly convey her confusion. "Something happened, I know that. But—I keep wondering and wondering about it, and nothing comes clear."

Three days later, as she watched the city militias march north from the bridge, she was still wondering. The High Marshal had talked to her again, and the paladin; the Duke had apparently talked to both of them. Dorrin had told of the incident in Rotengre, and Paks finally admitted that she'd tried to use the medallion to heal Canna. She could have had, if she'd wanted it, hours of instruction about Gird. She didn't want it.

"I want to stay with you," she'd told the Duke, while the High Marshal listened. "I joined your company; I gave you my oath. And my friends are here."

The Duke nodded. "You may stay, Paksenarrion, as long as you're willing. But I must agree with the High Marshal in this: some force—we need not agree on what—is moving you as well. The time may come when you should leave. I will not hold you to your oath then."

"My lord—" the paladin had begun, but the Duke interrupted.

"Don't bully her. If she's to leave, she'll leave, in her own time. You've seen she's no fool."

"That's not what I meant, my lord."

"No. I'm sorry." The Duke had sighed, looking tired. "Paks, think about it. I know it's not easy—but think. Talk to Arcolin or Dorrin, if you'd like; talk to Stammel. This company is not the only place you can be a fighter."

But she had been determined. From a sheepfarmer's daughter in Three Firs to a respected veteran in the Duke's Company, with friends who would die for her, or she for them—that was enough. Those childhood dreams were only dreams: this place, these friends, were real. It was all she wanted, and all she ever would.

She waved, nonetheless, to Sir Fenith the paladin, as he rode out. Canna's medallion was safe in her belt-pouch now. She would let it stay there. No more of those strange warnings to deal with, no more mysteries. And if she died, for lack of its warning—she grinned, not worried. Saben's red horse would bear her to the Afterfields.